Make You Beg

Christine Rae-Jones

Cliffside House Publishing

This paperback edition published by
Cliffside House Publishing 2021

ISBN: 978-1-8380863-1-2

www.christinerae-jones.com

DI Nick Morgan Reader Club

Why did DI Nick Morgan agree to move to Gullhaven?

If you'd like to know, sign up now to receive your free download of "FIRE FARM" the prequel to the DI Nick Morgan Crime Thriller Series

This download is exclusive to Reader Club Members ONLY and is absolutely free. You'll also receive news of upcoming publications in the DI Nick Morgan series and priority access to any discounted availability.

Visit https://www.christinerae-jones.com

and tell us where to email your download link.
If you change your mind, you can unsubscribe at any time

See you there!

DI Nick Morgan Crime Thriller Series

Fire Farm
(exclusive free download for Reader Club members)

Make You Sorry

Make You Beg

Make You Choose
(available Autumn 2021)

Make You Scream
(exclusive free download for Reader Club members available October 2021)

Chapter 1

Tues 31st March; midnight

They got out of his car and hurried down the long concrete path which sloped to the beach. Towards the east of the bay, they could see figures dancing in the pale light of the waning moon. The cool midnight breeze carried music, shrieks and laughter and the smell of woodsmoke from the early flickering of a fire which struggled for survival.

When their feet crunched on to shingle, she turned to him and raised her forefinger to her lips. She took his hand and started to lead him away from the gathering.

'No, they're over there,' he said, but she shook her head.

'We can join the others later. First, we're going to party alone.' He smiled and kissed her, pulling her close so she could feel how much he wanted her. 'We need to go further along,' she said, 'I'm not doing it next to public toilets.'

He decided to let her take the lead for a little longer. Once he'd got her clothes off, he'd show her who was in charge. He looked forward to hearing her beg. All his women begged; some for more and some for him to stop; but ultimately, they all begged.

Halfway down the short row of beach huts there was a wide gap. 'Through here,' she whispered. 'This is just right.'

He let himself be led to the back of the huts. He was tingling with excitement. She would pay for her assertiveness and the price would be high. He saw her reach into her beach bag and expected her to produce a condom. She needn't have bothered. He'd brought his own.

'Close your eyes,' she said. 'Let's play.'

He felt something ticklish brush across his cheek and lips and he smiled. Okay, he'd play … for now.

She leaned back against the wooden wall of the hut and took his hand. When she cupped it round her breast, he started to fondle and squeeze and he heard her sharp intake of breath.

Click!

His eyes shot open as the fluffy handcuff gripped his right wrist.

'Shhh,' she whispered. 'It'll be fun. You'll like it.'

He let her take his left arm and she applied the second cuff with precision and speed. She lifted his trapped hands to her face and ran his fingertips down her forehead and nose before pausing them at her mouth. She bit them softly.

'You said I was a mistake,' she whispered before her voice hardened. 'You were right.'

The thick hood came down over his head, and his arms were taken in a vice-like grip. His struggles were restrained by the handcuffs, and when he tried to kick, his feet were swept from beneath him. He landed heavily on the overgrown grass. His colleagues were nearby, he thought. Maybe this was a couple of them playing a game with him? He heard tape being ripped from a roll and as he took a deep breath and opened his mouth to yell, something round, the size of a tennis ball, was thrust in and a second pair of hands secured it behind his head. His lungs were screaming for air but he'd forgotten how to breathe.

‘You did well. We’ll take it from here.’ He didn’t recognise the man’s voice. This wasn’t a game. Maybe it was his time to beg.

Chapter 2

Wednesday 1st April

Dorothy Cooper watched from behind the curtains of her first-floor lounge window. She waited for her son-in-law to appear on the driveway below; needed to be sure he was leaving. Her eyes narrowed as she watched him make his way down the drive of Silver Sands Supported Living towards the visitor parking area. She had never hated him more than at this moment. How dare he threaten her family.

Since the day her daughter had returned from university with a police probationer on her arm and a ring on her finger, she'd done everything she could to get rid of him. She had told the boy to walk away from Samantha or she'd make him sorry. When threats hadn't worked, she'd offered him money. Now, more than twenty years later, they were still married … just.

Dorothy started to pace. She needed a plan. If DI Nick Morgan was determined to keep investigating Carl Raynor's murder, he would surely confirm her son's involvement. And Steven would never survive imprisonment. He was sensitive and weak. Morgan must be distracted and there were only two ways to achieve that. It was too much to hope that a big juicy murder case would turn up, so her only alternative was to punt another grenade into the Morgan marriage. Of course that would mean upsetting Samantha, but the stakes were high and collateral damage was inevitable.

She grabbed her phone from the table, scrolled through her contacts and tapped the number, starting to pace again as she waited for a reply.

Ellie Hughes parked her car in one of the disabled spaces near the exit of the clifftop car park. Two middle-aged women walked past and one of them glowered at her. Ellie ignored it. She reached into her handbag and produced the blue badge which she'd been using since her forced early retirement from her job as a police dog handler. The stab wounds she and Flame, her faithful German shepherd, received when they were ambushed by four teenage burglars had left them both with deep physical and mental scars.

Last night they'd walked along the clifftop before retiring and Ellie had spotted a concrete path which descended to the beach. If they made it down she suspected they would struggle to get back up. But this holiday was all about achieving new things, not failing.

Today, bright sunshine had beckoned them out of their holiday flat and down on to the beach, where there were already a few other dog walkers launching balls into the water for their pets. Ellie knew that swimming would help Flame but decided it could wait until he looked ready to leap in, so they continued walking along the wide path at the bottom of the cliffs.

Part way along the row of beach huts, Flame stopped. He lay flat, put his head between his outstretched front legs and started to growl. Ellie turned. This was his alert signal. She hadn't seen it since they became civilians. He had found something she should be interested in.

'Come on, Flame, it's only a rabbit.' She had already seen a few of them scampering through the vegetation on the cliffs. She continued walking, expecting to look down and find her dog at her heel. When she got to the end of the row of huts, she looked back. Flame had not moved; his eyes still focused on the hut. She swore and started to limp back but Flame did not acknowledge her return. He continued to stare straight ahead.

Ellie saw that this hut was shabbier than its neighbours. When she got closer, she noticed a rusty bolt dangling from the door by one screw. If there had ever been a padlock securing the bolt, it was gone. The door was held closed by a chunk of rock, similar to those scattered around the edges of the path.

'It's probably a homeless person, Flame. Let's leave them alone.' She gripped the dog's collar and tried to make him stand. Flame continued to growl. She tried to reason with him. 'We're on holiday.' Ellie bounced the yellow ball, confident that this would be the answer. Flame ignored it.

'You win,' she said, and edged the rock away from the rotting door. The hut was dark inside and the open door blocked most of the sunlight coming from the east. She could make out some striped sun-chairs, or maybe they were loungers, stacked against the wall on her left. On her right was a worktop with a single-burner camping stove and a small kettle. Across the back of the hut was a bench with beach towels thrown over it.

'Hello?' She used her police voice: the one needed to wake vagrants seeking shelter at the coach station. 'You shouldn't be here. Hello.' Flame was behind her and he started to bark. Ellie jumped. He hadn't barked since they were injured.

She lifted the edge of one of the towels and saw the backs of two legs and feet which extended beyond the bench. One of the trainers was missing. She shook the covered torso gently and called out another greeting.

Flame growled again from his sentry position at the door. Ellie sighed and put Flame's lead into her bag, which she hitched across her body. She eased the right jeans leg up to expose bare flesh above the sock, and touched it with the back of her fingers. It was stone cold.

Chapter 3

Wednesday 1st April

As DI Nick Morgan drove to the beach, he seethed. Visits to his mother-in-law never ended well and today's was no exception. He had confronted her with his suspicions of Steven's involvement in the recent murder at Cliffside House. Her reaction to the news convinced him that he was on to something. Steven must have been there that night, and with a weapon which matched the pathologist's description of the one used to stab Carl Raynor. Dorothy's reaction to his accusation convinced him that she had been aware of it and had kept quiet. Maybe he could take them both down at the same time. The thought pleased him, although he knew Samantha would be devastated.

He glanced down at the speedometer and applied the brakes. He refused to give Dorothy Cooper the satisfaction of having an accident or getting speeding points because she was in his head.

When he got to the public car park on the clifftop, he joined the queuing cars. The entrance was manned by two uniformed officers. They were having difficulty persuading the dog walkers who used the facility every day that, not only could they not park in their normal spot, but also that the beach was closed.

Morgan waited patiently then pulled out of the queue and abandoned his Volvo on the double yellow lines on the other side of the road. He knocked on the window of the car he had been behind and showed his identification to an elderly lady with two excitable Jack Russell terriers caged in the boot of the muddy estate vehicle.

'I'm sorry, Madam, there's been an incident and the car park and beach are closed. I'm afraid you'll have to walk them elsewhere today.' He stepped back from the car, intent on working his way forwards through the half dozen or so vehicles in the queue.

'What's happened?' the lady shouted after him. He ignored her and was about to knock on the next window when he heard a car door open. When he turned back, she was advancing towards him. 'I asked what happened,' she said.

'And I told you that there has been an incident, Madam. Please get back in your car and find somewhere else to exercise your dogs.'

'Well, when will the beach be open again?' The window of the car he was standing beside opened and two women tuned in to the conversation.

'I can't answer that, I'm afraid. Both the beach and the car park will be open when we have completed our investigations. Now, if you'll excuse me.' Morgan now understood why it was taking so long to deal with each car, and to his dismay he saw that another four had joined the queue.

He walked to the front and spoke to one of the uniformed officers. 'Radio for Traffic to come. I want the clifftop road closed from the first junction to the east of here through to the first junction to the west. Just tell the people who are already here that there's been an incident and that we're about to close the road. If they are still here when the block goes on, they will have to leave their vehicles and come back for them when the scene is released.' He started to walk away before calling back, 'And tell them that could take a week.'

The elderly lady was in deep conversation with the two women, and he heard the words 'illegal' and 'immigrants' as he approached. 'I'm asking you to get back in your car and leave now, please. I have arranged for the road to be closed and I'm giving you fair warning.' She narrowed her eyes at him. Another elderly lady who hated his guts; perhaps his mother-in-law should get T-shirts printed.

The threat of road closure did the trick and after five minutes he was able to drive into the car park. He walked back to the uniformed officers and asked who was in charge of the scene log.

'PC Gomez has it. Down on the beach. We thought it made more sense.'

Morgan wasn't so sure, but let it go. 'And who discovered the body?'

'Her name's Hughes. I didn't catch her first name. She was in the job: retired dog handler. She agreed to wait until the SIO arrived.' He pointed to a gate that partially blocked the concrete slope which descended to the beach. As he passed it, Morgan noted that the padlock which secured the gate was hanging loose but didn't seem damaged. He looked down at the row of beach huts at the bottom of the cliff. Several crime scene vehicles had already parked and spilled out teams of technicians in their usual uniforms of white coveralls, masks, nitrile gloves and overshoes. Some were standing and others crawling along the path compacted by the passage of millions of feet, paws and hooves over many years. In the distance, there was a black vehicle with red chevrons across the tailgate and yellow and black checks across the side. The harbourmaster had turned out for this one. He heard the sound of an outboard motor starting and saw a black inflatable dinghy heading out into the bay.

At the bottom of the concrete slope, DS Dave Spence was sitting on a bench talking to a woman who was stroking the black-and-tan German shepherd dog lying at her feet. Morgan always marvelled at how Spence arrived before him at every crime scene, the only exception being when Morgan had woken to find a body in his own home. He looked down with sorrow at his newly cleaned black shoes and made his way down the slope.

Waves were lapping on to the shingle beach, the sound barely noticeable on this bright spring morning. A few weeks ago, when his family first moved into Cliffside House, Morgan had brought Truffles, their springer spaniel, here every day. It happened less now, as the job had got busier and Samantha had reclaimed her role as chief dog walker.

'This is Ellie Hughes,' said Spence, getting to his feet as Morgan reached them. 'And this is Flame. They retired early from the job after sustaining injuries.' Morgan nodded and held out a hand, which she shook.

'I'm sorry not to get up, Sir,' she said, 'I've been sitting here for a while and by the time I'm up you'll be halfway back to the station.'

'I'm DI Morgan, Ms Hughes. I'm not Sir, not to you anyway.'

'Sorry. It's a difficult habit to break.'

He nodded and sat beside her. 'I expect you'll have given your account a few times already, but I'm going to ask for it again. I'd like to hear it for myself.'

Ellie Hughes started from when she parked at the top of the cliffs. She detailed the reproachful looks she'd received from the women in the car park, and anyone observing would see that her disability still angered and distressed her. When she got to the point of finding the body, she made it clear that she had touched it only briefly and with the backs of her fingers so she would not leave her prints.

'Once he got the scent, Flame refused to leave it be. He has always been focused. That's what made him such a good tracker. I know he misses it as much as I do.' Hughes reached down and stroked the dog's head again.

'How long have you had him?' asked Morgan.

'Four years in June.'

'And how long since you retired?'

'We were forced out thirteen and a half months ago.'

Most people would have said 'a year', he thought; this woman was still counting the days.

'I should have asked earlier,' said Spence, 'how long will you be staying at Gullhaven? We'll need to get a statement.'

'We'll be here for two weeks. Do you want me to come in?'

Morgan stood. 'Just get the address please, Dave.' He turned to Ellie Hughes, reaching down to let Flame sniff his knuckles. 'One of the DCs will be round at three this afternoon. I've no wish to inconvenience you any more than necessary on your holiday, and I hope you don't let this spoil it.'

She smiled for the first time since meeting him. 'It's the most exciting thing that's happened since we retired. And it's good to feel useful.' They shook hands again and Morgan walked towards the taped-off area where the white-suited army was mustering.

‘PC Gomez?’ He approached a tall woman who looked uncomfortable in her uniform. Dark wavy hair escaped from a cap and the warm brown eyes which turned to him were wide. She must be from the new intake, and he’d startled her. ‘I’m DI Nick Morgan. Can you log me in, please?’ She offered him gloves, shoe covers and white overalls, and added his name to her clipboard as he dressed. When he was ready, she lifted the inner cordon tape and he ducked under.

‘DI Morgan?’ His attention was grabbed by a woman’s voice which he recognised. It was just a matter of finding which of the white-suited clones it belonged to. He scanned the wide path and saw her walking towards him.

‘You made good time, Nick,’ she said.

‘I was visiting my mother-in-law over at East Gullhaven and there wasn’t much traffic. The biggest problem was negotiating with the dog walkers up at the car park. How are you, Morag?’

Like her father, Dr Morag Mackenzie was a Home Office forensic pathologist who worked with the Central and Southern Major Crimes Team. Since Morgan’s recent transfer to Gullhaven Cove, either father or daughter had attended all of his crime scenes where a death had occurred.

‘I’m well, thanks for asking. You’ve caught yourself an interesting one here,’ she said, pointing to a beach hut with peeling blue paint and weeds poking through broken patio slabs. They walked to it, picking their way between grass verge and areas of decking which fronted some of the other huts.

‘Shoe-prints everywhere. Too many for CSI to take casts, but they are photographing the more recent ones,’ said Mackenzie.

‘What are your first thoughts?’

‘Not killed in the hut. He was dragged from over there.’ She pointed to the rows of rocks deposited along the shore to limit erosion of the cliff face. ‘He lost a shoe in the process but we’ve found and bagged it. There’s vomit in his mouth and nostrils, and a strong smell of alcohol. His jeans are soaked in blood, and they’re undone.’ She looked out towards the bay, then back at Morgan. ‘I’ll know more after the PM, but I’m estimating life extinct between midnight and maybe four this morning?’ Her voice rose at the end of the sentence as if she was questioning herself. ‘And I’ve saved the best till last.’

‘And that is?’

‘His wrists are bound by pink fluffy handcuffs.’

Chapter 4

Wednesday 1st April

Dorothy let Graham Fletcher into her flat and pointed him towards her small sofa. 'I'll make us some coffee,' she said, ignoring his discomfort.

'I haven't got long. I've got a client coming in an hour.'

She clicked the switch on the kettle and, while she waited for it to come back to the boil, straightened the delicate cups, saucers and milk jug on the tray.

Until his clumsy suggestion to Samantha Morgan that she move in with him, Graham Fletcher had visited Dorothy frequently, but now he was keeping his distance.

'Your message sounded urgent. What's the matter? Is Sammy okay?'

Dorothy smiled and allowed herself a small nod as she poured the steaming water into her cafetiere. If he was concerned for Samantha, he still cared for her, and she could use that to her advantage.

She went to the door. 'Can you carry the tray through for me please, Graham. I'm not as steady as I once was.'

Fletcher eased himself out of the sofa and came to the kitchen. She touched his arm as he reached for the tray. 'Where have you been, Graham? I've missed our little chats.'

Back in the lounge, he placed the tray on the dining table and pulled out a chair. She preferred her armchair at the window but she needed him on side, so joined him at the table. She poured the black coffee he had asked for and pushed the cup towards him.

‘I came straightaway because it sounded urgent, Dorothy.’ He pointed to his watch. ‘I haven’t got long.’

She struggled to mask her impatience. If he hadn’t been such a prat … if he’d taken his time resurrecting his adolescent romance with Samantha, DI Nick Morgan would have been so obsessed with winning her back that he wouldn’t have noticed Steven’s pocket knife and they wouldn’t be in this mess.

She smiled at him, choosing her softest conciliatory tone before embarking on her plan. ‘I spoke to Samantha a couple of days ago. I think she’s missing you.’

‘I don’t think that’s very likely. She’s not replying to emails or texts and she’s not picking up the phone when I call.’

‘So you’ve given up.’ Dorothy’s voice hardened and she pursed her lips. With the exception of Nick Morgan, all the men in her life were such wimps. It frustrated her. ‘You said she was the love of your life, but now she’s starting to play a little hard to get, you’ve given up.’

Fletcher put his cup down and stared at her. Dorothy could see the pain in his eyes. ‘I pushed her too hard and too soon. She’s not playing hard to get, she’s weighed up what might be on offer with me and what is on offer with her family, and she’s picked them. Time to move on.’

‘I think you’ve misinterpreted what the choice is. It’s not you or her family, it’s you or Plod. The children will be with her whatever decision she makes. You’re a family lawyer, for God’s sake. Can you really see a court giving my son-in-law full custody of twelve-year-old twins with the hours he keeps?’

Fletcher’s head dipped to one side as he considered this. ‘No, I can’t, but I don’t think it’s as straightforward as custody of the children. She's had the choice of him or me twice now, and she's picked him both times.'

'If she was happy with him, do you think she's have leapt into bed with you at her first opportunity? He neglects her. She's told me that there are days when they hardly see each other, and since he found out about you two he doesn't even share a bed with her.'

Fletcher's eyes widened. 'I didn't know she'd told him. Why did she do that?'

Dorothy cringed at her error. She flicked her hand as if swatting away a pesky insect. 'I don't think it matters how he found out, does it? He knows, and he's sulking. If you can't steal her away now, when are you going to get a better opportunity?'

Fletcher was shaking his head in disbelief and Dorothy felt uncomfortable under his scrutiny. If he was going to insist on asking how Plod had found out about their affair, she was torn between admitting she had told him herself, and lying.

'I don't know, Dorothy. I love Sammy and getting her back would mean everything to me, but I can't see it happening.'

'Leave it with me. I just needed to be sure you would be there to pick up the pieces before I made a move. Now that I know, I'll think of something. Did you want more coffee?'

Chapter 5

Wednesday 1st April

Dave Spence had left Ellie Hughes and was approaching Morgan and Mackenzie. 'Like sex-toy handcuffs?' he asked, and they turned to him.

'And what would you know about sex-toy cuffs, DS Spence?' Morag Mackenzie was smiling. Spence gritted his teeth and cringed. Morgan noticed that his ears had reddened.

'I read a lot,' he replied.

'Ann Summers catalogues, I take it?' said Morgan. He was still feeling his way in the relationship with his sergeant, and took care with banter.

'They don't look right to me, Nick,' said Mackenzie. 'Have a look, but don't touch. There may be fingerprints and CSI haven't done that yet.'

'I think getting fingerprints from pink fluffiness will be beyond even our crack team,' said Morgan.

'The fabric has puckered up in a few areas and underneath I can see metal. They may even be standard-issue nickel-covered steel.'

Spence whistled through his teeth. 'That's taking sex-toy to a whole new level.'

'Quite,' said Mackenzie.

'Are you joining any dots between the cuffs and the blood on the jeans? Is this some sort of sex game that went wrong?'

Dr Mackenzie shrugged. 'If it is, it went very wrong considering the amount of blood he's lost, and …' she leant towards Morgan, her voice lowered, 'I'm pretty certain there's still something inside him.' Morgan and Spence exchanged a glance and both men grimaced.

Brian Bingley, one of the squad's crime scene managers, joined them, his feet crunching on the shingle. Morgan turned to him.

'Do we know who he is? If the harbourmaster's here, they may be thinking he's an illegal immigrant.'

Bingley shook his head. 'The only thing we've found on him is a keycard for the East Gullhaven Country Club. There's no wallet, car keys or phone, and no sign of a jacket. He's wearing jeans and a long-sleeved sweatshirt with a logo I don't recognise. And one of his trainers is missing.'

'Not many illegals stop off to book into the Country Club, I shouldn't think,' Morgan observed.

Spence turned the conversation back to the way the body was clothed. 'April's a bit early in the year to be out without a coat, I'd have thought, especially after dark.' As usual, he was immaculately turned out in a dark grey three-piece wool suit paired with a white shirt and light grey tie.

'Any chance of it being a romantic skinny-dip that went wrong?' Morgan looked to both Mackenzie and Bingley.

'Nothing romantic about steel handcuffs,' said Mackenzie, and Bingley nodded his agreement.

'I've sent you both the best picture of his face we can get under the circumstances. It might help with ID,' said Bingley. The keycard has gone into exhibits. It was in the jeans pocket and is bloodied so I'm not hopeful of any DNA except his own. Prints, maybe.'

'And the PM?' Morgan turned back to Morag Mackenzie.

‘Tomorrow at nine,’ she replied. ‘I’ve got a couple of victims from a suspicious house fire scheduled for this afternoon. Tomorrow’s the earliest I can fit him in.’

‘Okay. Tomorrow at nine.’

She picked up her metal case and made her way to the inner crime scene tape, where she stripped off her gloves, shoe covers and coveralls. The men watched as she logged out and disappeared from view at the bottom of the concrete slope.

‘Any word about Mack? I didn’t like to ask her,’ said Morgan.

The team differentiated between the father and daughter pathologists by referring to them as Mack and MoMack. Dr Hugh Mackenzie was recuperating at home after recent knee replacement surgery. MoMack was picking up all of the major crime work and Morgan wondered how long she would be able to cope.

‘He’s out for at least six weeks, I’d say. That’s how long he’s not supposed to drive. After that, it’s hard to say. So much of the job is standing, kneeling and getting into the awkward places that people dump bodies. It takes its toll on the joints.’ Bingley looked down at the ample belly which strained the seams of his white coveralls and Morgan wondered how long it had been since he had seen his knees and feet. ‘Anyway, I must get on.’ He turned from the detectives and plodded back to the beach hut.

‘Can you organise door-to-door along the clifftop please, Dave? Get hold of some uniforms. It’s a long shot, but maybe someone saw a light or heard some frolicking.’

‘What about ID?’ Spence took his phone from an inside jacket pocket. ‘Brian’s email’s arrived.’ He tapped the phone and looked at the photograph attachment before holding it up for Morgan, who frowned.

'No way of hiding that he's dead,' said Spence, 'but at least the face isn't injured.'

'On second thoughts, can you take that to the Country Club? See if someone recognises him. I'll ask one of the DCs to sort out the door-to-door.'

'On it,' said Spence, and made for the crime scene boundary. Morgan watched him stop and speak to Ellie Hughes, who was still sitting on the bench at the edge of the path. It was a short conversation which ended with him helping her stand. They linked arms and slowly made their way towards the bottom of the slope. Morgan allowed himself a small smile. Spence could be blunt and abrasive but he had a good heart. From the rear, they looked just like any one of the elderly couples who lived in Retirement-on-Sea embarking on their daily constitutional.

Chapter 6

Wednesday 1st April

Samantha Morgan stood in the car park at Silver Sands Supported Living and waited for her brother to catch up. Their mother, Dorothy Cooper, had summoned them and made it clear that failure to attend was not an option.

'Where's your car?' she asked, and looked beyond him in the direction from which he'd come. At five feet two, she struggled to see over the first few rows of vehicles.

'I came on my bike,' he replied. 'Can't afford the petrol since Mum stopped paying my wages.'

'She only stopped paying you because you stopped turning up for work. I've had to go in every couple of days to fill in. It's not on, Steven. I'm supposed to be working on our house. And I've got all the family stuff to do.'

Steven pouted. It was a look she associated more with her twelve-year-old twins than a brother who would soon celebrate his thirty-fifth birthday.

'She gave you the house and she wants you to run the business so she can give you that, too. It doesn't seem like a very fair split of the inheritance to me. You get everything and I can't afford petrol for my car.'

'She only gave Nick and me the house because she wants it fixed up. I've got a horrible suspicion that she's planning to move back in when it's up to her standards.'

'Poor you.' Steven's tone was sarcastic.

'Do you know what she wants today?' Samantha tried to change the subject.

'No, but I bet I won't benefit from it.'

When they got to the front door, Samantha rang the bell. After a brief wait, a young man appeared and opened it. He was small and wearing heavily stained chef's whites. He stood back and let them in. 'Do you know where you're going?' he asked.

Samantha nodded and made for the staircase. She waited at the top for Steven, and they walked together to the end of the long corridor which led to their mother's suite. She knocked on the door and tried the handle. Locked. Another knock – louder this time.

'I'm coming. I'm coming.' The siblings glanced at each other. Their mother's tone was angry. When the door opened, her face confirmed it.

'Get in, both of you.' Samantha entered first, then her mother reached out and grabbed Steven's jumper, pulling him over the threshold before she slammed the door closed. 'I'm furious; I hardly know where to start.'

'I'll put the kettle on,' said Samantha, pulling her yellow fleece over her head and making for the small kitchen.

'You will not,' said Dorothy. 'Sit at the table. And you too.' She pointed to Steven, who rolled his eyes and plonked himself down on the nearest upright chair.

Dorothy waited for Samantha to sit. 'I've had your bloody husband here this morning,' she said.

'Nick? What did he want?'

'This is nothing to do with me,' said Steven, pushing his chair back from the table and getting to his feet.

'Stay where you are,' Dorothy shouted. 'This is everything to do with you. Your brother-in-law was here this morning accusing you of murder and accusing me of covering up for you. We're in a lot of trouble and it's your fault.'

Chapter 7

Wednesday 1st April

DS Dave Spence waited in a queue at the reception desk of the East Gullhaven Country Club. If the background music was meant to soothe and relax, it wasn't working. He wanted to push everyone aside and get on with the important business of identifying the body in the beach hut. But it was lunchtime and they were busy. He needed the goodwill of the staff, particularly in these early hours of the investigation, so he waited. When his turn came, a young girl appeared from the office and called him to the desk. Her auburn hair was pulled back into a ponytail and she wore tiny gold stud earrings. Spence thought it might be 'Bring Your Daughter to Work Day'. As he approached the desk, he decided it wouldn't be appropriate to show her the picture.

He leant over the counter and spoke quietly. 'I need to speak to the manager. It's a sensitive issue.'

The girl, whose name badge read 'Monica – Trainee Receptionist', stiffened. 'I'm sure I'll be able to help you, Sir. What do you need?'

Spence swore under his breath. Monica either had a history of calling on management too often, or she was intent on proving she was up for any proffered challenge. He reached into his jacket pocket and showed her his warrant card. She took a step back from him and seemed unsure what to do next.

'The manager?' He reminded her of his original request.

'Perhaps I can assist?' A middle-aged woman who had been helping another guest stepped across.

‘Are you the manager?’ Spence asked.

‘I’m sorry, but Mr Thorne is not here this week. Our duty manager is in charge.’

‘Then I need to speak to your duty manager.’ Spence considered himself a patient man, but he had a limit and it was fast approaching.

‘Our duty manager is off duty at the moment,’ she said, apparently unaware of the irony of her response.

Spence sighed. ‘I am trying to identify someone who was found with one of your key cards in his possession.’

‘Monica could have assisted you … if you had explained.’ She didn’t attempt to hide her irritation and neither did the guest who was waiting for her return.

‘I don’t have the card. It has gone into evidence.’

‘How am I supposed to be able to identify which room they were staying in if you don’t have the card?’ She was sneering at him over the top of her rimless spectacles and Spence no longer felt protective towards them. He produced his phone, laid it on the reception desk and twirled it around so it faced them.

Monica leant in for a closer look. When she looked up, she was biting the edge of her bottom lip. The woman beside her recoiled. ‘That man’s dead,’ she said through clenched teeth.

‘Do you recognise him? Either of you?’

‘It’s Mr Dennison,’ said Monica. Spence and the woman looked at her. ‘I booked him in and I remember him. He was funny.’

‘Was he staying here alone?’ asked Spence.

‘He’s attending the sales meeting we’re hosting.’

Spence dismissed the mature woman with insincere thanks and focused on Monica. ‘What else can you tell me about him?’

‘Not much, really. He was kind to me because I was having trouble with the computer. Some of the other reps who arrived with him were impatient.’

‘He was a sales rep?’

‘I think so, yes. Or a sales manager, maybe? He always seemed to have a lot of the other delegates around him, hanging on his every word.’

‘Can you give me access to his room?’ Monica looked doubtful and turned towards her colleague, who asked if he had a warrant. ‘No, I don’t. But I can be back in an hour with a warrant and with a team of uniformed officers wearing big boots, if that’s your preference.’ She asked him to wait and disappeared into the office. Spence guessed that the duty manager might be contactable after all.

Chapter 8

Wednesday 1st April

Samantha's eyes widened and her jaw dropped. 'You can't be serious. Murder? Why would he be accusing Steven of murder?'

'And you're not innocent in all of this.' Her mother reached over and prodded her shoulder with a bony forefinger. 'You married him.'

'Why would Nick be accusing Steven of murder, Mother?' Samantha persisted. 'You must have misunderstood.'

'Your precious brother got in a bit of a tussle.' Dorothy hissed her words through clenched teeth. 'He stabbed someone.'

'No!' Samantha stood up. 'I'm not staying here to listen to this. I don't know what's going on, but I'm not getting involved.'

'You're already involved. You married Plod.'

Samantha dropped back down on to her chair, flinching as her back jarred. 'I still don't understand.'

'Tell her, Steven.'

'No. You told me never to tell anyone.' She was behind him and he didn't see her hand rise to deliver the blow that he wasn't expecting. The strength behind it shocked Samantha. A lifetime in the funeral business moving bodies and caskets had given Dorothy upper-body strength which showed no signs of fading however much she played the frailty card.

'Tell her. Tell her what you did.'

Steven's eyes were threatening tears when he opened them. 'I hurt the lad who Nick found at Cliffside House on the day you were due to move in. But I didn't kill him.' The first sentence was spoken softly, but the second was loud and indignant. 'I didn't kill him,' he repeated.

'Then who did?' asked Samantha.

'The police arrested the right man,' said Dorothy.

Samantha pulled her chair closer to the table and reached out her hands to Steven. 'Tell me all of it. I can't help if I don't know the full story.'

Dorothy scoffed. 'You can't help anyway. It's about money now, and I'm dealing with it.'

Steven took his sister's hands in his. 'I'm sorry,' he said. 'Mum didn't tell me you were getting Cliffside House until you were about to move in. And then she told me that you were coming in to manage the business, too.' He flicked his head in their mother's direction. 'It just seemed so unfair.'

Samantha frowned at her mother, who responded with a shrug.

'So what did you do about it?' Samantha persisted.

'I went to Cliffside the night before you were going to move in. I don't even know why I went.'

'How did you get in? Did you have mum's keys?'

He shook his head. 'I went up the fire escape. Even when we were kids, I could always open that lock.'

'And then?'

'I saw someone bending over the cabinet.'

'I don't know how that was possible. It must have been dark.'

Steven sighed. 'There was a small fire in the grate. That's how.'

'Why did you hit him?' asked Samantha.

'He didn't hit him,' said Dorothy, making Samantha jump. In the intensity of watching Steven relive the moment, she had forgotten about her mother. 'He stabbed him.'

Samantha recoiled. The brother she knew was good-natured and easy-going, sometimes to the point of frustration. That he would stab someone was inconceivable.

'I was so outraged that he had broken into our house. He was living there when I wasn't allowed to. So I stabbed him.' He paused as his eyes searched Samantha's face for her reaction. 'He was using our furniture!'

'That doesn't justify it.' Samantha turned to her mother, who had gone to stand at the window. 'How did he die? I mean, if being stabbed didn't kill him?'

'He fought back,' said Steven, not waiting for his mother to answer. 'He kept punching and kicking me. I fell over and he started kicking my head. He could have killed me.'

Dorothy came back to the table and sat. 'Your husband's hypothesis is that Danny Easton saw Steven and followed him into Cliffside. He thought he was witnessing a break-in, and you know he felt about those. Plod thinks Danny was watching when they started fighting, and at some point, with the light from the fire, he recognised Steven. That's when he piled in. When the yob tried to do a runner, Danny followed him to the master bedroom and got him on the ground. Then he smothered him.'

Samantha raked her hands through her short blonde hair. She tried to remember the details of the case which had seen Danny Easton charged with the murders of prolific burglars. She didn't always listen when Nick spoke about cases, but this body had been found in their master bedroom.

'So Danny Easton killed him? You're sure he didn't bleed to death from the stabbing? I remember Nick saying there was a lot of blood at the scene. The flooring was ruined.'

'Steven stabbed him but Danny has admitted smothering him.'

Samantha looked at her mother. 'Why didn't he tell the police about Steven?'

'He and I reached an arrangement,' said Dorothy. 'And the money will be deducted from Steven's inheritance.' She scowled at her son as if daring him to argue. 'I told you when he was arrested that I'd be paying for his legal representation, and I've also agreed a monthly allowance for his mother.'

Samantha remembered being surprised when her mother had mentioned that she was paying Danny Easton's defence costs, but she knew they had been friends when Danny worked at the home and had accepted it as an altruistic act. 'Jesus,' she said, 'I'm struggling to take all this in. Come to think about it, why are you telling me now?'

'Because your Plod was here this morning spouting off about his theory. He also said he's not going to let it rest.'

'It doesn't sound like a theory, Mother. It's a pretty good guess at exactly what happened.'

'I don't care.' Dorothy's eyes flashed with anger. 'You've got to talk him out of it. Your brother wouldn't last two minutes in prison.'

Samantha shook her head. 'Surely it wouldn't come to that?'

'It won't now because Steven is going abroad,' said Dorothy, 'until this blows over.'

'News to me,' said Steven.

'I've been looking at an art school in France,' she continued. 'It's what you've always wanted, so don't start changing your mind now.'

'I've no money … and I don't speak French.'

'I can sort out the fees and the accommodation, but you'll have to pick up the language. I can't do the impossible.' She turned to Samantha. 'And you'll have to pull your weight in the business. Things have slipped without proper management.'

Samantha saw how neatly this solution played into her mother's hands, but she couldn't see a way around it. 'So he stabs a man and brings about his death and is punished by being sent to art school, and I end up slogging full time in the business.'

'You've got my house,' said Dorothy. 'How much more do you want.' The comment stung Samantha. She had argued with Nick about whether her mother would use the house as an ongoing bargaining chip and now it seemed he was right.

'You can both go now,' said Dorothy. 'This whole thing has exhausted me.' She made her way to her favourite chair, reaching out to items of furniture to steady her. When she sat, she immediately closed her eyes.

They looked at each other and rose from the table together. At the door, Samantha looked back and saw that her mother's eyes were open just enough to confirm that they had obeyed. She slammed the door behind her.

‘Do you think Nick’s serious about coming after me?’ asked Steven as they walked back along the corridor.

‘Who knows, Steven; he rarely speaks to me about work. He certainly didn’t warn me that this was about to happen.’

‘I’m sorry, Sam. I was angry and I lashed out. Can you speak to him about it?’

She paused to think about it before shaking her head. ‘Nick and I are working through something personal at the moment. He doesn’t owe me any favours. Come on. We’ll put your bike in my car and I’ll take you to your flat. You’ve got packing to do.’

Steven nodded and they made their way to the car park without speaking again.

Chapter 9

Wednesday 1st April

If the briefing room door was closed and the view through the square glass panels made it obvious that a meeting was in progress, it was customary to knock before entering. DCI Richard Johnson burst in and Morgan looked up from his notes, irritated by the interruption.

'Sir?'

All eyes turned to Johnson and then to the woman who had entered behind him. She was tall, thin and unsmiling. Her hair was dark brown and cut in a neat bob which framed a well-made-up face. Alert eyes returned appraising glances through stern, black-rimmed glasses. Her navy trouser suit looked as if it had been purchased when she'd carried a little more weight, and her white blouse was buttoned up to the collar.

'So this is where you all are,' said Johnson, as if he had just found the cool kids smoking behind the bike sheds.

'Yes, Sir, I'm holding a preliminary briefing for the case we picked up earlier. A body down at Gullhaven Cove in a beach …' Morgan stopped. As Johnson moved to one side, he caught a look at the woman and his mouth gaped.

'This is DS Alison Goddard.' Johnson indicated towards her with his hand before pointing to the front of the room. 'DI Nick Morgan.'

She acknowledged with a slight nod in his direction. 'DI Morgan,' she said softly. All eyes turned to Morgan as the audience waited for him to respond.

‘We know each other from several training courses, Sir. It’s good to see you, DS Goddard. Did the weather in North Yorkshire finally get the better of you?’

Johnson stepped forward. ‘DS Goddard applied to join Central and Southern some time ago but we’ve only recently had funding agreed to fill the vacant DS position. Happily, she was still available and keen to join us, and here we are. Where’s DI Patel?’

‘She’s at the Crown Court today, Sir, so I’ve picked up this one.’

Johnson nodded. ‘There will be more induction, of course, and equipment allocation, but it would be counterproductive for DS Goddard not to be in at the beginning of a new case.’ He turned to her. ‘I’m going to leave you in DI Morgan’s care for the moment. When the briefing’s over and you’ve been introduced to your new colleagues, come back up to my office and I’ll get someone to sort out the rest of the preliminaries with you. Thank you, DI Morgan.’ He made a gesture with his hand which might have been a wave, and left without closing the door.

DC Jennifer Smart had been late getting to the briefing and was standing at the back of the room. She nodded at Morgan, reached across and closed the door, smiling at Alison Goddard as their eyes met. It wasn’t reciprocated.

‘As I was saying …’ Morgan tried to recapture his train of thought. ‘God … what was I saying?’

‘You were saying that there were heavy-duty handcuffs on the wrists which were disguised to look like a sex-toy.’ Smart had been taking her usual detailed notes, and read them back.

‘Yes, of course. CSI have reported that they are nickel-plated steel cuffs and they’ve been covered by a pink fluffy fabric and darker pink feathery tendrils, maybe to make them look a lot less intimidating.’

‘Perhaps they should be standard issue if it means the perps struggle less when we’re trying to get them on.’

Morgan ignored the interruption.

‘Have we got a name, Sir?’ asked Smart.

‘There was an electronic room key from East Gullhaven Country Club in his jeans pocket,’ said Morgan. ‘DS Spence has gone there with the best photo we could get of his face –’ he pointed to the picture stuck to the whiteboard ‘– and we hope that someone can identify him.’

Jenny Smart held her head to one side as if assessing a work of art in a gallery. ‘I’m not sure I’d recognise him from that, even if I knew him,’ she said.

‘Well it’s all we’ve got at the moment, so let’s hope,’ said Morgan. ‘Lastly, CSI are suggesting that the assault started in a gap between a couple of beach huts further down the row than where the body was found. The vegetation, and that’s their word, not mine, was trampled and they found one of those advanced key things for an Audi and a couple of condoms still in their wrappers. There’s also blood on some rocks and the surrounding shingle opposite the gap where they found the key.’ He consulted his report again. ‘The body is wearing only one trainer. The other one was on the path between the rocks and the hut where the body was found.’ He saw a few members of the team exchange glances. ‘I’m ruling nothing out at this stage; I’m just telling you all we’ve got.’

‘So we’re looking for an Audi?’ The voice came from the back of the briefing room and Morgan turned over a page of the printout he was holding.

‘The key matches an Audi SQ5 that was in the clifftop car park when we got there this morning. Navarra Blue metallic, apparently.’

Brian Bingley stood. ‘In the absence of Dave Spence, our go-to petrolhead, I can tell you that it’s fifty-five grands worth of car,’ he said. ‘And before you judge me, I had to look it up.’ There was a ripple of laughter. Spence’s enthusiasm for the high-end cars which his salary would never afford was renowned.

‘They’re bringing it in,’ said Morgan. ‘And I don’t want to hear that any of you have been dribbling over it.’ He looked around the room. ‘That’s about it for now. Not much to go on yet. The PM’s at nine tomorrow morning. We’ll know more after that. Meantime, Jenny, can you please sort out door-to-door for the properties overlooking the beach. There’s a chance someone might have seen or heard something. Ask about vehicles parked by the roadside and in the car park, too. It’s a bit early in the year for tourists. Remember that a lot of the buildings have been split into flats.’

She gave him a withering look and he raised his hands and nodded his apology. She was local; she didn’t have to be told about the flats. He issued a few tasks to some of the other officers then closed the meeting. ‘Next briefing at eight tomorrow, please. We should have an ID by then.’

Chairs scraped across the floor and multiple conversations started as some of the team left to get on with action points from other inquiries. One or two who had sat at the back of the room came forward to get a closer look at the photos of the body.

'Who's doing the PM?' asked Smart.

'MoMack. She was at the scene when I got there.'

'Do you want me to attend?'

'I'll go.' Alison Goddard's soft voice was in contrast to her severe face and outfit.

'That doesn't seem a very nice way of welcoming you to the team,' said Morgan.

'It's okay. I'll go. Can you give me the mortuary postcode for my satnav? I haven't found my way around yet.' Morgan glanced at Smart, who nodded and grabbed her phone from her bag to access the information.

'I'd like you both to go,' he said. 'Perhaps you can carpool. Meantime, come with me, Alison, and we'll have a quick coffee and catch up. I'm sure DCI Johnson can wait a little longer.'

They left DC Jenny Smart juggling her bag, notebooks and pens and walked to Morgan's office. He opened the door and waited to let her pass. They were close enough for him to smell her perfume. Hints of freesia and ginger. He went to close the door, then changed his mind.

'Well, this is a surprise,' he said, moving a visitor chair from its place by the wall and dropping his phone on to his desk. 'You could have called to let me know.'

'I haven't called in twenty years.' She held his gaze before looking away. 'Anyway, I only found out a couple of weeks ago that you had transferred here. I thought you were still the golden boy at the Met. I think a call would have given you a bigger shock than me just turning up.'

‘Fair point,’ he agreed, draping his jacket across the back of his chair and sitting down, ‘but why are you here?’

‘If you imagine it’s because of you, you can think again. I was due to be transferred here last summer but they lost the headcount and I was told I’d have to wait or apply elsewhere. I decided to wait, and now, here I am. How long have you been here?’

‘Couple of months … just over. We moved so that Sam could be nearer her mother.’ He had become accustomed to this as the reason for transferring, although the emotional scars of Operation Fire Farm still itched. ‘We’re living in her mother’s house now that she’s gone into a home. I’m supposed to be doing it up when I get some spare time.’

‘Always the handyman, Nick. I remember that from back then.’

He cleared his throat. It felt awkward to be sitting in a room with her after all this time. The Morgan marriage had been in its early stages when he first met Alison Goddard. Their affair was brief but passionate before guilt had got the better of him. When he confessed to Sam, she packed her bags and returned to live with her parents for a week. He suspected that the affair had added to the undisguised loathing his mother-in-law had for him.

Goddard stood. ‘I think I’ll go and find DCI Johnson. Good to catch up.’ She left without a backward glance.

Morgan leant his elbows on the desk and covered his face with his hands. He wondered why life had to be so complicated. After Sam had returned home all those years ago, they’d gone to marriage counselling at her insistence. She had kept her word not to bring up the subject of the affair at every argument, and he had vowed never to stray again. Moving back to Gullhaven had changed everything. Sam had embarked on an affair with Graham Fletcher, and his relationship with Maisie Sangster, which had started as simple revenge sex, was developing into something deeper. The addition of DS Alison Goddard to the mix was unforeseen and unwelcome.

His phone skittered across his desk as it vibrated. He picked it up and glanced at the screen.

'Yes, Dave. What have we got?'

'Our unknown is a guy called Simon Dennison. He was here attending a sales conference. One of the receptionists recognised him.'

'Good work, Dave. I'll send DC Smart over to help you search his room.'

'No hurry, Sir. I'm waiting for the duty manager to come on duty.'

'You know that doesn't make sense, don't you?' He heard Spence sigh. 'No worries. I'll send Smart over now.'

Chapter 10

Wednesday 1st April

DS Dave Spence had been appeased by two cups of coffee and a salmon and cucumber sandwich while he waited to search Simon Dennison's room. When DC Jenny Smart arrived at the Country Club, he was leaning on the reception desk. Her cheeks were flushed as she hurried to him. 'Sorry, I'm right at the back of the car park. Got here as fast as I could.'

Spence pointed at the large carrier bag she was clutching. 'Did you bring me lunch?'

'Evidence bags, gloves, coveralls and shoe covers. Sorry.'

He smiled. 'It's okay. I've eaten.' He was about to say more but was interrupted by a short man who bustled towards them from the direction of the lifts. He stretched out a hand. 'Ben Lowe. I'm covering for the duty manager.' His accent was Australian although Spence didn't comment on it. He wasn't good with accents. He'd once bored a girl at a party with a detailed description of a holiday he had enjoyed in Australia. She had let him continue without interruption for what seemed like forever before cutting him down with, 'I'm from New Zealand,' and walking away.

Spence shook his hand. 'DS Dave Spence and DC Jenny Smart. Central and Southern Major Crimes Unit.

Lowe was the first person at the club not to be put out by the presence of the police and Spence liked him immediately. 'We need access to the room of one of your guests who was found dead this morning.'

'Of course. What room number?'

Spence apologised. 'None of your reception staff has felt they were authorised to give me that information.'

Lowe nodded. 'I know that wasn't helpful but we're very protective of the security of our guests. What's the name?' He leant across the desk at an unmanned position and lifted the keyboard up, balancing it on the narrow shelf.

'Mr Dennison,' said Spence. 'Simon Dennison.'

There was a loud clatter as the precariously balanced keyboard slipped from Ben Lowe's hands and dropped back on to the desk. 'Mr Dennison? Are you sure?'

'I'm afraid so, Mr Lowe. How well did you know him?' Spence watched the man's face as he answered the question.

'He's been coming here with his company for … well, as long as I've worked here.'

'And how long is that?

'About three years now. But he also entertained here. He brought customers for meals.' He looked around before speaking more quietly. 'Women friends, too. He's a generous tipper and that makes him memorable – and popular, of course.'

Spence nodded. He had done some bar work in his teens and remembered how nice it was to be told to deduct a drink for himself from the change owed.

'We need access, Mr Lowe, to find out as much as possible about Mr Dennison for our inquiries.'

Lowe excused himself and entered a five-digit code before disappearing through a door marked 'Staff Only'. Smart looked along the desk to where two receptionists were watching them.

'He'll be coming through the office,' the older one called, pointing to a door behind her. She was right. Seconds later, Ben Lowe reappeared.

'What's today's password?' he asked, resting a hand on the nearer woman's shoulder. She tipped her keyboard up and passed him a sliver of paper. He seemed about to remonstrate, but changed his mind and returned to the computer in front of the officers. 'I'll log on and sort you out a couple of keys. They will only work for today, but you can renew them at the desk if you need the room for longer. I'll designate it as booked until you've finished with it.' His fingers danced over the keyboard at a speed which Spence envied. He loved his job but hated the time it took to write reports. Maybe he should consider typing classes?

'Here you are,' said Lowe, handing two key cards to Spence. 'Room 122, on the first floor. What about his property? Will you be taking it with you?'

'It depends on what we find,' said Smart. We may have to send a team over to deal with it.'

Lowe's eyes opened wider. 'It was an accident, wasn't it?'

Spence had already taken a couple of steps from the desk. He considered pretending he hadn't heard the question but relented and turned back. 'I'm sorry, Mr Lowe. I'm afraid I can't answer that because we've just started our investigation.' He felt Lowe's eyes follow him across the foyer.

Chapter 11

Wednesday 1st April

The lift dinged and the doors opened on the first floor. They got out and pushed through the fire doors. Smart paused in front of the directions sign and pointed to her left. They walked side by side down the wide corridor, manoeuvring around a laden housekeeping trolley and a number of white and blue laundry bags piled beside an open bedroom door. The sounds of a TV game show blared out, punctuated by a woman's voice yelling a one-sided conversation. She appeared at the door as they reached it, thrust a mobile phone into her tabard pocked and smiled at them both. Grabbing a couple of toilet rolls, she turned back into the room and the door closed behind her.

When they got to Room 122, the officers put on blue nitrile gloves and opened the plastic packs containing the white coveralls. Spence was quick to dress and already had his shoe covers on when he noticed Smart look round for a surface to steady against while she slipped her legs into the bulky suit. 'Here,' he offered, and pointed to his shoulder. 'Don't want you leaving prints on the walls.'

When they were both appropriately suited up, Spence slotted a key card into the lock. He responded to the click and green light by pushing the heavy door with his shoulder.

The room was darkened by thick, floor-length curtains drawn across the window. Smart flicked the matt metal switch with the knuckle of her forefinger. Nothing happened.

‘It’s one of these,’ said Spence, opening the door to the corridor again so he could borrow the light. He slotted the key card into a wall-mounted box and the lamps flickered and hummed into life. ‘They’re supposed to save money by making sure that the lights and TV aren’t on when the room’s unoccupied. I bet the receptionists are sick of telling people about it.’ He used a whiny voice: ‘*My electrics don’t work.*’

Smart laughed. She walked across to the curtains and opened them. The glazing was from floor to ceiling and took up most of the width of the room. ‘Wow,’ she said, taking in the view of the golf course and the woods beyond. Even with the low cloud and hint of rain to come, the view was stunning. ‘How the other half lives.’

‘Room’s been made up,’ said Spence. ‘Bed’s made.’ He took a couple of steps backwards and opened the door to the bathroom. ‘Clean towels, too.’

Smart passed him on her way to the door. ‘Housekeeping,’ she said.

Spence took a few pictures of the room with his phone. If something had happened in here that had contributed to Dennison’s death, he wanted to have a record before anything was touched. Realistically, now that housekeeping had done their thing, he suspected that boat had sailed.

The door lock clicked. Smart had returned, pen and notebook clutched in her hand.

‘Any joy?’ asked Spence.

‘She’s Filipino, or is it Filipina because she’s female? I’m not sure. And her English isn’t great. I think maybe she understands it better than she speaks. Anyway …’ she read from her notes, ‘she remembers that the bed hadn’t been slept in, so she didn’t change the sheets.

They change the bedding after two nights. She told me that she looked at the sheets to make sure they weren't stained.' She screwed up her face. 'Management policy, apparently.' She looked up at Spence, expecting a wisecrack, but he didn't comment.

'She cleaned the bath and toilet and changed the towels. She said that not having to change the bedding helped her catch up because she was running behind.'

'We'd better stop the towels going to the laundry, just in case.'

'Already sorted. I've dragged the bag to just outside but there's no way of knowing which were his towels.'

Spence nodded. Of course she had. He had never met anyone so completely focused on the smallest of details. She hadn't been a Detective Constable for very long and he could see that she had her eye on the next promotion. If he didn't sit his Detective Inspector exam soon, she would pass him and he would be calling her Ma'am.

Smart jiggled the wireless mouse which lay beside a laptop computer plugged in and charging on the desk at the bottom of the bed. The screen demanded a password. 'That's a pity,' she said.

'He liked his electronics,' said Spence, pointing to the shelf at the side of the bed, where a phone and a tablet lay.

'It's a boy thing,' she replied. 'I hope I've brought enough evidence bags.'

'I don't have to put up with that, you know. That's sex discrimination.' His voice was harsh and it must have startled her because she shot him a look. 'Sorry, Jen,' he said, and turned his attention to a tan leather travel bag which lay on the floor in the hanging space. He lifted out a neat stack of underwear and laid it on the bed. He plunged his hand into a deep side pocket and produced another phone and charger. The final items were a paperback novel and a white bin bag with a couple of pairs of pants and socks and a crumpled shirt.

'Was there a phone found with the body?' asked Spence.

'No, just the key card.' She passed him an evidence bag and a pen. 'These should keep the techies busy for a while.'

Spence completed the label and dropped the bag on the bed beside the rest of Dennison's gadgets. He went into the bathroom and tipped the contents of Dennison's wash bag into the sink. Nothing out of the ordinary, he decided, but all the items were high-end brands. His wife, Penny, would have sneered at the waste of money. There was a box of condoms, which Spence counted. Five missing. It looked as if Dennison had had plans for this conference. He looked up to see Jenny Smart watching him from the bathroom door.

'The boss said they'd found a couple of condoms not far away from the body, and an Audi key, too.'

'Used?' asked Spence.

'The Audi or the condoms?'

He rolled his eyes. 'Come on, Jen.'

'The condoms were still sealed.'

'So he fancied his chances at the beach party?' said Spence. 'If he was planning to bring someone back, he'd have just left them here.'

'Guess so. Not for me, though. Sand gets everywhere.'

'Sounds like the voice of experience. Anyway, it's shingle down there.'

There was a timid knock on the bedroom door and Smart opened it. The Filipina housemaid stood there with a knotted bin liner in her hand. She offered it to Smart and said, 'From this room, I remember. Too full to tip into my bin so I take all.'

'Thank you,' said Smart, and returned her shy smile. 'That's very helpful.'

She held the thin bag up to Spence, who screwed his face up. He could see lots of scrunched up paper, a couple of apple cores and a sandwich wrapper. Wet teabags had smeared the sides of the bag and stained the paper inside. He didn't want to speculate whether there might be three used condoms in there, too. 'We'll take it back with us,' he said.

Chapter 12

Wednesday 1st April

There were no lights at the front of the house when Nick parked his Volvo on the drive. He selected his key as he approached the front door and was surprised when Sam opened it.

'Where have you been?' she hissed. 'I sent a couple of texts.'

'I was busy. There's a lot going on.' He glanced at his watch and saw that it was nearly half past nine. Not unusual when a new case was in its initial stages, but suspiciously late if Sam found out that Alison Goddard was back on the scene. He decided he would break the news another time. 'What's so urgent, anyway?'

Sam was walking away from him towards the kitchen. 'We may have a problem.'

Nick felt his heart sink. He thought they were working on getting things back on track after his wife's affair. Admittedly, they still slept in different rooms, but that was his choice at the moment. It didn't feel right to share a bed with his wife whilst he was still figuring out his relationship with Maisie. Sam let him pass her at the kitchen door and closed it behind them.

The room was lit only by a couple of under-cabinet lights, which might have been romantic but for the frown on his wife's face. She had poured him a glass of red wine, although he had no idea how long ago. It sat on the island next to an almost empty bottle.

'You started without me, then?' he said, taking his first sip. He was more comfortable now. If Sam had found out about Alison's return, or worse, his relationship with Maisie, she would surely have tipped the wine over him.

She held out a sheet of paper and as he took it; he recognised the logo of the school that their twins, Alexander and Victoria, had been attending for the last couple of months. He was surprised – this was unexpected.

'Don't give me the look … Just read it.'

He took it over to the light, scanned the words and looked up. 'What do you make of it?' he asked.

'I've no idea. It says that they have sent Alex home with a couple of letters but we've not replied. Has he given them to you?'

'Of course not. I hardly see him without you being there.'

'I could say that you hardly see him at all.' Her comment was mumbled, but it was loud enough for him to hear.

'That's not fair.'

'The appointment with his year leader is for ten o'clock tomorrow. I think we should both be there.'

'It's not much notice. I've got an early briefing and interviews tomorrow, but I'll try to get there if I can. What did Alex say when you asked him about the other letters?'

'I haven't asked him. If he's hiding letters from school then I don't think I can trust what he says. Have you eaten?'

Nick shook his head and took a bigger swig of the wine. 'I think I'm beyond wanting to eat. You go to bed. I've got a couple of reports to read.'

She rinsed her glass and put it into the dishwasher. 'Have you remembered that Mum's coming for tea on Sunday?'

'She told me.'

'You didn't tell me you were going to see her.'

He sighed. 'I visited her this morning. I needed to talk to her about something.'

Sam stared at him and he saw from her expression that his visit had not come as a surprise. His mother-in-law had circled the wagons and as usual he was on the outside.

'About what?' she asked, although he could see she already knew.

'It's a police thing.'

They locked eyes and Morgan braced himself. Sam's mouth opened, but no words came out. She slammed the dishwasher shut and marched past him. 'I'm going in to work tomorrow, after I've been to the school. I might not have time to organise dinner.'

'Okay.' He poured the last of the wine into his glass, picked up his briefcase, and carried both into the lounge. He was humming softly; he couldn't remember the words; something about another day in paradise?

Chapter 13

Thursday 2nd April

'I don't even want this.' Luke Armstead pushed his plate away, the full English breakfast barely touched. 'What are we going to say?'

'Say to who?' snapped Rachael Robinson, her accent betraying her Glaswegian roots.

'The police. There's a group of them at the reception desk. The hotel has given them a whole suite of rooms for interrogations.'

'Don't be such a drama queen. They'll just ask a few questions. It hardly qualifies as interrogation,' said Gareth Evans. 'Anyway, all we did was go skinny-dipping after a few beers. There's no law against it. Just tell them the truth.'

'I did a line before I went. What if they do drug tests? Armstead looked around his colleagues, in obvious need of reassurance.

'Why would they do that?' Robinson's voice was louder than she had intended.

'Shhh,' said Evans, replying to the other diners' looks with placatory smiles. 'Simon suggested a few of us went to the beach after dinner. It seemed like a fun idea and we went. Someone thought skinny-dipping was a good idea and I went in. It wasn't. It was bloody freezing. I didn't actually see Simon at the beach and that's what I'm going to say ... if they ask me.'

'Of course they're going to ask you. They're going to ask all of us,' whined Armstead.

Evans smiled at the memory. 'All I know is that I froze my nuts off in that water and when Rachael said she was coming back here, I didn't have to think twice. I went straight to her car with the two guys from Germany. When I got back, I had a shower and went to bed.'

'That sounds too well-rehearsed,' said Rachael. 'I think I was over the limit when I drove to the beach.'

'That's what I'm saying,' insisted Armstead. 'They can do you for that, too.'

'For fuck's sake, Luke. Of course, they can't. They need evidence of me being over. Even if I tell them I was over, they can't do me. Get a grip.'

Armstead pushed his chair back from the table. 'I'm going to be sick,' he said, and hurried towards the dining-room entrance. He pushed past a man and two women without noticing them.

'Here comes trouble,' said Gareth Evans. He looked back down at his breakfast, avoiding eye contact with the group who were being shown to a table by the wall.

'I often imagine them as a ménage à trois.' Robinson spoke softly with her hand in front of her mouth in case her lips could be read.

'That's a thought that will stay with me for the rest of the day,' said Evans. 'You might have let me finish my breakfast first. You can't really see Gary Fox sandwiched between his secretary and his marketing director. Who would be doing what to whom?'

'I'll bet Melanie Meyer has a strap-on. You know what marketing are like. She'd have to fuck rather than be fucked.'

'Girls on top, is it? Poor Gary.'

***

Gary Fox, Managing Director of Forest-Fox Analysis, took the breakfast menu from the uniformed waitress with a smile which didn't reach his eyes. He thought back to yesterday, when they had last sat at this table to enjoy a working breakfast. That meal had been all about the new product launch and the sales awards. There had been banter and laughter. Then Simon Dennison hadn't shown up for the meeting and what he thought was going to be a disciplinary matter had turned into something more sinister.

The tall, well-dressed detective who had asked him to come out of their meeting in the afternoon had been reluctant to give details, but Fox knew that a DS from the local Major Crime Team would not be investigating anything trivial. What he hadn't anticipated was that Dennison was dead and that the circumstances were suspicious.

'Gary.' Becca Yates's voice was gentle and concerned. 'What are you having for breakfast?' He looked up from the unread menu and saw that the waitress was back with her order pad and pencil.

'Just coffee, thanks.' He handed the menu back.

'Mr Fox will have coffee, and one poached egg on wholemeal toast,' Melanie Meyer, the Marketing Director said, 'and I'll have the same. What about you, Becca?'

Rebecca Yates grimaced. She had been ahead in the 'who can be the most empathetic and supportive staff member' competition, but that crown seemed to have been snatched away. 'I'll have a sausage and bacon sandwich, please,' she said. It was the last thing she felt like eating, but if Melanie Meyer wanted to crash her breakfast with Gary Fox then she would have to overcome her Jewish sensitivity and watch her eat it. She called after the departing girl. 'Can you bring tomato sauce as well, please?'

Chapter 14

Thursday 2nd April

Neither DS Goddard nor DC Smart was keen to car-share for the journey to the mortuary so they agreed to meet in the car park. Jenny Smart arrived first and backed her red Renault into the last space. She knew how difficult it was to park at this site and had set off early.

When Alison Goddard appeared, she didn't appear to hesitate. She parked in front of Smart, blocking her in. 'Pick your battles,' Smart muttered under her breath as she got out of the car. She hurried to Goddard's door and opened it for her. 'Good morning, Alison,' she said.

'Morning, Jenny.' Goddard was shuffling through her handbag, lining up her phone, wallet and purse. When she'd finished, she pulled down her visor and checked her make-up before getting out in her own time. Smart felt that the gesture of kindness she had offered had been developed into a demonstration of rank.

'Good morning, Ladies.' Dr Morag Mackenzie extended a hand to Smart, who shook it and introduced DS Goddard. 'Where's "The Suit" today?' asked MoMack of two uncomprehending faces. She laughed. 'It's what Annie and I call DS Spence.' Annie Geeson, one of the mortuary technicians, looked across from the metal dissection table she was hosing down and nodded.

Goddard looked at her watch. 'Will you be starting promptly at nine?' she asked, 'Because I have some calls I can be making if you think there'll be a delay.'

MoMack and Geeson exchanged glances before the pathologist replied. 'Nine o'clock is what we agreed and I see no reason to change it, thank you. I'm sure DC Smart will show you to the viewing gallery in time for you to make yourselves comfortable.' Smart was sure she felt the temperature of the dissection room drop by a couple of degrees.

The body from the beach hut, now formally identified as Simon Dennison by his brother, who had driven down from London, was occupying the dissection table nearest the viewing gallery. Beside it was a table covered with separate sheets of paper. On top of each was an item of Simon Dennison's clothing. A T-shirt, sweatshirt, jeans, boxer shorts and socks. Smart noticed that the jeans and boxers were stiff with the brown staining of dried blood.

'The crime scene guys are coming to collect the clothing any minute now. You can have a look if you want,' said MoMack as she finished her preparations.

Smart and Goddard declined and took their seats as MoMack started a detailed macroscopic examination, once or twice wheeling an illuminated magnifier into place.

'Can you pass me the small forceps and a rack of universals, please?' said the pathologist. She took close-up photographs of the white face while she waited.

Annie brought her a tray with sterile plastic pots, forceps, and a number of syringes pre-filled with distilled water. She unscrewed the white lid from the first pot and MoMack dropped a swab from Dennison's left nostril into it before rinsing the same nostril with distilled water into the next pot. The procedure was repeated for the right nostril, each pot being labelled by Annie as she was handed it.

Next, they turned their attention to the bagged hands. Scrapings were taken from each fingernail, and the fingertips were swabbed. More pots filled and labelled.

When the technicians turned the body, MoMack took a number of photos. 'Nice tattoo,' she said, following the large Celtic knot design which ascended from the small of Dennison's back, up his spine and across his shoulders.

She parted Dennison's buttocks and flinched. 'There's a lot of damage here.'

'Consistent with anal sex?' asked Goddard.

'Violent anal sex, so I'd err towards rape. I can't see any obvious evidence of semen or lubrication, but obviously I'll still swab. You never know: even if they used a condom, it might have split or leaked.' She moved her head and adjusted the lighting. 'I can see something inside him. I'll let you know soon enough what it is.'

'I'm ringing the boss,' said Smart. 'He needs to know about the rape thing before he starts the interviews.'

'You'd best be accurate and report it as an "err towards rape" thing,' said Goddard. 'Maybe he just liked it rough.'

Smart left the viewing gallery, scrolling through her contacts for Morgan's number.

Chapter 15

Thursday 2nd April

When Morgan arrived at the East Gullhaven Country Club early on Thursday morning, he was directed to their conference suite, where he was told they had set up three small breakout rooms for interviews. When he got to the suite, he found DS Dave Spence and DC Lynn Greenfield waiting, each with a coffee in front of them. The aroma promised an expensive blend of real coffee rather than imitation instant.

'Morning, Nick.' said Greenfield. She held up her cup. 'Can I get you one?'

'It's okay, I'll get it.' He dumped his briefcase and followed her pointing finger to a long table which had been laid out with insulated jugs of tea, coffee and hot water. Both brown and white sugar had been provided as well as fresh milk. At the far end of the table was a stand filled with fruit-based teabags, decaffeinated instant coffee and individually wrapped biscuits.

'This is kind of them,' said Morgan, sitting in one of the pink velour and gold chairs ubiquitous to function venues.

'They've put bottles of still and sparkling water in each of the rooms as well. We told them to take away the mints.' Morgan wasn't sure if Spence was joking, but let it go.

'How many are at the conference?' asked Greenfield.

'Fifty-eight,' replied Spence without having to refer to the clipboard he had on the low table in front of him. 'Including French, German, Spanish, Italian and one from Belgium.'

Morgan nodded. 'Does everyone speak English?'

'The European Sales Director I spoke to yesterday said they do, but whilst we were together, a very excitable Glaswegian girl joined us and I didn't understand a single word she said.'

'You'll go down as a stuck-up Sassenach,' warned Greenfield.

Spence was unconcerned. 'I've been called worse. And that's just by my mates.' He reached down and opened a box on the floor containing more clipboards. Morgan saw that they each had the club logo on the back. 'They've given us six of these. Lists of names and positions in the company. They were all here for the annual sales and service conference and a new product launch which was scheduled for this morning. The company has cancelled the razzmatazz, but they want to do some training of the salespeople when we're not speaking to them.'

'I'd prefer them kept separate,' said Morgan, 'at least till we've spoken to everyone.'

'Too late for that, Boss. When I left yesterday, I asked Mr Fox – that's Gary Fox, the Managing Director – to try to keep everyone apart last night, but he told me that some of them were room-sharing. When I saw him on his way to breakfast this morning, he said they had all eaten dinner together in the ballroom as that's what the meeting package included.'

Morgan tutted. 'When does the conference end?'

'It was due to end with a gala dinner this evening and awards for sales performance et cetera. They still plan to have the dinner, but without the awards. I understand that the deceased was due to pick up three of them and it will take a while to recalculate who gets them now.'

'Christ! Life moves on quickly in the commercial world, doesn't it?' said Morgan. He finished his coffee and was placing the cup and saucer on the table when his mobile rang. He reached into his jacket pocket before realising it was his personal mobile, which was in his trouser pocket. He guessed it was Sam wanting to know if he was going to get to the school in time for the meeting, and ignored it. He took the clipboard Spence was offering and was starting to look down the list of names when his work phone rang.

'Good morning, Jenny. What have you got for us?'

'Sir, sorry to interrupt, but I … er, I mean, we … thought you should know about this before you start the interviews.' Morgan wondered if Smart really did mean 'we', or if she had felt obliged to include Goddard because she was standing next to her. He waited.

'MoMack thinks he might have been raped.'

'Explain, please.'

'There's anal tearing and bruising and she can't see any signs of lubrication. His clothes are covered in blood and there might be something inside him.'

'Okay. We'll ask about sexual orientation and preferences. Anything else?'

'She likes his tattoo.' Morgan didn't respond to that and Smart filled the silence quickly. 'MoMack's just starting and I'll send a text if there's anything else I think you should know urgently. Do you want us up at the club when we've finished here?'

He glanced down at the list and sighed. 'Yes, please. We've got fifty-eight, and that's before we get to hotel staff and any guests who are still here and who might have seen something on Tuesday. There are three rooms available and Dave and Lynn Greenfield are already here. On the up side, the coffee is great, so get here when you can.' He ended the call and updated the others.

'Handcuffs and anal sex,' said Spence. 'Each to their own, I suppose.'

'MoMack's thinking he might have been raped.' Morgan frowned and looked back and forward between Spence and Greenfield.

The DC spoke first. 'How do you want to prioritise the interviews, Nick?'

Morgan's eyes scanned down the list. 'Let's start with those who were with Mr Dennison on Tuesday evening, or, at least, those who will admit to it. Lynn, can you set up a sort of triage system out here on the sofas? We'll start with general information and preliminary alibis. Just the usual questions. How well did they know him? When did they last see him? When did they last speak to him? Do they know who could have done such a thing? When we get an idea of who knew him best, you and I will do longer interviews in the meeting rooms. Jenny and Alison Goddard are coming over after the PM.'

'I'll start screening with Lynn, then pick up on the in-depths when we get a few possibles,' said Spence, 'but I'll pour us all another coffee first.'

Chapter 16

Thursday 2nd April

Samantha Morgan delayed getting out of the car for as long as she could. Nick had promised to get to the meeting with Alex's year leader but there was no sign of him. In fairness, she knew that his actual words had been that he would be there if he could, but that was before they'd argued about her mother. He had slept in the spare bedroom again and she knew there was little chance of him making time to turn up, even if it was for the benefit of their son. He would leave it to her, as he'd done so often in the past.

The main doors to the school were locked and it took her a moment to realise that she had to announce her arrival over a security monitoring system. Random gun and knife attacks had made schools very different from how she remembered them.

When the door clicked, she went through into a waiting area. The wall on the right had a hatch through to what looked like the school's administration office. Glazed sliding doors were closed across it. Samantha sighed. She assumed that one of the three women who were fixated by their computer screens must have authorised her entry and that ignoring her now must be some sort of power trip. She looked again at her watch. Now she was late for the meeting.

'Mrs Morgan?' A thin man with boyish features and brown wavy hair was walking towards her, hand outstretched. He was wearing a white lab coat over grey trousers and a white shirt, open at the neck. 'I'm James Newton, Alexander's Head of Year. They told me you were here. Please follow me to somewhere we can talk in private.' He gave a slight nod to one of the women in the office, whose returning smile was warm and wide. Samantha was glad she hadn't hammered on the glass and made a fuss.

At five feet two, Samantha Morgan was at least a foot shorter than the teacher. She had to take two steps for each of his, and she struggled to keep up as they progressed along the wide corridor. Neither spoke, for which she was glad, as she was getting out of breath. At last he opened a door into a large room with wooden benches scarred by years of spills, burns and the carvings of disengaged pupils. The smell brought Samantha's adolescent struggles with science lessons crashing back.

'This lab's free at the moment.' Newton entered first before standing back to let her pass and closing the door with a loud click that made her start. Her mouth dried and she started to sweat. She felt trapped, terrified he was going to interrogate her on the laws of thermodynamics. He pulled two stools out from under the front bench and invited her to sit.

'Are you okay, Mrs Morgan? Would you like some water?'

'I'm fine, thank you. It's the smell. It brings back difficult memories.'

He smiled at her. 'I don't smell it anymore. The first ten years were the worst.'

She saw he had soft brown eyes and full lips. Samantha guessed he would feature in the fantasies of many of his students. She put her bag on the bench beside her, crossed her legs and clasped her hands around her knees, waiting for him to start.

James Newton seemed anxious and Samantha thought that if she didn't get things going she might be here all day. 'I'm sorry my husband wasn't able to make it. He's a police detective and is tied up with a new case.'

Newton nodded and tried to adopt a sage expression. His youthful looks made it unconvincing. When he eventually spoke, he was looking down. 'I wondered … well, that is, *we* wondered … if everything is okay at home?' When he looked up again, he was blushing and his eyes pleaded for her help.

Samantha was taken aback. 'What do you mean, exactly?'

She watched him swallow hard before taking a deep breath. 'We've got some concerns about Alexander's behaviour at school and we wondered if there are issues at home. He seemed to be settling nicely, and now his work, when he does it at all, is of a very poor quality. He is rude and can be aggressive. He's not the lad who started with us six weeks ago.'

Samantha tilted her head to one side and looked beyond him to a poster of the Periodic Table on the wall. So many more elements than she remembered from her own schooldays.

She was trying to think if she had noticed any changes in Alex's behaviour at home but nothing was coming to mind. 'He's twelve and the onset of his adolescence has coincided with us moving him away from friends he's had since nursery. He's going to need time to adjust. I'm sure there's nothing to worry about, Mr Newton.' It felt strange to call him 'Mister' when she thought she could be old enough to be his mother.

She reached out to pick up her bag; this had been a waste of time. He held out a hand to stop her.

'We understand he will need time to settle, but some members of staff have concerns about his choice of coping mechanism.'

'We haven't just dragged him away from his friends, you know. He was with me when we found a woman's body in the woods.' She knew she was exaggerating. They had found a bridal garter belonging to a missing solicitor. It was a police dog that found the body while they were tucked up in the car. 'And his grandmother had a seizure when she was held hostage by a serial killer.'

'Mrs Morgan … I know your family have had quite an unusual introduction to Gullhaven, and I'm sorry for that. My reason for asking you to meet with me is to see what we can put in place to support Alex as he learns to cope.'

Samantha closed her eyes and nodded. It was difficult to remain outraged when this man was so calm, his expression so sincere.

'Has any alcohol gone missing from home?'

'What do you mean?'

'A few of my colleagues have come to me and said they believe they may have smelled alcohol on Alex's breath, particularly in lessons after break and lunch.'

She was immediately reminded of the day before they relocated. When the twins got back from their last day at that school, she thought she'd caught a whiff of alcohol when Alex had pushed past her on the way to his room. It had surprised her but she'd forgotten about it in the excitement and trauma of the move, followed by the body being discovered in their house. She wanted to leap to Alex's defence; she wanted to slap that handsome, boyish face; but she knew he might be right. If Alex was turning to alcohol to help himself cope, he could only have learned it from his parents. She thought of the two half cases of wine in the boot of her car, courtesy of the shopping trip she had fitted in on her way to school, and felt her face flush.

'My husband should be here. I don't quite know what to say to you. You're making a serious allegation against my son and I'm not sure if you're suggesting that I may have been complicit.'

'No!' He threw his head back, grabbing it with both hands, his eyes closed tight. 'I'm not suggesting anything of the sort. I asked you to come in so that we can find out what is going on with Alexander. I'm not accusing you, or him, come to that. I don't teach Alexander after break time, and I have never smelled alcohol on him.'

'I don't know what to say to you,' said Samantha. 'We can have a word with him at home, but I don't expect he'll admit anything.' A more disturbing thought crossed her mind. 'What's the school's position on something like this?'

'Substance abuse on the premises, and we include alcohol in that definition, is a one-week exclusion on the first occasion. If it happens again, we expel the student and involve social services. I'm sorry.'

Samantha was speechless. Exclusion was bad enough, but expulsion and the involvement of social services would surely harm Nick's career. The tabloids would have a feeding frenzy if they found out. She got up and put out her hand, which he shook then enclosed in both his hands. 'The school is here for you and

Alexander. We will support you in whatever way you need. Now, let me take you back to Reception.'

'I can find my own way.'

'Rules, I'm afraid.'

They retraced their steps through the corridors. Samantha could hear a piano being played badly in the distance and she cringed.

'They're supposed to be the happiest days of your life,' he said, 'but not everyone feels that way.'

'I hated school. When I got to fifteen, I was more interested in make-up and boys. Couldn't wait to get old enough to leave. Then, in my last year, we got a new history teacher and she inspired me. I stayed on and ended up with a degree in it. Not honours, but it's still a degree.'

'Well done you.' His voice was soft and when she looked at him to see if he was being sarcastic, his smile was friendly. 'The right teacher can be an inspiration.'

They were back at reception now and he reached again to shake her hand. 'I'll do whatever I can to keep Alex on the straight and narrow. I know it's hard when everything around seems to be changing.' For a moment, he looked as if he was going to say more, but nothing came. She thanked him and looked through the window expectantly, but the women in the office made her wait before releasing the door lock.

Chapter 17

Thursday 2nd April

Gary Fox entered the conference suite accompanied by two women. All three were dressed in black trousers and white sweatshirts with the Forest-Fox Analysis logo embroidered on the left breast. Morgan took a couple of paces towards the group but Fox held up a hand to stop him in his tracks.

'One more coffee,' he said, 'then I'm all yours.' His smile was more of a grimace, and Morgan suspected that he and many of his colleagues were experiencing the consequences of a late night in the club bar.

DC Lynn Greenfield approached them as they poured drinks and added their preferences of sugar and milk. 'I seem to be in charge of the register at the moment. And you are?' She fixed her gaze on the shorter woman, who Morgan put in her forties. There were early signs of crow's feet around her blue eyes, which were red and sunken from tears and lack of sleep.

'I'm Becca. Rebecca Yates, that is.' She pointed to the man beside her. 'I'm Mr Fox's Personal Assistant.' Morgan noticed a sneer cross the taller woman's features at the mention of the job title. Greenfield looked down her list and ticked off the name on the second page.

'I'm really sorry to hear what happened to Simon. He was one of our best.' The taller woman spoke, her voice deep and husky. 'I'm Melanie Meyer. I'm Marketing Director at Forest-Fox Analysis.' She stressed the word 'director' in her title and gave a condescending glance across at Becca Yates. Morgan wondered if the animosity between these women would help or hinder their investigation. He approached the man, who seemed uncertain whether to add sugar to his drink.

'Mr Fox, I'm DI Morgan and I'm in charge of the investigation into Simon Dennison's death. There will be questions for everyone attending the conference, but I think it'll help if you and I sit down and run through a few basics first.' He nodded at Greenfield, and as he led Gary Fox to one of the meeting rooms, Spence closed in on Rebecca Yates.

The meeting room was brightly lit but there was a low and insistent grinding noise which came from the direction of the window. Morgan peeped through a gap in the rose pink velvet curtains and saw a man in shorts which were at least one size too small, shovelling sand into a cement mixer. He predicted that the noise was going to give him a headache before he was finished here. Beyond the mixer and the piles of supplies that would feed it, he saw men laying bricks for what looked like a large extension to the conference suite. It reminded him of all the work needing to be done at Cliffside House. He drew the curtains fully closed and turned to see Gary Fox making himself comfortable in one of the chairs pulled up to a large round table in the middle of the room.

'Thank you for supporting us in our inquiries, Mr Fox. We're going to undertake a sort of triage process today and we'll be speaking to everyone at the conference as well as hotel staff. Once we get a feel for who knew Simon Dennison and who might know something about what happened to him, we'll be able to let some of your delegates get on with the conference, or get home. I know there are flights and trains booked.'

Morgan felt Fox's eyes on him as he came back to the table and sat. 'Perhaps we can start by you telling me a bit about Simon and how he came to work for you?'

'Okay. He came to me at a trade exhibition, about three years ago; Becca can probably give you the exact date. He was working for one of our competitors and he'd been done out of the commission on a large deal he'd closed. He'd done all the work, and with the order about to come in, the management moved the account to an in-house portfolio, which meant that he missed out earning the sales commission. Simon was ultra pissed off. He told me it was the last straw and he was going to leave.'

Morgan's elbows were on the table, his clasped hands supporting his chin. Fox's attention seemed to be drifting, but he waited for him to continue.

'I told him I couldn't afford him. He was at the top of their salary scale. I couldn't get close to their benefits package either, but he insisted that he wanted to come and work with us. Eventually, we negotiated a deal we could both live with. I made it light on the basic salary and generous with the commission. If he was as good as he said he was, he would break even.'

'And was he?'

'Was he what?'

'As good as he said he was.'

Fox nodded vigorously. 'He was better. He was popular with his customers and they brought their business over to us to stay with him. We screwed his old company that year in the South-West territory, and every year since. They spent a few months sending me 'without prejudice' letters: accused me of poaching him and all sorts of other crap. But that died down and Simon thrived with us. He was going to pick up a few awards at dinner tonight.'

'Yes, I'd heard that. How did his success go down with his colleagues?'

'Selling is a competitive business and we encourage that. It brings out the killer instinct in them.'

Morgan thought it was either an unfortunate expression to use under the circumstances or a very telling one. 'Enough of a killer instinct to tempt someone to attack him?'

Fox rubbed his face and Morgan noticed that he hadn't shaved. 'I buy the trophies online and I don't think I spend more than a tenner on each of them. Again, Becca would be able to tell you. Each award has something a bit more valuable as part of it, but even those aren't very generous. A case of wine; a spa day; meal for two; that sort of thing. I like the prizes to include the spouses because they put up with a lot. I don't think anyone I employ would kill him for the sake of winning a meal for two, really I don't.'

'Okay,' said Morgan, 'but over the years I've come across people who kill for the most unexpected of reasons and envy is one of them. To go back a minute …' Morgan frowned as he tried to remember Fox's exact words. 'You said that the letters from Mr Dennison's previous employer had stopped?'

'I said "died down", I think. There was another flurry of legal threats back in October. Simon won a European tender to supply instruments that we'd recently started marketing. Up until last summer, his previous company would have been a shoo-in to close the deal, but Simon came to me with a fully costed case for us to source the item and put our badge on it. We responded to the tender and won it. They were really pissed off. Didn't even see it coming. I heard they'd responded at list price.'

Morgan thought Fox's smug chortle was inappropriate.

'You said there were legal threats?'

'From Giles Clooney, or Clueless Clooney, as I like to call him. He was Simon's previous boss.'

Morgan jotted the name down. 'Just legal? Nothing more personal?'

'I heard that someone sent Simon a photo of a removal van outside Clooney's house. I believe he had to put it on the market when he lost his job. Simon thought it was funny.'

Morgan frowned. 'Is it normal to be sacked if you lose a tender? Seems a bit harsh.'

'He wasn't sacked. The company ceased trading last Christmas. Pity, really. They'd been going for thirty years or more. Still, it's an ill wind and all that, because we picked up a chunk of their service contracts. Two of their service engineers, too.' He grinned at Morgan before looking at his watch. I don't think there's a lot more I can tell you. I'll miss him. He was good for business.' Fox made to get up from his seat.

'Just a few more questions.' Morgan waited until he sat again. 'You've known him for three years, so I'm bound to ask. What can you tell me about his private life?'

Gary Fox shrugged his shoulders and splayed his hands out to his sides. 'Not sure what to say to that. Simon was in his early thirties; single; lots of relationships but nothing seemed to last. Having said that, I don't think he was that bothered about women. He –'

'What do you mean? Are you saying he was gay, or maybe bi?'

'No, I don't mean that. He just never seemed bothered whether he was in a relationship or not. The girls in the office swarmed around him and I've seen him be a bit flirty, but nothing serious. I think he was a bit of a user where women were concerned. More interested in the chase than the result.'

'Broken a few hearts, maybe?'

Fox shrugged. 'I couldn't say for certain. I don't know.' He leaned forward and placed his arms flat on the table before continuing. He seemed to be choosing his words with care. 'I know he lived on his own. I was talking to him about taking on some of the export work, which would have meant a bit of travel. I asked about home, even about pets, in case he had responsibilities. He said he was ready to do whatever we needed. I was going to announce it at the awards dinner.' Fox sighed and his head dropped. 'I'll have to find someone else to do that, too. For fuck's sake.'

Morgan asked if there was anything else that Fox knew which he thought would be useful for the inquiry, and was answered with a curt negative.

'I'm still getting my head around it,' said Fox as he picked up his empty coffee cup and made for the door.

The wave of raised voices and clinking crockery which invaded the room told Morgan that a lot more of the conference delegates had arrived, and he followed Fox to the door to see who he would be interviewing next.

Chapter 18

Thursday 2nd April

DS Dave Spence was leading Becca Yates towards him and he could tell that she had used the time to collect herself and control her emotions.

She sat in the chair recently vacated by Gary Fox. ‘May I have some water?’ She pointed to the bottles, which were beyond her reach.

‘Of course.’

Morgan opened one of the green plastic bottles and handed it to her. She filled a small glass tumbler and took a delicate sip. ‘How can I help?’ she said.

‘We’re trying to build a picture of Simon Dennison. Anything you can tell us about him will be useful, and if you know how he could have ended up dead in a beach hut, that would be even better.’

Spence frowned. He pulled a chair up to the table and sat down.

‘Simon was well liked within the company. A little full of himself sometimes, but one-to-one he could be charming.’

‘How did the “full of himself” manifest itself?’ asked Morgan. He hadn’t started taking notes; he concentrated on Yates as if Spence wasn’t in the room.

‘He could be over-confident. He would sometimes say things that put the other sales guys down. I thought that Gary – Mr Fox, that is – let him get away with things because he brought a lot of business in.’ Morgan continued to hold her eyes, putting her under pressure to say more. ‘He could be over-familiar with some of the young girls as well; the girls in the office and in production. He said they liked it but I wasn't sure.'

The red flush which Morgan had spotted on her neck when she came into the room started to spread to her cheeks. He leaned forward. 'And did that over-familiarity extend to you?'

For the first time since striding confidently into the room, she looked away from his penetrating stare. He sat back, giving her a little more space.

Becca Yates cleared her throat. 'I suppose you'll find out about it anyway, so I may as well be the one to tell you. Yes, you could say we'd had a bit of a thing.' She looked back up at him. 'But it was over before it started. I don't know how many people know about it, and if you can keep it to a minimum I'd be grateful.'

'Who started it?' asked Morgan.

'Him, of course. It was at a sales conference, just like this one. Too much to drink; too much dancing; my divorce had just come through. It just happened.'

'Just the one night?' Morgan noticed Spence wince and threw him a disapproving glance.

'A few nights,' she sighed. 'A few weeks.'

'You'll forgive me, Ms Yates, if my next question seems overly intrusive. I have sound reasons for asking it.' Morgan saw a flicker of dread cross her face before she composed herself, wriggling in her chair as if preparing to absorb a physical blow. 'Did you find any of Mr Dennison's sexual demands or preferences to be in any way unusual?'

Her reply surprised him. 'I've always thought that one person's deviance can be another's preference.'

'Yes,' Morgan nodded, 'that's one way of seeing things.' He rested his clasped hands on the table. It was obvious that this closeness was making her more uncomfortable than the line of questioning. 'Did he ever ask you to engage in any activity involving sex toys?'

'No!' The volume of her reply startled both men.

'Or to physically abuse him in any way?' Morgan was undeterred.

'I believe I already said no.' Becca folded her arms around herself, her face flushing deeper. Morgan could almost feel the heat from across the table.

'During your relationship, did you ever notice marks of physical abuse on him?'

She shook her head and when she answered this time, her voice was soft and tears were threatening her eyes. 'I was older than Simon by more than ten years. I always tried to make sure that our liaisons weren't overly lit.'

'Who ended it?' Morgan sat back again and heard Spence exhale.

Her laugh was bitter. 'It was Simon. He told me I was a mistake and he apologised. He said he was stepping aside so I could find a new life partner. All very amicable, all very civilized. A few days later, I found out I'd been replaced by a skinny twenty-two-year-old apprentice in the production department. That was that.' Morgan saw pain and humiliation etched on her face, but he also detected a steely hardness.

'Is there anything else you can tell us about Simon that will help our investigation? Anything about why he would be on the beach late at night?' asked Spence.

Yates shook her head and Morgan stood. 'I think that's enough for now, but we'll probably need to speak to you again.' He showed her out, making eye contact with Lynn Greenfield, who started to make her way towards him. He shook his head and closed the door then turned towards Spence.

'She's angry and she's not trying to hide it.'

Spence exhaled through barely parted lips. 'She's not angry enough to kill him, I don't think. At the time, I'd have been a bit worried about what she might do to the skinny apprentice, but not now. Now, I think she's just angry with herself.'

'Okay. Who's next?'

Chapter 19

Thursday 2nd April

Morgan and Spence returned to the table where the pots of coffee had been replenished. DC Lynn Greenfield approached. She looked down as she spoke, so that only they could hear her.

'I think you should speak to this guy.' She pointed to a name on her clipboard. 'There's something not right about him.'

Morgan nodded. 'Okay. Where is he now?'

'I asked him to wait for you. He's the one sitting over there, by the door.'

Morgan's eyes scanned the room. Lots of men and a handful of women, all in their Forest-Fox sweatshirts and black trousers or jeans. They stood around in groups, some openly monitoring the detectives as they singled out their colleagues for interview. The officers had done their best to keep those they had spoken to away from those yet to be interviewed, but it had proved impossible. Forest-Fox staff were coming and going at will. Some who had been interviewed had gone back to their rooms whilst others were hanging around as if expecting a murderer to be unmasked like in an Agatha Christie denouement.

The man who Greenfield was referring to was sitting on his own. His long legs were stretched out in front of him and he was fiddling with his phone. Morgan thought his regular glances round the room made him look furtive.

'What don't you like about him?' he asked.

Greenfield grimaced. 'He's answered all my questions, but he's evasive. He was at the beach that night with Dennison and about twelve or fifteen others. He can't remember exactly who was there; he can't remember when he left or who was still there when he left; he can't remember how he got back the club, or when. Oh, and he smells of sick.'

'Okay. Get him and yourself a coffee and wheel him in.' He turned to Spence. 'Can you overlook the initial information that's coming in? I'd like to narrow the crowd down as soon as possible. Lynn can help me with "vomit man".'

Greenfield handed her clipboard over to Spence and crossed back to the man on the sofa. Morgan waited to see how he would react to being told he was to be questioned further. He saw panic cross his face before he stood, lowered his head, and trailed behind Greenfield towards the meeting room's open door with the enthusiasm of a man facing his execution.

Morgan poured himself another coffee. Before resuming his interviews, he spoke to each of the officers in the reception area. He saw that their qualifying questions were working well and that many of the Forest-Fox staff, particularly the service engineers and European salespeople, were being excluded from further inquiries. He took a final sip from his coffee and crossed to the meeting room, where Greenfield was pouring a glass of water for the man.

'DI Morgan, this is Mr Armstead, Luke Armstead,' said Greenfield. 'He is the Forest-Fox sales rep for Greater London.'

'Technical Sales Specialist,' Armstead corrected her. 'And my area is inside the M25 motorway.'

Morgan greeted him and sat about a third of the way around the table. 'I believe you've already spoken to my colleague, DC Greenfield.' He looked to his side, where Greenfield was sitting with pen and notebook at the ready. 'Let's start with what happened on the beach on Tuesday evening. You were there with Simon Dennison.'

'Not just me, there was a gang of us.'

'And who was in that gang?'

'I remember that a couple of the Germans came, but that's about all.'

Morgan smiled his encouragement. 'Well, that's an improvement on what you could remember when you spoke to DC Greenfield earlier, so let's see if we can build on that. What made you go to the beach in the first place? We're hardly in the height of summer.'

'Who knows why you do things when you've been drinking,' said Armstead.

'Whose idea was it?' asked Greenfield.

Armstead gave a decent impersonation of someone who was thinking hard, but Morgan wasn't fooled. 'Was it your idea?'

'Definitely not.' He sounded outraged.

'How did you get to the beach? Gullhaven Cove is a drive away, so who drove?'

'I didn't drive. I sat in the back of someone's car.'

'Which someone?' asked Morgan. 'You must remember who drove you there and who brought you back?'

Armstead looked across at Greenfield, then back at Morgan. He shook his head. 'I can't remember. I can't remember very much at all. I shouldn't have gone because I'd already had quite a lot to drink. I remember that we started with shots up in Simon's room, and I think there was Prosecco too. Gary's a bit tight with the wine served at dinner so we mostly have a few before we meet up.'

'And this is in the rooms, not at the bar?' asked Greenfield.

'Not at their prices,' said Armstead, and Morgan allowed himself a small smile.

'Did you car-share with Simon?'

Armstead frowned again before shaking his head. 'No, I'm sure I'd remember if I had.'

'Was Simon there when you arrived or did he come later?' asked Morgan, and he watched as Armstead frowned and tilted his head to the right, looking upwards. Morgan had been on enough neuro-linguistic programming courses to know that a glance in that direction was supposed to indicate that the person was trying to access a memory and would, as a result, tell the truth. He was sceptical.

'Now you mention it, I actually don't remember seeing Simon.'

'Not even in the beach hut?'

Armstead looked bewildered. 'What beach hut? I wasn't in a beach hut, or if I was, I don't remember it.' He looked across to Greenfield. 'What beach hut?'

'No matter,' said Morgan before asking Greenfield if she had any other questions. She shook her head, the movement almost imperceptible. 'Okay, Mr Armstead. Thank you for your help.' Both men stood, and with a small smile back at the detectives, Armstead scurried to the door. As he reached for the handle, Morgan called after him. 'I think we'll probably have more questions for you later this afternoon, so please don't leave the club until we've spoken again.' The smile dropped from Armstead's face and his shoulders slumped as he made his escape.

Chapter 20

Thursday 2nd April

Dr Morag Mackenzie was warming both hands around a mug of steaming tea when Goddard and Smart joined her in the mortuary office.

'I probably don't have a lot more to give you,' she said. 'I think I covered most of the findings during the examination. There are gastric contents evident in his mouth, nose, oesophagus and bronchi. There's also bruising around the mouth, I'd say from some sort of hard gag, like a ball, perhaps, or a large bore pipe. He had a lot of blue fibres in his hair and around his nose and I've taken samples for comparison when you get that far. Annie noticed that there were more of them on his sweatshirt, so the crime scene guys will be reporting that too, I'd imagine. I've also washed out the nostrils and taken scrapings from his fingernails and swabs from his fingertips.

'You saw me remove the ... well, I suppose it's a dildo, but it's a frighteningly impressive size.' She took a mouthful of her tea. 'I'm no expert, but I would say you'll have difficulty sourcing one like that on the high street. And the force with which it was inserted? I wouldn't associate it with a lovemaking activity, but it was certainly personal.' Jenny Smart winced but Alison Goddard's face remained expressionless.

'I've taken samples for toxicology, of course. He reeks of alcohol and there's damage to the nasal septum, so I've asked for cocaine and its metabolites. In fact, I've asked for a full drugs screen to make sure we don't miss anything.'

'Time of death?' asked Goddard.

'Between twelve and two, I'd say.'

'Cause of death?'

'I think he vomited when the dildo was inserted, and because he was gagged, he aspirated on it, even though I suspect he was face down.'

'Murder or misadventure, then?'

'Whoever skewered him with that sex toy inserted it with enough force to burst through the wall of the bowel. That's where the blood and other staining on the trousers and pants originated. And, on the subject of the clothing, someone from CSI has arrived to bag up and take the items. They'll report back separately.'

'Murder or misadventure?' Goddard persisted.

MoMack turned away from her and rolled her eyes at Smart. 'I wouldn't rule out manslaughter,' she said. 'Okay, Ladies, if that's all, I'll get on with my next case. I'll email my provisional report. To DI Morgan?'

Smart nodded and thanked her.

MoMack beamed back. 'Always a pleasure, DC Smart.' They shook hands before the pathologist left the office.

'She's a bit abrasive,' said Goddard.

'You think so? The team really like her,' Smart replied.

Chapter 21

Thursday 2nd April

At three o'clock, and with the expected headache hammering behind his left temple, Morgan turned on his personal mobile and braced himself for the list of missed calls and increasingly abusive texts from Sam. He was still smarting from last night's argument about her mother, but then he was still smarting about a lot of things when it came to Sam. He typed in his password and waited for the boot-up process to complete.

Nothing.

No texts; no messages; no emails to his private account. He shook it, and then looked around, hoping that nobody had noticed. He wasn't behaving logically. He took his work mobile out of his jacket pocket and studied the screen. It had been on silent during the interviews, but emails and voice messages had arrived and were awaiting his attention. He knew that the two phones used different service providers. That was it, he thought. As soon as he got a signal, he would be deluged. But no, four bars told him he should have received anything she chose to fire at him. He called her.

'Hello, Nick.' Her greeting was formal and he could hear that she was driving. Lynn Greenfield was walking towards him but he shook his head and pointed to the phone. She nodded and headed for Dave Spence instead.

'I'm sorry I couldn't get to the school this morning. We've been flat out with these interviews.' No harm in being placatory, at least not at first. 'How did it go?'

'I don't want to talk about it over the phone,' said Sam. 'I set off early to get some shopping. It's Film

Night for the twins and Mrs Bradley's taking them with her kids. Can you get home at a reasonable time so we can talk over dinner?'

Morgan's heart sank. Sam was usually out on Thursday evenings, and unless it was their turn to ferry a group of children to the local cinema he usually spent a few hours in the welcoming arms and warm bed of Maisie, the manager of the nearby Park Homes Estate. The promise of it had kept him going all day.

'Is it serious?' he asked.

'The word expulsion was used.'

Morgan knew when he was beaten. 'I've probably got another hour here, and then I'll head for home. I may even be there before you, so is there anything I can do to start dinner?'

'I'm going to get a Chinese on my way back,' she said, 'I don't feel like cooking tonight.'

'God, it must be bad,' said Morgan. Cooking was something Sam usually enjoyed.

'Yes, Nick. I think it is.' She ended the call before he could say anything else.

He sighed as he looked around the remaining Forest-Fox staff who were waiting to speak to the officers. DS Spence was finishing up with a middle-aged man and caught his eye. He beckoned him over.

'I've got a bit of family trouble and need to get away,' he told Spence. 'Can you finish up here?'

'You're not planning a late briefing?' asked Spence.

'Not unless something unexpected turns up. If that happens, send me a text and I'll come back in. Make it for six or half past.' He went into the meeting room where he'd spent most of the day and collected his briefcase before heading for his car.

Chapter 22

Thursday 2nd April

Cliffside House was silent when Nick Morgan got home. It wasn't often he had the place to himself. He enjoyed a leisurely shower and changed into clean jeans and his Met Police Rugby Club shirt.

He paused at Alexander's bedroom door. What could a twelve-year-old boy from a loving and supportive family be doing to make a school consider expulsion? He went in. This was his opportunity to see if there were any available clues to whatever Sam was going to tell him when she arrived. He lifted the mattress. In his teenage years, that was where he'd hidden contraband, which usually comprised well-thumbed magazines. Of course, now, it was all delivered to mobile phones and tablets, so he wasn't surprised that his search was fruitless. He sank on to his knees and looked under the bed. Nothing there either.

He heard Sam's car on the drive. Taking a last look around the room to ensure he hadn't left any signs of his visit, he went to greet her.

Sam lit the oven and put the takeaway containers on the top shelf to heat through. They stood in the kitchen, uncomfortable in each other's company. 'I went to see mother after I finished at the school,' she said.

'Okay.' Nick realised that his wife was going to take a while to get down to what had happened at her meeting with Alexander's Head of Year. 'She said you were horrible to her yesterday.'

'Did she say that she was horrible to me, too?'

'She can be a bit difficult, but that's just her way. Can you not make more of an effort?'

'What part of saving her life a few weeks ago doesn't qualify as me making an effort?

She sighed. 'You're not going to keep on about that, are you?'

'Only as long as she keeps on about me living in her home as the handyman. What happened at the school?'

Sam recounted the staff's suspicion that Alex had been drinking alcohol on the school premises. Morgan looked across to the worktop where he'd laid out a bottle of wine for them to share. He turned his back on it.

'But in his defence,' she said, 'he's had a lot to contend with. Not just the relocation and loss of his friends, but having to stay in a caravan …'

'It was a park home,' Morgan corrected her, 'and lots of kids live in them throughout their school life without being driven to drink. Vicky's not drinking.'

Victoria was the younger twin but they had matured at different rates and seemed separated by years rather than minutes. Sam sometimes accused her of being needy, but Nick was keen to preserve her childlike innocence for as long as possible.

Sam reached into the oven and removed the foil containers. She peeled lids off egg fried rice, sweet and sour pork and beef with cashew nuts. 'Shall I serve it, or do you want to help yourself?'

Morgan was opening the bottle of wine. He glanced at his watch. Twenty past seven and he had heard nothing from Spence. He filled two glasses as Sam spooned the food on to two plates. If he was called in, he would take a taxi.

‘How do we tackle it?’ she said, perching on one of the chairs at the breakfast bar.

‘Is that what the school is expecting? I mean, they’re the ones making the accusations.’

‘I believe it.’ Sam spoke quietly before putting another forkful of rice and beef in her mouth.’

‘Well, I’m not sure I do,’ said Morgan.

‘The day you drove down here, Alex was upset about leaving all his friends in London. When he got home from school, I thought I could smell alcohol on his breath.’

‘And you kept it to yourself?’

‘With everything else that was going on, I forgot.’

‘You mean with everything else that was going on with you and Graham Fletcher.’

She slammed her fork down on the worktop. ‘Not again, Nick. I’ve told you it’s over and done with. This isn’t about me or what’s missing in our marriage that made me start that relationship. This is about Alex.’

Morgan looked up from his meal, his eyebrows raised. This was a new slant on his wife’s perception of her affair. He prepared to remonstrate then decided against it. She was right: this was about Alex.

‘I had a look under his bed. I didn’t see any bottles,’ said Morgan. ‘What did you think he’d been drinking back in February?’

She shrugged. ‘I didn’t think about it. I just caught what I thought was alcohol as he went past me. The removal men were there and I had so much to do.’

‘Maybe we should be grateful it’s not drugs,’ he said.

‘He’s twelve, Nick. This is every bit as serious. We need to present a united front, and that should start with us sharing a bed again. I’ve told you that I won’t see

Graham again, and you've said you want to make a go of it. Prove it by coming back to our bed.'

He could tell she was being genuine and it should have been easy to agree, but he couldn't. As he searched for a reason she would accept, he heard a key turn in the front door lock and the twins bounded in, full of excitement about the film they had seen and the pizza they had eaten. It didn't stop them falling on the takeaway containers, and Morgan marvelled at their appetites. He told them that he had work to do and took his glass of wine upstairs to the spare bedroom, where he logged on to headquarters and ploughed through the uploaded interview reports until he fell asleep.

Chapter 23

Friday 3rd April

For the first time in weeks, Morgan had slept well and was feeling optimistic as he opened the briefing room door. It was a few minutes after seven on Friday morning and he had already been at the office for an hour. He was going to add some updates to the whiteboards before the team arrived.

'Good morning, Nick.'

He wasn't completely surprised to find DC Jennifer Smart already seated at the front, a sheaf of paper on her lap and a couple of notebooks on the floor. When he got closer, he saw that only one of the books was standard police issue.

'And good morning to you. Did you make it home?' He laid the case policy book on the table at the front and opened it at his most recent entries.

'I had a few things I wanted to get straight in my head before everyone else got here,' she said without looking up. She laid her papers on the floor, on top of a book with a sparkly cover.

'What's in the glitter notebook?' Morgan could tell that he wasn't supposed to have seen it but still felt justified in asking the question. He knew that some officers kept private notes about cases. Perhaps they had plans for a future autobiography. Smart's ambition was obvious, but he didn't think that would be her reason. Through the thick make-up she wore to disguise her acne scars, Morgan saw her blush.

'It's just some notes I make in case I forget something. I find it helps me, especially at the beginning of a case. I do mind maps and stuff.'

He reached out his hand. 'Can I see it?' He softened his tone to ensure that she wouldn't think he was angry with her. 'I might learn something.' She flinched. 'If that sounded patronising, Jenny, it wasn't meant to. Seeing someone else's thoughts committed to paper would be very helpful, that's all.' His hand was still out.

Jenny Smart's jaw shifted to one side and she bit her lip. As the senior officer, Morgan knew he could make it an order, but he wanted her to hand it over voluntarily. She reached down and picked it up.

'I don't want you to read too much into it,' she said, holding it to her chest before handing it to him. The silver cover sparkled under the overhead lights and he read the three words embossed in black surrounded by grey glitter. "Believe Achieve Succeed."

'It was a present. I wouldn't have chosen it.'

'If it works, I'll buy us all one,' he said, opening it.

'The Dennison case starts where the bookmark is.'

Morgan turned to the marked page and saw that he had glitter on his left hand. 'You don't take this to crime scenes, do you? The CSIs would have a fit.'

'I keep it at home. I don't even bring it into the office, but there was such a lot of information flying around yesterday, I wanted to make sure I was on top of it before the briefing. You won't see it again, I can promise you that.'

He riffled through the completed pages before looking back up at her. Smart had wrapped her arms around her body and was biting her lip.

'It's not just mind maps and personal thoughts, is it?' She shook her head. 'How long have you been doing this?'

'Since I joined the Unit.'

'I'm impressed,' he said. 'If I'd known you were completing your own policy book, I might have asked you to complete mine.'

'It helps me get my head round the cases if I act like I'm the SIO.'

Morgan read in silence. He turned to the next page.

'Lust, love, loathing and loot. That classification goes back about fifteen years, doesn't it?'

'I like to use it as a starting point.' She spoke sharply, defensive of her methods.

'I'm not criticising, Jenny, we're discussing a case like two professionals who need to solve the same problem.'

'I know you think I'm getting ahead of myself and –'

The door to the briefing room opened and DS Dave Spence came in.

'Looks like none of us could sleep,' he said. 'Anything come in overnight?'

'Nothing new,' said Morgan, who had checked with the Ops room on his way into the building. He had been told that it was DCI Johnson's habit to do this, and made sure he was never caught out.

Spence came to the front and pinned a photo of an unsmiling Simon Dennison to the whiteboard. 'It's the picture from his passport and driving licence. A bit miserable, but at least he looks alive.'

'Where was the licence?' asked Morgan.

'Glove compartment of the Audi. CSI have emailed a list. Licence, wallet with about fifty quid and credit cards, house keys and a mobile phone. Nothing unusual or unexpected,' said Spence.

'Another phone? How many does that make?' asked Smart.

'Three.'

Chapter 24

Friday 3rd April

The briefing room was filling up with voices and the smell of cheap, machine-dispensed coffee. Morgan bent down and slipped Smart's glitter notebook under the pile of papers lying at her feet. 'I'm not done with your notes. I want to read them in more detail.' Smart flushed again and he wasn't sure if she was embarrassed or pleased. He raised his voice over the escalating hubbub. 'Lots to get through, so let's settle down so we can get on with it, please.'

He leafed through his notes as the scraping of chairs died down and conversations were cut short. He opened his policy book and ran a finger down the fold. When he looked up, expectant eyes were fixed on him.

'As you can see, courtesy of DS Spence we've now got a better picture of our victim, Simon Dennison.' He pointed over his shoulder to the board. 'And copies are available for those of you who are staying with this investigation.' He glanced across at Spence, who nodded. 'What I want to collate this morning is what we know about this man, so far.' He selected a black marker pen, snapped the cap off and approached the whiteboard. 'I'm going to start with single, successful salesperson and ambitious.' He jotted the words as a list on the right of the picture.

'Ruthless, smug and philanderer,' said Spence.

'Wow, that's a bit damning at these early stages.' Alison Goddard scowled at him. 'Based on what?'

Spence counted off his reasons with the fingers of his right hand. 'He ditched his previous employer whose business went to the wall because of it. Numerous colleagues described him as smug and arrogant during yesterday's interviews. He seemed to think he was better than everyone else and didn't let them forget it. And he drifted in and out of relationships … well, sexual encounters more like, without a glance over his shoulder at the wreckage he was leaving behind. I stand by the words.' He returned Goddard's stare and Morgan wondered who was going to burst into flames first. He was relieved when Smart took her pen out of her mouth and spoke.

'Potential drunk driver, assuming he drove his own car to the cliffs. Maybe even a drug driver. MoMack found nasal septum damage. The alcohol level will be back today, drugs will take longer.'

Morgan nodded. 'He organises a skinny-dip party at the beach, but when he arrives he goes down the slope and walks away from the party? Why would he do that?'

'Needs to take a leak?'

'It's possible, but why does he walk past public toilets and venture into the dark where he can't see?'

'Maybe the toilets are locked overnight?' It was Smart's suggestion.

'Can you check with the Council please, Jenny?' said Morgan. She nodded and made a note.

'Perhaps he was meeting someone and didn't want the others to know?'

'A dealer, maybe? We haven't found any drugs in his hotel room or his car. He might have needed to replenish his supply.'

'There were condoms found near his car key. He left his driving licence in the car but took condoms to the beach. He must have been meeting someone for sex.'

‘The size of that,’ said Spence, pointing to the photo of the dildo positioned beside an exhibit measure, ‘looks like he got more sex than he was expecting.’

‘Why choose the beach?’ Morgan thought it best to change the subject. ‘He had a perfectly serviceable hotel room. And let’s face it, with most of his colleagues at the beach he had less chance of being caught at the club.’ Nobody volunteered an answer. ‘Okay. What else have we got?’ He looked around and caught Jenny Smart’s eye again. ‘Jenny?’

She picked up her police issue notebook from the pile by her chair. ‘We took the contents of the bin in his hotel room to the lab yesterday. There are cotton buds and tissues they will be working on, but one of the things they have drawn attention to is a screwed-up letter from the club management. It seems that when Simon Dennison arrived at the club, he parked his Audi in the space reserved for the captain of the ladies’ golf team. She reported it and they wrote to him expressing their displeasure.’

‘I wouldn’t like to think he was killed for a parking misdemeanour,’ said Morgan. ‘Why do you think it’s important?’

‘When DS Goddard and I arrived at the club yesterday, we waited in the foyer with some of the Forest-Fox team. There was a lot of talk about that car.’ She looked over at Alison Goddard but received no encouragement. Morgan felt the muscles in his jaw tighten. Jenny Smart was a good detective. He respected her and trusted her judgment. Why was she suddenly so hesitant?

‘The consensus was that he had parked it in the captain’s space so that everyone else would see it on their way in. They were saying he did it to piss everyone else off.' She gave a small nod as she finished the sentence. Job done.

'We'll need to ask Gary Fox why Dennison's car is better than everyone else's, and who gets it now he's dead.'

'I'll do that,' said Smart.

'While we're waiting for the PM report and anything CSI turn up, we need to have a look around his flat.' Goddard seemed to perk up at the thought, but Morgan pointed to Spence. The team's next case would be allocated to his colleague DI Maggy Patel and he felt it best if Goddard was part of her team rather than his. Besides, as the weeks had passed he'd got used to working with Dave Spence and had grown to like him. He didn't imagine that it was mutual, but they might yet get there. He drew the meeting to a close by scheduling a follow-up for later that afternoon. There was the usual outbreak of noise as the team broke up and left.

'Can you wait a minute, Jen, please?' Morgan called out as she got to the door. She smiled her thanks at Brian Bingley, the crime scene officer who was holding it open for her. As she turned, Alison Goddard made her way purposefully towards the whiteboard, where Morgan was adding a note about the Audi.

'DI Morgan?' The words were clipped and he turned, shocked to see her flared nostrils and angry eyes, framed by those severe glasses. 'I'm available to search the flat.'

'I don't expect to have the luxury of two experienced Detective Sergeants on my team for very long. You need to be available to pick up the next job with DI Patel.'

She moved towards him, closer than professionally appropriate, and looked directly into his eyes. 'I hope we're not going to have a problem here, Nick.' Her lips barely moved; teeth clenched as she spoke.

He tilted his head down towards her and replied, mirroring her tone. 'So do I.'

As Goddard moved away, he looked up and noted Jenny Smart's look of surprise.

Chapter 25

Friday 3rd April

When he returned to his office, Morgan booted up his laptop and opened his emails. Considering he had been away from his desk for a couple of hours, there were fewer than he expected and nothing relevant to the Dennison case. His phone rang and he snatched at it, answering with his name.

'Hi, Nick, it's Morag. I've got initial tox results on Simon Dennison for you.'

'Anything in there that surprises you?' Morgan was fascinated by the fact that, face to face, Dr Morag Mackenzie's engagement and enthusiasm for her work completely sucked him into her world. It was only when he spoke to her on the phone that her east coast accent reminded him that she was Scottish.

'Well, it's just the routine screens and the alcohol result. I won't get the controlled drug screen for about a week.'

Okay, fire away.'

'Blood alcohol one hundred and eighteen milligrams per hundred millilitres, so over the limit, obviously. He had recently eaten, so if he'd lived I've no reason to think that the peak results wouldn't have been higher. The lab hasn't found any evidence of prescription drugs in his stomach contents, but we're doing a blood screen too.'

'Cheers, Morag. Is the alcohol high enough for him to have choked on his vomit without the gag?'

'I'd say it would depend on his tolerance to alcohol. If he was a party man, it's unlikely.'

‘I’ll get the team to find out,’ said Morgan, and was reaching across his desk for a pen when he heard her theatrical sigh.

‘I’m a pathologist, Nick, and I’ve handled his liver. Trust me … he was a party man.’

He thanked her and put his phone down.

There were times when he found it difficult not to make judgments about people, especially when their secrets were exposed after death. They weren’t there to defend themselves; to explain. He made one exception and that was for those who put their own lives and those of other road users at risk by driving whilst drunk. And what if Simon Dennison had exacerbated the risk by snorting cocaine, too? It wouldn’t stop Morgan giving everything he had to bring whoever was responsible for his death to justice, but he would never be endeared to him.

His computer pinged: another incoming email. Johnson wanted to see him immediately.

Morgan knocked on DCI Richard Johnson’s office door and entered without waiting to be invited.

‘Sir, he said, ‘I’m sorry for the delay. I was on the phone.’ He wasn’t sorry, and he hadn’t been on the phone. He had taken some time to reply to a few emails and to speak to Maisie. After missing his evening with her yesterday, he hoped to find time to spend with her later. Sometimes you had to make a senior officer understand that they couldn’t snap their fingers and have you come running.

‘Yes, Nick, of course. Coffee?’ Johnson rose from behind his desk. There was already a strong smell of what Morgan thought of as proper coffee in the office, and he thanked him. 'Black, no sugar?'

'That would be great, thank you.'

Johnson nodded over towards the comfortable seating area of his office and Morgan's heart sank. He hadn't been invited to sit there since his first week, and his relationship with Johnson had swung from formal, through polite to terse, and back again many times since then.

'How is DS Goddard settling in?' asked Johnson.

'It's only been a few days, Sir, but she seems to be getting on with things.'

'What about her management skills?'

'I haven't had an opportunity to see her in that context so far.'

'Mmm.' Johnson brought his coffee and placed it on a coaster on the low table. He took the chair at right angles to Morgan before continuing. 'DI Patel has asked for some personal time. She's applied for an Extended Leave Break of two months to go to India and spend time with her family. I believe her mother is ill.'

'When does she plan to go?' Morgan's thoughts turned to the whiteboard in the team's designated area of the open-plan office. Maggy had a couple of outstanding cases, including a fire which was still being assessed for criminal intent.

'She's gone, Nick. Her case at the Crown Court finished yesterday and she came to me straight afterwards. I know it's short notice, but she's taking unpaid leave to cover for the time until the ELB is authorised.'

Morgan felt sad that he hadn't had a chance to speak to Maggy before she left. He found her input and opinions useful and she wasn't scared to tell him when she thought he was being an arse.

'So I'm asking if you think DS Goddard is ready to act up as temporary DI during DI Patel's absence. She's passed the modules and she's completed the SIODP. She's waiting for confirmation of her registration.'

Morgan placed his cup back on its matching saucer. It gave him a few moments of thinking time. Alison Goddard was a career copper; he'd known that from the first time they'd met back in training. This would be an opportunity she would relish. But he also knew how DS Dave Spence would react. Hungry for promotion and quick to feel overlooked, this would feel like another slap in the face to him.

Johnson intruded into his thoughts. 'If you're thinking about Spence, then I agree, he would have been my first choice. He's been a DS longer than Goddard and his local knowledge puts him in front. But he's not due to sit the DI exam for another few months and I need an Acting DI now.'

Morgan knew then that the posh coffee and the comfy chair were not the bargaining chips of a negotiation. This wasn't even a discussion. Johnson wanted his support for a decision that had already been made.

'I'm aware of DI Patel's current workload and I'm confident that I could be across all the cases until she returns. It would help if we could draft in another DS, or maybe two. If not, perhaps we could have a couple of uniforms acting up as DCs?'

Johnson stared at him, then cleared his throat and got up. 'I'll speak to Goddard this morning and you can brief her with any information you have about DI Patel's cases. She'll pick up the next major case that comes in. She's going to need someone familiar with the territory on her team, so DS Spence will transfer over. DC Smart has been on the body at the beach case, so you can keep her, and DC Greenfield will work with Goddard.'

'DS Spence is on his way to Simon Dennison's flat with DC Smart.'

Johnson sighed. 'Then he transfers to the suspicious fire as soon as they get back. Tell him.' He walked back to his desk and jiggled his computer mouse. Morgan assumed the meeting was over. He got up and left, abandoning his half-drunk coffee on the table. He wasn't bothered; it had turned bitter as soon as the conversation had started.

Chapter 26

Friday 3rd April

'Did you want a cup of coffee, Mrs Cooper?'

Dorothy had been for a walk around the grounds of Silver Sands House and was sitting on the wooden park bench by the front door. She flinched at the inappropriate use of the past tense of the verb, but when she turned, she saw it was Mary, one of the carers she liked, so she forgave it. Most of the others called her Dorothy and spoke to her in a tone she associated with talking to babies and puppies, but Mary was neither patronising nor deferential, so they got on.

'Not really, thank you. I was just taking a moment before I go in and review the company accounts.'

Mary came down the stone steps and stood beside her. 'It's a lovely day,' she said. 'I can't blame you for wanting to be outside. I think spring is my favourite season.'

Dorothy allowed a rare smile to cross her face. 'Mine too, dear. Why don't you sit and keep me company for a minute. Tell me what's going on in your busy life.' She missed the conversations she used to have with Danny Easton, the maintenance man who was now in custody undergoing psychiatric assessment after killing several burglars.

Mary looked nervously to both sides, and then up at the windows of the building. She whispered, 'I'm not supposed to.'

'Nonsense,' said Dorothy. 'A couple of minutes won't harm.'

‘But I’ve already had to take some time out to talk to the police today. You know what they’re like here. She said I’d have to take a shorter lunch break.’ Mary nodded her head in the direction of the manager’s office window.

‘That’s outrageous. Do you want me to have a word?’ asked Dorothy, who could smell gossip and was determined to get the full story.

‘No … no … it’s okay. Her lights are off.’ Mary glanced at her watch. ‘She must be with Chef, in the kitchen.’ She sat down on the bench. Dorothy could tell that Mary was as keen to share her story as she was to hear it.

‘These detectives came and asked Jackie and me about a shift we did at the club on Tuesday night.’

‘Do you mean at the Country Club? I didn’t know you worked there.’

‘I do the odd shift when I can. It’s just waitressing and bar work and stuff. I’m not clever like you.’

‘What did the detectives want?’ asked Dorothy, no longer holding out much hope that the story was worth hearing.

‘They were investigating an incident.’ Mary pronounced the last word carefully, as if she was nurturing it.

‘What incident?’ Dorothy asked, and was frustrated when Mary responded with a shrug. She crossed her arms and shuffled further along the bench.

‘They didn’t say, but Jackie told me there was a body found on the beach the next day and that the man had been staying at the club. She’s mates with the receptionist, who recognised his picture.’

Dorothy decided that the story didn't merit any more of her time. She started to get up. 'I'd better get on,' she said, 'and maybe you should, too.'

Mary had a far-away look on her face. 'I've never helped the police with their inquiries before. She was really nice.'

'Must have been one of the Detective Constables who works with my son-in-law,' said Dorothy, keen to show her familiarity with the workings of the local detectives.

'Oh no,' Mary corrected her, and reached into the small pocket on her tabard. 'She was a Detective Sergeant. Look.' She held a business card out for Dorothy to read.

Detective Sergeant Alison Goddard. Now that was a name Dorothy had never forgotten. She had been a threat to her daughter's marriage when it was in its infancy and now it looked as if the bitch was back. She gave the card back to Mary, who read it again before thrusting it deep into her pocket and scurrying away.

Dorothy sat down again. She clenched her hands into fists and rubbed them together with glee. Her relationship with Samantha had been damaged when she'd told Plod of her affair and it had not yet recovered. But now, she had information, and information gave her power. A way back into her daughter's affections had just presented itself and she would take full advantage.

Chapter 27

Friday 3rd April

Spence's satnav guided him to a public car park near Simon Dennison's flat overlooking the harbour. The building's concierge, whose uniform was rather more elaborate than the role required, unlocked the glass doors and scrutinised their identification as if his life might depend on it. When Spence explained that he and DC Smart were investigating Mr Dennison's death, the elderly man clutched at his chest. Smart leapt forward, took the man's arm and led him back to his chair. 'Tell me where I can find you some water,' she demanded.

'I'm fine … I'm okay. It's just that … nobody told me. It's a bit of a shock.'

'We're going to have an initial look around,' said Spence. 'I expect there will be another team who will come and do a formal search, but we're the advance party.'

'I should be there with you,' said the man, undoing the top couple of buttons of his uniform jacket. 'Mr Dennison won't want you going up there on your own.'

Spence and Smart exchanged a glance before she spoke. 'I'm afraid that won't be possible, Sir. We need to preserve the scene and that means limiting access to it.'

'Are you saying something happened up there?'

'At this stage we're keeping an open mind. Now, please, where can I get you that water?'

The concierge pointed to a door, and behind it Smart found a small kitchen with a sink, kettle and microwave. She grabbed a mug which wasn't as badly stained as the others and ran the tap until the water was cold. She returned with the filled mug and placed it with care in the man's shaking hands.

'That's Jerry's mug,' he said.

'I'm sure he won't mind,' said Smart. 'Just this once.'

The officers watched him take a few sips of the water before Spence decided he wasn't prepared to wait any longer. 'We're going up now,' he said. 'If our colleagues come while we're up there, tell them to ring my mobile.' He jotted the number down on a pad by the side of the concierge's phone and led Smart away from the desk.

'Who are we expecting?' she asked, keeping her voice low.

'Nobody, but he'll be distracted from worrying about us being up there if he has a job to do. I've given him that job.'

'Blimey. That's a course I haven't been on yet,' she said.

They arrived at the door of the penthouse flat via a lift which smelled of lavender and eucalyptus. They put on the nitrile gloves and shoe covers which Smart produced from her handbag, and Spence took the keys out of the evidence bag she held out to him. He unlocked the mortice first, then had a couple of unsuccessful attempts at the dead latch before selecting the key which released it. The door opened on to a large hall with a centrally positioned roof lantern. Bright spring daylight filled the area.

'How can he afford a place like this?' asked Smart. 'This is bigger than my sitting room – and look at the size of this.' She'd opened the oak-faced doors leading to an open-plan living space which included the kitchen and dining areas and bi-fold doors to a sun terrace with an uninterrupted view of the harbour. The room was double height and a glass and metal staircase led to a mezzanine level, where they could see a desk and filing cabinet.

'Not for the first time, I think I made a bad career choice,' said Spence. 'How much do you think he paid for this place?'

Smart nodded towards the view. 'Not a lot of change out of a million, I would guess, and a hundred grand of that is going to be just for that view. Where do you want to start?' Spence looked around and pointed to the kitchen. 'Okay, I'll head for the bedroom. Do you want to take a bet on whether there are black sheets?' Spence's mouth twitched but he shook his head. 'Did the boss say what we're looking for?'

'He said it was an open remit. We're looking for something that's here that we wouldn't expect to be here, and to see what's missing, if anything.'

'His keys were in his car, weren't they? We don't think he's been burgled, do we?'

Spence shrugged. 'I think we're just covering the bases.'

When DC Smart had left for the bedroom, Spence started on the three black sofas, lifting the cushions and thrusting his gloved hands down the sides. He unzipped the scatter cushions and squeezed the pads before carefully reassembling each sofa to its original state. There was a wall unit and he flicked through the pages of the two books which lay on it before opening three empty drawers. He lifted each drawer out and checked to see if anything had been taped round the sides or underneath, then ran his hands around the space in the unit.

Spence was aware that his heart wasn't really in this search. Nothing had happened here. The man had died at Gullhaven Cove and that's where he wanted to be. This was a waste of time.

He wandered into the kitchen and opened a few of the cupboard doors. Penny, his wife, would love a kitchen like this, but on police and teacher salaries it was never going to happen.

It was obvious that Simon Dennison mostly ate out, or maybe ordered takeaway food. There didn't seem to be any of the half-used packets of pasta and rice he had expected. No tins of tomatoes, or pulses, or even baked beans. Spence wondered what this man had eaten when he'd come back from work late and knackered. He opened the fridge and found two bottles of Prosecco and a bottle of champagne. No milk, but that wasn't a surprise because Dennison had planned to be away for a few days at the conference. But where were the 'past its best' cheese, the jars of pickle, jam and mustard? Did the man even live here?

He stood by the doors to the sun terrace. His attention was caught by a small boat setting off towards the harbour entrance. Two women were waving to a man in shorts on the quay. Lives were going on out there as if Simon Dennison had never existed. He returned his focus to the terrace. How likely was it that there would be anything hidden out there, and if they were going to look, how would they get out? There were no keys. He went back to the ring of keys they had used to get in and tried the two that were left. Neither fitted the bi-fold lock. He took a couple of photos of the two sun loungers and a glass-topped table with a stack of four chairs to one side. If there were repercussions later about overlooking this area, he would be able to show why he had made his decision. It crossed his mind that if there were cushions to make the outdoor living more comfortable, Dennison must store them somewhere else.

He stood at the foot of the staircase to the mezzanine. He knew it was ridiculous, but he'd always been suspicious of glass treads. He took them singly, holding on to the banister rail. When he got to the top, he wiggled sweaty fingers in the gloves before try the top drawer of the filing cabinet. Locked.

Now that he was up here, he could see that there were two desks, a wide bookcase with a corkboard above it, a locked metal cupboard, and a black leather office chair on wheels. The chair had worn a path between the two desks. It was the first sign Spence had seen of Simon Dennison ever being here. He wondered if Smart had found pyjamas under a pillow.

The first desk was under a window which was too high for anyone seated at the desk to see through. There was a laptop-sized gap in the middle of the desk, and a monitor on a raised shelf to the right of a keyboard and mouse. Cables dangled over the edge of the desk. There were scraps of paper with names and phone numbers in untidy piles, and an A4 refill pad with doodles, a couple of which looked overtly sexual when Spence looked more closely.

The second desk had a tower PC under it and the largest computer monitor Spence had ever seen. The single filing tray contained bills and statements. At the bottom of the pile was a letter from the block's Residents' Association, informing Dennison that there had been complaints received from neighbours about noisy partying. He looked for a date on the letter but couldn't see one.

Spence made his way gingerly down the stairs and returned to the large hall. The next door he tried opened towards him: an airing cupboard containing a gas boiler, hot water tank and a stack of towels, linens and carefully folded laundry. The boiler was lit and the tank, hot. Dennison's life had ended abruptly and it would be someone else's responsibility to shut everything down and clear any evidence of his existence from this flat. As Spence prepared to remove the pile of shirts and underpants from the cupboard, he was startled by the soundless reappearance of Smart.

'You should come and see this,' she said, and turned away without waiting to check if he was following.

Spence followed her into what he assumed was the master bedroom. The double-height sliding doors to the sun terrace and mirrored wardrobe doors made it seem bigger than it was. She had removed all of the clothes and laid them on the bed, which was made up with a dark grey duvet cover, not black. Spence saw that she had started her search with Dennison's footwear, and she handed him a black Chelsea boot.

'I thought these went out of fashion forever ago,' said Spence, manipulating his gloved hand inside. Smart shrugged and waited. He pulled out a red gingham cloth bag held closed by drawstrings. She took the boot back and watched while he pulled the bag open.

'What do you think it is?' asked Smart.

'I think it's the reason he can afford to live this lifestyle,' said Spence, producing one of about thirty deal bags of white powder and holding it up to the light.

'Call the boss. We're going to need the technicians in here after all.'

Smart called Morgan's mobile. She put her phone on speaker so Spence could contribute to the conversation.

Morgan listened to the description of Dennison's flat and the stash of baggies they had found. 'How many, do you think?' he asked.

'Twenty-five, or maybe thirty,' said Spence.

'It's hardly Pablo Escobar territory, is it?'

Spence rolled his eyes as Smart continued.' We are still searching, Sir. There may be more. We're checking in to make sure you want us to carry on. You may prefer to send a CSI team.'

'Is there anything to suggest that the flat's been searched already?' asked Morgan.

'I'd say no,' said Spence.

'Okay. Bag up what you find and bring it back for CSI, especially any technology that's still there. If he was dealing, he may not have carried his contacts with him.'

'Okay.' Spence and Smart spoke together.

'And Spence?'

'Yes?'

'Come to my office as soon as you get back, please.'

'Sure.'

Smart ended the call. 'Well, that went well.'

'He's in a mood. It's gone on for weeks and I'm getting pretty sick of it.'

'What do you think you've done to piss him off this time?' Jenny Smart's smile showed that she was offering support. He thought that she too had noticed their boss's recent edginess.

'Anybody's guess,' he replied. 'I'll let you know.'

He left her and continued his search in the second bedroom, which was much smaller than the master. It was furnished with a bed and a set of drawers. Compared to the rest of the flat, Spence thought this looked like a cell. No curtains at the windows, or pillows and covers on the bed. Like the lounge, the drawers were empty. He opened the fitted wardrobe and shouted Jenny's name.

Chapter 28

Friday 3rd April

Morgan looked up from his telephone conversation and beckoned Spence in. He mouthed the words 'two minutes' and carried on listening, punctuating the call with an occasional 'mmm' and 'of course'. When he'd finished, he put the phone on the desk, screen downwards. Spence towered above him. 'That was a great find, Dave. Grab a chair.'

Spence's shoulders tensed. 'I'll remain standing, if that's okay.' Morgan realised this conversation was going to be even more difficult than he'd feared.

'What did the scene investigators say when they turned up?'

'We only spoke to one of them briefly. She said that the cameras and sound system were top of the range. She also said that covert filming of bedroom activity is never above board. At least, that was the gist of what she said. You know how guarded the techies can be.'

Morgan nodded. He'd have preferred to talk more about the unexpected discovery at Simon Dennison's flat, but the tense atmosphere developing in his office stopped him. 'Where are you with applying for your Inspector's exam?'

Spence had spent the journey back from Dennison's flat sifting through his memory for any short-cuts he might have taken or unfortunate things he might have said; anything that might have caught up with him. Nothing had come to mind. He had prepared a few catch-all phrases which he hoped would cover all eventualities, but nothing was suitable for this.

‘I’m applying for the October exam. I missed March … obviously.’

Morgan nodded. ‘You’ve got my support. You know that, don’t you?’

‘Sir.’ Spence put his hands behind his back. He was looking over the top of Morgan’s head.

Morgan tutted, got up and lifted one of his visitor chairs over to face his desk. ‘I’ve asked nicely, Dave, now I’m telling you.’ He returned to his side of the desk and sat back down. Spence sat opposite and the two men looked at each other before Morgan broke the silence. ‘DI Patel is taking some personal time.’

Spence looked concerned. ‘Is she okay?’

‘Yes, I believe so. Her mother’s not well, so she’s gone to India for a while to support her.’

‘I hope it’s not to nurse her. She once put a sticking plaster on my finger and missed the cut altogether.’ Both men smiled at the thought.

‘DS Goddard will be acting up.’

The smile dropped from Spence’s face. He stood and his chair toppled backwards. The clatter of plastic hitting the floor filled the room. ‘She’s only just got here.’ He turned away from his boss and kicked the recumbent chair before bending to pick it up and replace it at the wall.

‘I’m told that she passed her Step Two exam eighteen months ago. They didn’t have the headcount in Yorkshire to promote her.’

‘We don’t have the headcount here,’ Spence snarled. ‘When is Maggy back?’

‘Couple of months, maybe.’

‘And then it’s back to normal?’

‘Whatever “normal” means,’ said Morgan. Spence started to head for the door but Morgan was still speaking. ‘Johnson’s allocated you to her team. She’s upstairs being updated by DC Greenfield and you should probably join them.’

‘And what about tomorrow?’

Morgan had forgotten that he and Spence had arranged to go to the Country Club to speak to Mr and Mrs Thorne, the managers, who were returning from their holiday cottage in Dorset later today.

‘Yes, of course. I’ll do it. I’ll need DC Smart to come with me. Can you ask her to pop in?’

Chapter 29

Saturday 4th April

Morgan and Smart met in the Country Club car park. He got out of his car and looked up at the windows, wondering which room his wife had been in when she had begun her affair with Graham Fletcher. DC Jenny Smart parked her car in the space opposite and got out to join him.

'Morning, Nick.' She was wearing a navy dress and blazer with white edging. He noticed that she was also wearing jewellery: gold earrings with a line of three sapphires descending, alternating with tiny diamonds. At her neck was a gold chain. As if she was reading his mind, she said, 'I'm visiting my mother after we've finished here. She likes me to make an effort. I find it's quicker to dress up than have her go on about how being a police officer has robbed me of my femininity.'

He smiled. 'I'm not going to make the sexist mistake of commenting. I hope we get what we need quickly enough for you to have a worthwhile trip to your mum's.'

'Don't hurry on my part,' said Smart, following him up the steps to the entrance.

The officers showed their warrant cards to the receptionist, who was reading a newspaper at the desk. Morgan glanced at his watch. Nine fifteen. On a weekday, he would have expected the foyer to be busy with people paying their bills and checking out, as well as others arriving for meetings and conferences.

'Is this the calm before the storm?' he asked.

‘Certainly is. We’ve got two wedding receptions later. Hairdressers and beauticians have been here since eight.’ She looked at her screen. ‘It says you’re here to see Mr Thorne. Is that right?’

‘Yes, although I believe we’re meeting Mr *and* Mrs Thorne.’

She shook her head. ‘I’ve seen Mr Thorne this morning, but not his wife. He was with Hugo.’

‘Hugo?’ asked Morgan.

‘Their son.’

‘I see. Can you let Mr Thorne know we’re here, please?’

‘He’s waiting for you in the Shanklin Suite. He said to tell you to go straight through.’ She pointed to their left. ‘Through the double doors and down the corridor to the end. The Shanklin Suite is on your right.’

The detectives thanked her and followed her directions. They progressed down the long corridor, passing piles of chairs and folded tables, a couple of vacuum cleaners, and separate piles of blue and white laundry sacks.

‘I hope they’ve sorted this out before the bride and groom get here,’ said Smart.

The door to the Shanklin Suite was labelled ‘Fire Door’, but was being held open. Morgan was tempted to kick the wedge away and see who came to remonstrate. He heard raised voices from a room leading off the suite’s foyer. An older man and the higher pitch of someone younger; could be a boy or a girl, he wasn’t sure. When the door opened, a young man, older than Morgan was expecting, with short brown hair and flushed cheeks appeared. He was the same height as Morgan, but not as broad or muscled. Through the fashionable red-framed glasses, Morgan could see that he had been crying. He stopped and stared at them.

'Mr Thorne?' said Morgan, although he thought that this man was too young to be the manager of the club.

'Not the one you want,' he replied. 'Not the one anyone wants, it would seem.' He turned to point to a second man, who was following him.

A large man. A bear of a man.

'Hugo. Don't be silly. Come back,' said the man before noticing the officers and smiling his welcome. He crossed the lobby at an enviable speed for a man of his size and held a beefy hand out towards Jenny Smart. Morgan noticed a slight hesitation on her part before she took it. He didn't hear the crunch of breaking bones, so when the offer was repeated, he too shook Mr Thorne Senior's hand. He was amazed by the gentleness and control of the handshake.

'Come through, officers. I've got coffee and tea of every description waiting for you.' He held out an arm in invitation for them to make their way to a table set with vacuum flasks and mugs. He called out to Hugo that he would catch up with him later before returning his attention to them. 'My son can be a little hot-headed. It makes for fireworks. Now, what will you have?'

Morgan chose a black coffee and Smart asked for the decaffeinated version. Once they had their steaming mugs, Thorne pointed towards a couple of sofas in the room and he sat on a third. Smart put her coffee on the floor and took her police notebook out of her bag.

'I expect you're here to talk about Simon Dennison,' said Thorne, 'but I'm not sure how I can help. My family and I have been in Dorset all week.'

'Mr Thorne …' Morgan began.

‘Roddy,’ said Thorne.

Morgan flashed an insincere smile. ‘Thank you. And that was your son, Hugo, who’s just left?’

‘That’s correct.’

‘I had hoped to speak to both yourself and your wife today.’

‘Francine stayed in Dorset. We have three holiday lets down there and we went to do the necessary to get the last of them ready for the season. Hugo and I did a bit of decorating and the girls stayed on to finish the cleaning and to buy some new accessories. Linens, kitchen bits and pieces, that sort of thing. They’ll be back in a few days.’

Morgan looked over to check that Smart was keeping up with her note-taking.

‘Are they your own properties, or are they part of the same portfolio the club is in?’

Roddy Thorne’s expression showed surprise. ‘Done your homework, I see – so you probably already know that the club is owned by a hotel chain based in France. Our head office is in the Dordogne; in Périgueux. My wife’s father is one of a board of six owners. Hotels are in her blood, not mine. I married into them. The holiday lets are ours. I inherited money when my mother died, and my wife made the business case for investing in property rather than stocks and shares. We don’t make a fortune, but enough to make them worth keeping.’ It was more information than Morgan either needed or wanted, but if Roddy Thorne was in the mood to talk, he wasn’t going to stop him. He saw that Thorne was following Jenny Smart’s pen, and when she paused and looked up he continued. ‘I don’t quite see how I’ll be of any help to you. We left on Sunday after Francine had overseen lunch, and Hugo and I only got back last night.'

'I appreciate that,' said Morgan, 'but I understand Mr Dennison was something of a regular at the club, so you must have known him.'

Thorne rocked his head from side to side. 'Not sure I would say I knew him, as such. I could recognise him in a crowd, and we always acknowledged each other, but we never socialised.' He pointed to Smart. 'I think I served him in the bar a couple of times. You should write that down … in case it's important.'

Two small circles of pink appeared on her cheeks. 'Was Mr Dennison popular with the staff?' she asked.

'You would have to ask them.'

Morgan took back control of the questioning. 'We have, but we find that people are less willing to give their honest opinion about someone after their death. You'd be amazed. Aggressive and violent thugs can become lovable rogues. But you seem like a man with his ear to the ground. You must know what was being said.'

Thorne smiled broadly and stretched his large frame back in the sofa, which emitted an alarming creak. 'I don't think I can help. I can't recall anything being said. Now, if that's all …' He put one hand on each side of his wide thighs and pushed himself up. 'I've been away for a week. Lots to catch up on.'

'Just one more thing,' said Morgan. 'I believe there was some unpleasantness regarding Mr Dennison parking in a spot designated for the captain of the ladies golf team?

'You're surely not suggesting that he was killed for a parking space?' said Thorne. 'Not in Gullhaven.'

‘I’m not suggesting anything. I’m asking about it.’

Thorne shrugged. ‘I’ve heard about it, but I wasn’t here.’

‘I think we’d like to know what happened,’ said Smart. Morgan thought she was sharing his growing impatience with Roddy Thorne.

‘The space you’re referring to is by the front entrance and Mr Dennison had parked his car in it. When it was reported, the Duty Manager put a note under his door and the car was moved. I’m told that there was a bouquet of flowers at reception for the captain the next day. All blown over. Nobody died. Oh, God … I’m sorry. That was tactless. It’s just an expression I use.’

‘Quite,’ said Morgan. He looked across at Jenny Smart, who gave a small shake of her head. ‘Before we go, I should just ask … How involved is Hugo in the business? Would he have known Simon Dennison?’

Thorne gave the matter considerable thought before he replied. ‘He will probably have served him at the bar, much like myself. He helps out when we have conferences and big events, but he’s mostly involved in marketing.’

‘And your daughter?’ asked Morgan.

‘We’ll involve her when she’s older. She’s recently turned sixteen, so she can’t serve alcohol. It’s easier if we keep her out of the banqueting rooms and the bars. The punters get impatient if they think a member of staff won’t take their order.’ He raised his hands as if surrendering. ‘I should admit that she has helped out in the cloakroom a couple of times. Cash in hand. Not reported to the revenue.’ He presented his arms as if expecting handcuffs. ‘I’ll come quietly.’

Morgan looked at his watch and stood. ‘Maybe later,’ he said. ‘DC Smart?’ She nodded and closed her notebook, then reached across for her shoulder-bag and put the pad and her pen in it before zipping it closed.

‘I’ll show you out,’ said Thorne.

‘That’s okay; we’ll find our own way.’ Morgan was sure he detected a relaxation in Thorne’s body language as they made for the door. Had they missed something?

They made their way back to reception and out into the fresh air, maintaining silence until Morgan spoke. ‘What did you make of him?’

‘Hmmph. I don’t know if you’d like to hear what I make of him.’

‘He didn’t seem that bothered, did he?’ Morgan frowned. ‘Dennison was a regular and, from what we’ve heard, was generous with the staff.’

‘He’d have been more upset if Dennison had been murdered in the building. Bad for business.’

‘I’m sure you’re right,’ said Morgan. ‘Thank you for fitting this in at the last minute. DS Spence was coming with me, but he’s not going to be working on the case. He’s partnering up with Acting DI Goddard.’

‘I’ve heard,’ said Smart. Morgan waited for more, but nothing was forthcoming.

‘I know he’s upset, Jenny, but my hands are tied on this one.’

‘He’s not said anything about it. Well, not to me.’

Morgan applauded her loyalty. ‘What have you got planned for the rest of your weekend, once your visit to your mum is over?’

‘The usual. Washing, ironing, shopping, cooking.’

‘And the sparkly notebook? What will you be writing in there about Roddy Thorne?’ They’d reached the point in the car park where they would have to part company to get to their vehicles, and both stopped walking.

'I think I'll write that we need to speak to Hugo and to Mrs Thorne on her return, and that both of those conversations would be better in the absence of Mr Roddy Thorne.'

Morgan nodded. 'I agree, and I'll put the interviews in the formal policy book. We'll do it when she gets back from Dorset, and you can lead. Okay?'

'Thank you.' Smart flushed a little. 'And your weekend?'

'I'm laying laminate flooring in a cramped en-suite,' he said. 'My knees will be glad to get back to work on Monday.' He raised a hand as a truncated goodbye wave and walked in the direction of the west car park.

Chapter 30

Monday 6th April

Morgan started Monday's Dennison case briefing by telling the team about DS Alison Goddard's temporary promotion to Acting DI. Nobody seemed surprised; the rumour mill must have done its work over the weekend. There were a few murmurs about her only being here five minutes, and he was sure he heard someone say 'Poor Dave'. He looked to the back of the room, where Dave Spence stood, face impassive, next to DC Jenny Smart, who had her notebook open as usual. No sign of Acting DI Alison Goddard.

'I'm sure you'll join me in hoping DI Patel's mother makes a speedy recovery and in anticipating her early return to us,' he said, and was rewarded with a few nods and smiles.

'Let's start with a catch up on what's happened over the weekend. Dave and Jenny ... can you please tell us about your findings at Dennison's flat.'

They presented their findings together. The expensive flat; the drugs; the locked cabinet which had been forced open by the CSI team to reveal more DVDs than Spence had ever seen in one place; and finally, the high specification camera and computing in the second-bedroom wardrobe. Spence's voice was flat and unemotional, as if feigning disinterest protected him from the disappointment of being removed from the case. When their report ended, Morgan asked the team if they needed any clarification, and, with no questions being put forward, thanked Spence for his work. The sergeant nodded curtly and left the room, closing the door more loudly than necessary.

Morgan turned a page of his policy book. 'Okay. I'll move on to the visit DC Smart and I made to the Country Club on Saturday. We spoke to the manager, Roddy Thorne, but if I'm honest it didn't really help us. Simon Dennison was a fairly regular visitor who Mr Thorne knew by sight but not much more than that. It was a bit of a waste of time, really.' He felt the eyes of the room on him. It was less than a week since Dennison had died and they seemed to have run out of ideas.

'I've spoken to Digital Forensics and they will take at least another week to get around to what was submitted from the flat,' said the exhibits officer.

'Easter will add a few more days to that,' said Smart.

'God. Yes. It's this weekend, isn't it?' Morgan raked his nails through his hair, realising that the school holidays must be starting soon. Maybe they already had? Again, a difficult case had meant he'd lost touch with family life. 'Has anyone got anything else before I allocate tasks?'

'I'm still trying to trace the sex toy, but no joy yet.' Morgan almost missed the input and looked at the group to identify who had spoken. His eyes fell on Lee Tyler, the newest member of the team.

DC Tyler was in his early twenties, but might still get away with paying half fare on public transport. Morgan had heard some of the female officers speculate on whether he had started to shave, and, on one occasion, whether he was still a virgin. Morgan thought of him more as a heat-seeking missile. Give him a problem and make sure you're not standing in his way as he seeks to solve it.

‘Settle down.’ Morgan was struggling to make himself heard over the ribaldry and laughter that Tyler’s comment had generated. His heart went out to the lad. ‘Keep trying, Lee. If we could connect the purchase of that dildo to someone who knew Dennison, we’d be well on our way. Anyone else?’ He looked around the room at shaking heads and eyes that were avoiding his. ‘Right, then.’ He picked up his policy book and bent back the spine to hold it open. When he looked up again, he noticed that Dave Spence had reappeared.

‘Yes, Dave?’

‘I’ve just been emailed the address for the owner of the company that went into liquidation after Forest-Fox Analysis won a competitive tender which they were counting on.’

Morgan smiled and thanked him. He knew that Spence could have simply forwarded the email, either to himself or Smart. But once DS Spence was involved in a case, he took ownership of it. That was one of the qualities which would make him a great DI and Senior Investigating Officer. Acting DI Goddard was going to struggle to prise him away from this case.

Chapter 31

Monday 6th April

Dorothy Cooper was nervous. Neither of her attempts to enrol Steven on the art course in France had received a response, and Plod had gone very quiet. She didn't know if he had abandoned his investigation, or was on the point of arresting her son. She'd thought of little else all weekend and had woken up angry and prepared to meet fire with fire.

When she rang Samantha to arrange a shopping trip, her daughter was reluctant. 'I've got the kids with me,' she said. 'Easter holidays.'

Dorothy was sure that her own schooldays hadn't been peppered with such a generous number of holidays. No wonder today's kids couldn't read or add up.

'Is there nobody you could leave them with ... even just for the morning? What about Plod?' She heard Samantha's sigh of disapproval at the nickname.

'He's got a big case on at work, Mum. Where else would he be?'

Dorothy didn't answer. This gave her some breathing space. If Plod was tied up with a case, he might not be worrying about Steven. At least, not for now.

'I haven't seen you for so long. You don't visit me.' Dorothy used the whiny tone which always succeeded in prodding Samantha's conscience.

'I'm living in a building site, raising two kids who won't stop bickering, and I'm running your business. If you needed to shop for something, you should have told me before I went yesterday, when Nick was here to look after the kids.'

‘I just want to spend a bit of time with my only daughter. Surely that’s not too much to ask?’

She heard Samantha sigh. ‘Okay. A couple of hours. I’ll ring round for someone to take the twins – but I don’t know how long that will take.’

‘Thank you, darling. It means a lot. It can be quite lonely here.’

Samantha ended the call without saying goodbye and Dorothy put her phone down on the arm of her chair. She was smiling. Her plan was coming together.

Chapter 32

Monday 6th April

With the transfer of DS Dave Spence to Alison Goddard's team sorted, Morgan accompanied DC Smart to interview Giles Clooney at his home, just west of Southampton.

Smart parked her car outside the modern, end-of-terrace property. The front garden had a small patch of grass which hadn't had its first cut of the season. The rest was covered by paving slabs and tarmac. An integral garage on the left of the property looked too small for the converted van which was parked in front of it.

'Homely, rather than executive,' said Smart as they walked up the path. She pointed to a disabled sticker on the back of the vehicle.

Morgan shrugged. They knew nothing about this man apart from the fact that he had reason to be angry with Simon Dennison. He pressed the doorbell and heard a faint noise from inside. They stepped back and waited.

'I'm coming. I'm coming.' The voice preceded the jangling of a chain being released and the door opening. 'Thank you for waiting.'

Giles Clooney was probably in his mid-sixties, although the lank grey hair which hung to his shoulders made him look older. His complexion was pale. A nasal cannula was delivering oxygen to both nostrils from a small cylinder mounted on his wheelchair, which took up most of the width of the hall.

The detectives held out their identification for him to look at but he waved them away before reversing down the hall. 'Whichever of you comes in last, can you please close the door.' He carried out a speedy three-point turn in the lounge doorway and led them into the kitchen.

'We're sorry to bother you, Mr Clooney,' said Morgan. 'We're here about Simon Dennison.'

'What about him?' The question came from a woman who appeared through an arch. She had a paintbrush in her hand and her hair was tied up in a scarf. 'It's a name we don't usually use in this house.'

'Gina,' Clooney's voice was soft but carried a warning, 'don't do this.'

'Why not?' she asked. 'He should pay for what he did to you.'

Morgan felt as if he'd arrived on a film set without a copy of the script. He decided to try a different approach. 'I believe Mr Dennison worked for you at Specify Solutions Limited? Up to around three years ago?'

'Correct,' said Clooney. 'Would you like some tea? Have you come far?' Smart shook her head and Morgan declined on behalf of them both. 'In that case, come through here where we can talk without disturbing my wife.' He opened an unpainted door and Morgan inhaled the smell of new wood as he stepped through into what had been the attached garage. Now, it was a tiny bedroom with an adjustable bed and hoist, as well as a narrow sofa. There was no space left for the storage of clothes or display of personal nick-nacks. The room was hotter than the hallway.

'We've not been here long,' said Clooney by way of explanation. Morgan sensed he was also apologising. 'When the company folded, we couldn't keep the other place. This will do us. Once we've completed the renovations I need.' He pointed to himself. 'I can't get up the stairs, you see.'

Morgan nodded. 'Was it an accident?' he asked.

'Stroke. Two days after the business folded. I'm getting able to do more, but I'll never be on my legs again.' He pulled the cannula tubing from his face and rested it over the arm of the wheelchair. 'What about Simon Dennison? What's he done?'

The detectives sat on the small sofa and Smart produced her phone to record the conversation. 'Do you mind?' she asked, and Clooney shrugged one shoulder in response.

'I'm sorry to tell you that Mr Dennison was found dead a few days ago. We believe he was attacked,' said Morgan.

Clooney gave a short laugh which developed into a fit of coughing. 'Since this happened,' he again pointed to himself, 'I've read a lot of crime books; fact and fiction. I know how it works. So ...' He dragged the word out as if it had multiple syllables. 'I grant you that I have motive, but I'm going to come up a bit short on means and opportunity.'

'I wasn't accusing you, Mr Clooney; I was informing you of what has happened to him.'

'Okay. I'm sorry.'

'Have you had any communication with Mr Dennson since he left your company three years ago?' asked Morgan.

Clooney motioned for Smart, who was nearest the door, to close it.

'If Gina found out, she'd go spare,' he said.

With the door closed, Clooney reached for a packet of rolling tobacco and then changed his mind. Morgan was relieved. It was oppressive enough in this small, windowless room, and he hadn't seen Clooney close the tap on the oxygen cylinder.

'I met him a couple of times for a pint.'

'When was this?'

'Last year. Late summer, I'd say ... September, or it might have been October?' His intonation rose at the end of the reply as if he wasn't sure.

'Who got in touch with who?' asked Smart. Morgan cringed at her grammar. It was one of the few foibles he shared with his mother-in-law.

'He rang me and we met in a café in Lyndhurst, surrounded by American tourists. The taxi cost a fortune, but I didn't want Gina taking me. She'd have killed him.' His brain caught up with his words and he apologised. 'Figure of speech. Don't read anything more than that into it.'

'What did he want?' asked Morgan.

'He wanted to come back to Specify. Said Gary Fox was running him into the ground. Said they were milking him.'

Morgan sensed that Smart was trying to catch his attention, but being seated side by side and this close, it was difficult to be sure without being obvious. 'And what did you say?' he asked.

'I told him he'd stitched us up and that I wouldn't trust him even if I could have afforded him. I said he could ask again after our tender had come in and I'd see what I could do.'

'But the tender went to Forest-Fox?'

'Yes. And we went under as a direct result of that.'

‘Did you blame him?’ asked Smart.

Clooney frowned as he considered his answer. ‘Gina blames him. I think I blame Gary Fox more than Simon. They both knew we were relying on that tender to survive, but only Fox had the power to source an instrument to compete.’ He nodded slowly. ‘Yes, I blame Gary Fox.’ He looked at Morgan and Smart in turn. ‘But that doesn’t mean I approve of what Simon did to him.’

Chapter 33

Monday 6th April

From her lounge window, Dorothy watched Samantha approach the Silver Sands' main building. Her daughter's head was down and it didn't look as if she'd taken a lot of trouble with her appearance. She crossed to her kitchen and flicked the switch on the kettle she'd already filled. She tipped a few chocolate biscuits on a plate, brushed her hair, and while at the mirror, practised a few sympathetic facial expressions.

Samantha's arrival was accompanied by the smell of cigarettes. Dorothy screwed up her face.

'Don't start, Mother.'

Samantha slipped her raincoat off her shoulders and hung it behind the door while Dorothy busied herself with the coffee. When it arrived, Samantha sniffed at it and scowled. This is instant,' she said, putting the mug on a flowery coaster on the table.

'I'm not wasting my best Blue Mountain on someone whose tastebuds are paralysed by nicotine. Take it or leave it.' Dorothy immediately wished she hadn't added the last words. She was supposed to be in sympathetic mode, wasn't she? Sometimes, she just couldn't help herself. 'What's he done now?'

'It's Alex,' said Samantha. 'There's been a bit of a misunderstanding at school.'

'What sort of misunderstanding?'

Samantha shook her head. 'Doesn't matter. And it's not something you can help with. Nick needs to have a word.'

‘If he can find the time, of course,’ said Dorothy, her eyes fixed on her daughter. She was waiting for her moment.

‘Did you hear about the body in the beach hut? Nick’s investigating that one. I’ve not seen much of him since they found it.’

‘It’s a “him”, Samantha. How often do I have to remind you? Just because he’s dead, he doesn’t cease to become a person in his own right. He’ll always be someone’s son, or father, or brother. He’ll always be a real person to someone.’

It was a lecture she had given both her children over the years. Although she was becoming increasingly entrenched in the family funeral business, it seemed that Samantha hadn’t yet developed a respect for the deceased clients, and it annoyed her.

‘Was there anything you were particularly looking for when we’re shopping?’ asked Samantha as she passed her mother to get more milk for her coffee. Dorothy cursed silently. The conversation had moved past DI Nick Morgan and it would be difficult to get back to him without her motive seeming obvious.

‘I thought I’d look for a pair of sandals for the summer,’ said Samantha.

‘For the beach?’ Dorothy seized her opportunity to claw her way back to her own agenda. ‘I don’t know if I’d feel good about going there after a body turned up. Has Plod found out who he is yet?’

Samantha was rummaging in her handbag for her car keys. She looked surprised when she looked up. Her mother wasn’t usually interested in Nick’s work activities. ‘He hasn’t said.’

‘Has he returned to your bed, or is he still sulking about Graham?’

‘We’ve spoken about it and he says he’s not ready. I know I hurt him.’ She sounded defensive.

‘It’s not natural for a married couple to sleep in separate rooms,’ said Dorothy, confident now that she was back on track. ‘Your father and I shared a bed until the day he went into hospital. Samantha opened her mouth to speak, but Dorothy continued. ‘You need to make sure he’s not getting his fun somewhere else.’

Samantha shook her head. ‘I can’t see that happening.’

‘I don’t think you should be so confident.’ Dorothy was carrying her mug into the kitchen when she called over her shoulder, ‘Especially now that Alison Goddard is back on the scene.’

Chapter 34

Monday 6th April

'We're not sure what you mean, Mr Clooney,' said Morgan. 'What did Simon Dennison do to Gary Fox?'

Clooney's laughter was without humour. He stretched back into the cushion of his wheelchair. 'He didn't tell you, then?'

'Tell us what?'

'I'm not sure it's my place.'

'Tell us what?' Morgan persisted.

'It's difficult for someone who didn't know Simon Dennison to make sense of what he did and who he did it to. My Gina and I used to lie awake at night and talk about him. She said he had tunnel vision. Reckoned if he saw something he wanted on the other side of a motorway, he'd stop his car and run across the lanes of traffic without looking left or right.' He looked again at both detectives, as if checking their understanding. 'Don't get me wrong. That's not a bad thing if you want to be successful in sales. But it's crap if you want to be a decent human being.'

There was a soft knock on the door and Clooney's wife entered. 'Shall I make tea?'

'Honestly, Mrs Clooney, we're fine,' said Smart.

'Please don't overtire him.' Gina Clooney looked near to tears as Smart guided her back out of the door and closed it.

'She fusses,' said Clooney. 'Just a moment.' He brought the cannula tubing back to his nose and took a few breaths before removing it again and, to Morgan's relief, turning the oxygen cylinder off.

'This is all hearsay, of course. It wasn't a party I was invited to.'

'Okay,' said Morgan. 'What party?'

'The Forest-Fox Christmas party, last year. It was a big night because they weren't just celebrating Christmas and end-of-year figures, they were celebrating winning the tender. It was still held at the Country Club because they get a good rate there, and Gary Fox has never seen a pound he doesn't want to hang on to.' Again, Clooney was checking to make sure he had their attention. Morgan decided that there couldn't be many visitors to this house. Giles Clooney was relishing being the centre of attention.

'It was a masked ball. Ridiculous, really. Everyone recognised each other straightaway. Complete waste of time and money. Then this woman comes in: dress slit to her crotch and her boobs shoved in everyone's faces – and Simon does his thing. He barges across the ballroom, probably with his tongue hanging out, and starts to charm her.'

'And it's Mrs Fox,' said Smart. Clooney looked disappointed at having his punch line stolen. 'What happened?'

'How well do you know the Gullhaven Country Club?'

Morgan shook his head. He knew it was where Samantha had shared Graham Fletcher's bed two months ago. That was as much as he needed to know.

'There's a paved area at the side with picnic benches and a kids' play area. You get to it through bi-fold doors in the ballroom where the main bar is.'

Morgan closed his eyes and looked down. He sensed what was coming and felt sorry for Fox. It seemed they had something in common.

'He had her over one of the benches, and when he was done and he looked up, Gary Fox was watching from the doorway with his puppy-dog PA standing right beside him. Anyway, they never went back to the party and she went home with him. If you ask me, it's Gary Fox who had the motive. You should have a word.'

'How do you know this, Mr Clooney?'

'I have my spies.'

'Which particular spy?' asked Smart.

'Simon Dennison, of course. He was that pleased with himself when he told me. I just thought that at least I wasn't the only person he'd fucked that week.' He turned to Smart. 'Sorry, Miss.'

Chapter 35

Monday 6th April

Once back in the warmth of the car, DC Jenny Smart checked the address of the Forest-Fox Analysis head office. 'It's in Basingstoke,' she said.

Morgan looked at his watch. 'What do you reckon ... half an hour?'

'Nearer three quarters,' she said, pointing to the satnav.

'Let's take the register first.' Morgan dialled the number and waited while the automated response offered him several options. When he was transferred to a human, he asked for Gary Fox.

'Mr Fox isn't in the office today. I'll put you through to his PA'

Morgan ended the call. 'One out of two. Fox isn't in, but Becca Yates is. Let's go and ask her if she enjoyed the Christmas party.'

Morgan wasn't sure what he expected, but it wasn't this. Forest Fox Analysis's HQ was at the far end of a run-down industrial estate. The few windows of the two-storey building which faced the front were covered by rusting grills and looked as if they had never been cleaned. The double-height roller door, which, he assumed, must be the goods entrance, was defaced by graffiti. There were three cars including one in the space designated for visitors.

‘Block it in,’ said Morgan, looking up at the darkening sky and hearing the first drops of rain on the car roof. ‘We won’t be long.’

They got out and hurried to a metal door with an intercom. Smart pushed the button and they waited.

The threatened downpour started in earnest and Smart pushed the button again. She pressed her ear against the speaker in case she missed the reply. When the door buzzed, Morgan pulled it towards them and they stepped in.

The hallway was unwelcoming. No sofas or phones, and no magazines, elevator music or aroma of coffee. There was another metal door through which they could hear the unmistakable sounds of machinery and loud voices. It was secured by a digital keypad. On the left was a staircase with a sign on the wall which was an arrow pointing upwards. Morgan thought he had never seen a more pointless sign in all his life. Faced with no alternative, he led Smart to the next floor.

The stairs ended with a tiny landing and a fire door through which things improved. The security-glazed door was being held open by Melanie Meyer, Forest-Fox’s Marketing Director.

‘We weren’t expecting you,’ she said. ‘Mr Fox isn’t in the office today.’

‘That’s okay,’ said Morgan. ‘We’ll speak to his PA.’ Morgan had noticed back at the original interviews that the relationship between Melanie Meyer and Becca Yates was frosty. Better to give the impression that they were only speaking to the PA because Fox wasn’t about.

‘Follow me.’

It was clear that any money invested in the building had been spent on the office accommodation. The area was open-plan but split into designated areas by shoulder height, padded partitions. Signs hung from the ceiling: Sales; Marketing; Purchasing; Quality.

They reached a closed door which Meyer opened without knocking. Becca Yates was sitting at a desk facing them. She jumped at the intrusion, and her eyes narrowed when she saw it was Melanie Meyer. When she noticed the detectives, her expression changed to dismay. 'My Fox isn't in the office today,' she said.

'I've already told them. They're here to make an appointment.' Meyer backed out of their way and Morgan smiled and thanked her. The reason she had given for the intrusion meant that Becca Yates would be in personal assistant mode. The diary would come out; her defences should be down.

'He's working from home today,' said Yates. 'He asked not to be disturbed.'

'That's okay,' said Morgan, taking a seat on one of the visitor chairs. Smart had already sat on the other one and was poised to take notes.

'I've already told you everything I know.' Her eyes darted between the detectives. Morgan reached across from his chair and closed the door. When she started to remonstrate, he shook his head at her.

'You see, Becca, I already know that you're good at your job. When I spoke to Mr Fox last week, most of his answers were "You'll need to ask Becca," or "Speak to Becca." From that, I have to believe that you're a good organiser and that you have a good memory.'

She sat back in her chair, shoulders relaxing a little, but still wary.

'I also believe that you're loyal, both to the company and to Mr Fox personally.'

She nodded. Just once. Morgan inferred that this was as much acknowledgement as he was going to get. He kept his voice soft, conscious that walls have ears and that there were people at their desks only a few feet away who would be curious about the visitors.

'So when we spoke last week, I have to imagine that it was your loyalty to Mr Fox that prevented you telling us about last year's Christmas celebrations at the Country Club.'

Her eyes opened wide and her hands flew to her mouth.

'I think it's loyalty, but of course it could be an attempt to pervert the course of justice.' He heard Smart's sharp intake of breath and saw her head snap in his direction; but his cold blue eyes remained on Yates.

The door opened and Melanie Meyer appeared. 'Can I offer you tea or coffee? You seem to be staying longer than I was expecting.'

Morgan exhaled and cursed. What was it about refreshments today? It was the second time he had been interrupted at a crucial moment. Smart had looked away again and was concentrating on her notepad. She gave a slight shake of her head. 'No thank you, Ms Meyer.'

'Becca?'

'No thank you, Melanie. And please close the door behind you.'

They waited, listening for her receding footsteps.

'I get the impression she doesn't make your tea very often,' said Smart.

'Never.'

'The Christmas party.' Morgan was keen to get the interview back on track. 'Am I right in thinking that you were no longer in a relationship with Simon Dennison by then?'

'Correct.'

'Was he in a relationship with anyone else, to your knowledge?'

'No. Well, not to my knowledge. But why would I know? I was just a mistake.' Morgan heard her resentment; saw the hurt in her eyes.

'Can you tell me what happened at the party?'

'It was a good night. We were celebrating winning the tender. Gary put more money behind the bar than he usually does. That's all, really.'

'What can you tell me about Simon Dennison and Mrs Fox?'

Becca Yates looked up at the ceiling, then back down to the office door, as if ensuring it was closed. Morgan couldn't imagine that in a company of this size, Dennison having sex with the boss's wife in a beer garden would still be a secret.

'I think they sat together at dinner,' she offered.

Morgan waited. He'd already heard the sordid details. What he wanted was a witness account of Gary Fox's reaction to what they had both seen.

Becca Yates's demeanour changed, her voice raised. 'I don't know what you want me to say. You must already know what happened or you wouldn't be asking me about it.'

He felt her pain. What was hurting more? Was it that the man who had unceremoniously dumped her had indulged in public sex with another woman, or was it that the other woman was the wife of the most important man in Becca Yates's life, Gary Fox?

‘I saw Claire, that’s Gary’s wife, slip behind the curtains of the ballroom where the doors open on to the picnic area. Then Simon went out into the hall.’ The anger had passed and tears were forming. ‘I knew what was going to happen, I’d been watching them all evening. He couldn’t take his eyes off her. I looked around for Gary to see if I could warn him. He was in front of the stage, talking to Roddy Thorne, but I could see he was watching the curtains where Claire had disappeared.’ She was talking now as if she was back in that ballroom.

‘It sort of happened in slow motion. He finished speaking to Roddy and walked across to the curtains. I tried to get there first, but someone stopped me. I can’t remember who. When I got to Gary, he was standing in the doorway. He was watching. They were ...’

‘It’s okay. We don’t need all the details at this stage, but we may need a statement later,’ said Morgan. He wanted to be out of the cramped little office as soon as possible.

‘He could have gone out and stopped it. I don’t know why he didn’t. After it happened, Simon looked up at us. I think maybe the curtains were open wide enough to throw light on them. He smiled at Gary. I wasn’t sure, but I thought he might have winked, too. They didn’t come back to the ballroom. In fact, I didn’t see Simon again until after the Christmas break.’

‘And what did Gary do?’ asked Morgan.

She looked down at her lap, where her hands were clasped. ‘He said he’d kill him.’

Chapter 36

Monday 6th April

Roadworks on the M3 slowed their return trip. Morgan felt a vessel in his temple start to throb when they joined stationary traffic waiting to pass a broken-down car transporter in the middle of the two-lane section. They used their time to talk through their interview strategy for Gary Fox. When they finally hit open road, Morgan asked Smart if she wanted to lead.

'I'd like to, yes, but I'm a planner. If I'd seen this coming yesterday, I'd have spent my evening planning it out on paper. And it would have been good.' She glanced across at Morgan and he could see she was conflicted. 'It's not that I don't think I can do it. I would just prefer to have time to plan.'

Morgan nodded. He understood her concerns and could see why she might be reluctant to demonstrate her skills to her boss without prior notice. But when you were in the field, planning was a luxury that was not always available.

'I've been considering applying to be a specialist interrogator,' she said, changing the subject as she changed gear and took advantage of a gap in the outside lane to gain a bit of ground.

Her face didn't show if she was serious or attempting to wind him up. Morgan decided it was safest to ignore it. She would be brilliant in the role of interrogator, but she was also a damn good detective in the field and he didn't want to lose her from his team. He did what he always did when he wanted to avoid a conversation. He got out his phone and scrolled through messages.

When the satnav told them they had reached their destination, they seemed to be in the middle of nowhere. Smart parked on the grass verge so that other vehicles had a chance of squeezing past and they both got out and looked around. One side of the road was edged by a low fence with fields beyond; the other had a tall privet hedge of about seven feet.

'Well, we haven't passed anything,' said Smart, 'so I'm guessing it's coming up somewhere beyond this bend.' Morgan nodded and they got back into the car, Smart driving slower now in case of oncoming traffic in the middle of the road. Soon, there were tall iron gates on the left and the hedge gave way to a wall on which hung a green ceramic plaque. The white lettering read "Forest House".

The building came into view about halfway down the wide drive. Morgan was struck by the contrast between this lifestyle and the one now enjoyed by Giles Clooney. He wondered what sort of house Clooney had owned before liquidating his company.

The woman who answered the door was dressed in white denim jeans and what looked like a cashmere jumper. Black leather boots and a heavy gold necklace completed her outfit. She would have been frowning if her Botox injections had allowed it. 'We don't buy at the door, and we donate to charities directly on their websites. Thank you.' She made to close the door and her mouth dropped open when Morgan took a step forward thrusting his ID out in front of him.

'I'm DI Morgan, Mrs Fox, and this is DC Smart. We've come to speak to your husband.'

'He's busy.'

'I doubt that he's too busy to speak to us,' he said. 'Although if he is, I can always arrange for a car to bring him in for questioning.'

'Are you the bully who interviewed him last week?' she asked, still blocking their entrance.

Morgan stared at her. 'I'm investigating the violent death of one of your husband's staff. Sometimes that role involves asking difficult questions. If your husband found that process uncomfortable, then I'm not about to apologise for it.'

Claire Fox stood to one side and Morgan entered, followed by Smart.

He's in there.' She threw a hand towards closed double doors on their left and started to walk away.

Morgan called after her. 'Please make yourself available for us when we have finished with Mr Fox. I have questions for you also.' When she turned, Morgan noted that her injectables weren't blocking the flush to her cheeks. Guilt, embarrassment or temper? He looked forward to finding out.

Either Becca Yates had lied when she had promised not to contact Fox and warn him of their visit, or he had heard Smart's tyres crunch on the shingle-covered parking area under his windows. As a result, Fox was halfway across his spacious home office to greet them as Morgan opened the door. 'I wasn't expecting you,' he said, but Morgan wasn't convinced. 'Have you found anything?' Fox's smile fell short of welcoming.

It seemed an odd question to Morgan. He was expecting something more along the lines of 'Do you know who killed him?' 'No, Mr Fox, but a few things have cropped up which I need you to clarify.'

Gary Fox returned to his chair behind a black desk which dwarfed him. He motioned the detectives towards an unfussy sofa which faced a flip chart. The set-up was exactly what Morgan expected of a managing director, but not in his own home. When Morgan needed to work from home, he sat with his feet up on the spare bed and supported himself with a pile of pillows, his laptop on the duvet beside him and papers spread out on the bed and the floor. He looked at Smart, who clicked her biro and sat, opening her notebook.

'When we asked you about Simon Dennison last week, I remember you concentrated on his work ethic, and, indeed, his success.'

'Yes, we'll miss him. In fact, I was just looking at some CVs that a recruitment company have sent me and now I can appreciate just how *much* we will miss him. There's not a lot of talent out there.'

'No doubt.' Morgan took a large breath in. 'Today, I want to ask you more about his private life and –'

'I told you already that I don't know much about that.' Fox looked away from the detectives and started to fiddle with a pen.

'What you told me was that he had paired up with some of the female members of the Forest-Fox staff.'

'But nothing serious.'

'You don't have anything in your employment contracts to say that such liaisons aren't allowed?'

'We're too small a company to worry about that. Our HR is contracted out, along with payroll.'

'I see.' The men stared at each other, the light coming from the window behind Fox catching Morgan's eyes and making them glint.

Fox wriggled in his chair, no attempt to smile now. 'This is obviously leading somewhere, so just get on with it.'

'It's leading to last year's Christmas party, Mr Fox.' Fox closed his eyes. His face and shoulders dropped. 'What can you tell me about that?'

The door burst open and Claire Fox strode into the room. Morgan thought that if she had come to offer them tea at this crucial point of the interview, he might strike her. She passed the detectives without acknowledging them and rounded Fox's desk, where she stood beside him, a hand resting on one shoulder. 'If this is about the party, you should be asking me, not Gary.'

'And I intend to,' said Morgan. 'As I told you, we have questions for you when we've finished speaking to your husband.'

Fox reached up and patted his wife's hand. 'It's okay. Go and sit in the lounge and I'll come for you when we're done.'

She looked doubtful, but left them, again without acknowledging Morgan or Smart.

'How much do you already know?' asked Fox.

Morgan nodded to Smart, who read out the version of events they had heard from Becca Yates. She stopped before she mentioned Fox's threat.

Fox nodded. 'Yeah, that's pretty much how I remember it. Who told you?'

'We've more than one source,' said Morgan.

'Your sources have omitted to mention that I said I'd kill him.'

'And did you mean it?'

'Not really. I was angry. Of course I was angry. But that was mostly with myself. Becca had come to me when Dennison dumped her and I'd played it down. I told her we couldn't afford to lose him and that I'd talk to him. You know, get him to rein himself in a bit.'

'Did you?'

'No. And I think him shagging my wife was the universe's way of telling me I should have been more supportive of Becca. She was in bits when they split.'

'Who might have heard you threaten Simon Dennison's life?'

Fox shook his head as he trawled through the uncomfortable memories of that night. 'Becca was standing behind me. I don't remember if I actually said it to her, or if she was just there when I said it. Does it make any difference?'

At this stage of the inquiry, Morgan didn't know the answer to that. Could someone else have overheard the threat and killed Dennison themselves, confident that there was a fall guy?

'What did you do then?'

'That, I can prove. I looked at my watch and it was after one o'clock, so I went to the bar and closed the tab, paid the bill and went to bed. I paid with the company credit card, so that's proof.'

Morgan stayed silent, allowing Smart her opportunity to break into the conversation. 'We don't need proof of your whereabouts at that party, Mr Fox. Mr Dennison was alive for nearly four months after it.'

'Of course. Sorry.'

'How were communications between you and Mr Dennison after that party?'

‘Hmph. You could say they were businesslike.’

‘Meaning?’

‘He sent me an email at the end of the first week in January complaining about the size of the target I had set him for the next twelve months. His wording was disrespectful and I called him into the office. He said he had customer appointments and I told him to cancel them and be there.’

‘Is that a usual response from a salesperson when they find out about their target?’

Fox gave a rueful smile. ‘I think I can say that it’s not unusual.’

‘And how did that meeting go?’

‘It was loud and he got angry. Told me that he had to make at least the same amount of commission as last year or he wouldn’t be able to afford his flat. I don’t remember being very sympathetic.’

‘Would it surprise you to hear that he had spoken to Giles Clooney about going back to work for him?’ asked Morgan.

‘I don’t think anything you could tell me about Simon Dennison would surprise me.’

‘Okay. I think that covers it for now. You’re not planning any foreign travel in the near future, are you, Mr Fox?’

‘Are you asking me or telling me?’ Fox looked at both in turn before raising his hands in surrender. ‘I’ll be here.’

Smart left the room first, and as Morgan followed, Fox called after him. ‘I’m not sorry he’s dead, but I didn’t kill him. The business needed him.’

Chapter 37

Monday 6th April

The door across the wide hallway was open and Claire Fox was standing inside the lounge with what appeared to be a gin and tonic in her hand. Morgan looked again at his watch, wondering if it was later than he thought. The twins would be getting home from school soon and he had told Alex they would kick a ball about on the clifftop this evening. Another promise made and broken.

Claire swirled the drink, ice cubes making a delicate tinkling noise against the crystal glass. She reached out to a gin bottle on the side table and added a generous glug before beckoning them in. She threw herself into a white leather armchair and folded her legs to one side of her. The contents of her glass sloshed and she mopped the spillage off the leather with her sleeve. Morgan wondered whether she would have licked it had she been on her own.

'I don't know why I did it,' she pre-empted the questions Morgan had planned. 'Gary and I had rowed in our room before we went downstairs. I was angry with him. I'd spent a lot on that dress and he didn't like it. He said I looked like a tart.' She looked at Smart. 'How is it that the less fabric there is in an evening gown, the more expensive it is? Can you answer me that?' Smart offered a small nod of empathy.

'Anyway, I didn't want to sit with Gary for dinner, so I moved down the table and sat next to Simon Dennison. He was very attentive. Kept telling me how sexy I looked and how lucky Gary was. Kept filling my glass up, too. He made me feel special. And when I looked over at Gary, he was being looked after by that Meyer woman. I'm not trying to make excuses, but I suppose that's how it happened.'

'I'm sorry to press you, Mrs Fox, but we're going to need more.' Jenny Smart spoke before Morgan had decided how to say the same thing. He nodded his thanks to her. It was better coming from a woman.

She sighed and started picking at her manicured nails. 'We had sex in the picnic area. Is that what you need?'

'And after that?' Smart stopped writing to watch her.

'We went to his flat.' She looked at Morgan now. 'I don't know how we got there. I know I didn't have a coat, because Gary and I were staying at the club and I just expected to go back upstairs to bed with him. I don't remember anything about the rest of that night, really.'

'What about the next day?' asked Morgan.

'Before you answer that, Mrs Fox, can I just clarify something?' Morgan and Claire Fox turned to Smart and she gave a small apologetic smile. 'Do you remember having sex outside the club, or have you just been told about it?'

She paused, frowning as she replied. 'I hadn't thought about it, but you're right. I don't remember. Gary told me when I got home.' She took a large swig of her drink and nodded as if she was having a conversation with herself. 'I don't remember.'

Smart started writing again and Morgan picked up the questioning. 'And the next day?'

'I remember that. Simon was already showered and dressed when I woke up. He brought me a cup of coffee. Black coffee because he said he hadn't any milk in. He sat on the end of the bed as if he couldn't bear to be near me. He apologised and told me I had been a mistake. I remember that specifically. Not *it* had been a mistake, but *I* had been a mistake. I think that hurt even more than what he'd done to me.'

'What do you mean?' asked Smart.

'I mean that he couldn't have been the most gentle of lovers. I was sore for days.'

'Thank you, Mrs Fox. That's been very helpful. Have you any more questions, DC Smart?'

Jenny Smart blushed and shook her head.

Morgan stood and waited while Smart packed her notebook and pen away. When he opened the door, Gary Fox was waiting outside.

'You think she was drugged, don't you?' he said.

'I'm disappointed that you were eavesdropping, Mr Fox. I'll make sure that if we need to speak to either of you again it'll be in an interview room under controlled conditions.'

'You think she was drugged,' Fox repeated. 'It would explain a lot, wouldn't it? My wife's not a slag.'

'Mr Fox, the half-life of any of the drugs which are commonly used in date rape is pretty short. It's been four months since that party, so we're never going to know.'

'I didn't kill him, but if he drugged and raped my wife, I wish I had.'

Claire Fox hurried to her husband and clasped his hands in hers. 'Don't, Gary. It's over now.'

'We'll need you both to come in and make statements,' said Morgan.

'I've got a meeting tonight,' said Fox. 'I'll come in on my way to the office tomorrow.'

'What about you, Mrs Fox?'

'I'll drive over tomorrow afternoon,' she said.

The couple turned towards each other, Claire looking up into her husband's eyes, searching for his understanding and forgiveness.

'We'll see ourselves out,' said Morgan, and Gary Fox nodded his agreement as he hugged his wife close to his chest to muffle her sobs.

The detectives walked to the car in silence before Smart apologised for interrupting Morgan's flow of questioning.

'No need to apologise, Jenny. You have as much right to ask questions in an interview as the lead, and anyway, I think you might be on to something. Maybe he did drug her. We've certainly identified his kiss-off line. "I'm sorry. You were a mistake." He told Becca Yates the same thing. Not very flattering, is it?'

Smart unlocked the car. 'I suppose it's better than "It's not you, it's me",' she said.

DC Jenny Smart dropped her boss off in the station car park and waved as she reversed into the space opposite and drove back to the barrier. Morgan leant on his Volvo while he decided whether to go into the office or drive straight home.

'Are you arriving, or leaving?' He turned to see DCI Richard Johnson approaching from the direction of the building. He was wearing a dinner suit and the shine on his shoes reflected the car park lighting.

'Arriving, Sir.' DC Smart and I have been on a bit of a road trip.'

'With what result?'

'We uncovered a strong motive, only for the next two interviews to stomp on it.'

'So, no further forward.'

Morgan wondered how high up the greasy pole he would have to climb before he would only see the end result without recognising or respecting the work it took to achieve it. He contemplated remonstrating but realised he was too knackered to be bothered.

'I'm off to a Rotary dinner at the Country Club,' said Johnson, 'and you should get off home, too. Time with the family helps recharge the batteries, you know.'

'Sir.'

'We'll talk about progress in the morning.'

Morgan watched him walk to his car, start the engine and flick the headlights on. He saw Johnson's brake lights as he used his security pass at the barrier, then again as he waited for a gap in the traffic to exit. He put his car keys back in his pocket and headed for his office.

The door to the lounge was closed when Morgan got home and he could hear urgent voices and a police siren from the television. He went into the kitchen and found a cereal bowl with what looked like pasta in a tomato sauce. He thought he could also see cubes of something which could be chicken, or maybe a vegetarian protein, and there were mushrooms. He covered the bowl and put it into the microwave while he poured a glass of red wine.

The microwave pinged as Sam came into the room. She was yawning. 'I must have fallen asleep,' she said.

'You should go to bed. You don't usually wait up when I've got a case on.'

‘I waited up to tell you that Alex sat by the window for two hours with his football beside him. He went to bed disappointed. You promised.’

‘I don’t think I did,’ said Morgan. ‘I never promise. This job means I don’t have that luxury. You know that.’ He dug his fork into the pasta. The texture was rubbery and the sauce needed salt. He put the bowl down again.

‘You promised,’ she said. ‘You’d better not have been with *her*.’ She closed the door behind her.

Chapter 38

Tuesday 7th April

The corridor outside his office was noisy this morning. People were shouting and there was a lot of laughter. Morgan got up and slammed the door. It didn't make him feel any better.

What had Sam meant? 'You'd better not have been with her.' How had she found out about Maisie? He felt a cold chill at his neck. An angry and shouting Samantha he could handle. It happened often and it blew over quickly. But last night had been something different. 'You'd better not have been with *her*.' She'd said the words quietly; there had been a calmness about her that made him apprehensive.

Jenny Smart came into his office and closed the door behind her.

'I couldn't hear myself think,' he said by way of explanation.

'Digital Forensics just got back to Dave and told him they won't have time to look at the hard drives and SD cards from Simon Dennison's flat for at least another month.' She held out a hand to bar any interruption. 'And Dave has told them he's no longer on the case and has given my contact details.'

Morgan thumped his elbows on the desk and rested his chin on clasped hands. 'I don't know where else to go with this one. When that Christmas party came up, I thought we were there. Gary Fox was a slam dunk.'

'Have you slept?' asked Smart.

'Not really.'

Smart tutted and shook her head. 'I'll get you a coffee,' she said.

Morgan frowned at the screen of his ringing mobile. 'Yes. Dave.'

Smart made for the door, but he waved to catch her attention and beckoned her back. She waited for him to end the call.

'There's another body on the beach,' he said. 'We'll take my car.'

'Can't Acting DI Goddard sort it? She's got Dave to help.'

'Dave's already at the beach and he recognised the victim.'

Smart smiled. 'As always. I'll need my boots from my car.' Something in his expression must have told her there was more.

'It's Gary Fox,' he said.

Chapter 39

Tuesday 7th April

Samantha dropped the twins off at Silver Sands and drove back into town. Her mother hadn't ask where she was going, or why, but she'd smiled and patted her hand when she kissed her at the door of her suite.

She parked her car in the multi-storey and slapped the ticket on to her dashboard. When she slammed her car door, the noise woke a baby whose mother was struggling to settle her into a pushchair at the back of the car opposite.

'Thanks for that,' the young woman shouted after her. The baby's howls grew louder but Samantha didn't hear them.

She didn't pause until she was standing at the door to the office, pushing the button for entry.

'You've not got an appointment,' said a metallic female voice. 'He's very busy, Mrs Morgan.'

'He'll see me,' she said. The door buzzed and she pushed it.

When she got out of the lift, a short woman in compensating high heels was waiting for her. 'Please follow me,' she said, and turned, walking away before checking that Samantha was following. They passed through a reception area and down a corridor with doors on both sides. Her escort reached the door at the end and knocked, pausing for a couple of seconds before opening it. 'Mrs Morgan,' she announced, and left, closing the door behind her.

Graham Fletcher rose from his desk and walked towards her. He seemed unsure whether to shake her hand or gather her up in an intimate embrace. He smiled. 'You look well, Sammy.'

The moment she heard his rich, warm voice, she knew she'd made a mistake coming to him. She blushed, unsure of what to say or do.

'Let me take your coat.'

'I'm fine,' she said, and wrapped it tighter around herself. This morning, she'd thrown on the same clothes she'd worn yesterday and she remembered the jumper had spatters of tomato sauce from the pasta dish she'd cooked for dinner. Graham, in his immaculately creased trousers and starched white shirt, made her feel dowdy. He pointed to a sofa behind a coffee table in the corner, but she shook her head and dropped into a visitor chair pulled up to his desk.

'I was going to ask if it was business or pleasure,' he said, 'but you may have answered my question.'

'I think Nick is having an affair and I need a solicitor to represent me. It's going to be complicated, what with us living in mum's house and everything.'

Fletcher exhaled through pursed lips, the noise coming out as a whistle. He returned to his chair and closed the lid of his laptop. 'If you want to divorce him using adultery as the reason, it may be difficult unless he admits it. And without wishing to alarm you, he could at this very moment be talking to a solicitor about our indiscretion. Dorothy told me that you admitted it to him, so he has grounds. And we're still within the six-month period of him knowing, and that's relevant to the court. As far as I can tell, you just have supposition.'

She got up. 'I thought you'd want to help me,' she said. 'If you don't, I'll find someone who will.'

He rose again and moved to cut off her path to the door. This time, he didn't hesitate; he wrapped his arms around her and pulled her in to him. She started to cry.

'Sammy. Oh my God, Sammy.' His hands held her arms as he eased her away to look at her more closely. 'What has he done to you?' He took a step back and leant on his desk, reaching out for the box of tissues which were a permanent fixture. She snatched one and dabbed at her eyes.

'He refuses to share a bed with me. And now his old girlfriend is back on the scene. It doesn't take Miss Marple to put two and two together.'

Fletcher grimaced. 'You'll have to talk to him about it. You may be worrying needlessly. But if you really have decided that it's over with Nick, we could try for unreasonable behaviour. Or, if you can hang on a bit longer, there's supposed to be new legislation coming to make "no-fault" divorce easier.'

'There is fault. His fault. I was ready to make a go of it.'

'Take a breath, Sammy. Speak to him. And if you still think that divorce is the way you want to go, come back and of course I'll help.' He hugged her close again before releasing her and pulling another tissue from the box. He dabbed her eyes. 'Your visit will certainly be giving my secretary something to think about. I never see clients without an appointment and they are usually crying on the way in, not on the way out.'

On her way back to the car park, Samantha replayed the conversation in her head. She had been sure that Graham would jump at the chance to free her from her marriage. Why the reluctance? She was almost back at Silver Sands when it struck her: Graham must be afraid that Nick would cross-petition, using their affair as grounds. He was looking out for his professional reputation rather than her future happiness. She didn't need him; she'd do it herself.

Chapter 40

Tuesday 7th April

Morgan drove Smart to the scene, passing Cliffside House on the way. He noticed that Sam's car wasn't there. She hadn't mentioned she was going out when they had breakfast. But when he thought about it, she had barely spoken at all.

The kerbside parking was all taken and Morgan was forced to leave the Volvo in one of the expensive car parks. He put his police sign on the dashboard and hoped for the best. They changed their footwear leaning on the sides of the open car boot and picked up the personal protective equipment they needed. At the top of the slope, they could see that this crime scene was to the east of the hut where Simon Dennison had been found. Their rubber boots made hollow trudging noises as they progressed down the concrete slope.

The sun was shining on calm water which was struggling to lap on to a ridge of exposed sand. In stark contrast, there was frenetic activity to his left.

The CSI circus was in full swing behind DS Dave Spence as he descended the cliff face, setting off an avalanche of soil and small stones. He strode towards Morgan and Smart.

'Morning, Dave,' said Smart. 'I know you wanted to be on this case, but pushing our suspect over the cliff is taking it a bit far, isn't it?'

Spence acknowledged her words with a small smile but spoke directly to Morgan. 'MoMack's up there,' he said, pointing.

'Any chance it's suicide, or an accident?' asked Morgan. 'Have you seen the body yourself?'

'Yes. Big head wound, and his legs look broken. They're at odd angles. MoMack says there are broken ribs, too. She doesn't think there's enough blood up there for that to be where he died.'

The three detectives stared back up at the cliff, shielding their eyes from the bright sun rising on their right.

Gullhaven Cove was prone to cliff-falls and there were signs everywhere warning people to stay away from the edge. Morgan had seen a couple of field trips of geography – or maybe geology – students photographing, measuring, but mainly frolicking on the beach while lecturers did their best to engage them.

Gary Fox's body lay beneath a large bite out of the cliff face which had happened long enough ago for some of the vertical faces to have grassed over. If he had come over the edge, he would have been bounced and deflected a few times on the way down. Like a cliff face pinball machine, thought Morgan.

'Morning, Nick.' Dr Morag Mackenzie stripped her white hood back and lowered her face mask as she got closer to the three detectives. 'It's slippery up there with shoe covers on. I've nearly ended up on my backside a few times.' She turned to Spence. 'I thought you were picking this one up.'

'It may be connected to last week's guy in the handcuffs,' said Morgan, pointing back in the direction of the beach hut.

'Oh, him? Yes, he made a lasting impression on all of us,' said the pathologist.

‘Not as lasting as the impression made on him,’ murmured Smart.

Mackenzie smiled and nodded. ‘You’re not wrong.’

‘So, who am I reporting back to? You or DI Goddard?’

‘Acting DI Goddard,’ corrected Spence.

This guy –’ Morgan pointed up the cliff face ‘– was beach-hut guy’s boss.’

MoMack rocked her head from side to side. ‘Okay. So you need the post mortem sooner rather than later?’ Nobody replied; their answer was obvious. ‘Well, I was due to take my nephews Easter egg shopping this afternoon, but I’ll give it a miss and do it at two thirty. That okay?’

Smart nodded and tapped an entry into her phone planner.

‘Where is Acting DI Goddard, anyway?’ asked Morgan.

‘She asked me to come and take a look and said she’d come out if she needed to,’ said Spence.

Morgan paused before his bottom lip protruded and he said, ‘Funny way to approach your first case as a DI. How did she react when you told her you were ringing me?’

‘I didn’t tell her,’ said Spence.

Chapter 41

Tuesday 7th April

Morgan and Smart sat in his car, which was facing across the bay. He drummed his fingers on the steering wheel. 'Shall we go to her, or shall we wait for her to come to us? She said she would come in and give her statement this afternoon.'

'It depends on whether you've got a heart,' said Smart. 'Would you want to hear that your spouse is dead while you're sitting in an interview room? Thanks for your statement, Mrs Fox. Oh, by the way ... not sure if you know this, but ...'

Morgan's nod was decisive. 'You're right. M3 it is. Can you ring her and make sure we don't pass each other on the way.'

'I don't have her number.'

He got out of the car and retrieved his case notes from the boot. He handed them to Smart and started the car. 'You'd better ring MoMack and tell her you may not be back by two thirty. Tell her we're sorry.'

'I thought I was coming to you.' Claire Fox was wearing more make-up than yesterday; her clothes more tailored; jewellery more expensive.

'Can we come in, Mrs Fox, please?'

Her face was expressionless, but she shrugged her shoulders as she stood back and pointed them towards the lounge.

'Gary's at the office,' she said, 'or he may be with you, giving his statement. Is there a problem?'

Morgan and Smart exchanged a glance. They had agreed in the car that he would deliver the death message and Smart would make the tea.

'You should sit down, Mrs Fox,' said Morgan.

Claire Fox's head pivoted between Morgan and Smart. 'I don't want to sit down. What's going on?'

'Please, Claire,' said Smart, and Morgan sat on the sofa by way of encouragement.

'Is it Gary? Has he had an accident?' She reached out for her mobile and swiped at the screen. 'I've not heard from him this morning.'

Morgan exhaled. 'I'm sorry, Claire. It is Gary. He was found at the bottom of the cliff at Gullhaven Cove this morning. I'm afraid he's dead.'

She stared at him and then up at Smart, searching their faces for an explanation. 'I don't understand. Is this some sort of test?'

'I'm going to make some tea,' said Smart. 'Milk and sugar?' Claire Fox looked as if Smart was speaking in a language she didn't understand. 'I'll put a couple of sugars in.'

Smart had reached the door when Claire called after her. 'I don't take sugar.'

Once Smart had left to find the kitchen, Morgan moved a bit closer to the edge of the sofa so he could speak quietly, but Claire Fox started before he had got his words together.

'What happened? This isn't still to do with the Christmas party, is it?'

'All I can tell you at the moment is that Gary was found partway down the cliff face. He was dead when he was found and there are some serious injuries to his body. A pathologist will be able to tell us more after the examination.' Morgan never called it a post mortem when he spoke to relatives.

'Oh, God. Poor Gary.' She needed both hands to push herself out of the low armchair. She crossed to a nest of black tables, where she grabbed what Morgan could now see was a box of tissues covered in a frilly sleeve. 'Gary hated this,' she said, 'but it was a present from my mum, so I needed to keep it.' She stroked the starched white lace and gave a small laugh. 'He used to hide it in cupboards, and when I missed it I'd have to go looking for it and put it back without saying anything. Like a war of attrition. Do you and your wife do silly stuff like that?'

Morgan shook his head a couple of times. He didn't tell her that his marriage was more like a nuclear war, certainly at the moment.

Once she had lowered herself back into her chair, the tissues on her lap, she seemed to no longer need them. 'It wasn't suicide,' she said. 'After you left yesterday, we had a long chat. He said he was confident that I'd been drugged and that he forgave me. He asked me to book a weekend away. Not Easter, but the one after. We were back on track. It's not suicide.'

Was she talking to him, or thinking out loud? Morgan wasn't sure.

'I've been on those cliffs,' she said. 'It's pitch-black at night. Maybe he went for a walk and got dizzy, or didn't see how close he was to the edge. That could happen.'

'I'm sorry, Claire. We'll know more later, but for now we believe he may have been murdered.'

Chapter 42

Tuesday 7th April

Another late finish at work. Morgan's mobile rang while he was sitting at his desk, catching up on his paperwork and preparing for tomorrow's briefings.

'Are you on your own, Nick?'

'I'm at my desk, Jenny. I'll be going home soon. What have you got?'

'I was checking you weren't with your kids. I've got the PM results.'

'That was thoughtful. Fire away.'

'The wound to the back of the head was the fatal blow and MoMack reckons it was delivered using something with a sharp edge.'

'She's sure he didn't get it on the way down?'

'She seems confident. She looked at the stones and rocks between where he was found and the edge he came over, and didn't see any that matched the wound.'

'What about the other injuries?'

'All sustained after death. And no blood up on the top of the cliff, so she thinks he was killed somewhere else and his body dumped over the edge. Full tox screen to follow, and I've asked for it to include benzodiazepines and GHB.'

'Johnson's going to love that. "Think about my budget".' It was a passable impersonation. 'Why do you think he'd have a date rape drug in his system?'

'When we questioned his colleagues after Simon Dennison was found, everyone I spoke to seemed edgy. If someone can drug the MD's wife, who knows what else is going on?'

‘I trust your judgement, Jenny, but I’m not sure about that. We don’t even know if he was with people from work last night.’

‘We don’t know he wasn’t.’

Cliffside House was silent when Morgan got home. The lounge was dark and the kitchen was lit only by the under-cabinet spotlights. He went to the breadbin and grabbed a sourdough loaf. He sawed off a couple of slices and posted them into the toaster before putting the kettle on. He fancied a cup of tea rather than his usual glass or three of red wine.

It wasn’t until he perched on one of the breakfast bar stools that he noticed it. An unsealed C4 envelope sitting right where he usually sat to eat when he was home late. It wasn’t addressed to him; it wasn’t addressed to anyone. He buttered the toast and took two bites before pulling the papers out.

Application for a divorce, dissolution or (judicial) separation.

Morgan stopped chewing, the toasted bread and salty butter turned to cardboard in his mouth. He placed the papers down on the countertop and pushed them away from him. He put the main downlights on and re-read the heading, but it hadn’t changed.

There was a section in the top right-hand corner which said it was for court use only and the boxes underneath were blank. Did that mean that the petition hadn’t yet been filed? He didn’t know.

He flipped through the pages of Sam’s contact details, then his own, and stopped to read the details of their marriage more slowly, remembering their happiness and excitement at embarking on a new life together. He remembered Dorothy Cooper's eyes narrowing when she looked at him and how happy he was. He had won. Against all odds, he had stolen her precious daughter from under that pert little nose and there had been nothing she could do about it.

He skipped the jurisdiction section and arrived at the reasons page. The adultery box was ticked and a couple of pages later Alison Goddard's name filled the co-respondent box, with the address of the police station provided as her contact information.

He put it back on the counter and made his mug of tea.

How had Sam found out that Alison had moved south? He hadn't told her. The right opportunity hadn't presented itself.

Was she spying on him? Surely not, or it would have been Maisie's name on the papers.

He took a sip of the hot tea, noticing its temperature only when it burned his mouth. He slammed the mug back down and headed for the stairs.

Sam Morgan was reading, propped up by a pile of pillows which included those from his side of the bed.

'Been to see your boyfriend, have you?' He brandished the petition at her, the gesture wasted when she didn't look up.

'You're late. Been to see your girlfriend, have you?' The edge of her lip twisted in the sneer she had inherited from her mother.

'Alison Goddard is not my girlfriend.' He picked his words carefully, intent on not being caught out in a lie.

'She's followed you the length of England. I don't think it's for your mentoring skills.' Her voice was louder now and Morgan wished he'd taken more care when choosing the time and location for this discussion. The twins were only feet away and they shouldn't have to hear it.

'She applied for a transfer to here before we had even thought of moving. It was delayed because the headcount was cut. I didn't even know she was coming until she turned up. She wasn't my appointment.'

'But you didn't tell me she was here. What am I supposed to think?'

'Think what you want.' He crossed to the bed and grabbed the book out of her hands, tossing it across the room. 'You started this when you wrapped your legs around Graham Fletcher, and for all your assurances, when you find out Ali Goddard is here, it's him you go to rather than asking me. Something wrong with your priorities, Samantha.'

'Stop! Stop it! Just stop!'

Neither of them had heard the door open and they were shocked to see Alex standing there, his hands over his ears and eyes gripped shut. His bare feet poked out of the bottom of pyjama trousers that were too long for him, and the buttons of his top weren't in the correct holes.

Samantha leapt out of bed and hurried to comfort their son. 'Darling.' She held him close to her and rocked him like she had when he'd come to her after a nightmare. 'Mum and Dad were just talking. Shhh now.'

As Alex's body spasmed in time with his sobs, she looked up at Morgan. 'See what you've done?'

Alex pushed himself free from her arms. 'It's not him. It's both of you. You're always arguing. Ever since we moved here. Why can't we go back to London? You loved each other then.' He padded back to their bedroom door, and as he was closing it behind him, Morgan saw Victoria reach out to hug him. When his daughter's eyes met his own, he recognised the look: an angry determination that had been passed from Dorothy to Sam, and now to Vicky. He was afraid that future battle lines were already being drawn and he wasn't on the winning side.

Chapter 43

Wednesday 8th April

Alison Goddard was waiting in his office when Morgan arrived at the station. She held a C4 envelope in her hands which matched the one he'd opened last night.

'It was handed in yesterday. Care to explain?' she asked, her right eyebrow arching above the frame of her glasses.

'I wish I could. All I can tell you is that she hasn't filed at court yet. We had a brief conversation about it, which Alex interrupted. After that, I went back to the spare room and I came to work before the others got up this morning.' He didn't tell her that he had packed a bag before leaving and had no intention of returning home that night.

'I'm not going to be the sacrificial lamb in your marital difficulties, Nick. It would affect my career and my relationship with my son. Fix it!' She slapped the envelope down on his desk and left, ricocheting off Jenny Smart in the doorway.

Smart watched her stomp her way down the corridor. 'She has got some emotions then ... I thought she was the Ice Queen.'

Morgan let it pass.

'I came to give you this and to ask what time you're holding the briefing this morning. I've got things I need to catch up on.'

He looked at his office clock, surprised that it was already this late. Perhaps he'd sat longer than he'd realised drinking that takeaway coffee in his car. 'Let's make it nine fifteen,' he said. 'And what have you got there?'

'It's from Digital Forensics. It's the download of texts from one of Dennison's phones for the last six months. They can go back further if we ask.'

'Which phone?' he asked, holding his hand out for the sheaf of papers.

'It's his work phone. Issued by Forest-Fox. It was in his hotel room.'

'Anything interesting?' Morgan started to read. 'Christ, could they have picked a smaller font? I must need my eyes tested.'

'I think they're trying to save paper. Mr Dennison texted a lot.'

He flicked through the sheets of paper. 'But it's all invoice information, quote numbers, and a few confirming appointments.'

'I've highlighted some that I thought were more interesting.'

He thumbed his way through the pages until he came to words underlined in fluorescent yellow.

Fuck you You R finished
You'll get yours
Good luck with finding another job
Your time is coming
Youre a dead man

'I've seen worse,' said Morgan.

'Agreed. Maybe there's worse on the other phones?

'When will we get that?'

‘I rang them this morning. Apparently, there’s some super-serious encryption on one of them. No time estimate yet.’

‘Okay, thanks.’ He looked again at the clock. This morning was running away from him. ‘Let’s do the briefing at ten. Can you sort that for me please?’

The briefing room was fuller than yesterday morning, and noisier. Making his way to the front, Morgan heard officers greeting each other and saw some handshakes. There were some new faces, too. Johnson must have authorised the extra personnel he’d requested when Gary Fox’s body was discovered. He called them to attention and reminded them that they were dealing with two separate deaths which may or may not be connected. Then, for the benefit of the newcomers, he reviewed where they were with each case. When he got to the information about the texts on Dennison’s work phone, he pinned a printout of them to the murder board.

‘Five texts from two different numbers. All received during a weekend in December. The weekend of the Forest-Fox Christmas party. I can tell you that the first three were sent from Gary Fox’s phone. The other two are from a pay-as-you-go that we haven’t identified yet.’ He looked around the room. ‘We should remember that these texts were found on Dennison’s work phone. It makes sense that Gary Fox would use that number, even if it was to issue threats. But the other two messages? Well, who else would use his work phone rather than either of the two personal phones we found? A customer? It’s likely to be someone whose relationship with him is business rather than personal. Having said that, the threats are pretty personal. Any thoughts?'

The room stayed silent; glances were exchanged and shoulders shrugged.

'If you do think of anything, don't be shy. There are no stupid answers at the moment.' Morgan pointed to DC Smart. 'Jenny and I will be going back to visit Mrs Fox this morning. We broke the news of her husband's death and drove her in to identify his body yesterday. DS Hillier and DC Young –' he looked up to put faces to the names of these new additions to the team '– can you work your way through the UK-based employees at Forest-Fox? Start with the office staff and then the field-based. I want to know who knew about Dennison and Mrs Fox's display at the party. You'll need to use a bit of sensitivity with that. I don't want people told who aren't already aware. Claire Fox is dealing with enough at the moment. I also want to know who Gary Fox was meeting on Monday night. Maybe he has a regular meet-up with one or more of the staff.'

He worked his way down his list of tasks, apologising to those who were going to be scouring CCTV for sightings of Fox's car on Monday evening. 'Any questions?' He scanned the room again and received a few shakes of the head. 'Okay, next briefing at five thirty. I'll be on my mobile for the rest of the day.' He crossed to where Jenny Smart was talking to DS Hillier. 'I'll meet you in the car park in ten, Jenny. And we'll take your car this time, okay?' He didn't want her to catch a glimpse of the overnight bag and suit covers in the boot of his Volvo.

Chapter 44

Wednesday 8th April

Jenny Smart indicated and was preparing to turn into the Foxes' driveway when she had to stop for a grey van covered in stencilled daisies which was nosing its way between the gateposts. The driver waved her thanks and sped off.

'It starts with the flowers, then the cards, then the funeral arrangements and all the financial stuff, and then it just stops. Everyone else's life goes on. Their consciences are clear; they've done their bit. And you're left to pick up the pieces of your own life.' She was staring straight ahead as she spoke and Morgan risked a glance in her direction. There were no tears, just a far-away look, as if she had left him for a moment. Should he pry? He was getting to know her better, particularly now they were working together without a sergeant. If only DI Maggy Patel was around. He could ask her for more of Smart's story.

When they had parked up and were walking to the front door, he said, 'You can talk to me at any time, Jenny. Door's always open.'

She ignored him and made herself busy, plunging into her bag and producing an Android tablet. 'I'm going to use this to take today's notes,' she said, 'so don't go too quickly.' It was as if her earlier words hadn't been spoken.

Claire Fox opened the door before they got to it. She was dressed for comfort today in dark grey cuffed joggers and a matching hoodie. Her feet were bare, toenails painted a pale opalescent pink. 'I saw you at the end of the drive,' she said. 'Any news?' Her voice was flat. She closed the door after them and led them to the lounge, where they sat on the same seats as on their previous two visits. The sickly sweet smell of lilies was overpowering and Morgan counted four flower arrangements dominated by them.

'I'm thinking that I'll be able to open my own florist's by the end of the week.'

Morgan nodded and looked at Smart, but her head was down, her eyes focused on the screen of her tablet.

'Have Family Liaison been in touch?' he asked.

'Someone rang and said they would be coming over, but I told them I don't need anyone here. I'll be okay.'

'We'd like to have an officer with you in case you get any calls or visits from someone who might know something about what happened,' said Morgan.

'That's not likely, is it?'

'I appreciate it's a long shot, but you never know.'

'I don't want anyone here.'

He decided he would leave it for now and come back to it later. 'Have you had any thoughts about where Gary might have gone on Monday evening?'

'Nope. I asked him not to go because we were still talking through what you said about the party. He said it was important. I think he said something about needing to consider other sources of money, now that Simon was no longer with us. But I wasn't paying much attention. We'd lived very separate lives since that damned party and I'd stopped caring where he was going.'

Her words stabbed at Morgan's conscience. That's how his life had been since Sam's affair with Fletcher and the beginning of his own relationship with Maisie.

No wonder the twins were upset. They were old enough to figure out what was going on.

'Do you have children, Mrs Fox?' he asked.

'Is that important?' He sensed both women watching him.

'No, of course not. I just wondered who was supporting you.' He hoped that covered it.

'No, no children. Gary never wanted them, and I accepted that before we married.'

'What might Gary have meant about the money?' Smart must have sensed the direction of Morgan's questioning was veering off their agreed plan and butted in to fix it.

'I know that Simon brought in enough business to contribute more than sixty per cent of the profits. Forest-Fox might not survive without him. You saw what happened to Specify Solutions. She waved her arms around her. 'I may have to sell up now that they've both gone.'

When he'd found out about the Christmas party, Morgan had thought it likely that Gary Fox had assaulted Simon Dennison for what he did to his wife. The loss of face; the death threats; the overheard, angry conversations. Now that he understood how much the company, and, in turn, the Foxes' lifestyle, depended on their best salesperson, he was doubtful. Fox had worked with Dennison for more than three months since the party. He would have had other opportunities to attack him if he was going to.

'How was he dressed?' asked Morgan. 'When we found him, he was in jeans and a jumper, but he had a white shirt underneath. Was he wearing suit, shirt and tie when he went out? Like for a business meeting?'

She shook her head. 'I didn't see him go. I was lying on the sofa and he shouted from the hall. Said he'd see me tomorrow and left. I didn't even look up. I was upset he was going out after all.'

Morgan thought of the gin bottle that had been by her side on Monday. Maybe she hadn't been capable of looking up.

'If that's everything,' she said, 'I've got a lot to sort out today.'

The house phone rang and she excused herself and went out into the hallway. The conversation was short and composed mostly of her agreeing before she ended it and returned to where she had been sitting.

'Gary's car is at East Gullhaven Country Club. They want me to move it because it's blocking a space they need for a wedding.'

Having assured Claire Fox that the crime scene technicians would take care of moving Gary's car to a secure location, Morgan and Smart left her and scrunched across the shingle parking area to her car.

'Are you thinking what I'm thinking?' asked Morgan.

'I'm wondering who Gary Fox was meeting at the club on Monday evening.'

'Mmm. But I was thinking more along the lines of why did they ring the Foxes' house phone? We haven't released Gary Fox's ID yet. The news reports have been referring to him as "unidentified male". So why not contact Gary Fox and ask him to move his car himself? With all the times he used the club, they must have his mobile, and the business number.'

Smart stopped walking, her eyes wide, eyebrows raised. 'When's the press release going to happen?'

Morgan looked at his watch. 'We said midday, so another hour.'

'Local gossip, maybe? There were enough journalists on the clifftop. Someone might have recognised him.'

'So how did that information get back to the club?'

'Maybe they had been trying to contact Gary. We know he wouldn't have been answering his phone. Called her in desperation because they needed the space for the wedding.'

They reached the car and got in. 'Where now?' asked Smart.

'Back to the office, I think. I'll arrange for collection of the car while you're driving. And I'll speak to CSI and ask for the club's CCTV from Monday evening. Let's see who Gary Fox was meeting.'

Chapter 45

Wednesday 8th April

There were no cars outside reception at Gullhaven Park Homes Estate and Morgan could see Maisie was on the phone. Whoever she was talking to was making her laugh as she typed on her keyboard. He remembered how kind she'd been when he'd booked his family in. That was the day he'd found Carl Raynor's body in their house; the day his life had started to fall apart.

He watched until she ended the call then got out of his car. The reception doors were locked and he had to ring the bell. When she looked up, her smile was broad and welcoming and he opened the door when it buzzed.

'Nick. I wasn't expecting you. What a lovely surprise.'

He approached the counter, head turned slightly to his right so that his identity wasn't immediately obvious to anyone watching a playback from the CCTV camera mounted high on the wall.

'I need somewhere to sleep,' he said.

She frowned. 'You're always welcome here. You know that. Park round the back and I'll open the staff door.'

He should have thought more carefully about his words. He knew that now, but it was too late. 'I meant that I need somewhere to rent, Maisie.' A black cloud crossed her face. He'd hurt her.

'Oh. Okay. Let me look.' She returned to her side of the counter and typed on the keyboard. 'I've got the same home you had in February,' she said. 'Are the others coming too?'

He shook his head. 'I'll be on my own. I need to be on my own.'

She scrolled down a long spreadsheet before looking back up at him. When their eyes met, he could see her pain, could anticipate all the questions she wanted to ask but wasn't going to.

'I've got a two-bed in Sector C,' she said. 'It's clean, but the heating's not on. The previous guests moved out on Saturday.'

'I'll be fine. It's better than sleeping in the car.'

She opened a cupboard on the wall behind her by tapping in a code and produced a single key on a ring as big as a saucer. 'It's something I'm trialling,' she said. 'It helps guests remember to hand them in when they don't fit conveniently into their pockets.' She laid it on the counter and turned away as if he was just another punter. 'If you wait a moment, I'll fetch you some linen.'

He thanked her and glanced down at the worn map which was sticky-taped to the counter. He located Sector C and then walked to the window while he waited. Outside was empty and dark, just like he felt.

Chapter 46

Thursday 9th April

Dorothy placed the mug of coffee on the table in front of her daughter. Having seen the state of her, she didn't want to risk her china. Sam wrapped her hands around it and pulled it closer to her.

'You could have brought the twins,' said Dorothy. 'I like to see them.'

'I dropped them off at the sports centre. They're going rollerblading this morning, then Alex has football training this afternoon and Vicky's swimming. I gave them money for drinks and baked potatoes for lunch, and I hope they come back in better moods.'

'Why am I thinking that you've got more to tell me?'

Samantha took a tentative sip of the steaming drink but it was still too hot. She put it back on the coaster as Dorothy sat down opposite.

'Nick and I had a bit of a row on Tuesday and they heard it. Alex had a meltdown. They've barely spoken to me since.'

'Are they speaking to Plod? Have they taken his side?'

'He left for work yesterday morning and didn't come home last night. He's taken a couple of suits, some shirts, the usual. Toothbrush has gone, too.'

'So he's gone to that Goddard woman?' Dorothy grabbed her opportunity to plant the thought in Samantha's head in case she hadn't thought of it for herself.

'I don't know.'

'What was the row about this time?'

Samantha put her elbows on the table and washed her face with her hands. Dorothy focused her attention on the mug, preparing herself to save it if she knocked it. She didn't want to spend the morning mopping up coffee.

'I went to see Graham about a divorce but he wouldn't help me, so I drafted a petition online and printed it out. I left a copy for Nick to read.'

Dorothy resisted the urge to sing and dance and high-five her daughter. That would give Plod something to think about. He wouldn't have the headspace to come after Steven now. She was a bit miffed that Graham Fletcher hadn't played his part. She'd put him straight later. 'I'm sorry to hear that, Samantha, but it's probably for the best.' It was as placatory as she could manage.

'I'm citing bloody Alison Goddard as co-respondent. I dropped a copy off for her at the station.'

Dorothy hesitated. That wasn't so good. She was sure there wasn't anything between Plod and the Goddard woman, not now anyway. She simply wanted him distracted until she got Steven out of the way. If Samantha was serious about getting a divorce, the timing was helpful. It had taken over twenty years, but she'd won. Now it was important to make sure the reason on the petition was something he couldn't defend. Unreasonable behaviour; that was the one she'd read about.

'If the twins are at the centre until later, why don't we go shopping? We could make a day of it. I'll buy you lunch to celebrate.'

Samantha glowered but Dorothy was undeterred. She would celebrate enough for both of them.

Chapter 47

Thursday 9th April

The morning hadn't started well. An email had arrived in Morgan's inbox to let him know that CSI had been unable to retrieve CCTV from the country club for Monday evening. They put it down to a partial system malfunction. Then his briefing hadn't produced any new lines of inquiry, and his team hadn't seemed fully engaged. Morgan had lost his temper and shouted at them. Sitting at his desk now, with the door to his office closed, he held his head in his hands.

Marriage – dead.

Relationship with Maisie – dead.

Respect of his team – maybe not completely dead, but in need of resuscitation.

The knock on his door was tentative and he looked up as DC Jenny Smart entered, balancing two steaming cardboard cups in the palm of her hand. She placed them on his desk and dropped her shoulder-bag on the floor before going back to close the door. 'I want to talk about Giles Clooney,' she said, and sat on a visitor chair without waiting to be invited. When she reached out to lift one of the cups to her lips, Morgan saw a slight tremor in her grip. Her face was flushed under her customary heavy make-up. It drew attention to the acne scars on her cheeks and it made him feel like a shit. Whether she was here of her own volition or because she'd pulled the short straw, coming to his office after his temper tantrum was making her uncomfortable. *He* was making her uncomfortable.

'Thanks, Jenny,' he said. 'I appreciate it. And I'm sorry. I'll tell the others at this evening's briefing. There's stuff going on at the moment which I shouldn't be bringing to work.'

Smart gave a single nod before reaching down and retrieving her notebook. 'Before you say anything,' she started, 'I know you think Dennison and Fox's deaths are linked. But what if they're not?'

'Well ...'

She held up her hand, palm facing him to halt his interruption. Morgan was surprised into silence. If she had been feeling uncomfortable, she'd soon got over it. Good for her. He watched her flick back through the notes she'd taken during their recent interviews.

'When you asked Giles Clooney about the demise of his company, he said that his wife blamed Dennison but he blamed Gary Fox.'

Morgan nodded. 'I remember. But he also sat in a wheelchair in an insalubrious house and pointed out that he didn't have the means or the opportunity to attack Dennison. I can't see that will have changed. He won't have been in any position to kill Gary Fox.'

'His wife was pretty angry. Could she have fixed it?'

'Gina? Possible, I suppose. Do you want to go and speak to her?' he asked.

'I don't want to waste time, but I keep coming back to it.'

Morgan nodded. He knew that feeling. That intuition that nagged at you, no matter how unlikely the direction it was pointing you in. He wasn't getting it in this case, but if Smart was, he wasn't about to overrule her.

'Okay. Take one of the new lads with you and have a word. Give me a ring when you're on your way back.'

***

Smart and DC Rob Vine pulled up at the kerb across from the Clooney's house. There was a bright yellow skip on the grass, and no sign of the converted van which she'd seen on her previous visit. She rang the bell, half hoping that nobody was in. This was feeling like a wasted trip.

The footsteps seemed to be coming from a long way off and echoed in the uncarpeted hall. When Gina Clooney finally opened the door her irritation was obvious.

'He's not here. He's at a hospital appointment.'

'That's okay, Mrs Clooney. May we come in and wait?'

Gina Clooney answered by standing to one side so they could enter. 'I don't suppose I can stop you. First on the right,' she shouted after them.

The detectives entered what Smart assumed was the lounge by the presence of a sofa and too many chairs for the size of the room. Piled against the wall were boxes with the name of a removals company on the side. One or two had been opened but most were still taped shut.

Smart was moved by the sight. The Clooneys had once filled a house much bigger than this one and they must still be adjusting. With Giles Clooney's disability, the responsibility of downsizing would be sitting on his wife's shoulders and it didn't look as if she was coping well.

'Wait here,' Smart whispered to her colleague, 'then follow me in about a minute.' She went into the hall and allowed the sound of a radio to lead her to the back of the house. Gina Clooney was peeling carrots and tossing them into a slow cooker.

'Is this where you tell me you need to use the bathroom so you can have a nosy round my house?' she asked without looking up from her task. 'Go ahead. Look wherever you like. We've got nothing to hide.'

'It must be hard for you,' said Smart. 'Having to do everything, I mean.'

'"For richer, for poorer, in sickness and in health." I meant it when I said it twenty-five years ago next month. I've not changed my mind and neither has Giles. We'll get through this. He's responding well to physio.'

'That's good to hear. I hadn't realised he was able to drive.'

Gina looked at her as if assessing whether she was being sarcastic. 'Of course he can't drive. Our son's home on leave for a couple of weeks; he's taken him for his appointment so I can get on with stuff.'

'I see,' said Smart, conscious that DC Vine was now standing behind her.

They both turned at the sound of a key in the front door. When it opened, Smart had a clear view of the male who was entering backwards. He was broad-shouldered with tanned and muscled upper arms complemented by a white sleeveless T-shirt. Smart judged him to be a poser; that season-inappropriate shirt was for show rather than warmth. Then she thought of his potential as a suspect. He would have no difficulty shoving Gary Fox off a cliff, nor, come to think of it, inserting an oversized sex toy where she'd rather not think about.

He pulled Giles Clooney's wheelchair over the doorstep and turned it in the lounge doorway. When he looked up, Smart saw that he had achieved his tan whilst wearing sunglasses, or goggles, if he was a tanning salon client. Bright eyes which were closer to indigo than blue were shielded by pale eyelids.

'We've got visitors, Dad,' he said.

'DC Smart. Hello again,' said Clooney, and nodded to Vine. 'No DI Evans today?'

'DI Morgan's office-based today,' said Smart.

'Sorry, not good at names, even before the stroke. This is our son, Ian. He's back from Cyprus for a couple of weeks.'

The detectives introduced themselves and Giles Clooney asked his wife if she had offered refreshments.

'That's okay, thanks,' said Smart. 'We're just here to clear up a few points.' She turned to Ian Clooney. 'Have you been home long?' She kept her tone light and conversational.

'Monday,' he said. 'I flew back to the UK last week, but I was visiting my sister in Portsmouth. She's just had a baby.'

'You're on leave. Is that from the forces?'

'Royal Artillery.' He nodded in his mother's direction and Smart turned to see that Gina was holding up the kettle. 'What is this? Why all the questions?' He bent down to make eye contact with his father. 'Why are the police coming to the house?'

'One of my ex-salesmen was killed last week.' Clooney Senior laughed heartily as he pointed to himself. 'They think I did it.'

'Seriously?' Ian Clooney didn't share the joke. He straightened up and Smart wondered if he was about to throw them out.

‘You probably heard yesterday that we found the body of Gary Fox at the foot of the cliffs over in Gullhaven Cove.’

‘No, I hadn’t heard that,’ said Giles Clooney. ‘Suicide?’

‘We’re working on the likelihood of murder, Mr Clooney.’ She turned her gaze back to Ian. Now she abandoned all pretence of this being a light-hearted conversation. ‘Can you give me a few more details of your travel arrangements since your leave began, please? We can go and sit in the lounge. That way, we’ll be out of everyone’s way.’

Chapter 48

Thursday 9th April

'Are you sure you didn't argue? You can tell me, I won't be angry.' Samantha Morgan waited until Victoria met her gaze. Unlike Alexander, her daughter had never been a persuasive liar.

'No! I told you. We queued up for lunch together because he had the money.' Her tone was accusatory and Samantha made a mental note to give them separate amounts next time. If there was ever going to be a next time. The way she felt now, Alex was going to be grounded until his eighteenth birthday.

'Well, where is he, then?' Samantha knew her instructions had been clear. Football practice was due to end at three thirty, which meant that Vicky had to be out of the pool and showered and dressed by then so they could all meet up in the car park, then straight home for tea.

'Did he say anything at lunch?'

Victoria looked back at the windows of the cafeteria. 'Once he'd paid for my lunch, he told me to clear off. He said he wanted to sit with his football mates. Except he didn't say "clear off" exactly.' Her last sentence was spoken softly as if she knew she had to say it but preferred her mother not to hear it.

Samantha saw the hurt on her daughter's face. Vicky and Alex had been close before their move from London. She was struggling to accept her brother's new need for independence.

She looked at her car and decided to risk leaving it without paying at the machine. The rates were ridiculous, especially if Alex was going to appear at any minute. 'Let's go back to the hall and see if he's just chatting to someone.'

The receptionist stepped forward to charge the entry fees.

'My son hasn't come out after football practice,' said Samantha. 'Do you mind if I go and hurry him along?'

'I think they finished a bit early,' said the girl. She shouted to a young Asian man in a red tracksuit trimmed with black piping. 'Are any of the football lads still in the hall?'

'No. And I checked the changing room as well before I locked up. Next session's not until five. Is there a problem?'

'This lady's son hasn't come out.'

He strode across to Samantha, hand outstretched. 'I'm Rav. I run the football training. Which one's yours?'

'Alex. Alex Morgan.'

'He's not been before, has he?'

'No. We only moved here a couple of months ago.'

'As far as I know, he left with the others. There's nobody in the hall now. He probably got bored of waiting and went home on his own.'

Samantha thanked him although she would have preferred to check for herself. She couldn't see how Alex would have got home. It wasn't as if there were any buses he could have caught. Maybe a parent of one of the other lads had offered him a lift. Please, God.

Chapter 49

Thursday 9th April

'Okay, everyone. Let's get on with it so we can get home.' Morgan stood at the front of the briefing room where around half of the team working on the Dennison and Fox cases were seated. He knew that a few had been called away to assist in another couple of inquiries. It was a fact: as your investigation got older, you were less able to justify ring-fencing your team. The good news was that they seemed more animated this evening.

'Sorry.' DC Jenny Smart burst through the door. Her eyes were bright and she was waving papers at him. 'Forensics. I was waiting for the printer.' She made her way to where Morgan was waiting and handed him the report.

'Just give me a sec,' said Morgan, and turned away from his audience to concentrate on the words. When he had finished reading, he turned back and held a hand up to attract their attention.

'I'll summarise,' he said. 'Simon Dennison's jeans, socks and shoes were saturated with blood; his own blood. The lab says that if there's anyone else's DNA on them, they would struggle to find it with this level of contamination.' There was a low groan in the room and he stymied it by holding his hand up again.

'His top ...' he looked back at the report, 'sorry, sweatshirt has a small smear of black mascara. Supermarket own-brand, nothing expensive.'

'Sex worker?' asked one of the DCs.

'That's a big stretch,' said Morgan.

‘Just thinking cheap cosmetics applied thick enough to come off alongside the use of sex toys. You know ... the cuffs and the ... thing.’

‘I’m open to all suggestions,’ said Morgan, a comment greeted with a wolf whistle and laughter. He shook his head and sighed. When the noise had died down, he continued. ‘Talking of the cuffs. It seems that they were nickel-covered steel as we thought, and under the fluffy fabric they found a partial print.’ He saw glances exchanged and a few eyebrows lift. The room was silent, waiting for the punch line. ‘It matches to a retired detective in Greater Manchester who died six weeks ago.’

‘Boss ...?’

‘Don’t ask me ... I’ve no idea. I’m just reading what’s here.’ He flicked through the last couple of pages before looking up again. ‘Jenny, can you follow up our deceased colleague and see if he has links to either Forest-Fox or Simon Dennison. You’ll need to be a bit sensitive with who you speak to, and what you ask.’ He knew he didn’t have to spell it out. Jenny wasn’t just Smart by name.

‘What about the mascara?’ asked the young woman who was looking after the data entry for both cases.

Morgan looked at Smart who shook her head. ‘Way too many girls use cheap cosmetics. We’d never narrow it down,’ she said. He nodded his agreement and ended the meeting with the allocation of a few tasks he had in his policy book and some words of encouragement which he struggled to inject with sincerity. He was facing an evening on his own and already missing his children and the music they played at an annoyingly loud volume.

Chapter 50

Thursday 9th April

When his mobile rang, Morgan was installed in a lumpy armchair, surrounded by paperwork, his laptop on a coffee table beside him. He'd eaten a microwave curry and reached a lifestyle decision never to buy another one. He'd also made a deal with himself not to open the bottle of Rioja until his policy books were up to date and he had prepared for tomorrow's briefings.

The number was withheld and he didn't answer it. He wasn't on duty, and if it was urgent they would ring back.

They did. Immediately. He grabbed at it and growled his name.

'DI Morgan? It's DC Mihika Bindra.'

'Yes?' He didn't recognise her name.

'I'm at Cliffside House.'

Morgan sat up, the call now demanding his full attention. 'And?'

'I'm a Family Liaison Officer, Sir. I'm ringing to ask you if your son, Alexander, is with you.'

Morgan looked around the room before he answered, although he knew Alex wasn't with him. 'No, he's not.' He searched the floor for his shoes as Bindra continued.

'Have you seen him today?'

'What's happened?' he asked.

'When your wife went to collect your children from the sports centre this afternoon, Alexander wasn't with his sister. They waited for him then came home in case he'd made his way back on his own. But there's no sign of him here. Uniformed officers have had a quick look round, although we'll need to do a full search.' He heard her embarrassment. 'Sorry, Sir. You'll be familiar with the procedure, of course.'

'I'm on my way,' said Morgan.

'Just to fully inform you, DI Morgan ... Mrs Morgan has said that it's not necessary for you to be here. She has her mother and a friend with her. But I would prefer it if you came ... Sir.'

He ended the call without answering. Samantha had contacted her mother but hadn't bothered ringing him. If she'd hoped to hurt him, she'd hit the bullseye. And a friend? What friend? It had better fucking not be that smarmy solicitor boyfriend of hers. He grabbed his jacket and keys and headed for the door.

There was no space outside Cliffside House when Morgan arrived. Sam's car was where she always left it and a metallic blue BMW X7 blocked the rest of the drive. He parked on the double yellow lines, shoved his 'Police On Call' card on the dashboard and hurried to the house. It didn't seem appropriate to use his keys, so he rang the bell. He heard heavy footsteps on the tiles in the hallway: a man's footsteps. As the door opened, he heard a woman's voice shouting from the direction of the kitchen. 'Please don't answer it, Mr Fletcher. I'm on my way.'

Too late.

Morgan pushed his way through, pinning the left side of Graham Fletcher's body to the wall. He heard a satisfying gasp and hoped that Fletcher would have the sense to leave and take his flashy car with him. If not, he'd deal with him later. For now, Sam and the twins were his priority.

'DI Morgan?' The woman who was walking towards him had the height, looks and elegance of a catwalk model. 'I'm DC Mihika Bindra.' She extended her hand for him to shake.

'What's happening?' asked Morgan.

'We're going through the CCTV at the centre and talking to the lads at the football practice. I'm waiting for the SIO.'

'Who's coming?'

'I don't know. I'm sorry.'

Morgan looked around. He'd lived in this house for a couple of months but it all felt very foreign to him this evening. His wife's lover in his hall and an investigation kicking off into his missing son.

'Where's my wife?'

As Bindra nodded in the direction of the lounge door, it opened. Dorothy Cooper stood, arms crossed, blocking his entrance. 'Samantha has all the support she needs,' she said. 'You can go back to Detective Sergeant Slut.'

Morgan had time to register the surprise on Bindra's face as he rushed past her and grabbed Dorothy by her arms. He lifted her off the floor and dumped her to his side. She squealed but he didn't pause to enjoy it.

Samantha rose from the sofa as he strode towards her. She was crying and her face was pale. 'God, Nick. Where is he?'

Morgan folded her small body into his arms. He felt her trembling and hugged her tighter, whispering meaningless words into her ear to comfort her. Dorothy had started to speak, but he wasn't listening.

'I'm making tea,' said Bindra. 'Who'd like a cup?'

Sam wriggled and Morgan relaxed his grip and let her go. They stood, side by side, facing the FLO, whose intelligent brown eyes were taking everything in.

'Not for me, thank you,' said Morgan. Sam shook her head. Bindra nodded and continued to dry her hands on the towel she was carrying.

'You should go now.' Dorothy Cooper had recovered her composure and her voice, but Morgan took comfort that she was keeping her distance from him. Fletcher stood behind her, teeth clenched and rubbing the side of his groin. That must have been where the door had made contact. On any other day, Morgan would have laughed. He took a couple of steps towards Bindra. 'When is the SIO coming?' he asked. 'Are we contacting his school friends? What about hospitals? What was he wearing?'

Bindra didn't reply and he realised that he had stepped into the role of distraught parent. They always asked the same things, as if they knew how to conduct the investigation better than the police.

'There's a team from Major Crimes coming. We may have to reassess that, now that we know Alexander is your son. I can tell you that he's not in any of the local hospitals and he's not with any of the friends Victoria knows about. Your wife has told us what he's wearing and we've forwarded his description to all mobile units.'

'Is that Dad?' Victoria's voice came from the stairs and everyone turned towards her.

'I'm here, Vicky,' shouted Morgan. Fletcher and Dorothy parted to let her through and she ran to her father and clung to him.

'It's not my fault.'

‘I know, Vic. We’ll sort it out.’ Years of visiting parents of missing children had impressed on him that he must never promise their return.

‘Let me call you a taxi, Dotty,’ said Morgan. ‘If the police need you, someone will be in touch.’

‘She should stay if she wants to,’ said Fletcher.

Morgan kissed his daughter on the cheek and gently eased her away. He walked to the door. This time, Dorothy stepped aside without assistance.

Fletcher stood his ground as Morgan got closer, although his face and body language betrayed his discomfort. The men were of a similar height, but twenty years of part-time property renovation had given Morgan visible upper-body musculature. Fletcher’s strength was in his eloquent speech delivery. No competition in this scenario.

‘I’ll drive you to Silver Sands, Dorothy,’ said Fletcher, and Morgan relaxed his fists. Sam went to them. ‘I’ll see you both out.’ She frowned at Morgan as she passed but he didn’t care. His phone had started to ring and he was reaching into his pocket.

Chapter 51

Thursday 9th April

Morgan felt four pairs of eyes on him as he glanced at his screen. The caller ID said 'DC Ivybridge'. It was the name in Morgan's contact list for Maisie. 'Excuse me, I have to take this.'

Sam continued to show her mother and Fletcher to the front door and there was an untidy confusion of bodies as Morgan made his way past them to get to the kitchen.

'Is everything okay?' Maisie's voice was quiet as if she had already anticipated his answer. 'I drove up to your park home for a chat but it was dark.'

'Alex has gone missing.' He couldn't think of anything else to say.

'Christ. What can I do?'

'There's nothing, but thank you. I'll be here for a while.'

'Will you be there all night?'

'I expect so, yes.' Morgan's voice cracked as he spoke. This was all such a bloody mess. If they had never moved here ... if Sam hadn't slept with Fletcher ... if he hadn't fallen in love with Maisie ... He felt his shoulders stiffen. Love? When did that happen? He realised that she was still speaking. 'I'm sorry, it's a bad line. Can you say that again?'

'I just asked you to let me know what happens,' she said, and he could tell that she hadn't believed the excuse about it being a bad line.

'I'll do that,' he said, and ended the call.

When he turned to go back to the lounge, his way was blocked by DC Mihika Bindra, who came into the kitchen and closed the door behind her.

'I'm sure that somebody more senior than me will want to talk to you, Sir, but it will help me get a handle on what's going on here if we can have a chat.'

'Of course. What do you need to know?'

She stood behind one of the breakfast bar chairs, her hands resting on the back support. Morgan thought it odd. Maybe she sought the reassurance of something between them.

'It's not unheard of for the mother of a missing child to ask me to summon someone who isn't the father, but it's rare,' she said. She looked even more uncomfortable now. 'Can you tell me why Mrs Morgan wanted her mother? Is it because she knew you were tied up with a case?' Providing an answer for her own question seemed to comfort Bindra. Her eyes looked hopeful.

'My wife and I argued a few days ago. I would guess that she's not yet over it.'

'Was the argument in the hearing of the children?'

He nodded and looked down. He felt guilty. 'The twins were in the house, but not in the room. But when my wife is angry, her voice is inclined to carry. I was quieter. I was trying to placate her at first, but ... my wife knows how to push buttons. I was shouting, too, in the end. Alex came into the room and he was upset.' Bindra cleared her throat and exhaled the breath she had been holding. He continued without waiting for her question. 'Samantha had been told that I was having a relationship with a colleague. She consulted the gentleman who was here, Graham Fletcher, who is a family solicitor and a childhood friend of hers. At some point, a draft divorce petition was drawn up. I was angry that she hadn't spoken to me first and we argued.'

'And you packed a bag and left?'

'Correct.'

'How will Alex have responded to that, do you think?'

It wasn't as if that thought hadn't already crossed Morgan's mind, but to hear it from a stranger – from a professional who was here to prod and pry and scratch the scabs off family wounds – made him feel defensive. 'It will depend on what my wife has said to him, and to Victoria as well, of course. It will also depend on how much time my mother-in-law has spent here in my absence. She's not my biggest fan.'

Bindra's face broke into a wry smile. 'You're not kidding.' She crossed her arms and took a step back from the chair. 'Might Alex have gone looking for you? Would he have known where you had gone?'

'I didn't know myself when I left for work yesterday, but I've moved into accommodation that'll suit for a little while.'

'Accommodation?'

He had to hand it to her. She didn't miss much.

'On the day we moved here, I discovered a body upstairs. We had to move into a park home until CSI released the scene. I've rented one on the same site for a week.'

'Alex would know where that was. Is it possible he's gone there?'

'I don't see why he would, but I can try.' He felt his pocket before remembering he'd laid his phone down on the arm of the sofa in the lounge. He excused himself and went to fetch it. He'd have to play this carefully. If the search for Alex extended to Gullhaven Park Estate, the risk of exposing his relationship with Maisie was high. But it was a risk he'd have to take. If Alex was up there, he would spend a cold, wet night in the dark and Morgan didn't want the mess his parents' lives had become to impact him like that.

Sam was sitting on the sofa, his phone in her lap. She held a glass of red wine in her left hand. It was already half-drunk.

'It needs a password,' she said, picking it up and waving it at him. 'Secrets?'

He took it and nodded at the glass. 'Starting early?'

'My son is missing.'

He held his phone and scanned his finger to activate it. '*Our* son is missing. I'm working on finding him. You're working on a bottle of red.'

As he made his way back to the kitchen, he listened to the reception phone at Gullhaven Park Estate ring and wondered if it would be better if Maisie answered or if she didn't. While he waited, the front doorbell rang. He opened it and faced Ali Goddard. They stared at each other before she spoke. 'Your son is missing? I've been appointed Deputy SIO.'

Chapter 52

Thursday 9th April

Just when he thought his life could not get any worse, the patron saint of 'What the Fuck' stepped in to prove he was wrong. Morgan moved aside and let Goddard in, followed by DC Lynn Greenfield. He closed the front door and introduced them both to DC Bindra, who had appeared from the kitchen again.

'My wife is in here.' He led them into the lounge and braced himself.

When she heard Goddard's name, Samantha's face froze. Morgan counted to four in the silence. 'I don't know you, DI Goddard ... but I feel as if I do. We have things in common.'

Ali Goddard blinked slowly and adjusted her glasses. 'DCI Johnson asked me to come tonight. It may be that a new team from one of the neighbouring areas will take over tomorrow. Of course, he could be back by then.' She opened a black plastic wallet which Greenfield handed to her. 'We've brought some stills from the CCTV at the sports centre. Can I ask you both to look at them and confirm that they are Alexander? Also, there are pictures of vehicles which left the car park soon after your son left the building. Do you recognise any of them?'

She handed the pictures to Samantha, who was forced to put her glass of wine down to go through them. Morgan moved to the back of the sofa so he could look over her shoulder.

He realised that the camera must be mounted above the doors to the centre, which meant that the pictures were distorted. He recognised Alex, but only because he knew him and that hunched way of standing which he'd developed since he'd started to grow taller. When Sam had finished with the first picture, he reached over to take it from her and he carried it to the table lamp on the drawer unit.

'It's definitely Alex,' he said. 'But those aren't his trainers. He asked us for them, but we said we wouldn't buy them until his feet stopped growing at the rate they are now. Alex can outgrow trainers in a few weeks, and these are over a hundred pounds.'

Samantha put her hand out to have the photo returned to her. She screwed up her swollen eyes and brought it close to her face. 'He's right,' she said, handing it back to Goddard. 'I didn't notice.' She examined the next two photos, which were also of Alex, with more care than the first. When she handed them over, Morgan saw that his son was on the phone.

'Do we know who he was ringing?' he asked, although he knew the answer. It was too early for that level of information to be available.

'Not yet,' said Goddard.

Samantha asked for another look at the first few photos of their son. When she'd done that, she left the room and stood at the bottom of the stairs.

'Vicky! Come back down. And bring your phone.'

'What have you spotted?' asked Morgan.

'That's not his phone. His phone is the same as Vicky's, with a camera on the back. There's no camera on that one. The back's smooth.'

'Could be a different style of phone case,' said Greenfield.

'You can't seriously imagine that a teenager is going to put up with taking a phone out of its case every time they want to take a photo,' said Samantha.

'I don't have kids,' said Greenfield.

'Obviously.'

They looked at the photos of the cars while they waited for Vicky to appear. These were taken at the exit from the car park and Morgan saw that whoever had positioned the camera had prioritised revenue collection over security. Registration plates were clearly visible; vehicle occupants were not.

A red Toyota, a black Range Rover and a silver Golf.

'We've established ownership for each and I've got uniform out to interview them.'

Vicky arrived and handed her phone to her mother. 'He hasn't rung me. I promised I'd let you know if he did, and he hasn't.'

'That's not why we want it,' said Morgan. 'We're not checking up on you.'

Samantha turned the phone round and held the back panel up for everyone to see. 'Like I said ... it's a camera phone. She pointed to where the photos of Alex lay by the lamp. 'That one's not.'

DC Lynn Greenfield took a few photos of Vicky's phone using her own while Goddard guided Vicky to the pictures of Alex.

'The phone your brother is using ... have you ever seen it before? Has he ever talked about having another phone?'

Vicky frowned and shook her head. 'No. I've only seen him with the one we both got for our birthday.'

Goddard smiled at Victoria and thanked her, and Morgan was shocked to realise that it was the first time he had seen her smile since she'd arrived at Gullhaven. Greenfield returned Victoria's phone and she disappeared back to whatever she'd been doing when they'd interrupted. Morgan was willing to bet that it wasn't homework.

'I'll get on to Digital Forensics in the morning,' said Goddard. 'Assuming the clock is accurate on the CCTV, we should be able to trace the numbers of all the live calls at that time. Are you staying?' she asked DC Bindra.

'Yes, she is,' said Morgan. 'And I'm going to the Park Home Estate to make sure he's not there. I suppose you've checked where his own phone is?'

'It's not switched on, Nick. Hasn't been since we started calling it,' said Goddard.

Chapter 53

Thursday 9th April

Morgan and Bindra returned to the kitchen after Goddard and Greenfield left.

'We'll send a patrol car.' DC Bindra was insistent. 'If he's gone to the park home you were staying in, they'll find him.'

'If he's gone there, it's because he thinks he might find me there. He's not going to respond to a strange voice, but he will to mine.' Morgan had made his mind up and wasn't going to let her stand in his way.

She lowered her voice. 'Your place is here, with your wife.'

'After a couple more glasses, my wife won't know or care whether I'm here or not. I need to be out looking.'

Bindra looked appalled by his answer and he raised his hands, aware that he had crossed a line in her eyes, whilst knowing he had spoken the truth. He pointed to the window, where raindrops were gathering into rivulets before running down the glass. There was also a steady dripping noise near the back door. He'd not noticed it before. A blocked or broken gutter. Another problem to fix, but not tonight; tonight he had to fix his family.

The rain was getting heavier and he increased the speed of his windscreen wipers from intermittent to low. They started to judder and screech across the glass. Another task he hadn't prioritised.

The lights were on in the Park Home Estate reception, but he didn't look to see if Maisie was there. He followed the narrow road to the Lakeside sector and pulled up in the parking space for A-20, where the family had spend the first few days of their new life in Gullhaven. When he turned off his headlights, he was plunged into complete darkness. If there had been a moon tonight, it had long since given up and retreated behind the heavy clouds. At least the rain had stopped.

Morgan got out of the car and walked to the boot, trying and failing to avoid contact with the wet bushes he'd parked beside. He delved into the grab bag and produced the Nightsearcher torch he used at crime scenes. Sploshing through the puddles, he scanned the light from side to side, yelling Alex's name.

After thirty minutes of fruitless searching, Morgan drove round to the back of the reception building and parked in the area reserved for staff. When he was locking his Volvo he saw that Maisie was already standing in the open doorway, her body silhouetted by the light behind her.

'I heard your car,' she said as he approached.

He remembered the excitement and anticipation he'd felt when he'd first hid his car in this secret area, shielded from public view. That night had started the affair which was developing into so much more for him. He suddenly realised that he didn't know if Maisie felt the same. She looked serious. Was this how it was going to end?

'Do you want a drink?' she asked as she led him through to her office.

He picked up her glass of cola and took a sniff. There was a shot of something in there. Dark rum was his guess. He had never seen her drink alcohol and a sense of dread enveloped him like an ice bath. 'No, I'm okay.'

'Is there any news?'

'No. Nothing yet.'

Maisie sank into her worn office chair and took a large mouthful of her drink. When she looked up at him, he saw she had been crying. 'Did we do this, Nick?'

He crouched down in front of her and took her hands in his. 'Why would you think that? This is nothing to do with us.'

'Boys need their dads, and you've been here a lot. If you'd been at home, you might have spotted something was wrong before he ran away.'

'We don't know he's run away.' Morgan's throat constricted and he dry-swallowed. 'It's possible that he's been taken.' Nobody had asked for it yet, but he was already compiling a mental list of people who had grudges against him or scores to settle. He topped that list with Dorothy Cooper. She was more dangerous than any of the so-called hard men he encountered in his job.

'I've packed your things,' said Maisie, nodding at his bag on the floor, and the suit covers which were folded over the back of a chair.

'Why did you do that? I'm not going back.'

Maisie stood and picked up his car keys from where he'd thrown them on her desk. She took his hand and prised his fingers open, placing the keys in his palm and closing his hand around them. 'You're going back, Nick. Tonight. You need to be with Samantha and Vicky while this is going on, and when Alex is back, you need to be there to find out what happened and why. Because if this is because of us, I will never forgive myself.'

'I want to be here,' he said, watching the tears run down her face but knowing she wouldn't welcome his touch.

'But that's not true, is it,' she said. 'Because if you wanted to be here – here with me – I mean, you wouldn't have rented a home yesterday, you'd have come to share mine.' Maisie's tears were coming faster now as she surrendered to the emotion she'd been controlling. She gulped air noisily and grabbed at the support of her desk.

He knew she was right and he forced himself to watch her distress as punishment for what he'd done to her. As she crumpled into her chair, he left her, his vision starting to blur with his own tears.

Chapter 54

Friday 10th April (Good Friday)

DS Spence was pacing Morgan's office. He had heard about the disappearance of Alexander Morgan on last night's late local news and watched Alison Goddard make her TV appeal. It should have been him.

Johnson came in and pulled the sleeve of his jacket back to emphasise the look at his watch. 'No sign of DI Goddard yet?'

'I expect she had a late night,' said Spence, hearing footsteps advancing down the corridor.

Ali Goddard came in, flushed, sweaty and apologetic. 'I was on the phone,' she murmured.

Johnson closed the door and leant on it. 'I've asked for a team to come and take over the investigation into DI Morgan's missing son. But with it being Good Friday and so many staff being on holiday abroad with their families, I've not had any success, at least not so far. So Alison, I need you to stay with it until that changes. You've not known DI Morgan for as long as the rest of us, so you're best placed to keep an emotional distance. Please make sure your policy book is kept up to date so that you can hand it over without any break in the progress of the investigation.'

Goddard nodded. 'Sir.'

'And Dave, I know this is going to be difficult but I need you to take over the Dennison and Fox cases that Nick was working on. I've sent a patrol car to collect his policy books so you'll have them within the hour. I'm SIO for all three cases and I want to be informed of any progress. But to be clear, Nick's missing boy is the priority for both of you, particularly over this Easter weekend.' He sighed. 'I can't imagine what that family is going through. Let's hope we can find the lad soon. Any questions?'

When Spence and Goddard shook their heads, Johnson stood straight again and turned to leave. 'I think you'll be surprised how many of our colleagues have come in to help. The briefing room's packed.'

With Johnson gone, Spence asked Goddard how Nick was when she had gone to his home.

'Detached and business-like,' she replied. 'He insisted on going to the place they'd lived when they first moved here. I didn't find out till it was too late to go with him. Stupid, really. I'm told it's in the middle of nowhere, and it was pitch black last night.'

Dave Spence bridled at her choice of the word 'stupid'. He'd had his differences with Nick Morgan. He had sometimes found him cold, unemotional, and inclined to bend rules, but not stupid. He'd never thought of him as stupid. 'Who knows how we'd react in the same situation,' he said, and left her to think about it.

DCI Johnson had not been lying. The briefing room was fuller than Spence had ever seen it. The windows had started to steam up until someone figured out how to open a few.

Acting DI Goddard came in and jostled her way to the front, where DC Lynn Greenfield was waiting. The hubbub died down, everyone intent on what she was going to say. Johnson slipped into the room and remained standing at the back.

Spence noticed a tremor in Goddard's voice as she greeted her colleagues and thanked them for coming in on a Bank Holiday. She started the briefing by taping photos of Alexander outside the sports centre to a whiteboard. Spence could still see some writing from the Danny Easton case which hadn't been cleaned off properly. It distracted him until her voice broke into his thoughts.

'Neither Mr nor Mrs Morgan recognises them except to say that they are Nike Sportswear AIRMAX Plus III trainers and that Alex had wanted them but they'd refused to buy them until the growth of his feet slowed. Cheapest I could find them online last night was £160.' The comment produced some sympathetic murmuring from parents of teenagers in the room.

'Ditto, the phone. Alex has a Samsung with a camera lens on the back. This enlarged photo shows the phone he is using doesn't have that.' She pinned the blurred image to the board. 'We're trying to trace all calls made at that time in that area, but not getting anywhere so far and Bank Holiday isn't helping.'

'That's a burner,' said one of the uniformed sergeants.

'Why do you say that?' snapped Goddard.

'My son is fifteen. If I gave him a phone without a camera, or even two cameras, he would never leave the house. The shame would kill him. That phone is for short-term use, maybe only single use, then discard. Mark my words.' The chorus of agreement overwhelmed any voices of dissent, and Goddard wrote a question mark beside the photo, followed by the word 'Burner'. The addition of the word to the board started a debate which threatened to take control of the briefing.

Spence thought about helping her bring them back under control, before changing his mind. He guessed she would think he was drawing attention to her lack of confidence and would hate him for it.

'Moving on to the cars.' Goddard's voice was barely audible at the back.

'Pack it in, everyone. This is important.' Johnson's words brought the room to order and Spence watched Goddard's face crumple. Maybe he should have helped her out before their boss felt he had to.

'Three cars left the sports centre car park at about the time Alex was leaving. We've traced and discounted one of them and uniform are still trying to contact the owner of the Golf. The registration plate on the Range Rover comes back to a white Ford Transit whose owner is a plumber called Jasper Amir.' She checked her notes before looking back up. 'He lives in Peterborough. No surprises that I have asked all patrols to keep a lookout for that Range Rover.'

'Unless the plate was a fake just used to lift Alexander Morgan,' said a woman's voice. It was the first time anyone had publicly said that this might be an abduction, and the room fell silent.

'I don't want to think about that,' said Goddard.

'Well, you should.' This voice was more familiar to the team and came from the open doorway, where DI Nick Morgan stood, legs parted and arms rigid by his sides. 'I really think you should.'

Chapter 55

Friday 10th April (Good Friday)

Spence held the door open and watched Johnson escort Nick Morgan away from the briefing. Goddard was staring at the door, her mouth open but without words. The background chatter had started up again and he caught a few snippets. 'Looks rough', 'hasn't shaved', 'slept in those clothes'.

Spence pushed his way through the crowd until he was standing beside Goddard. He shouted over the noise. 'Come on, guys, listen up. We need to get on with it.'

When she could be heard, Goddard started to divide her lines of inquiry between uniformed officers and detectives. 'NPAS are going to be with us from ten,' she said. 'They're going to fly over the Park Homes Estate and take a turn round the golf course and along the cliffs and the beach. We've also got two dog teams out already.'

The news that the National Police Air Service was involved raised a few eyebrows. Goddard ignored them and started to pass round printouts of contact details for the classmates of Alexander and Victoria. It wasn't a complete set as the Head Teacher was waiting for permission from the governors and their legal team before they would assist. This list was down to Greenfield, who had made some progress by asking each parent she spoke to if they could give details of other parents, and so the list had grown. Greenfield had also managed to speak to the plumber whose number plate had been cloned. He was angry and she shared the highlights of his long diatribe about the uselessness of the current Home Secretary. Spence had some sympathy with the sentiment.

There was a team trying to trace the purchase of the trainers, and another looking at mobile phone calls made near the centre between a quarter to and a quarter past three the previous afternoon. Four detectives who had come in on their day off were bent over a map tracking the roads around the sports centre for the likelihood of CCTV of the Range Rover and who was in it.

'What's going on?' Jenny Smart arrived and made her way to where Spence and Goddard were going through a list, making sure everything was covered.

'Where have you been, Jenny?' asked Spence.

'I asked the boss if I could come in a bit late today. I was babysitting my niece last night and I needed to take her home before work.'

'When did you speak to him?' asked Goddard.

Smart frowned and looked back over her shoulder at the activity and concentration in the room. 'Is he okay?'

'His son's missing,' said Spence. 'It was called in late yesterday afternoon.'

'I think I spoke to him at about four. I'd left him a message to say we might have a suspect for Gary Fox, but I didn't hear from him, so I rang. He apologised. Said he'd picked up my message but hadn't got round to calling me back. He said I didn't have to come back in and that he'd see me at this morning's briefing at nine thirty. I thought I was early.'

Goddard gave her a summary of what they already knew and what was planned for the morning.

'What can I do?' she asked, her eyes darting between Goddard and Spence.

‘Nick’s in with Johnson,’ said Goddard. ‘Perhaps you could take him home?’

‘I’m going to speak to James Newton,’ said Spence. ‘He’s Alexander’s Head of Year, or whatever they call themselves. I’ll take Jenny with me so she can update me with the Dennison and Fox cases on the way. I think that’s a more appropriate use of her time and skills.’ He led Smart away without looking back.

Chapter 56

Friday 10th April (Good Friday)

Spence and Smart made it to her car without speaking. He heard her taking deep breaths and expelling the spent air from her mouth. He didn't think it was caused by excitement at their planned visit to James Newton.

'If it's any consolation, I don't think she meant anything by it,' said Spence, reaching round to grab his seatbelt.

Jenny Smart pulled her driver's door closed and Spence cringed at the slam. He knew she loved her car and would be regretting venting her temper on it.

'I'd have driven him home. That's not the problem. *She's* the problem.' She huffed another deep breath out and started the engine. 'How far back do you need me to go with the Dennison and Fox cases?' She turned to him as she selected her gear and set off towards the barrier.

'Not as far as you think. I've been keeping a watchful eye.' Smart looked more closely at him as they waited for the barrier to rise. 'What?' he asked. 'I never wanted to be taken off the Dennison case in the first place. You can't blame me for having a sneaky peek at the boards.'

'If the Ice Queen found out, she'd castrate you.'

'Probably with just one glance.'

'Where are we going, then?'

'I can give you directions. My wife works at the school and we know James Newton socially, from fundraisers and stuff. He lives just off the motorway, so head north.'

Their conversation during the drive showed Smart that Spence really had kept himself well informed. The only details she could add were Gary Fox's post mortem findings, and her conversation with Giles and Gina Clooney's son, Ian.

'He's a big lad,' she said, pulling up outside a modest new-build house with a front garden the size of a postage stamp. 'He looks as if he works out. He's on leave from Cyprus; Royal Artillery.'

'Big enough to clobber Gary Fox?'

'Easily, I'd say. Now, are you going to lead this one, because I've been thinking about the two deaths? I haven't got my head around Alex Morgan going missing.'

'Sure, but it'll be off the record because, as I say, we're friends.'

'If he gives us anything, we'll fix up for someone to come and take a statement,' said Smart, this time closing her door with more care.

James Newton came to the door with a cordless drill in his hand. He greeted them warmly, despite Spence's laughter.

'I made a deal with the missus. I could carry on buying books, as long as I started building shelves. Happy Easter!'

He showed them into a small lounge and invited them to sit on a two-seater sofa which fitted under the stairs. Spence and Smart changed places to avoid Spence banging his head when he stood back up.

'This is just awful,' said Newton. 'I couldn't believe it when the Head rang.' He lowered his voice. 'She advised me not to speak to the police until she's heard from the school's lawyers, but I figured a quick chat can't harm. Can I say "off the record", or is that just in films?'

'Quick informal chat is what we're here for,' said Spence. 'No notes; no recordings. Just any clue you have as to where he might have gone, or who with?'

With obvious reluctance, and qualified with protestations of Alexander Morgan being a nice lad, polite and bright, Newton got round to repeating the allegations of alcohol abuse during the school day.

'You spoke to Alex's parents?' asked Smart.

'Just Mrs Morgan. She said he was busy. That was a week ago yesterday.'

'DI Morgan was doing interviews. We'd picked up a suspicious death case the day before,' said Spence.

'I remember. The kids were calling it The Body in the Beach Hut. There was some silliness in school that day. Everyone goes to that beach. It felt a bit close to home.'

'Was there anything different about Alex after you spoke to Mrs Morgan?' asked Spence.

'I saw him for registration the next morning, and then we broke up for Easter. Sorry.'

'Don't be sorry, James. That's been very helpful. We may need a statement.' Spence raised himself out of the sofa slowly, conscious of the height restriction. Both detectives handed over their cards and Newton promised to be in touch if he thought of anything else.

Back in the car, Smart looked out of the windscreen. 'What do you make of that?'

'Useful information,' said Spence, 'but I wish I didn't know it.'

'Me too. It'll make trouble for the boss. Let's hope Alex turns up soon.'

***

Alison Goddard brought the evening briefing under control by welcoming everyone and thanking them for their hard work that day. There were significantly fewer people in the room. Some were still out on visits or searching, and others, who had holiday commitments which could not be rearranged, had reported in and gone home. Spence and Smart sat together at the back.

Goddard pinned a photo of the local train station on the board. 'CCTV shows Alex arriving at the station at 15.15 hours. He didn't purchase a ticket at the station, but he was seen to pass through the barrier with a ticket. The next train due was for London, but we've no confirmation he actually got on it. Not all the cameras at the station are working.' Her news was greeted with the usual groans and tutts of disgruntlement. 'It's not perfect,' she snapped, 'but it's better than nothing.'

'We're waiting to hear from South West Trains about ticket purchases, or any coverage of the barriers at Waterloo.' The reply had come from a young woman with spiky blonde hair dyed purple at the tips. Spence thought she looked tired.

Other officers updated the group with their findings, although nothing could compete with the station sighting. Smart nudged Spence and whispered in his ear. He shook his head. 'Let's give it another few hours. He hasn't gone to London to buy a better brand of vodka, has he. What we've got might not even be significant. It could send the investigation off in a whole different direction. Let's sit on it for now.' Smart gave him a look that told him she wasn't comfortable with the decision but would go along with it. For now.

Chapter 57

Saturday 11th April (Easter Saturday)

'Look at him. And they say it's a dog's life.' Nick Morgan used his launcher to hurl a chewed-up ball across the shingle, and they watched Truffles, the family springer spaniel, bound after it, unconcerned when his paws got wetted by the incoming tide. 'Thanks for coming, Jenny.'

Jenny Smart didn't reply. She'd not slept, still concerned that the information about Alex's drinking in school hours was relevant to his disappearance and that she and Spence were harbouring it.

'This Ian Clooney,' said Morgan. 'Does he need a closer look?'

'I'm not sure. He says he was with his parents from last Monday, but he'd been with his sister since he flew back from Cyprus the week before. Sister's in Portsmouth. Neither of the places he's been since he got back is a million miles from Gullhaven.'

'Which could put him in the frame for both Dennison and Fox. Is that what you're saying?'

Truffles dropped the ball at Nick's feet and looked up expectantly. He obliged, and the delighted dog raced after it again. 'I sometimes wonder who's training who,' he said. 'Have you ever thought of having a dog?'

Jenny Smart shook her head and cleared her throat. 'I'm not sure about Dennison, but I like him for Gary Fox. It was Fox that Giles Clooney blamed for the demise of his company, and the day after Ian Clooney turns up, Fox is at the bottom of a cliff with his head split open.'

‘What does Dave say?’

‘Dave says we need to concentrate on Alexander and that we’ll speak to Ian Clooney once he’s turned up safe and sound.’

Morgan snorted. ‘And you want to bring Ian Clooney in?’

‘He’s on leave and I forgot to ask when he’s going back.’ She looked across at him for his reaction. ‘Sorry, no excuses.’

‘Ring Clooney Senior ... You’ve got the number, haven’t you?’ She nodded. ‘Just ring and ask. And if he’s due on a plane soon, ask him to come in. I know Johnson has told everyone that Alex comes first, and he does, but our other cases are important, too.’

They had reached the end of the beach, where there were signs warning not to go any further. Beyond, it was rocky and the risk of cliff falls increased. They stopped while Nick Morgan bent and ruffled his dog’s fur before offering him a treat from his pocket.

‘I don’t think you’re here for me to tell you to ring someone for a bit of information, and I also don’t think you came to help me walk my dog. Why don’t you tell me what’s really bugging you.’

They paused at a bench with an engraved brass plaque which told them it was the favoured spot of a couple, both now deceased. As they sat, Morgan noticed that the husband was widowed for eight years before he too died. If Sam persisted with the divorce, he would face a solitary life too. Unless Maisie ...

‘Dave and I went to speak to James Newton yesterday. He’s –’

‘Alex’s Head of Year. I know. And I also know what he’ll have told you.’

‘We’ve not told anyone else. I wanted to ask you about it.’

He leant forward, rested his elbows on his knees and chin in his hands. ‘What about last night’s briefing?’

‘We didn’t say anything.’

‘You should have. You don’t owe me anything. And if it comes out and Ali Goddard finds you concealed something from her ... on her first case in charge ... she’ll never forgive you. Either of you. And she knows how to bear a grudge.’

Chapter 58

Saturday 11th April (Easter Saturday)

Dorothy Cooper answered the knock on her door, purse in hand and ready to pay for her delivery.

'It's okay, Mother, you don't have to pay me for coming.'

Steven Cooper breezed past her and dropped into her chair at the window. Dorothy remained at the door, her eyes wide. She looked down the corridor before poking her head out to check the doors on either side. 'What are you thinking? I told you not to come back here,' she hissed. 'You were supposed to wait in Suffolk until the art school accepted you.'

Steven put his hands behind his head and arched his back.

'Of course I came back. Samantha rang me and told me my nephew was missing. Frankly, I was a bit surprised you hadn't told me yourself. She asked me if I thought he might be hiding in our holiday home and I was able to confirm that he wasn't. Because I was.'

Dorothy's eyes narrowed. She didn't like this confident incarnation of her son, and she didn't want him here. In a few more days she hoped to have confirmation of his place in France, and she'd wave him off with a smile, knowing he was safely out of Plod's grasp. She made her way to one of her dining chairs and winced as she sat. She'd missed her last two walks around the grounds of Silver Sands. The exercise helped her arthritis and it was a good way of staying on top of the gossip. But for now, leaving her flat was too risky.

Steven's brow furrowed. 'Your grandson is missing. My nephew is missing. Sam is in bits. Have you no heart at all?'

'You can't be here,' she insisted. 'People know who you are.'

He shook his head. 'It doesn't matter. It's only family that know I stabbed Raynor, and the only member of our family who wants to do something about it is Nick. I don't suppose he comes here for many social visits, does he?'

'Not usually,' she conceded, 'but we're not in usual times. Her eyes lit up. 'What if Alex goes to find you at your flat and you're here? You should get back there.'

'Alex doesn't know where I live.'

There was another loud knock. 'Delivery, Mrs Cooper.'

'I'll get it,' said Steven.

'No! Keep quiet. They'll go away.'

'Don't be silly, Mother. It's a delivery. You might have to sign for it.'

Before she could stop him, Steven had opened the door and taken the flat pizza box from a young man in fluorescent purple dungarees. He handed her the bill. 'Pay the man,' he said, taking the box to the dining table.

Dorothy's hands were trembling as she counted the money into the deliveryman's hands. She watched him take a few steps away from the door before closing it. When she turned back, Steven had opened the box and was staring at her.

'You don't like pepperoni, Mother. You don't even like pizza. What's going on?'

Acting DI Alison Goddard logged on to the computer in Morgan's office willing something ... anything ... to have been reported that would throw light on Alexander Morgan's disappearance. She clicked on the photos of him outside the sports centre, then those that had been taken at the train station. Was he in London, or had he caught a later train going in the other direction? The local news had shown the pictures on their late bulletin, but how many people were up at that time? They'd promised to show them again at breakfast, but had qualified the offer with 'if there's air time'. She'd missed the broadcast, and judging by the lack of response from the public she assumed it hadn't happened.

She sat back in Morgan's chair and swivelled it from side to side.

Yesterday, a lot of effort had gone into tracing the current whereabouts of people who might have a grudge against DI Nick Morgan. But assuming nobody had a gun trained on Alex's head when he went into the station, she had to believe that he'd not been taken by anyone who wanted to harm him. That only left the options that he'd left home because he'd fallen out with his parents, or for a prank. She already knew that Alex had burst in when his parents were arguing about the draft divorce petition. Did it come back to that? It seemed a big leap. What about school? Maybe he was being bullied? She flicked through the policy book. Spence and Smart were supposed to have spoken to one of the teachers yesterday, but they'd not reported back and she'd forgotten to ask at the briefing.

She picked up her phone and flicked through her contacts. Jenny Smart's mobile diverted to voicemail without ringing.

Chapter 59

Saturday 11th April (Easter Saturday)

'Is that my pizza?'

Dorothy's bedroom door opened without her hearing it. She whipped round. 'Get back in there,' she shouted.

'What the fuck?' Steven was out of his chair and across to the door before she could reach it.

Alex was wearing jeans and a sweatshirt, and socks without shoes. He padded across the carpet and took a piece of pizza from the box. 'I only had orange juice for breakfast.' He directed his comment to Steven. 'I'm starving.' He folded two slices together and shoved them into his mouth as if afraid his lunch might be whipped away from him.

'How long have you been here? Your mum and dad are frantic with worry.' Steven put his hand on Alex's shoulder and positioned himself between the boy and his grandmother.

Alex chewed a couple of times before swallowing. 'Grandma says they're furious with me and it might not be safe for me to go back until they've calmed down. But she says I can stay here until it blows over, so it's okay.'

Dorothy lifted the pizza box and shoved it towards Alex. 'Take it and eat it in the other room. Uncle Steven and I need to talk.'

'Talk about me, you mean.' Alex tilted his head back, thrusting his jaw out in a gesture of defiance Dorothy recognised from her own children. 'Anyway, you've told us never to eat or drink in your bedroom.'

‘I think you’d better do as Grandma says, Alex,’ said Steven. ‘I won’t go without speaking to you again.’ Alex shrugged, the petulant look still on his face as he retreated and closed the door behind him.

Dorothy felt her palm itch with a desire to slap him. She rubbed her hands together and sat at the table. ‘Before you start,’ she said, ‘all of this is your fault. If you hadn’t stabbed that junkie, I wouldn’t have had to do this.’

‘Do what? What exactly is *this*?’ Steven was shouting at her, although Dorothy noticed that he had stayed beyond her reach on the other side of the table. He threw an arm in the direction of the bedroom door. ‘Is “this” kidnapping? Your own grandson? While your daughter is in agony less than ten miles away.’

‘She brought it on herself when she married Plod. Anyway, I don’t know why you’re so concerned about her. You’ve always accused me of making her my favourite. Now she’s hurting because I’m helping you.’

‘We’re your children. You shouldn’t be pitching us against each other. What are we going to do? The police have thrown everything they have at this. And he’s been here all the time?’

Dorothy wiggled her forefinger at him, her denials issued at machine-gun speed. ‘No, no, no, no, no. He rang me late last night and told me he was at the station. I sent a taxi for him. He was scared to go home in case he made his so-called parents argue again. He’s only been here –’ she looked at her clock ‘– about twelve hours.’

‘And where was he before that?’

‘He won’t tell me.’

'Christ! There's been helicopters and everything. What are we going to do?'

'Be quiet and let me think. You caused this problem, not me.'

Steven started to remonstrate but Dorothy held up her hand. She needed a plan and it had to be a good one.

Goddard bit into a cheese and pickle sandwich that was so dry she feared for her teeth. She tossed it into Morgan's waste bin and had just put the second salt and vinegar crisp in her mouth when the desk phone rang.

'DI Goddard, it's DC Mihika Bindra.'

Goddard's brain spun. She recognised the name but couldn't remember who she was.

'Family Liaison at Cliffside House.'

Bindra must have sensed her memory lapse. She felt bad. 'Of course, I'm sorry, Mihika. Any news?'

'Alex has just rung his mother. He's at the train station.'

'I'll send a patrol car for him. I want him brought to the station, preferably before anyone else speaks to him.'

'Too late for that, DI Goddard. I tried to stop them, but DI Morgan and his wife set off a moment ago. Your patrol car will need to select warp speed to beat them.'

'Okay. Thanks for trying. I'll ring him.'

She wasn't confident that Morgan would answer his phone, and was preparing to leave a message when she heard Samantha Morgan's voice. 'I need to speak to Nick, Samantha.'

'He's driving. Fast. We're going to fetch Alex.'

‘I know, but I’m concerned about preservation of evidence. He might have something on his clothes, and if he has, I want it. I don’t want it compromised.’

‘I’ll put you on hands-free,’ said Samantha.

The line went quiet and Goddard checked to see if she had lost the signal before she heard road noise and the engine.

‘This is my case, Nick. I need Alexander’s clothes and that’s before he’s smothered with either Samantha’s DNA or your own.’

‘What if it’s not a case? What if he just wanted to get away from us?’ Goddard hardly recognised Nick Morgan’s voice. He was shouting, but his tone and pitch were high: excited and alarmed.

‘I want coat, trousers and those damn shoes. They’re at the centre of this.’

Samantha’s voice was tinny and further away than Nick’s. ‘I’m not stripping my son in the middle of the road.’

When Nick chipped back in, he was calmer. ‘I’ve got evidence bags in the boot. I’ll take the jacket and shoes, and you can come to the house for them. He’s not a criminal and I’m not having him treated like one. Come to the house and we’ll get to the bottom of it.’ He must have ended the call and Goddard threw her mobile down on the desk. She drummed her fingernails on the scratched wood beside her notes. Then she called the Duty Officer and arranged for a patrol car to be despatched to the station. It might still get there before the Morgans. Miracles sometimes happened.

Chapter 60

Saturday 11th April (Easter Saturday)

Morgan opened the front door at Cliffside House at Goddard's first ring. She barely looked at him as she stepped over the threshold. 'Where is he?'

'Kitchen,' said Morgan, standing back to let Lynn Greenfield follow.

'We're going to speak to him together,' said Goddard, pointing behind her towards Greenfield. 'Samantha can sit in, as long as she doesn't interrupt.'

'Fair enough,' said Morgan. He pointed to the brown paper bags with clear panels which lay on the floor at the door. 'Jacket, sweatshirt and jeans, as you requested.'

'I want the shoes, too.'

He nodded to two other bags. 'One in each. I've done this before, you know.'

Alexander Morgan was sitting at the breakfast bar facing a full cup of tea which looked cold. He was wearing a grey tracksuit and kicking his bare feet back and forward in a gesture which made him seem younger than his years. Samantha sat beside him, the morning's mascara now set in the wrinkles at the edges of her eyes. Goddard thought it looked theatrical; she could be playing the witch in a pantomime. She placed her bag on the countertop and gave Alex her best attempt at a sincere but closed-mouth smile.

'Alex, I'm Alison. I'm please you're back. We were all really worried.'

Alex didn't look up. Smile wasted.

Lynn Greenfield took a notebook out of her pocket and stood behind Alex in case he was spooked by having his words documented. But she hadn't escaped Samantha's notice. 'Is that really necessary?'

'Yes, until we have an understanding of what happened, Samantha,' said Goddard.

'Nothing happened,' said Alex, and when she looked back at him, Goddard saw that he had inherited Nick's eyes. Samantha's eyes were blue, too, but more of a baby blue. Morgan men had eyes at the grey end of the scale, with flecks that caught the light.

'Why did you go?' snapped Samantha.

Goddard put up her hand. 'I'm sorry, I can't have this. If you want to stay, you'll have to remain silent.' Samantha's glower reflected more than her annoyance at being silenced, but Goddard was unconcerned. She turned her attention back to Alex. 'Let's go back to the sports centre and football practice. What happened after that?'

'One of my friends offered me a lift to the station.'

'Which friend? Can you give me his name?'

Alex shook his head. 'I don't know their name.'

Goddard made eye contact with Lynn Greenfield, who replied with a single nod. She had caught it too: 'their name', not 'his name'.

Goddard softened her voice. 'Not much of a friend, then, if you don't know their name?'

The look Alex Morgan gave her was calculating. He knew he'd let something slip and was strengthening his barriers.

'So, they drove you to the station. Did you notice the make of the vehicle?'

'I'm not good with cars.'

Goddard nodded. She'd check that with Nick Morgan later. 'Why did you ask to go to the station?'

'I wanted to get away from here. They're doing my head in.' He threw a pointing hand in Samantha's direction and Goddard watched her die a little.

'Where did you go?'

'London. I went to London. But I didn't like it and I came back. Will that do? Can I go now?'

'Where did you go when you got to London?'

'Nowhere, I just walked about.'

Goddard's patience was close to running out. Her last forty-eight hours had been a sleepless nightmare. She'd known that if Alex Morgan had turned up in a shallow grave, everyone would have said she wasn't up to the job of leading an investigation. And that same Alex Morgan was treating it as if it was no big deal. He'd just fancied a trip to London.

'You were gone for nearly two days, Alex. That's a lot of walking about.'

Alex lifted his head enough to make eye contact with his mother, who nodded and stood. 'That's enough,' she said, and reached an arm around him. 'He's been through enough.' She shouted for Nick and the speed of his arrival showed he hadn't been far away.

Goddard felt that she, too, had been through enough. 'Okay. We'll let him rest, but I'll need to speak to him again.' She followed Nick Morgan to the door. 'Is Alex into his cars?' she asked.

'Probably more of a petrolhead than Dave Spence,' said Morgan. 'He's already asked for one for his seventeenth. Why do you ask?'

‘Just curious,’ said Goddard as she followed Lynn Greenfield out of the house.

Chapter 61

Tuesday 14th April

Morgan grabbed a chair and wheeled it across to Jenny Smart's desk. She sat back from her computer screen and took a mouthful of coffee. 'I'm glad he's back home safe and sound,' she said. 'How is he?'

'Hard to tell,' said Morgan. 'We've not seen much of him. He's playing computer games in his bedroom or watching TV. If you decide to have kids, Jenny, take my advice. Don't put a TV in their bedrooms.'

Smart laughed. 'I don't even want the responsibility of a dog, remember?' Morgan smiled, but it was an effort. 'Forgive me for saying it, but you look as if you could have done with a few more days off.'

'It's a bit tense at home. I've spent the last two days on the roof, when it wasn't raining. There were more tiles to be replaced than I thought, and the scaffolding rental is getting ridiculous.' He didn't tell her about the calls he'd made to Maisie Sangster, all unanswered. He hadn't left messages. 'Where are we with the Dennison and Fox cases?'

Dave Spence strode through the open office door. 'I can help with that.'

Smart looked at Morgan. 'Did you just rub a magic lamp or something?'

'I've got the records for Gary Fox's mobile, which is still missing, by the way, and I've forwarded you an email from the lab. They've found particles consistent with brick dust in the wound to Gary Fox's head.'

Morgan accessed the message on his mobile. 'Straight-edged and heavy,' he said. 'A brick fits with what MoMack said. So, we just have to find someone who's carrying round a brick with Gary Fox's blood on it. Should be solved by lunchtime.'

'There's building work going on at the country club,' said Spence. 'Bound to be bricks there. And that's where Fox's car was.'

Morgan remembered looking through the curtains of the room he'd done his interviews in. He'd seen pallets of bricks, and breeze blocks, too. Testing all of them wasn't feasible, and anyway the deadly brick would be long gone by now.

'And what about Ian Clooney?' He directed his question to Jenny Smart.

'He's agreed to come in this afternoon. He's a bit angry, but he's going to talk to us. What about the phone, Dave?'

Morgan rolled his eyes. He'd forgotten Spence had mentioned the records from Gary Fox's phone. He'd have to sharpen up or he'd be no use to the team.

'I've not had time to go through everything in detail, so I concentrated on the day he died. Monday the 6th. He spent a lot of time on his phone during the day. The texts were all work-related. Then, just after six, he phoned the Country Club. It's not a long call ... maybe a dinner booking? Twenty minutes later there's an incoming text from a PAYG phone confirming a meeting at eight p.m.'

'Too much to hope that we know whose phone that is, I suppose,' said Morgan.

Spence shook his head. 'But we do know it's the same phone that was used to make the two threats to Simon Dennison that weren't from Gary Fox's phone. You remember? He had five threatening texts after the Christmas party.'

Morgan's mobile rang. He answered and listened before speaking. 'No, Alison, I've no idea where he got the trainers. We didn't buy them for him. No, I'm as certain as I can be that he didn't shoplift them.'

When the call ended, he slapped the mobile down on Smart's desk and exhaled. Spence and Smart were looking at him, their faces expectant.

'The pictures of Alex at the sports centre and at the station show him wearing expensive trainers we didn't buy him. He says a friend didn't want them and gave them to him. Alison doesn't believe him.'

'And neither do you,' said Smart. 'Or you don't look as if you do.'

'Would you not rather be at home with him? Just till you know what happened?' asked Spence.

'I'm better here,' said Morgan. 'Right. We need to stay on top of that phone – and who wants to come with me to the country club to inspect bricks?'

Chapter 62

Tuesday 14th April

Hugo Thorne was talking to one of the receptionists when Morgan and Spence approached the desk. He grabbed a tissue from a box and started to polish his glasses.

'Mum and Dad have gone to see my sister,' he said. 'She's back at the clinic again.'

'I'm sorry to hear that, Hugo, and I hope she gets better soon,' said Morgan. 'Hopefully, you'll be able to help us and we won't have to bother them.'

Thorne put his glasses back on and waited.

'I'm interested in the construction site,' said Morgan.

'Planning a wedding, are you?' asked Thorne. 'It'd better not be any time soon, the number of setbacks we've had.'

His comment reminded Morgan that he was probably nearer to booking a divorce than celebrating a wedding. 'Was Gary Fox interested in the new venue? Maybe for his next sales conference?'

'As I said, we don't have a completion date.'

'But you're advertising it for bookings later this year.' Spence held his phone screen towards Thorne. It showed an artist's impression of a single-storey building bathed in bright sunshine and surrounded by colourful flowerbeds. It was a page on the club's website.

'That was dad's idea. I said we should wait.' Hugo's face took on a sulky expression he should have grown out of. 'I'm supposed to be in charge of marketing and business development but my dad thinks that means moving tables and bundling up the laundry.'

‘Were you here last Monday evening, Hugo? Did you see Gary Fox in the building?’ asked Morgan.

‘Yes, I was here. I wasn’t on duty, but chef asked me to stay behind after my shift. We hadn’t got enough vegan meals for a party of thirty financial advisers. I had to source some ingredients and go out to fetch them.’

‘So you weren’t here the whole evening?’

‘No.’

‘When our technicians came to collect Mr Fox’s car, they asked about CCTV and they were told there had been a problem with the system on Monday evening. What do you know about that?’

‘It’s fixed now. We had to get a new hard drive.’

‘How much of Monday’s coverage was affected?’

Hugo Thorne shifted his weight from one foot to the other and shook his head. ‘You’d have to ask my father. Not my department.’

‘When do you expect him back?’

‘I don’t know.’

‘You’re aware that this is a murder inquiry, Hugo?’

‘I can’t tell you what I don’t know.’

Morgan exchanged a glance with Spence, who moved a couple of steps closer to Hugo Thorne. Not all pressure had to be applied with words.

‘We’d like a closer look at the building site,’ said Morgan.

‘What for?’

‘Is it covered by CCTV that was working on Monday?’

‘Of course not. It’s a building site.’

‘Materials can go missing. There’s vandalism, too. If you’re falling behind due to other issues, I’m surprised to hear you’re not taking every precaution.’

Hugo Thorne rolled his eyes. 'If I take you to the site, is that it? I haven't got all day to be chasing round after you.'

Morgan smiled at him, but it wasn't a friendly smile. 'Let's go,' he said.

They walked down the corridor towards the ballroom, Morgan on Thorne's left and Spence, once he'd caught up, on his right. Hugo Thorne looked to one then the other before speeding up. Morgan knew he wasn't trying to out-march them; he just wanted their meeting to be over.

They crossed the ballroom and went out into the lobby. Thorne made for the double doors with fire exit signs above them and entered a code into a keypad before throwing them open. 'The doors are alarmed unless we override it,' he explained.

The builders had made progress since Morgan had first seen the site. Now, the foundations were hidden by walls of brick and masonry blocks. He thought there were more men on site today. Different trades, too, according to the logos on their fleeces.

'How do your builders access the site?' he asked, looking at the mud and slurry outside and comparing it to the cleanliness of the carpeted lobby.

'There's going to be a new entrance for the suite. We've made a hole in our perimeter fencing in preparation for it. The contractors use that as their entrance.'

'Is it covered by CCTV?' asked Spence.

'No, but it will be when the work's finished. What is this obsession with CCTV anyway?'

‘Gary Fox was here last Monday. We want to know why. Who did he meet? Who was it that wanted him dead?’

‘We’re open to the public. He could have arranged to meet anybody,’ said Hugo Thorne.

Morgan remembered Claire Fox’s comment about the fragility of the couple’s finances without Simon Dennison’s contribution to the business. ‘You said there were financial advisers here on the night?’

‘Yes.’

‘Perhaps he came looking for advice. We’re going to need their contact details.’

‘Well, that’s not going to make us very popular. We’re trying to run a business here, you know.’

‘And I’m running a murder investigation,’ said Morgan. ‘You’ll need to close this site until CSI can send a team to go over it.’ Thorne’s protestations rang in his ears as he and Spence walked away.

‘Do you mean it? About sending a team over, I mean?’ asked Spence. ‘They’re not going to find anything. It’s like a paddy field out there.’

‘Then why is he so obstructive? You’d think he’d want us to get our investigations over as soon as possible but he fought us every step of the way there.’ He stopped walking as they got to the double doors which would return them to the reception area. ‘Can you get someone to have a closer look at the Thorne family for us?’

‘But they weren’t here when Simon Dennison was attacked,’ said Spence.

‘That could be coincidence or it could be very convenient. Get Lee Tyler to do it, would you?’ Confident that his ‘heat-seeking missile’ DC wouldn’t let a firm alibi stand in his way, Morgan led the way back to the car.

Chapter 63

Tuesday 14th April

'Is he worthy of further investigation, or not?' asked Morgan as he was packing up for the day.

DC Jenny Smart had spent an hour with Ian Clooney and had checked with the car hire company he'd used at Gatwick. She'd been given the start of hire mileage and had arranged for a patrol car to go out and photograph the current mileage. Clooney had been adamant. He'd driven from Gatwick to Portsmouth, and a week later, from Portsmouth to Southampton. There had been no trips to Gullhaven to kill Simon Dennison or Gary Fox, however much he might have wanted to.

'He could have used another vehicle,' said Morgan. 'His sister's?'

'She doesn't have one or, he says, access to one.'

'What was your gut feel when you spoke to him?'

Smart considered her answer before she spoke. 'Now I've spent a bit of time with him, I believe him. But I think he's disappointed in himself that he didn't kill Gary Fox. Maybe he feels he should have? To avenge his father's ruin and disability and all that.'

'When does he go back?'

'Monday. And he's with his parents until then.'

'Okay, we'll keep him in mind, but we'll also keep looking. It's good work, Jenny. I like the way you follow your instinct.' She thanked him and left him going through his files and packing his briefcase.

Alison Goddard's text arrived on Morgan's phone as he was taking a last look at his emails. Digital Forensics promised a preliminary report on sample files from

Simon Dennison's computers in the morning. He also got a commitment that a CSI team would be at the country club site as soon as one was available. They would also make sure they collected some bricks for comparative analysis with the residue found in Gary Fox's head wound.

Nothing more to be achieved today. But now this text. He decided it would be quicker to ring her.

'You could have texted me back,' said Goddard.

'I wanted to thank you for letting me borrow Spence from your team this morning.'

'It's okay. I've only got a suspicious death in town that I'm on my way to, and Alex's disappearance, of course.'

'I'm not sure why that's still ongoing. He's back now.'

'Aah, you've not heard, then?'

Morgan's heart started to pound. 'I don't know. Heard what?'

'Alex didn't get off the train from London on Saturday. He arrived at the station from the roadside, not the trackside.'

A trickle of fear ran down his spine. 'Was it the black Range Rover; the one we saw on the sports centre CCTV?'

'It's out of shot. All we see is Alex walking towards the station and then he gets out his mobile. I'm guessing that's the call he made asking to be collected, but I'll be confirming that.'

'Where are we going with this, Alison? I'm not sure what you're looking for. He's a kid who ran away from home when his parents had a row and then came back as soon as he saw that he doesn't have it so bad after all.'

‘I think there’s more to it and I’m doing it as much for his protection as anything. Who gave him the trainers? You know yourself how expensive they are. There’s more to it.’

‘Will you let me speak to him? As a favour, that is, and I know you don’t owe me any.’

‘If he’s in the shit, you can’t really believe he’s more likely to tell you than me, surely? You were the one having the row that made him leave.’

Morgan wasn’t sure if she’d planned her words to be that hurtful. He hoped not. He was going to be working with her for the foreseeable future, and when all this stuff with Alex was done, he didn’t want residual resentment on either side.

‘Will you let me speak to him tonight? If I can’t get any sense out of him, I’ll bring him in tomorrow and see if putting him in an interview room is more persuasive.’

She didn’t agree immediately, but he built his case and eventually she relented, but with the parting sentence, ‘I expect to see you both tomorrow.’

Chapter 64

Tuesday 14th April

'You're on time, for once. I've made a fish pie. I'll put it in the oven while you're showering.' Sam's voice greeted Morgan from the lounge. He heard her get up, and the noise of a wine bottle touching her glass. He could smell cigarettes. Since Alex's disappearance, she wasn't attempting to hide that she was smoking again.

'Have the kids eaten?' he asked.

'They had a massive burger and chips for lunch. I said I'd make them a snack later.' She appeared at the lounge door. She was wearing dark jeans and a black T-shirt with long sleeves. Her cropped hair was tousled and he could see that she hadn't bothered with make-up.

'I'm going to speak to Alex before we eat.'

'Good luck with that,' she said. 'Mum came this afternoon and he refused to come out of his room.'

'What did she want?'

'To see if we were all okay.'

'Mmm.' Morgan knew that Dorothy didn't give a toss if he was okay and he wondered what her real reason for the visit had been. 'I'll give you a shout when I'm getting in the shower,' he said, and made his way up the stairs.

When the Morgan twins celebrated their eleventh birthdays, the family had made an agreement about bedroom doors. If a door was closed, a knock was required to gain entry, but that knock was always to be answered.

Morgan knocked.

'Go away.'

'It's Dad, Alex. Come to the door.'

'I said, go away.'

'That's not going to happen. Come to the door.' Morgan knew the door wasn't locked – none of the doors had locks – but if Alex opened the door himself it was an acceptance that this conversation was going to take place.

He knocked again, not too loud, but confirming that he wasn't going away. 'I'm going to sit here until you come to the door.' He slipped his jacket off and hung it over the banister then squatted down, his back against the wall.

A couple of minutes later, and just when Nick Morgan was thinking his knees would give in before Alex did, the door opened with a soft click. By the time Morgan stood up and entered, Alex was back in his bed, his duvet clutched to his neck by tightly closed fingers.

Morgan pulled the chair out from his son's untidy homework desk and straddled it. He laid his arms across the top of the backrest and lowered chin to rest on them.

'Mum's made a fish pie. Would you like me to bring you some?'

Alex shook his head.

'You know, I'm really sorry we upset you ... Vicky, too. I'd give anything for your mum and me not to have had that argument.'

They sat in silence, Alex looking at the wall and Morgan looking at Alex.

'Please speak to me. Tell me where you went. We were so worried about you. There's a lot of bad stuff out there.'

Alex's reply was a derisive snort and Morgan wondered when his sweet-natured son had become so cynical. He rested his chin again and waited. He was trained to play the silence game. Alex wasn't.

After looking over at him as if checking he was still there, Alex seemed to reach a decision. He thrust his clenched fists down and heaved himself into a sitting position, the protective duvet discarded. 'Nothing has been right since we moved here. Why did we have to come? You've done nothing but argue ever since.'

Morgan blew his breath out through parted lips. This was progress. His son had chosen an uncomfortable topic, but it was a start.

'We didn't *have* to come, but I hoped it would make your mum's life a bit easier if we did. Grandma was missing her, and Mum was getting more and more stressed every time she had to come and see to her.' Morgan didn't tell him about Operation Fire Farm and the contribution its outcome had made to his decision to relocate. 'Anyway, I want us to talk about you. Did you go to London with one of your new friends?'

Alex shook his head. 'No. And Vicky wouldn't come so I went on my own. You were both doing my head in.' Morgan sat up straighter again but it didn't ease the pain these words were causing. 'Mum's started smoking again. I hate that, too.'

'She'll stop soon. She's just stressed.'

'You said we came here to stop her stressing and it hasn't. Why can't we just go back home to London?'

'This is home now.' Morgan felt as if he was betraying his son when he said it. He didn't want to believe it either. It was time to change the subject before he gave himself away. 'Where did you get the posh trainers?'

Alex shrugged but Morgan wasn't deterred. 'The detective who came on Saturday is still looking into this. If you tell me now, I might be able to persuade her to wind it up.'

'My friend gave them to me.'

'Which friend?'

'I don't know his name.'

'You're telling me that a friend gave you trainers that cost £150 and you don't know his name?'

'I've seen him at school, but we only started speaking on Thursday. At football practice. I said I liked them and he said I could have them.'

Detective Inspector Nick Morgan's heart broke. He stared at his son and saw a boy he didn't know. A boy who could look his father straight in the eye and lie without flinching. He got up, replaced the chair at the desk and left the room, closing the door behind him.

Chapter 65

Wednesday 15th April

Morgan's phone rang while he was driving to work and the voice of Brian Bingley the crime scene manager boomed around the car. 'Gullhaven Country Club is on my way to work, so I dropped by. It's not good news. There's no point in me sending out a team. It's rained a hundred times since last Monday, and if that's where Gary Fox's blood was spilt it's long since been washed away ... and I mean long since.' He dragged the word 'long' out until Morgan's ears stopped listening. 'I've bagged up a few sample bricks for comparison, but that'll be it. The site is too rutted by heavy plant to get tyre marks; no chance of body fluids; no CCTV. Sorry. You're going to have to beat a confession out of someone.'

Morgan butted in while Bingley was still laughing. 'Or I could ask for every brick on the site, including those already used in construction, to be fingerprinted.' The laughter stopped.

'We'll be in touch when the lab's done the brick dust comparison.' Bingley ended the call and Morgan guessed it wouldn't take long for everyone in his team to hear that DI Nick Morgan was a humourless bastard.

He parked in his usual bay and walked to the station staff entrance, offering the security pass he wore round his neck to the control panel. It beeped and the door lock released faster than usual. Or did it just seem faster because he was dreading the conversation he was going to have with Acting DI Alison Goddard?

Morgan greeted DC Jenny Smart as he passed her desk. She held up a hand to halt his progress while she completed typing on her keyboard. 'I've had an email from –' she tapped a few keys to bring up the message '– a Hayley Glover. She wants to come and talk to us about Simon Dennison's computers.'

'Digital Forensics? I thought they couldn't look at our material for another couple of weeks?' It made him suspicious. He had been caught out a few times by devious journalists who wormed their way into inquiries, not by lying, but by omitting to tell the truth. He asked if she had checked the authenticity of the message.

'Yes. And her name is in the directory.'

'I'll give her a call. Maybe it's easier if we go to her?'

Smart's look said it all. It was never going to be easier for them to take a forty-minute drive to the labs, where parking was impossible and security clearance as intrusive as a rectal examination. Morgan got the message and trudged to his office, where his phone was already ringing. Goddard's name on the caller ID screen.

He answered it with his own name and started to decant the policy books from his case while she was talking.

'I've had a call from Crimestoppers,' she said. 'Someone filled in their online form to say they saw a lad getting out of a ... and I quote ... "posh black car" at the station on Saturday.'

Morgan's heart sank. Whatever his son had got himself into wasn't going away, not while Alison Goddard felt she had a point to prove. He didn't blame her. 'I've spoken to him, Ali, and I agree. There's something he's not telling us.'

'Did you bring him in? We need to get this sorted. It's for his own good.' She'd said it before and Morgan knew she was right. But Alex was his son and he wanted to protect him for as long as possible. 'If it was any other lad, you'd have sent a patrol car yourself.'

He rested his forehead in his left hand. 'Can you give me one more chance to speak to him tonight? I'm sorry to ask, but I'm scared for him. He's not a bad lad, but once he's in the system, you and I know how easy it is to become a bad lad.' He waited. She didn't answer immediately, but that was good. At least she was thinking about it. He heard her sigh; it was louder through his handset than if she'd been in the room with him.

'Last chance, Nick. And you owe me. Get that fucking divorce petition sorted today. Or I will, and it won't be pretty.'

Chapter 66

Wednesday 15th April

Hayley Glover didn't conform to Morgan's idea of a typical digital forensics investigator. He put her in her mid-forties. She had a mop of black curls and lines at the edges of brown eyes which deepened when she smiled. She placed an aluminium flight case on his desk and introduced herself.

'Thanks for coming, Hayley,' he said, getting up from his chair and shaking hands. 'It's not often we get a forensics report a couple of weeks earlier than expected.' He hadn't meant to be sarcastic, but she bristled and ended the handshake prematurely.

'I understand that your investigation was prioritised when there was a second associated death,' she said.

'Well, thank you. We appreciate everything you do for us.' He hoped that a small grovel would set the relationship back on an even keel, and it worked.

She smiled and relaxed. 'That's okay. It's nice to see daylight.' She nodded at his office door. 'Where am I setting up?'

Morgan led her to the briefing room, where Jenny Smart was already lowering blinds. When Dave Spence arrived, he closed the door behind himself.

'DC Smart and DS Spence are the detectives who searched Mr Dennison's flat and found the recording equipment and the media,' said Morgan, by way of introduction. 'I'd like you to give us an overview of content before we include the whole team, if you're okay with that?'

'It's your investigation, DI Morgan. My role is strictly supportive.' Glover cabled her laptop to the projector as she spoke. She selected one of the hard drives from her case and plugged it into a USB port before pushing another three drives across the desk to Morgan. 'I'll need you to sign for them,' she said.

'They are copies, right?' asked Morgan, and she nodded, confirming that the original drives and DVDs were in the evidence store.

Hayley Glover grabbed a chair and waited for her small audience to settle. She opened a file on her laptop and glanced at the screen behind her to make sure they could see what she was looking at.

'This is our evidence list for the investigation into the death of Simon Dennison. We have three mobile phones, an Android tablet labelled "Property of Forest-Fox Analysis", a tower PC and a laptop, and finally twenty hard drives and just under three hundred DVDs retrieved from a locked cabinet in his flat.

'And I should say we also have the filming equipment from the flat booked into evidence. Whether we look more closely at that depends on your thoughts after today. You might want to confirm that some of the content was definitely filmed with that equipment.' She made fleeting eye contact with Spence and Smart but saved her broadest smile for Morgan. 'If we're all sitting comfortably, I'm going to begin.'

Samantha wasn't pleased to find Graham Fletcher on her doorstep; even less so when he insisted on coming in.

She made coffee for them both and took a tray with two mugs and a plate of biscuits upstairs for the twins, who were competing at some sort of car racing game and hardly noticed her.

'I don't understand how you can have changed your mind so quickly, Sammy. This time last week you were full steam ahead for a divorce.'

Samantha Morgan shooshed him and turned the radio on. She pointed upwards. 'The twins are upstairs. One of them could come down at any moment.'

'I've never seen you so unhappy,' he continued, as if she hadn't spoken. 'And when did you start smoking again?' His tone was accusatory, as if she had taken up drowning puppies.

She gave it some thought. Since her mother had told her that bloody Alison Goddard was back on the scene, she was getting through about thirty a day. But she'd started smoking again when they came to Gullhaven. It was when Nick had accused her of sleeping with this man in front of her in his posh suit and whiter-than-white shirt. She ran her fingers through her hair, which she hadn't bothered to brush today.

'If all you've come to do is criticise, you can piss off. My husband's shagging some detective and my kid ran off last week. Smoking's the least of my worries.'

'Dorothy rang me this morning. She's worried about Alexander.'

'She came to visit him and he wouldn't come downstairs. I think she needs to prepare herself for a good few more years of that. He's going to be a teenager soon.'

'She's also worried that you've let Plod talk you out of a divorce. She just wants what's best for you.'

'Why are you even discussing it with her? It's none of her business.' He looked away and she caught a glimpse of the expression she remembered when they'd been boyfriend and girlfriend and she'd caught him out in a lie. 'I said, why are you discussing it with her?'

'She asked me to help you. I can file the petition this afternoon. Then you can concentrate all your attention on Alex. I won't even charge my fee. What do you say?'

Samantha reached across and grabbed his mug as he reached for it. She took it across to the sink and raised it to shoulder height so he could watch her pour it away. When she returned, she came to his side of the breakfast counter. She brought her face close to his and watched his eyes close in preparation for the kiss which wasn't going to come. 'I say and do whatever I want to, and when I want to, not when my mother and her lackey conspire to control me. Now, get out and report that back to her at your first opportunity.'

When he'd gone, she sat down heavily at the breakfast bar. She felt giddy, and cradled the mug of coffee in her hands, taking comfort from its heat. She lifted it to her mouth and recoiled from the smell. She just reached the sink in time before she was sick.

Chapter 67

Wednesday 15th April

Hayley Glover started her report by explaining that they had cloned Simon Dennison's work-issue laptop and prioritised its examination so that they could return it before the Forest-Fox Analysis business was compromised. She refused to confirm if Gary Fox, the Managing Director, had applied pressure. 'Knowledge of that is above my pay grade,' she said with a smile that suggested she could hack her way to any information if it piqued her interest. 'It was all work stuff. Customer relationship software; product information and specs; complaints – just what you'd expect on a company-issue system.

'Next, we looked at your victim's Android tablet. I understand we've already provided details of his finances that were on there?'

Morgan nodded. 'We've identified his Forest-Fox income, but we know he was living way beyond those means.'

'We also found some bagged-up drugs at the flat,' said Smart.

'In that in-between area,' added Spence. 'Too much for what I define as personal use, but probably not enough for serious dealing.'

'He was dealing all right, but not drugs. This is what we found on the PC.' Glover typed a web address she didn't need to check and her audience looked up at the screen. The video which appeared was professional and slick. The letters B, B and D appeared one by one and rotated on individual axes. They glinted red and silver as they turned. The briefing room was filled with the unmistakable sounds of panting and moaning. Glover returned to her keyboard and the screen froze.

'He was dealing in videos?' asked Smart. 'We knew he had a lot of partners and we guessed he was making recordings, but we didn't join the dots.'

When Morgan looked across at her, he saw she looked annoyed. She didn't like to miss anything.

'BBD?' asked Spence. 'Any idea what it stands for?'

Glover tapped on a couple of keys and the video continued. She muted the sound. 'I think we can do without that,' she said.

The three letters fragmented and vanished. They were replaced by four words. BIG BOY DENNI'S SECRET. And a mobile phone number. She paused it again.

'I was at the post mortem,' said Smart and I can tell you *that* –' she pointed to the words '– is a mis-set expectation. We should involve Trading Standards.'

Morgan ignored her. 'What about the mobile number?' he asked.

'It's the one you found in his travel bag at the hotel,' said Glover. 'It's a pay-as-you-go, but it had more than fifty quid credit on it when we got it. There were no calls made or received. All just incoming texts with letters and numbers. The texts are orders,' she explained. 'The website has excerpts of the films, and if you want to see more you have to buy the whole thing. Your mobile number is your member number and you use it as a reference when you pay. Then he attaches the mp4 file to a text and it's all yours.'

'But there's so much free porn on the internet ... I don't see why anyone would pay,' said Spence.

‘Simon Dennison had a USP,’ said Glover. ‘A unique selling point, that is.’ She reached out to start the film again, but Morgan had tired of the showmanship.

‘Just tell us,’ he said.

‘The next screen explains that he has had sex with females of all ages, sizes and nationalities. His USP is that none of them knew they were being filmed, and none of them consented to being filmed. That’s what the punters were paying for.’

‘Dear God,’ said Smart, and covered her face with her hands.

‘Why is that a turn-on?’ asked Spence.

‘Peeping Tom syndrome,’ said Morgan.

‘Does it not have to be live for it to qualify as voyeurism in law?’ asked Smart.

Morgan tried to remember, then gave up and shook his head. ‘I’d have to check. But don’t let’s forget, we’re investigating Simon Dennison’s assault. CID can chase after his clients.’

‘If one of the women he filmed found out, it would be quite a motive, wouldn’t it?’ said Smart. ‘If a bloke filmed me and put me on the internet, I’d go after him myself.’ She crossed to the murder board and pointed to a word. ‘MoMack said the attack on Dennison was personal. Whoever did it had to get close, strip him, and then ...’

‘You’re right,’ said Morgan. ‘And it was an overtly sexual assault. It could tie in with his sideline.’ He turned back to Glover. ‘How many downloads are available on the site?’

‘Four hundred and eighty-two. The last three were uploaded three days before his body was found.’

‘And how many have you looked at?’

'Me personally, or the team?'

'Both.'

'The team has looked at about three hundred so we could give you an initial content report, and I've looked at forty of them.'

'The excerpts or the complete films?' asked Spence, and was answered with a withering glare.

'And what's your opinion of that content? Based on what else you've seen that's out there?' asked Morgan.

'The quality is good. He's invested heavily in the equipment. Content isn't anything extraordinary. They all seem to feature your victim. No animals or children featured although there are a couple of girls whose birth certificates I'd like to see. A second guy appears in a couple of them. They were filmed somewhere different and I think it might be mobile phone footage. It's not the same quality.'

'Maybe he was on holiday?' It was Smart's suggestion.

'Could be. Anyway ...' Hayley Goddard powered down her laptop and started to disconnect the cables. She produced a sheaf of papers from her bag and slid them across to Morgan. 'Signatures on the last page of each copy, please.' She answered his questioning look by pointing to the hard drives. 'Maybe your killer's in there somewhere.' With one final wide smile for each of them, she agreed to DC Smart's offer to show her out, and was gone.

'What are the chances?' asked Spence, lifting the top hard drive from the pile and resting it in his hand as if weighing it.

Morgan shook his head. ‘If our murderer is in there, she’s one cold and scary woman to do what she did to him.’

Chapter 68

Wednesday 15th April

He was just about to go out for a lunchtime sandwich when his phone rang and Morgan saw it was Samantha. She started to speak without a greeting.

'I suppose I already know the answer to this, but can you come? Mother called in again and Alex went into meltdown, like he did before he ran away. He's upstairs crying his heart out. I can't make sense of what he's saying except he keeps talking about you and prison.'

Morgan frowned. He replayed yesterday's conversation with Alex in his head. He was sure he hadn't mentioned prison. Why would Alex think he was going to prison? 'Leave him to calm himself and I'll see what I can do.'

'I'll see you tonight, then,' said Sam, and he knew that if she could have slammed the phone down, she would have.

He dropped in to the briefing room, where Spence and Smart had made a start on the hard drives. 'I need to go home for an hour,' he said. 'I'll tell Ali Goddard, and I'll be on my mobile if one of those files shows a woman fighting back. Okay?'

Jenny Smart nodded, her eyes glued to her screen as she shovelled another spoonful of yoghurt into her mouth. Spence replied with a thumbs-up.

Alison Goddard wasn't in her office when he went to find her. He scribbled that he was going home for lunch and hoped she would be able to read between the lines.

***

He let himself in and paused in the hallway to listen.

Nothing.

He hoped Sam hadn't over-dramatised the situation.

She came out of the kitchen, drying her hands on her jeans. 'Well, this is a first.'

'Where is he?'

'In his room.'

'And Vicky?'

'I asked her to ring one of her friends. She's gone over there to do some project work, although I'm guessing there will be more girly gossiping and trying on clothes and make-up than schoolwork.'

'What happened?'

Sam Morgan shook her head and he could see she was genuinely baffled. 'Mum was in the lounge and I came out to make some coffee. She must have gone upstairs. Next thing I heard was Alex screaming at her to leave him alone. He slammed his bedroom door, but she must have gone in. Then all hell broke loose. He was throwing things at the door. Books, I think. I didn't hear anything break. She came back down and pretended nothing had happened. When I pressed her, she wouldn't tell me what she'd said to upset him, so I called for a taxi. It arrived, she got in it and went. We didn't speak again. She didn't even say goodbye.'

Nick saw that his wife was distressed. She looked pale. Was it appropriate to offer a hug? Somewhere in this house was an envelope with a draft divorce petition in it. He decided against the hug and made for the stairs.

'Can I get you some lunch?' she asked. He shook his head. Food wasn't on his list of priorities. He was two steps from the upstairs landing when she called after him. He stopped and leant over the banister. She was craning her neck to look up at him when she spoke, so quietly that he almost missed it. 'Thank you for coming.'

With a strong sense of déjà vu, he tapped on his son's door.

'Alex, it's Dad. I'm on my own. Grandma has gone. Vicky's with a mate and your mum's downstairs. This is just you and me.'

Alex opened the door immediately and stood straight, arms crossed in front of him. It was a demonstration of belligerence without the physical build to back it up. Morgan was torn between seeing the child he was raising and the man he was to become.

'This is shit,' said Alex. A clear breach of the family rules which forbade swearing in the house.

Morgan pushed him gently to one side and made his way to the chair he'd sat on yesterday. 'I don't doubt it, Alex. But quite a lot of life is shit. It's how we handle it that defines us.' He pointed to Alex's bed and watched him make a display of getting comfortable.

'In the nearly thirteen years you've been a member of this family, Mum has only once before rung me at work and asked me to come home because of you. You were little and it was the day we found out you were allergic to penicillin. They were putting you in an ambulance and your mother was beside herself. It's happened again today and I need to know what it's all about.'

Alex was unbuttoning and re-buttoning his duvet cover and it was starting to annoy him. 'What did Grandma want?' he asked. 'Because Mum says that's what started all of this.' Alex shook his head with a weariness Morgan could relate to. 'Your Grandma can be difficult, Alex, but I know she wouldn't want to hurt you.'

'She told me that you were mad at me for running away.'

Morgan shook his head. 'We're not. If anything, we're angry at ourselves for upsetting you so much you felt you had to go.'

'Why do you want to send Uncle Steven to prison?' Morgan had to hand it to his son. Maybe he'd been watching police custody documentaries? He'd picked up the technique of rapid changes of topic to unsettle the interviewee.

'I don't. I just want to find out the truth about something I think he did. Truth is important.'

'Are you and Mum getting a divorce?' When Morgan hesitated, Alex spat his own words back at him. 'Truth is important, Dad.'

'The truth is that I don't know. She's angry with me for something I haven't done.' As he spoke the last words, he wanted to take them back. Because they weren't the truth. His affair was real; it just wasn't with Alison Goddard. Not this time. 'Anyway, who told you I wanted to send Uncle Steven to prison?' He asked the question so he could get off the subject of infidelity, but as he asked it he realised he wanted an answer. He had only discussed his suspicion of Steven with Dorothy. He hadn't even spoken about it to Sam. How did Alex know?

Alex looked up from his buttoning task. 'I didn't say that.'

'Yes, you did. Who told you?'

'I overheard it,' he mumbled.

‘Not in this house you didn’t.’ Morgan stood and took the few steps he needed to get to the bed. He crouched down at the side of it. ‘And who told you we were mad at you for running away?’ Morgan reached across and lifted Alex’s chin so they were looking at each other. His son’s face was white.

Morgan stood and brought the chair to the side of the bed. He straddled it again and rolled his head around to release the tension that was grinding at his neck. When he was comfortable, he spoke. ‘From the beginning, Alex. And don’t make anything up, or miss anything out.’

Chapter 69

Wednesday 15th April

When DC Smart got back to the briefing room, she found Spence studying the photo of Simon Dennison that Becca Yates had provided from his personnel file. In it, the man was smiling: mouth a little open, as if he'd been caught appreciating the punch line of a good joke. Even teeth, bright eyes, strong jaw.

'I've brought you one.' She held out a cup. 'They've just serviced the machine. I can smell bleach.'

He turned towards her and took the cup anyway. 'I've gone off sex,' he said. 'I'm going to take up crochet.'

She laughed and sat down, grimacing after taking a sip of the coffee then putting it to one side. When she reached for her earphones, Spence held out a hand to stop her. He had more to say.

'Four hundred and eighty-two files. We have no chance of identifying every one of these women. There are some I've looked at where the faces aren't visible. There must be a way of whittling the numbers down to something more manageable.'

Smart jiggled the wireless mouse to bring her screen back to life and Spence pulled up a chair to sit beside her. 'You've got the most recent files. Mine are from two years ago. I think she's more likely to be on your list than the ones I'm looking at.'

'I don't know,' said Smart. 'A woman can hold a grudge for a long time.' Her tone made Spence look at her. He saw that Smart's eyes were still directed at her screen. Her face had hardened and he didn't doubt for a moment that she spoke from experience. He put the thought aside and bent closer so that he could read the file names. He reached across the desk and grabbed his laptop, pulling it so that the screens were side by side.

'What do you make of the file names?' he asked.

'I haven't given it much thought.' Smart used her mouse to return to the list of video files on the external drive she was reviewing. She ran her fingers down the list on her screen. 'Three letters and six numbers. Is that the same on your list?'

'Yup.'

'The numbers look like dates. Two for the year, then two each for the day and month.' She scanned down the list. 'Some of mine have an extra letter at the end: X, Y and Z.'

Spence looked at his own list and clicked on the properties of similar files on his own external drive. 'Same here – but look. The recordings were made at different times on the same day.'

Smart opened a couple of her files and watched a few minutes of the video. 'I think the first three letters are the girl's name, followed by the date of the film. The extra letters are where he has filmed the same girl more than once on the same day. Look.' She played the two files she had just watched and Spence nodded his agreement.

Smart grabbed a pen and reached for the papers that Hayley Goddard had left. She turned one over so she had a blank sheet. She jotted down a few of the file prefixes and showed the list to Spence.

DIA
SAR
CAT

ADA
PAT
'Girls' names,' he said.
She took the paper back and continued to write before handing it back to him.

DIAne or DIAna
SARah
CATherine
ADA
PATricia

'What about Ada?' he asked. 'I had a Great Aunt Ada, but she's been dead for twenty years, and she lived to a good age. Surely he had some limits.'

'Play it,' said Smart.

'I'd rather not.'

Smart tutted her disapproval and took control of Spence's laptop. When the file played, the sound was only just audible as it came through the headphones Spence had been using. The picture was of Dennison's bed, and the arms and legs wrapped around his body were unmistakeably black. Smart paused the action and turned to her own laptop, where she searched for Nigerian female first names.

Adaego; Adaeze; Adaku; Adaobe, and more.

'Okay.' Spence was warming to her theory. 'Scroll down to December and look for a file for the 18th. That's the day after the Forest-Fox Christmas party.

They looked at the file name together.

'CLA, for Claire. Claire Fox,' said Smart.

'Play it.'

Smart clicked the button reluctantly. She had met Claire Fox and to view the video seemed a massive intrusion of privacy. 'That's her,' she said, and was about to stop it when she noticed how this video differed from all the others she had sampled.

'Do any of your videos have Dennison's face in them?' she asked.

Spence closed his eyes as he thought, then he shook his head. 'You're right. This is the first one I've seen with his face. They looked at the paused frame. Dennison was looking straight at the camera, his smile jubilant.

'He had some balls to film himself screwing his boss's wife and selling the footage,' said Spence.

Smart shook her head. 'I've seen quite enough of Simon Dennison's balls today, thank you.'

Chapter 70

Wednesday 15th April

Morgan knew he still didn't have the full story. Like most liars, Alex had told him the version which didn't make himself look too bad. He'd watched his son look up at him to see how much of it he was buying. He'd seen a tiny smile on his lips when he was able to implicate Dorothy. He must have thought that was his trump card.

Alex was calmer when he left him and went downstairs to look for Sam. She was in the kitchen, cigarette in hand. She stubbed it out before he asked her to.

'He's okay. He's told me some stuff which I need to talk to DI Goddard about. With any luck it'll be enough for her to close the file. I need to go back to work now.'

'Thank you for coming to help. I didn't think you would.'

He picked up his keys and set off, aware that on this occasion family had been work. He'd just prioritised Alex's case over the Dennison and Fox killings. But it didn't harm that Sam had her own slant on it.

Alison Goddard was sitting at Maggy Patel's desk when he went into the office. He thanked her for waiting for him to speak to Alex again.

She pushed her keyboard to one side. 'I got your note. How did it go?'

'I've got a better understanding of what happened and where he went.'

Goddard sat back in her chair and crossed her arms. She didn't say 'This'll have to be good', but her body language screamed it.

He started slowly, conscious of limiting the version he was going to tell her to what she needed to hear to shut down the file. He would use the rest of it to sort out Dorothy Cooper once and for all.

'Alex was distressed when Sam and I argued about the draft divorce petition. He was still festering over it when he made a new friend at football practice. He says that this friend told him to teach us a lesson by staying away for a while.'

'Great friend. Great advice.'

Morgan shrugged. 'If I could get a name I'd go and have a word, but that's not happening at the moment. Anyway, this friend swaps trainers with Alex – or, I should say, lends his trainers to Alex – and –'

'Is that likely?' she asked. 'Are you buying that? At that age, designer trainers are status. I can't imagine my son would have given his away ... if I'd ever bought them for him.'

'I'm just telling you what he told me.'

'So he gets the new trainers ...'

'And his new friend's brother gives him a lift to the station and loans him money for the ticket.'

'But the ticket was pre-bought.'

'Will you just let me finish, please? I'm not saying I believe it all, but I'm coming to a bit I do believe.'

Goddard raised her hands then gestured the closing of a zip across her mouth.

'When he gets to London, he rings a few of his old friends.' Morgan watched Goddard jot down a few words. He'd predicted her issue. There were no outgoing calls on Alex's phone. 'When none of them can come into town to meet up with him, he walks about for a while. Until it gets dark, I think. He sits in Waterloo, but gets scared when strangers come and talk to him. Someone said they could give him a bed for the night. Thankfully, that's when his Spidey sense started to tingle and he gets on the last but one train back here.'

'We don't have him getting off that train on the CCTV.'

'The station isn't manned at that time of night, and the CCTV doesn't cover the exit gate they leave open. I went and had a look on my way back here.'

'Shit.'

'My exact thought. He comes through the gate and gets into a taxi: a taxi booked by Dorothy Cooper when he rang her to ask if he was in trouble. She told him it wasn't safe to come home to us.' Morgan's voice broke. All the fear and anguish that he and his wife had experienced during Alex's absence revisited him. He'd thought that he and Sam were to blame but now he knew different. As it had been ever since he met Sam, his worst problems originated with Dorothy Cooper. 'The taxi takes him to Silver Sands.'

'Where's that?'

'It's where my mother-in-law lives.'

'No, no. That can't be right. Why would she do that? Even if she does hate you, why would she put her daughter through that?'

'I'm sure she has her reasons.'

'How did he get back to the train station? Does she drive a posh black car?'

Morgan noted the edge of sarcasm in her voice. He stepped forward and rested his hand on her desk, leaning his weight towards her. 'No, she doesn't, but my brother-in-law has access to six posh black cars that belong to the funeral business. He took Alex to the station and told him to ring us when he'd driven away. That's the call he's making in the CCTV.'

She tapped on the note she'd made earlier. 'What about all these other calls? They're not on his phone.'

'He says it must be a problem with his phone, but you and I know that can't be true. I accept that there are holes in it, but I want ...'

'What is it you want me to do, Nick? It's not as if I can charge her with abduction. He went willingly.'

'What about wasting police time?'

'For a £90 fixed penalty. It can't be worth the earache you'd get from your wife. Knock it on the head. I'll put it down to a teenage tantrum and I'll tell DCI Johnson that I'm closing the file. Go and sort out this stupid divorce petition and let's all of us move on.'

'It doesn't stop me telling her she might be charged,' said Morgan.

Goddard shook her head. 'It doesn't ... but maybe it should. She's just an old woman who wanted her daughter to marry someone else. Move on.'

Chapter 71

Thursday 16th April

'You're both looking very pleased with yourselves.' Morgan could see that DS Spence and DC Smart had been waiting for him. They followed him into his office. 'Can I take my jacket off and sit down first?'

'Only if you're quick,' said Smart.

Morgan put his briefcase down without taking his policy books out. He dropped his work and personal mobile phones on the desk and draped his jacket across the back of his chair before sinking into it. Last night had been another late one and he still had work to do before this morning's briefing.

'Jenny and I had a look at some of Dennison's home movies,' said Spence.

'We're amazed he had time to do any selling,' Smart added.

'We've had a look at the file names. He had a system which might help us trace some of the girls. Or women. Well, both, I suppose. We looked at December of last year, and on the day after the Forest-Fox Christmas party there's a film of Claire Fox in his bed, at his flat. She looks a bit dazed.

'Where's this going?' asked Morgan, who was starting to feel a headache developing.

'We checked all the recordings from last year and none of them starts with a BEC,' said Spence.

'I'm sorry. Still not with you.'

'Becca Yates. She admitted they had a thing ... Remember?'

Morgan was disappointed. Was that why they were so excited? He'd hoped for something more. 'She's Rebecca. She'll be under REB. Or maybe the camera wasn't working, or maybe he wasn't happy with the recording and binned it ... or them. Maybe he was just ashamed of being with her? It was a good thought, both of you, but I'm not sure it's relevant. There might be loads more he filmed but wasn't selling.'

Spence exchanged a disappointed glance with Smart. 'I still think it's worth speaking to Becca Yates again,' he said. 'And if she gave us the right dates for their fling, then we've identified the girl in Production that he started the relationship with soon after. She looks very young and it's got a lot of orders.'

Morgan considered it, taking into account Spence's look of determination. If it was going to take one last interview to convince them, then it was quicker to agree than to argue. 'Ring her now to make sure she's at work, then leave straight after the briefing. When you get back, come and update me and we'll take it from there.'

They left him to his briefing notes and his bad mood and Jenny Smart rang the Forest-Fox main number. She asked for Gary Fox and was put through to Becca Yates, who explained that he had died unexpectedly and asked if she could help.

Smart nodded to DS Spence as she asked the questions that anyone who wanted to speak to Gary Fox would be asking, barely listening to the sanitised responses she was receiving. When she replaced her receiver, she smiled. 'She's there. We're on.'

Spence drove within the speed limit until he joined the northbound M3, when he put his foot down.

'Steady tiger,' said Jenny Smart as she grabbed the passenger door handle.

'He doesn't think this is worth doing,' said Spence. 'I think it is.'

'I thought you were getting on better with him now.'

'So did I, until he promoted the Ice Maiden.'

'Just sit the bloody exam, Dave. I'm sick of telling you. If you'd already sat it, there's no way she would be acting up now. Anyway, it must have been Johnson's decision, not Nick's.'

The rain started and Spence slowed to a more appropriate speed. It calmed him. 'What do you think is going on with their kid?'

'I've kept out of it. If you want to know, Lynn's your girl. She went with Acting DI Goddard to the Morgans' house when he was reported missing, but they've both been pretty tight-lipped ever since. I think we're safer not getting involved.'

Chapter 72

Thursday 16th April

Spence and Smart crossed the Forest-Fox Analysis car park, skipping over the puddles in the worn tarmac. Becca Yates held the door open so they didn't have to use the security system.

'I saw you from my window,' she said. 'Who are you here to see this time?'

'A couple of people, but we'd like to start with you if that's okay?' said Smart.

Yates led them into her office and closed the door even though nobody was sitting within hearing distance today. She moved some files from one of the visitor chairs and Smart sat before bending down to grab her notebook from her bag. She'd abandoned the tablet computer for now. Her keyboard skills weren't up to taking notes during interviews she was leading. Spence remained standing and leant against the doorframe.

'Can you confirm when your relationship with Simon Dennison started, and also when it finished, please?'

'Why are we back to that?' asked Yates.

'More evidence has come to light and we want to make sure we've got everything right.'

The screen of her computer came back to life when she moved the wireless mouse on its mat. Smart noticed it was a 'Little Miss Sunshine' mat from the Mr Men series. It seemed inappropriate for this scowling woman.

Yates turned her screen so that they could both see the diary she was looking at. 'This is the Q3 sales meeting, and that's the dinner. We spent that night together at the Country Club, and also three more nights during the following two weeks. I went to his flat the first time, and I invited him to my house after that, but he always insisted his flat was more convenient. My place; his place; I wasn't bothered. There was parking nearby.' Smart flashed a look at Spence, who nodded.

'Did you have any idea why he was so keen to entertain you at his flat?' she asked.

'No. But like I said, I wasn't bothered.'

Smart noticed pink blotches appear on Yates's cheeks, and at the throat of her jumper. She watched her rub her hands down her trousers.

'But you seem bothered now, Becca, or am I imagining it?' Smart clasped both hands around her pen and waited for her answer.

'Did you know Simon Dennison was filming his sexual conquests?' asked Spence.

Becca Yates jolted her head to face him. The colour in her cheeks darkened. 'I don't believe you.'

'It's true,' said Spence. 'He sold them online. We've watched quite a lot of them.'

Yates stood up, her hand to her mouth. 'That's terrible. I can't believe it. Why would he do that? I don't believe you.'

Spence stood up straight and took a couple of steps towards her desk. 'I think you do believe us, Becca, because I think you already knew. Yes?' His eyebrows arched with the question.

'When did you find out?' asked Smart. 'And did you make him destroy the ones he made of you?'

'I don't have to tell you anything. I haven't done anything wrong.'

‘It’s an investigation into his death, Becca, and you need to tell us everything you know,’ said Smart. ‘Here, or back at our place. I’m not bothered.’

Spence must have sensed that the story they were about to hear from Becca Yates was going to be long and detailed. He lifted some box files from the other visitor chair and put them on her desk before making himself comfortable.

‘Where would you like me to start?’ asked Yates.

‘Your call,’ said Jenny Smart.

‘I didn’t know about the filming, all right? I didn’t know until the day after the Christmas party. I knew how angry Gary was about Simon getting with Claire, so I went to his room to tell him to check out before Gary got up.’

‘What time was that?’ asked Smart.

She shook her head. ‘I can’t be sure. About seven, maybe?’ Smart nodded and made a note. ‘He didn’t come to the door, so I asked at the desk and they said he’d left at half past five that morning.’

‘Early bird, then?’

‘I think a lot of salespeople are. I suppose it helps to be up and about before the traffic gets too heavy.’

‘Then what?’ she asked.

‘I had breakfast and I spoke to some of the others. I sent Gary a text to say I wasn’t feeling very well and I was going home. There were activities set up for the day, but that’s never been my thing. I was pleased to make an early exit. Then I drove to Simon’s flat.’ When Smart looked up from her notes, Yates was picking at her nails.

‘Becca?’

'I got past the doorman because he recognised me. I told him that Simon had left something at the hotel and it would only take a couple of minutes for me to return it. He wasn't fussed. He was reading the paper. I went upstairs and knocked on his door. He didn't want to let me in. I thought that was because Claire Fox was still there. Then I heard it. He was watching porn.' She looked at them in turn. 'I was furious. I thought he was in there with Claire watching that stuff while Gary was back at the hotel breaking his heart. I shoved him out of the way and went through to the lounge to have it out with her. His laptop was on the settee. That's what he was watching it on. I ran over to it ... I was going to smash it ... I saw Claire Fox on the screen. Her posh dress was draped over the bottom of the bed and I saw his tattoo. He has a tattoo on his back.'

'I know,' said Smart. Becca Yates's eyes widened and she added, 'I've seen some of the videos. That's how I know.'

Assuaged by that, Yates continued. 'I picked it up and I hit him with it. I asked him who had done the filming. You could see from Claire's face she wasn't acting. She can't have known about it. That's when it struck me that he'd done it before. Long story short, when I said I'd tell Gary, he took me up to his office area and I watched him wipe my files off the drive. I told him if he'd kept copies, I'd tell all his customers about it, and that their wives and kids weren't safe.'

'What about the young lady from Production? Did you think about getting her films erased?' asked Spence.

The corners of Becca's mouth twitched before she replied with a simple, 'No.'

'Did you know he was selling the films on the internet?' asked Smart.

Her howl filled the tiny office. 'So my footage might still be out there?'

Smart would have been more sympathetic if she had attempted to destroy the films made of her colleague. Whatever happened to sisterhood?

The detectives asked a few more questions before Smart summed up by telling Becca Yates they were going to need a statement. Without bothering to hide her reluctance, she agreed to come to the station in the morning. 'Will that be an end to it?' she asked.

'That's not a promise I can make,' said Smart. 'Before we go, we need to speak to the young lady who works in Production. Can we use your office?'

Chapter 73

Thursday 16th April

Morgan read the text from Smart that said they were on their way back from the Forest-Fox offices. He looked at his watch and estimated their journey time before going to the water cooler. When he was almost back at his office door, DC Lee Tyler was just leaving.

'I've left you a note, Sir,' he said. He seemed flustered.

'Come back in and tell me instead.' He led the way. 'Have you brought the missing piece of the jigsaw?'

'I don't know about that,' said Tyler. 'The man didn't think it was anything, but you can never tell.' He rubbed a finger around the neck of his shirt, which looked tight and uncomfortable.

'Which man?' asked Morgan.

'I was asked to get in touch with the financial advisers who were at the conference between the 6th and the 8th of April.'

Morgan had assumed that Tyler was bringing information about the Thorne family, and struggled to hide his disappointment. 'I don't remember delegating that to you.'

'You didn't, but it landed on my desk anyway.'

Morgan didn't detect any sign of anger or resentment but made a mental note to have a word with whoever had originally agreed to complete the task.

'It's not been easy to speak to them. They're always in meetings or with clients. And if I hear the word Brexit again, I may scream.'

And the rest of the population, too, thought Morgan.

‘So today, I spoke to a ... God! I’ve forgotten his name.’

Morgan picked the note up from his desk and read it aloud. ‘Joshua Hanson.’

‘That’s him; thanks. Mr Hanson and his colleague Mrs Joanna Reade were outside the club having a smoke. Mr Hanson said they cut the fag break short when they heard the sound of arguing. They didn’t want to get involved, so they went back inside.’

‘Where was this? Did he say?’

‘Outside the ballroom. They used the fire-escape door.’

Morgan frowned. ‘I’m sure that door is alarmed.’

He shrugged. ‘I don’t know.’

‘Did he say if he recognised who was arguing?’

‘No, Sir, he said it was dark – but he heard men’s voices and it was a heated argument.’

Morgan asked him to forward the contact information for these potential witnesses. He would get Jenny Smart to question them both again.

‘That’s good work, Lee. Any progress on the Thorne family?

Tyler looked crestfallen. ‘I thought the financial advisers were the priority. Sorry. I’ll get on to it now.’

Morgan thanked him and watched as he scuttled away. He looked at his office clock and wondered how much longer Smart and Spence were going to be. Maybe there was just time to conscript DCI Johnson into his plans for Dorothy Cooper.

Chapter 74

Thursday 16th April

'Alison Goddard has updated me,' said Johnson when he sat with Morgan in the meeting area of his office. 'I'm glad your son is back and, I believe, none the worse for his adventure.'

Morgan wasn't sure about that assessment, but didn't argue. He felt Johnson looking at him, waiting for the reason for this visit to his office.

'I'd like to go and speak to Danny Easton about the Carl Raynor case.'

Johnson's mouth turned downwards. 'Not this again, Nick. It's becoming an obsession. Danny Easton pleaded guilty to all six murders, including Raynor. We can't keep reinvestigating closed cases, especially when we have a confession, and even more especially when I'm short of an experienced Detective Inspector. I don't know when Maggy Patel will be back and I can't sanction you going off and doing your own thing when you're the only experienced DI I've got.'

'I don't feel good about one man being sentenced for a murder when two men carried out the attack.'

Johnson sat back in his chair. 'If, and I mean if, you could prove who this second person was, what would you charge him with? Joint enterprise isn't going to stick. A solicitor is going to drive a coach and horses through that. How could this person know that Danny Easton was going to smother the lad with cushions, or whatever it was he found there. GBH? That's going to be an argument between experts. Yes, the victim lost a lot of blood but he might have got up and walked away if he hadn't been smothered. The pathologist said that the blood loss was post mortem. Gravity drained it out of him. Maybe ABH, or it might end up as possession of a bladed article. His solicitor will say that his client uses it at work and it was still in his work clothes. He tells the magistrates about his client's previous good character, the violins start playing and said client gets a suspended prison sentence. I understand that this is important to you, but you've got to let it go. It wasn't even your case.'

'It's unfinished business for me.' Morgan wasn't lying, it was unfinished business: family business.

'Have you spoken to the CPS?'

'I wanted to speak to Easton first.'

Johnson shook his head in disapproval. 'I sense there's more to this than you're telling me. I hope you're not trying to get one over on DI Patel in her absence.'

'Absolutely not. I have the greatest respect for Maggy Patel. In fact, I miss being able to talk through cases with her and I'm looking forward to her return.' Morgan was being sincere but Johnson looked doubtful.

'Okay. One visit.' Johnson moved his hands on his knees and pushed himself out of the chair. '*If* Easton gives you the name of this other person you keep going on about, and *if* he confirms that this other person did the stabbing, we'll look at it again. But I mean it, Nick, this is the end of it. I don't want you in here every week with this one. We've got enough on our plates without raking over the solved stuff.'

'Sir.' Morgan rose and made his way to the door as quickly as he could without appearing disrespectful. Johnson had been known to reverse his decisions as quickly as he made them.

‘Before you go ...’

Dammit. Not quick enough.

‘I’ve had a call from Roddy Thorne at the Gullhaven Country Club. He said you’re beginning to be a bit of a nuisance up there. Can I assure him you’ve completed your investigations up there?’

Morgan wondered whether Roddy Thorne’s direct route to Johnson was via the Rotary Club or the Saturday-morning ballroom dancing classes.

‘I’ll be sure to let you know when that’s the case,’ he said, and this time made it through the door to the safety of the corridor.

Chapter 75

Thursday 16th April

Arranging the prison visit took DI Nick Morgan longer than he'd expected. Danny Easton had a busy diary. There were pre-sentencing assessment sessions to avoid, and the prison welfare officer was coordinating with his solicitor to ensure he could attend the interview. Eventually, an appointment was fitted in after a work session the next morning. Morgan puffed a breath of air out of his mouth and picked up the phone he had just dropped on to his desk, to read the incoming text. At last, Spence and Smart were back and they were inviting him to the briefing room.

When he got there, Smart was cabling one of the hard drives into a laptop and Spence was kneeling under the desk, plugging it in. 'What did you get?' he asked.

'Becca Yates knew about the filming at Dennison's flat in December last year, and when she found out, she got him to delete the ones he'd made of her,' said Spence.

'We've also spoken to Louise Wallace. She's the girl who works in the Production department at Forest-Fox Analysis. Simon Dennison started a relationship with her after he told Becca Yates that she'd been a mistake,' said Smart, a little distracted as she scrolled down the list of files on the hard drive. 'What were the dates again, Dave?'

Dave Spence took his phone from his pocket and tapped the screen a few times. 'She said they started dating on September 14th last year and –'

'I'm not sure I'd call it dating,' said Smart. 'She was just film fodder.'

'And he told her she was a mistake on the 24th.' He turned to Morgan. 'She's insistent that she never saw him again, or had any further contact.'

'There are six films here that start with the letters LOU and fit between those dates,' said Smart, 'then one starting BRE and another two with JAC. But look, there are five more here that start LOU dated the 27th through to the 29th September. And I'm certain it's one of those that Hayley has highlighted as being a bit more –' she searched for the appropriate word '– worrying ... than the rest.'

'See if you can find it,' said Morgan. 'Maybe this Louise Wallace was spooked by what happened and she's forgotten the actual dates she was with him. Go to the last film that was taken on the 29th.'

They gathered round the laptop, nobody suggesting they project the film on to the large screen. The BBD logo appeared, accompanied by music which Morgan didn't recognise. They fast-forwarded through the introductory screens until the film started.

Dennison was sitting, fully clothed, on the side of his bed. He was watching a girl who appeared to be asleep. She was dressed in jeans and a white blouse, her face partially obscured by long dark hair. Dennison smiled at the camera before smoothing the hair to one side. He stroked her cheek, his fingers lingering on her mouth, then traced over her chin and down her throat.

The scene faded and when it returned the scenario had changed. This time they could see the girl's face. She was naked and gagged, struggling against ties which held her wrists and ankles to the bed. She was looking at something to the right of the camera and her eyes were wide with fear.

'She looks very young,' said Morgan. 'Jesus Christ!'

The image of the girl blurred as the focus of the lens adjusted to a large black dildo which was being held close to the camera. It filled most of the screen and it glistened with lubricant under the bright lighting. A man's hand came into view and started stroking it suggestively.

Morgan's phone rang.

'Turn it off,' he said as he answered the call and made for the door.

'It's not her, is it?' said Smart.

'Same hair,' said Spence, 'but Louise Wallace only looks young. I'd swear this one really is young. Very young.'

'Cherchez la femme?' said Smart.

'More like cherchez la fille.' He pointed at the screen, which was paused on the girl's terror. 'She's just a child.'

Chapter 76

Friday 17th April

Handing over his warrant card as identification, Morgan removed his wallet, phone and loose change and put them into a tray which went into a visitor locker. The officer at reception ran a metal-detecting wand over his body before patting him down with the expertise of a master masseur. He checked inside the manila folder before handing it back, then pointed to a plastic chair and mumbled something incomprehensible. Morgan sat, assuming he had guessed correctly.

When the uniformed escort arrived, she made him read the rules and regulations page again before letting him precede her through the heavy metal door. Morgan anticipated the clang of it closing but the noise still made him jump. He would be leaving in about an hour. He could not imagine how it felt to have that sound ringing in your ears and know you would not be leaving for years; or ever.

'He's one of our more popular lads,' said his escort. She walked smartly, acknowledging the trustees who passed them.

'What do you mean?'

'I mean that lots of people come to see him. I hope they keep it up when he's sentenced.'

'Who visits?' He wasn't that interested, more making conversation.

'There are the psychologists, obviously. Two of them, and they both come every week. And his mum comes as often as she can. I know Danny misses her.

There's an older lady, too; always well dressed. I don't know who she is. His grandma, maybe?'

'What does she look like?' asked Morgan.

The question seemed to worry her. She stopped walking and looked at him. 'I probably shouldn't say. You can get a list of his visitors if you put in a formal request.' He added an extra question to the mental list he had for Danny Easton and they completed the trip to the interview room without further conversation.

Morgan waited ten minutes before Easton arrived. He was wearing prison-issue tracksuit bottoms and a T-shirt which may once have been white. His face was fuller than when he had been in court, but he had already developed the pallor of those whose liberty is restricted.

One of the escorting officers took a seat in the corner of the room and did his best to look uninterested in the meeting. The other closed the door and Morgan heard the key turn in the lock.

'I've nothing to say to you,' said Easton, sitting back in the chair and extending his legs out in front of him. 'I did it; all of it.' The small smile that Morgan remembered from their previous meetings played around his lips. 'But I was suffering from an abnormality of mental functioning. I was grieving for my dad.'

Morgan recognised the wording of diminished responsibility as a partial defence to murder. 'Is that how you're going to play it?'

'My solicitor reckons it's a good defence.'

'Maybe for one death, but six is pushing it,' said Morgan.

Easton shrugged, the smile still on his face. 'We'll just have to see how it goes on the day, then.'

Morgan opened the folder and removed crime scene photographs taken in Cliffside House on the day he and his wife were supposed to be moving in. He turned the first one round so that it was the correct way up for Easton, and slipped it across the table.

Easton squinted at the picture without touching it. 'Yes, I did him,' he said. 'I told you.'

'That's the body of Carl Raynor, who we found in the front bedroom of Cliffside House.' Easton was unmoved. He continued to stare at Morgan with a 'So what?' expression on his face. 'You admitted to suffocating him.'

Easton sat forward and leant his chin on linked hands, elbows on the table. He was more engaged now. 'And I stabbed him,' he said. 'Had you forgotten?'

Morgan shook his head. 'I don't think you did.'

'DI Patel thinks I did, and it was her case.'

'Someone stabbed him. I agree with you there, but it wasn't you, was it.'

Easton turned to the officer in the corner. 'I'm bored now. I want to go back to my cell.'

'Why does Dorothy Cooper visit you so often?'

The officer had stood up and Morgan held out a hand to delay him.

'It's not been that often.'

'So she has been visiting you? Why?'

'We're friends.'

'Does she talk to you about Steven?'

'Who?'

'Her son. Does she talk to you about him?'

Easton pouted. 'She's not mentioned him.'

Morgan pulled a second photo out of the folder and placed it in front of Easton. 'Do you recognise this room?'

Easton held Morgan's eyes. His voice took on a surly tone. 'No.'

'I need you to look at the picture before you reply.'

'My answer is still no.'

'Okay. It's the room you say you stabbed Raynor in. Then he somehow got up and ran to the front bedroom, where you finished him off by smothering him.'

'I killed him.'

'I don't dispute that, Danny, but I don't think you stabbed him. I want to know who did.'

'I did.'

'Your knife doesn't fit the wounds on the body.'

Easton's eyes narrowed. 'I killed him. Everyone else is happy to leave it at that.'

Morgan opened his folder and shoved the two photos back inside. He turned to nod at the officer, who got up again and crossed to the table. 'I won't be leaving it at that, Danny. With or without your cooperation, I'm going to nail your accomplice.'

The officer knocked on the cell door, which was opened from outside. As Danny was led away, he turned back to Morgan. 'You don't know what you're taking on.'

Closing the folder and preparing to leave, Morgan mumbled, 'I think I do.'

Spence and Smart were in the briefing room reviewing more of the material from Dennison's hard drives.

Morgan tossed them each a greasy bag containing doughnuts he'd bought for them on the way in.

Smart sighed and pushed her bag away. 'I've been watching too many of these videos,' she said. 'My first reaction to a doughnut isn't entirely culinary and definitely isn't professional. I'll fetch some tea. It'll give me a chance to breathe uncontaminated air.'

Morgan and Spence stayed silent until she left the room.

'I'm not going to ask,' said Spence.

'I'm not even going to think about it,' said Morgan, pushing the bag containing his own doughnut away from him. He wasn't hungry anymore.

'How about –' Spence's suggestion was interrupted by Morgan's phone. The conversation was very one-sided, Morgan listening with a furrowed brow. 'Put him in one of the interview rooms and someone will be down in a minute.'

He responded to Spence's expectant expression with a shake of his head. 'Different case. My brother-in-law has come in to talk about Carl Raynor's death. I need to brief Alison so she can interview him. I'll be gone a while.'

'I thought we were just waiting for sentencing. Didn't Danny Easton admit to it?'

Morgan grabbed the doughnut and was opening the door as Smart appeared with the teas. She indicated which was his as he held the door open for her. 'I'm not sure when I'll be back,' he said.

Smart called after him. 'Are you okay with me going a bit early this afternoon? My mum and dad came for Easter, and with everything that's been happening I haven't had a chance to see them yet. They've booked dinner for us tonight and I want to make a bit of an effort.'

'Of course, Jenny. Have a lovely evening and apologise to your parents on my behalf.'

Chapter 77

Friday 17th April

Ali Goddard was pushing an arm into the sleeve of her jacket when Morgan got to her office.

'I need a word,' he said.

'It'll have to be a quick one. I'm on my way to Berat's Kebab House.'

'I thought a tuna wrap was more your thing.'

'This isn't lunch. This is assault with a bladed article. One of the cooks stabbed one of the serving staff because he was chatting up a customer when he's already engaged to the cook's sister. The guy's in hospital, doctor's not committing to his chances.'

'Family relationships are complex in any nationality.'

'Quite. What can I do for you?'

'There's someone who has come in for interview about a case of Maggie Patel's. The cause of death was suffocation, but there were stab wounds, too.'

'Is this the Carl Raynor case?'

Morgan was surprised she knew the name. 'That's the one.'

'The case that Johnson told you to keep out of but you're determined to keep investigating?'

'Who told you about it?'

'Johnson asked me to look at it yesterday.'

'I went to see Danny Easton this morning. He still insists he stabbed Raynor before he suffocated him, and I'm sure he didn't. The man I think stabbed him has come in voluntarily. I don't know what he wants to say.'

She looked at her watch. 'I need to get to the kebab place first, in case the guy dies; but if he's happy to wait, then I'll speak to him when I get back.'

'Would you have a problem if DS Spence speaks to him? He was involved in the case from the beginning. '

She shrugged. 'Of course not. I seem to remember he's supposed to be on my team.'

'Sorry. He likes to be where the action is.' Her lips pursed and he realised she may have interpreted his words in a way he hadn't intended. 'No offence.'

She picked up her bag and made for the door. 'If Spence does speak to him, ask him to report back to me. If this is going to turn to shit, I want fair warning.'

'It's a relief to get away from the videos,' said Smart as she followed Dave Spence to the interview room.

'Funny that, because I think investigating the boss's brother-in-law is a poisoned chalice. Whatever he says, we're going to get the blame, just because we were the ones who were there when he said it.'

Spence held the folder with the questions they had both planned after the short briefing Morgan had given them.

Steven Cooper was alone in Interview Room 1 when they went in. He looked up and asked them how long they thought he would be kept at the station.

'Depends what you're going to say,' said Spence, making himself comfortable in the chair directly opposite. Jenny Smart sat on his left and selected a new page in her notebook.

'I'm DS Dave Spence and this is DC Jennifer Smart,' said Spence. 'You may remember that we interviewed you about the deaths of Carl Raynor and Wesley Crook a few weeks ago. You denied knowing either of them. I understand you wish to change your mind and that you have information about Carl Raynor. Is that correct?'

'Nick Morgan went to visit Danny Easton in prison this morning,' said Cooper. Neither detective reacted. They knew that Morgan had been out, but not where he'd been.

Cooper banged his fists down on the table. 'This has gone on long enough. I don't want to go to France. And I was horrified when Mum hid Alex from his family. It's all got out of hand. Sam was beside herself. All because of me.' He looked around the room. 'Why aren't you recording this?'

Spence turned to Jenny Smart, who nodded and reached over to the recording system console. When everything was set up and the long beep ended, Spence identified himself and Smart and invited Cooper to do the same. He reminded Cooper that he had attended voluntarily and that he could leave at any time. He also asked him to confirm that he knew he could be represented by a lawyer before he spoke to them.

'What do you have to tell us about the death of Carl Raynor?' asked Spence.

'I didn't kill him, but I was there when Danny Easton smothered him.'

'Okay, Steven, I'm going to remind you again that you are entitled to legal representation before you speak to us.'

There was a knock on the door and Spence tutted. Smart was nearest, and got up to answer it. While she spoke in whispers, Spence and Cooper stared each other down until Cooper looked away.

‘Your brief is on his way,’ said Smart when she returned. ‘Interview suspended at 13:45 hours. She clicked the button and grabbed her pad and pen from the table. ‘We’ll be back after you’ve had a chance to speak to him.’

‘I haven’t got a brief,’ he said. ‘I just want to get this over with.’

‘Your mother has contacted Brian Gault. He’ll be here in about an hour.’

Spence slammed the cardboard folder shut and followed her out of the room. As they passed the Operations office, he called in to ask for someone to keep an eye on their visitor.

Morgan was waiting upstairs. He looked surprised to see them. ‘That was quick. What did he say?’

‘So far, he’s admitted he was there when Raynor was smothered, but that’s it. Mummy has called for reinforcements. Brian Gault’s on his way.’

‘How did she know he was here?’ asked Morgan. They shook their heads.

‘Is it back to the videos until we’re on again?’ asked Smart.

‘Looks like it,’ said Spence.

‘And I’m thinking it’s another takeaway for me. Looks like I won’t make it to dinner.’

Brian Gault arrived sooner than expected and was with Steven Cooper for only twenty minutes before Spence and Smart were called to the interview room.

‘Dinner might be back on again,’ said Spence as they descended the concrete stairs, their steps echoing around them.

‘Mmm.’ She didn’t sound convinced.

As soon as they entered the small room, Spence could see how the interview was going to pan out. There was a piece of A4 paper with a couple of short paragraphs written in Gault’s ornate script. He wasn’t surprised. It was Brian Gault’s signature approach to most of his cases. *‘I wasn’t there. A big boy did it and ran away. I don’t want to talk about it.’*

‘I have a prepared statement for you,’ said Gault after the recording system was restarted and the participants identified. ‘Would you like me to read it?’

‘Please do,’ said Spence.

Gault cleared his throat before adjusting his rimless glasses on his nose. He looked up, like a teacher checking that the class was paying attention.

‘I, Steven Ian Cooper, did not murder Carl Raynor, nor did I have any involvement in his death. I tussled with Mr Raynor when I found he had broken into my mother’s vacant property. We wrestled on the ground during which I believe that a small knife I use at work may have fallen from my pocket. I did not see Danny Easton pick up that knife and I did not see him stab Carl Raynor with that knife. I was not present when Danny Easton smothered Carl Raynor.

‘I do not wish to answer any questions at this stage. I have made this statement of my own free will and it bears my signature.’

Gault slid the sheet of paper over to Spence and pointed to it. ‘Which it does, as you can see.’

Spence already knew what his first question needed to be, and he also predicted Cooper's response, although that wasn't going to stop him asking it.

'Why did you tell us you were there when Carl Raynor was smothered?'

Cooper stared at him and Spence was struck by the change in his demeanour since Gault's intervention. He looked more confident now and less remorseful.

'We have it on the tape,' said Spence. 'You asked us to record your words, and we did.'

'You were interviewing him without legal representation. He was afraid and confused.' Gault's voice was quiet and smooth, in contrast to the strident tones he used to demolish the evidence of police officers in court.

'He was offered a solicitor and refused,' said Smart. 'That's also on the tape.'

'As I said, he was confused.' Gault smiled again, communicating that he empathised with the difficult situation the detectives found themselves in. 'I've explained to Mr Cooper that he shouldn't be out there carrying a knife for any reason, and he understands that now. I'm sure you don't need to bother the courts with this. You already have Mr Easton's confession to killing Mr Raynor.'

'Interview suspended at 14:55 hours,' said Spence, and nodded to Smart, who stopped the recording. 'Wait here.'

Morgan was leaving the viewing suite as Spence and Smart got to the door. 'How did Gault even know he was here? We could have been looking at joint enterprise, accessory after the fact, anything! Now we'll be lucky to make possession of a bladed article stick.'

Spence waited for a pause in the rant. 'Can we do this upstairs? They're only just in there.' He nodded back to the door of Interview Room 1.

Morgan glowered but led the way.

'Is there anyone from the CPS in today?' asked Spence.

'No, I checked before we went down,' said Smart.

'Pity.' Spence always fancied his powers of persuasion more when he dealt with prosecutors face to face. At the end of a phone line, an anonymous voice could say 'No' more easily.

'Do what you can and let me know,' said Morgan. 'If we have to release him under investigation, I'd rather do that than settle for anything less than ABH.'

Chapter 78

Friday 17th April

Nick Morgan got home in time to sit down with the rest of his family for their Friday evening meal of spaghetti Bolognese, garlic bread and a green salad. They sat at the table in the dining room and it felt good to be laughing and joking together. He remembered when the twins had first been old enough to sit at the table with them, and how, as they had got older, the meal became a messy competition. Who could suck strands of pasta up fastest? It resulted in sauce flying everywhere, including, once, into Alex's ear. Tonight, the family debated which parent made the best Bolognese sauce. Alex sided with his father and Vicky with her mother. Honours even.

When the meal was over and the twins were clearing the table, Nick and Sam took their glasses of wine to the lounge. Sam slumped down at one end of the sofa leaving room for him to join her. When he sat in an armchair, her posture stiffened.

'You didn't tell me you were investigating Steven,' she said.

'For obvious reasons.'

'Mum says it's to distract me from your affair.' The sentence hung in the air and he couldn't help laughing.

'She's putting a very interesting spin on things. She should have considered going into politics.'

'So, you tell me your side,' she said, taking another mouthful of red wine.

'Is it worth me bothering?'

‘If I’m being played, I want to know whose side to take.’

From past experience, Nick knew that his wife was on the side of the last person to speak to her, as long as that was her mother.

‘Your brother came to the station today to confess to his involvement in one of Danny Easton’s murders.’

‘The body you found upstairs,’ she said.

‘Yes. He told Dave and Jenny he was there when the lad died. Then suddenly your mother finds out he’s at the station, and your boyfriend’s mate Brian Gault turns up. After that, Steven’s memory plays tricks and he wasn’t there after all. We’ve let him go ... for now, but when I find out who told your mother –’

‘I rang her,’ said Sam. ‘Steven told me he was going to speak to you and I rang her because I thought she should know.’

‘You’ve interfered in an investigation.’

‘He was entitled to have a solicitor present when he was being questioned.’

‘He didn’t want one.’ He realised how loud his voice had become and apologised. ‘I’ve suspected he was involved for months and I made the mistake of telling your mother when she made me angry. I expect it was her who told you that Ali Goddard had joined the team, and I’m also betting that the divorce idea was down to her, too. That caused an argument which made our son run off to London, but ...’ He stopped. He hadn’t intended telling Sam about her mother’s involvement in Alex’s disappearance. He looked at his glass of wine. It had made him indiscreet.

‘But what?’ she asked. ‘Tell me.’

He took a deep breath. 'Alex came back to Gullhaven about eight hours after he disappeared. He rang your mother and she sent a taxi for him. She put him up for thirty-six hours while you smoked, drank and cried. She only let him go because Steven found out and shamed her into it. That's your precious mother.'

'I don't believe you.'

'Ask Alex. He'll tell you.' He looked around for the bottle before remembering they had left it in the kitchen. When he got up, his work phone vibrated, skittering across the coffee table. He wasn't on duty. It must be important.

'Yes, Jenny?'

'I've found the scared girl.' Jenny Smart's voice was a whisper and he struggled to hear.

'Can you say that again? Where are you?'

'I'm in the ladies loo at East Gullhaven Country Club. My parents booked dinner here.'

Nick Morgan's heart sank. The area wasn't particularly well served for restaurants, but why did they have to pick that one? Johnson would be on his back first thing on Monday.

'Has anyone recognised you?' he asked, and was surprised when she started her reply with a girlish giggle.

'I'm dressed for a night out, Nick. Even you wouldn't recognise me.'

He didn't comment. Best not to risk a rebuke from Human Resources and a three-day course on gender respect.

'She's changed since the video. She's lost a lot of weight ... and I mean a lot. Her arms are stick-thin and her face is gaunt. She's also had her hair cut. Some might say it's elfin now, but with the weight loss she looks like a boy.'

'You're sure it's her?'

'I recognise her eyes and her cheekbones.'

Morgan smiled. He knew there were still some misogynistic officers who didn't think women made as good a job of policing as men. They were wrong, and this was a case in point. How many men who viewed the sexual content of that video were concentrating on eyes and cheekbones? DC Jenny Smart had, and she put them all to shame.

'The name on her badge is Louisa. That fits with the LOU initials on her video. She's working on the cloakroom desk. What do you want me to do?'

'Go back to your mum and dad and enjoy your meal. If you can get away with taking a sneaky photo of her on your phone, it will help us when we follow it up, but don't take any risks, I don't want her disappearing.'

'Okay. Will do.'

'And that's great work, Jenny. Thank you.' He ended the call and tried to remember why he was standing at the lounge door when he had been in the middle of a conversation with Sam.

'Wine,' she said, holding out her empty glass. 'And it sounds as if you've got something to celebrate.'

Chapter 79

Saturday 18th April

Sam Morgan was having trouble concentrating as she poured orange juice into four glasses. The smell of toast was making her queasy and she'd already burnt one batch and had to scrape it into the bin. She kicked the kitchen door closed before the smoke detector in the hall activated.

Alex joined her and responded to her greeting with a grunt. He glugged his juice down before reaching out for the scraped toast. Sam remembered Steven at the same age: always hungry; boys seemed to have hollow legs.

'We're going shopping this morning,' she said. 'Just you and me. To replace the trainers that disappeared.'

'I've got trainers,' he replied. 'Why don't you just give them back to me?'

'Because you won't tell us where you got them. Anyway, the police still have them.'

He glowered at her and she held out her arms in a gesture that said 'Your fault, not mine'.

'Where's Dad going?'

'He's taking Vicky to choose some wallpaper for her bedroom.'

They had agreed on this morning's shared parenting responsibilities before turning in last night. It had been their most amicable conversation since the divorce petition, and partway down the second bottle of red she had thought they might even share the same bed that night. It hadn't happened, but he had kissed her cheek when he left her outside their bedroom door. The thaw in their relationship, if it was coming, was going to be slow.

'I smell burning,' said Nick. She hadn't heard him come in, and jumped. When she turned, she smiled. His hair was tousled and he still looked a bit sleepy. He was wearing a greyish-blue T-shirt with long sleeves. It had shrunk over numerous wash cycles and it magically reappeared each time she tossed it in the bin. It gripped his torso and arms, complementing his musculature, developed over years of hardcore DIY. She made a mental note never to throw it away again. It was the exact colour of his eyes and he looked good in it.

He crossed to the grill and saved the current batch of toast from cremation, moving the slices around so they coloured evenly. 'Any sign of Vicky?' he asked.

'She's putting her make-up on in the bathroom. I had to come downstairs to pee,' said Alex, rolling his eyes.

Nick gave his wife a warning look. Victoria's previous experiments with eye shadow, mascara and lipstick had resulted in her looking like a cross between a prostitute and a clown. He didn't want to suppress her creativity, but he wasn't taking her out in public like that.

'I'll go,' said Sam. 'Look after the toast.'

'I already am.'

The shops were busy, and Alex was being a pain. Sam swore that if he asked her again why he couldn't have his Airmax trainers back, she'd commit filicide. There wasn't a judge in the land who would convict her – those that were parents, anyway.

They were sitting at a table in the corner of a café. She had a pot of tea, and he was demolishing a buttered muffin, washing it down with cola.

The café was filling up and they would soon be under pressure to move on. No time like the present. She took a deep breath.

'Why did you call Grandma when you got back from London, rather than asking us to come and pick you up?' If he looked puzzled or confused, she would know Nick was lying about her mother.

Alex stopped chewing and swallowed. His expression was one she recognised, although she hadn't seen it for a while. It made him look vulnerable and he used it when he was in trouble.

'She said you were both furious and I was scared.'

'Did she say that when you rang her?'

He nodded, tearing a piece of muffin off and shoving it in his mouth.

'Then that doesn't answer my question. Why did you ring her first, and not us?'

'You're just like Dad. It's all "Why this?" and "Who that? And where did the trainers come from?" You should both be working on staying married, not getting on my back.'

His outburst surprised her, and when he made to get up from his chair, she only just managed to grab his arm and pull him back. She looked around, acknowledging the looks of disapproval and sympathy in equal numbers.

'Your dad and me ... We're adjusting to living here. He's given up a lot so I can be near Mum and help her. I think sometimes it gets to him.'

‘Vicky and I know you want a divorce. We’re living in the same house and we’re not kids. We hear what’s going on. Vicky says you’ve got a boyfriend and that’s why Dad is sleeping in the spare room.’ Sam felt her cheeks redden. This was not the conversation she had planned. ‘She told me he came to visit when I was in London, and he’s been back again.’

‘He came to the house with Grandma. That’s what friends do when they know there’s a problem.’

‘He’s not a friend of Dad’s.’

Sam had never wanted to be the sort of mother who used the phrase ‘You’ll understand when you’re older’ to get out of a difficult discussion, but now she was tempted. She realised she was still gripping Alex’s arm, and let him go.

‘If you’re getting a divorce, will we be able to pick who we live with?’ he asked.

‘We’re not getting a divorce, Alex. Now, finish your muffin and let’s get these trainers and go home.’ She squeezed the teabag in the pot and poured the last of her drink into the cup. She wanted to be somewhere quiet and on her own to think this through. Her mother had hidden Alex from her and had left her to picture the worst fates imaginable for him. Why would she do that?

Chapter 80

Monday 20th April

Morgan was taking off his jacket when DC Lee Tyler appeared at his open office door. 'You're keen. I hope you've not been here all weekend.' He'd meant it as a joke and was mortified when Tyler avoided his eyes and started to shuffle from one foot to the other.

'I didn't have anything else on,' he said.

'You need a work–life balance, Lee. You've got a long career ahead and I don't want you to burn out before it's started. What's that saying? "Nobody said on their deathbed that they wished they'd spent more time at the office."'

'I was looking into the Thornes, like you asked me to.' Tyler held out a folder for him to take. His bottom lip was protruding. He looked like a chastened child.

'I think they also say "Never listen to a man who doesn't take his own advice".' Jenny Smart's voice held a smile as she appeared and joined Tyler in front of Morgan's desk.

Morgan took the folder and thanked him. He laid it on his desk and opened it before turning his attention to Jenny Smart. He wanted to hear more about the girl she'd seen at the club on Friday, but Tyler seemed disinclined to leave. He relented. 'Can you give me the gist and I'll read it properly later?'

Tyler nodded, his speech breathless with enthusiasm. 'The club is late filing its company tax return, and it's not the first time. Last year, profits were down by sixty per cent and the current building is mortgaged to the hilt.'

‘Do we have anything on the family members?’ asked Morgan.

‘I’ve nothing on Mrs Francine Thorne, or the daughter, but there’s a historical conviction for drink driving against Mr Thorne ... Roddy, that is. It was 2002. And I did find this.’ He leant over Morgan’s desk and scooped the loose pages out of the folder, flicking through them until he found what he wanted. ‘There’s a DV marker on the family home.’

‘Saving the best till last, were you?’ asked Smart.

Morgan didn’t know what Francine Thorne looked like but he couldn’t imagine any woman being a match for the bulk of Roddy Thorne in a domestic violence scenario. ‘I wasn’t expecting that,’ he said. ‘Why isn’t it on his record?’

Tyler looked confused. ‘He hasn’t got a record.’

‘You just said he was done for drink driving.’

‘That was Roddy Thorne. The call-outs were for Hugo Thorne. Two of them. One was for an assault and the other was for threatening behaviour; both against his mother. She refused to press charges and the assault was before body-worn cameras, so there was no video or photographic evidence taken at the scene.’

‘Hot-headed,’ said Morgan. ‘That’s how Roddy described his son when we first met them. Remember, Jenny? When we got there, they were shouting at each other.’

‘Oh, I remember all right, and I saw more of that on Friday when I was at the club.’

Morgan held up a hand to stop her. He beamed at Lee Tyler. ‘This is great work, Lee. Well done and thank you.’

DC Lee Tyler left with a smile on his face that said his day had been made, and it wasn't even nine o'clock yet. Morgan waited until he'd gone. 'What have you got for me?' he asked.

'Oh, not the club again,' said Johnson. He threw his pen down and it bounced across his desk and landed at Morgan's feet. He resisted the urge to bend down and retrieve it. 'The Thorne family are very well connected locally. They can't possibly be involved in supplying participants for some sort of seedy sex film business.' Morgan opened his mouth to reply, but Johnson hadn't finished. 'And if there are hundreds of these questionable videos, why are you so desperate to follow up on this one?'

'Because, apart from Claire Fox and a girl called Louise who works at Forest-Fox, this is the only footage where we think we recognise the female. DS Smart saw her working at the club on Friday evening.'

'It's not as if we can prosecute Simon Dennison for making the films.'

Morgan wanted to shout that he was missing the point. He wasn't trying to build a case against Simon Dennison, he was seeking a motive for the attack which resulted in his death.

'Jenny Smart watched Hugo Thorne arguing with a young girl in the car park of East Gullhaven Country Club on Friday evening. He ended up dragging this girl to a car and shoving her in before he drove off at speed. We're checking the registration. Jenny thinks the girl features in one of Simon Dennison's films.'

'Lovers' tiff?' asked Johnson.

Morgan shook his head. 'I'm not interested in what happened in the car park, apart from the fact that it links Hugo Thorne to that video.'

'I don't see how.'

Was Johnson being deliberately obtuse, or could he really not join the dots? Morgan exhaled before spelling out the link that he and Smart had made.

'If I was of a hot-headed disposition – and I'm quoting his father's description of Hugo, not mine – and someone I was close to had been sexually assaulted with an XL-sized dildo, I might be tempted to return the favour.'

Johnson sat back in his chair. His shoulders dropped. 'Ahh, I see where you're heading. What are you planning?'

'I'm planning to bring Hugo Thorne in for questioning regarding the assault on Simon Dennison.'

Johnson took off his glasses and placed them on his desk with more care than the pen had enjoyed. 'I know you trust DC Smart's identification, but let's make sure the girl at the club is the girl in the video before we get ahead of ourselves. We need to be certain. Roddy Thorne has the ear of the PCC.'

'Of course. We wouldn't want to upset the PCC.'

Morgan relented and bent to pick up the pen. He placed it back on Johnson's desk, but just far enough away that he would have to stand up to reach across for it.

Chapter 81

Monday 20th April

Spence and Smart approached the reception desk at the club. Monica, the trainee receptionist who had helped identify Simon Dennison nearly three weeks before, gave Dave Spence a welcoming smile and asked how she could help.

Spence smiled back. 'I've got another photo,' he said. 'Can you help me identify one of your colleagues this time?'

Her smile vanished. 'No one else has died, have they?'

'No. Nothing like that.' He held out his hand and Jenny Smart put her phone into his palm. She had already selected the photograph she'd taken of the girl at the cloakroom desk. Monica took the phone and studied the screen carefully.

'She's not a colleague. That's Louisa Thorne. She's Roddy and Francine's daughter.'

'She was working on the cloakroom desk on Friday evening,' said Smart.

'Francine had to come in to help out and they don't like to leave her alone. She's not been well. Maybe she got bored in the office and went looking for something to do.'

'Is she here today?' asked Spence. Monica shook her head.

'What about Mrs Thorne?' asked Smart.

After consulting a screen on her computer, Monica confirmed that Francine Thorne had a shift in the dining room starting at six that evening.

'We're going to need her mobile number,' said Smart.

'I can't give you that, but I can ring her and ask her to get in touch with you.'

'Thank you for that offer. We'll contact her ourselves,' said Smart, reaching for her phone.

Back in the car, Dave Spence rang Morgan's mobile while Smart drummed her fingernails on the steering wheel.

'The girl in the video is Louisa Thorne, Hugo's sister.' Spence had got through to Morgan, who swore. 'What do you want us to do?'

DC Jenny Smart's phone started to vibrate. She reached through to the footwell behind her driving seat and retrieved it from her handbag. She got out of the car before accepting the call and Spence raised a hand in acknowledgement. He was waiting for Morgan's decision.

'I trust Jenny's identification skills, but this is sensitive and we need to be absolutely certain. I want you both to go to the Thornes' house and speak to the daughter. What was her name?'

'Louisa,' said Spence.

'Right. I want us all to be very clear that this isn't an interrogation. This is just to be certain that it was Louisa Thorne in that video. Understood?'

'I get it,' said Spence. 'Have you got the address?'

'Who's driving?'

'Jenny.'

'Okay. I'll get Lee to text it to your phone. Can I speak to Jenny before you go?'

'She's on the phone.'

'Okay. Tell her: softly, softly. This girl is a victim, not a criminal.'

'Hang on,' said Spence. 'She's just getting into the car. You can tell her yourself.'

He put his phone on speaker and rested it on the dashboard.

'I've just told Dave that we need confirmation of your identification of Louisa Thorne in that video. It's no reflection on you, it's DCI Johnson walking on eggshells again. Have a word with her, but be gentle, okay?'

'I've just had a call from Joanna Reade,' said Smart.

'Who's she?' Spence and Morgan spoke together, and with the speaker effect on the phone, the question seemed to bounce around the car.

'She's the financial adviser who heard the argument outside the ballroom on the night Gary Fox died.'

'Did she call to sell you a mortgage?' asked Morgan.

'No. She called to say she recognised one of the voices she heard.'

'Who was it?' said Morgan. Spence kept quiet this time.

'She recognised him because she had argued with him earlier that evening. Something about vegan meals? She said he overreacted and shouted at her in a high-pitched squeaky voice, and that's the voice she recognised outside. She says it was Hugo Thorne.'

The line went quiet and Spence exchanged a look with Smart. 'We're outside the club now. Do you want us to go in and pick him up?' he asked.

After a further short pause, Morgan's voice filled the car again, but he sounded thoughtful. 'We need to be a bit strategic here. I don't want Hugo Thorne's custody clock ticking down while my best interviewers are out confirming a victim identification to appease the PCC.' His voice changed. Decision made. 'Let's stick with the plan. You two should go and speak to Louisa Thorne. I'll get the address sent to Dave's phone and I'll drive over there and meet you. Then, Jenny, I'd like you to come back to the station to start preparing an interview plan for Hugo Thorne, and I'll go with Spence to pick him up at the club.'

They agreed the plan and Smart started the car.

'Alternatively, we could go in and grab him now,' said Spence, looking back with regret towards the main entrance to the club. His phone vibrated with the arrival of a text advising them of the Thornes' address.

Chapter 82

Monday 20th April

'How many houses is this?' asked Spence as Smart drove between the two brick gateposts at the end of the drive.

'There's only one number on the post.'

'But it's huge. It looks like the house Nick Morgan would be living in if the architect of Cliffside hadn't been a cokehead.' She gave him a warning look, but he could see she was amused.

Smart rang the bell and they waited. 'I'll bet you a pound it's a maid,' she said.

'You're on,' said Spence, who had already heard the unmistakable sound of high-heel shoes on a tiled floor. He was sure that staff would wear flats.

The door was opened by a woman who Spence put in her early forties. Her jeans fitted the curvature of her hips, their pale apricot colour highly impractical for a woman who did her own housework. An embroidered white shirt was open at her neck by just the right number of buttons to display a small gold cross on a chain.

'Good morning, Mrs Thorne. I'm DS Dave Spence and this is DC Jenny Smart. We need to speak to your daughter as part of our inquiries into the death of Simon Dennison.'

Francine Thorne ignored the proffered identification. 'My daughter is resting. Can you come back another time?'

'I'm sorry, Mrs Thorne. It's very important we speak to her now.'

'She is recently discharged from a private clinic. Her mental state is fragile.' Her French accent seemed to grow stronger as she pleaded Louisa's case, and Spence felt bad, knowing they were obliged to insist.

'I'm sorry,' said Jenny Smart. 'We must speak to her today and we'd rather do it here than have to take her to an interview room at the station.'

'Wait.' Francine Thorne closed the door and her footsteps retreated down the hall.

'Now what?' said Smart.

'We wait, I suppose. But I'm not going to wait for long.'

The door opened again less than four minutes later, but Francine Thorne was still blocking their entry.

'My daughter's mental state is fragile. She is being treated for depression, anxiety and anorexia nervosa. I have just now spoken to her therapist. He told me that any interrogation will set back her treatment by weeks, if not months. Please, can it wait?'

'We're not here to interrogate Louisa. We just have a few questions. It won't take long, and I promise, if she becomes distressed, we'll stop and come back another day,' said Smart.

'Are you a mother?' she snapped.

'Not yet.'

Francine Thorne looked surprised by Smart's answer and took a moment to consider it. She stood to one side and held out her hand to show that they should precede her. 'Door at the end ... Go straight through,' she called from behind them.

Spence followed Smart towards the back of the house and saw her rummage in her pocket. She produced a coin, which she offered him. He shook his head and mouthed that he'd cheated on the bet.

Smart opened the door into a large lounge with three designated seating areas. One set of matching sofas surrounded a coffee table which was bigger than Spence's dining table, the second had a leather sofa and chairs facing a wall-mounted screen, and the last was furnished with four armchairs and a wood burner as their focal point. Patio doors led out to a terrace, pool, and more than enough grass to justify a ride-on mower. 'It's beautiful,' said Smart. Her complete flat would fit in this room with space left over.

'But a lot of work. Please sit.' Francine pointed towards one of the settees at the coffee table. Spence sat next to Smart. His preference for wall-leaning wouldn't work here; he'd be too far away from the action.

Francine sat opposite. It looked as if she was hoping to answer their questions on her daughter's behalf.

'Can you please fetch Louisa so we can get started?' Spence recognised Smart's gentle voice and wondered if she used it to get her own way in her personal life; if she had a personal life. Francine looked as if she was going to start the argument again, but instead she harrumphed and left them alone.

'You okay with this?' he asked.

'I'm fine.' Smart grinned back. He envied her adaptability. He was much more comfortable questioning hard-assed villains than their victims.

Soft footsteps descended the stairs and Francine Thorne steered her daughter through the lounge door. Spence prepared to stand, before quickly changing his mind. He was afraid his height might intimidate her.

Louisa Thorne was wearing pyjamas with a cartoon character on the jacket pocket. Her white fluffy slippers dwarfed the small feet at the end of stick-thin legs. She sat next to her mother on the settee opposite them and grabbed one of the cushions on to her lap. She hugged her arms around it: a barrier and a comfort.

'My name's Jenny and this is Dave.'

Louisa looked at them with eyes that were too large for her gaunt face. 'I remember you from Friday at the club. Red fake fur jacket with sparkles on the shoulders.' Spence glanced across at his colleague. That was a side of her he'd never seen.

'That's right,' said Smart. 'You've got a good memory.'

Smart started asking Louisa about the work she did at the club. The answers she got were short and lacking detail until Francine interrupted. She told them both that Louisa helped out occasionally, but that they were always careful to stay within the licensing and employment laws. It had been drummed into Louisa that she shouldn't chat about work in case someone misunderstood and got them all into trouble.

'How old are you, Louisa?' asked Smart.

'Sixteen.'

'Are you still at school?'

Louisa looked to her mother for guidance and Francine answered for her. 'She's off sick at the moment.'

'I'll have to repeat the year. If I go back at all,' said Louisa.

'Of course you'll go back. You'll have to if you want to be a nurse.' Her mother reached out to put an arm around her.

‘Midwife.’ The volume of the word and the anger with which she spat it surprised them all. Louisa shook herself free of her mother’s embrace and hurtled out of the room. They heard her run up the stairs before a door slammed.

Chapter 83

Monday 20th April

'I did say,' said Francine as she hugged the same cushion to her chest. 'It's like this all the time.' She sighed heavily. 'Louisa loves kids, but she's had a few health problems and now we've found that she can't have them. She's devastated.'

Smart glanced at Spence. He gave her a nod of encouragement.

'Mrs Thorne, we believe that Louisa was the victim of a serious sexual assault last September. What can you tell us about that?' asked Smart.

Francine Thorne frowned. Her eyes darted between the detectives. 'What sexual assault? Who said anything about a sexual assault? So she went to a party. She sent me a text to say she'd be late back, but she stayed out all night. It was just the once. That's what happened.'

Smart shook her head. 'We believe it was more than that.'

Francine stared at them both and then looked down to her hands, which were white-knuckled and rigid.

'Louisa was always Papa's girl. He would let her do and say whatever she wished. If I said "Non" she waited for Roddy to come home to say "Oui". When she came back after the party, she was a bit out of it. They had a huge row. He accused her of using drugs and he called her a slut. After that, he wouldn't speak to her. It went on for weeks. I begged him to make up with her but he told me to stay out of it.

'When she stopped eating, I thought she was just trying to get his attention and I ignored it for a while, but the weight loss was rapid and I made her come with me to the doctor. He diagnosed anorexia and referred her to a therapist.' Francine had been waving her arms around with the enthusiasm of an airport ground controller, but she stopped now. 'We decided not to wait and paid for her to see a psychologist. After a few appointments, she sent us back to the doctor, who referred her to a gynaecologist at the hospital. That's when we found out she wouldn't be able to have children. Something to do with the damage done by the anorexia, I suppose.'

'Were you actually told that?' asked Smart.

'Louisa was already sixteen years and didn't want me in her appointments with her. So no, I was just the taxi driver.' Bitterness added an edge to her voice. She took a deep breath. 'Is that everything you need? I should go to her.' She stood again and waited for them to do the same.

'And how are things between Louisa and her father now?' asked Smart. Neither officer had risen from their sofa. Francine looked irritated. 'They started to get on better just before Christmas, and more recently they're closer than ever. She's been trying to eat to please him, but it's a long process.' She frowned at them. 'Nobody's ever mentioned sexual assault. It can't be. I won't believe it.' She looked up to the ceiling; reaching out to her daughter.

'Can you tell us the date of the party she went to?'

She shook her head. 'Not exactly. I know it was September because it was very busy at the club. The function rooms were heavily booked. We had to get the punters in and out within tight time windows so we could honour each booking without making us look like a sausage factory. We were all working double shifts.'

‘Including Louisa?’

Her eyes narrowed; she was wary now and didn’t answer.

‘Francine, this isn’t about employment law,’ said Spence, conscious that he’d given in to his impatience and interrupted when he’d promised Smart that he wouldn’t.

‘Louisa worked the cloakroom desk. She was amazing. Once you get a queue there, the whole system falls apart. Car park overflows because the first group are waiting to collect their coats and leave while the next lot are arriving. Drinks and canapés are late, so meals have to be delayed. Everything knocks into everything else. I think that’s why Roddy was so upset with her. We only needed her for two more evenings. She didn’t show up for the first, and she wasn’t fit to work on the second.’

‘Could you tell us which evenings she was missing?’ asked Smart.

‘If I log on to the club’s conference and events diary, then yes.’

‘Could you do that for us, please?’

‘And could you also give us details of all the bookings for five days before and five days after those evenings?’ Spence called after her as she left the room.

Jenny Smart got up off the sofa and followed her. ‘While you’re doing that, I’ll just make sure Louisa is okay. Which door is it?’

She was nearly at the top of the stairs when Francine reappeared. ‘What did you say?’

‘I asked which door is Louisa’s room. I want to make sure she’s okay before we leave.’

Francine's mouth dropped open, but Spence was now at her side. 'The dates, Francine, please?' He steered her back through the open door into a home office.

Jenny Smart opened the first door she came to and popped her head in.

'Hi Louisa. Are you okay?'

Chapter 84

Monday 20th April

Morgan pulled into a parking space at the entrance to East Gullhaven Country Club.

'Reserved parking for the ladies' golf captain,' said Spence.

'I'm not dragging the manager's son halfway across the car park in handcuffs. This is the nearest space and I'm sure she'll understand. Come on.'

Spence had one foot on the tarmac when his phone rang. 'Yes, Jenny?'

Morgan was walking away from his car when he heard Spence wind up the conversation.

'I'll tell him.' Spence got out and walked to where his boss was reading the menu board while he waited. 'Jenny has spoken to Louisa and she's confirmed that she was at Dennison's flat in September. She's coming in to make a statement this afternoon. Francine's going to bring her.'

'It's going to be a real family outing. We should have booked a charabanc.'

When they got to the top of the steps, a concierge stepped forward to open the doors.

'I'm afraid you can't leave your car there, Sir,' he said, his expression a perfect blend of insincere regret and self-importance.

Morgan had his ID ready and flicked it open. 'This says I can. Now where will I find Hugo Thorne?'

'Ask at reception.' He waved a dismissive hand in the direction of a woman who was waiting at the end of a long queue.

Morgan thanked him and strode straight to the desk. He held his ID up and made his apology to a man who was undertaking a close analysis of his bill with the receptionist.

'I'm looking for Hugo Thorne,' he said.

The young man behind the desk was already flustered. He looked around for support, but Morgan saw that the other staff members were suddenly engrossed in their current task.

'Hugo Thorne. *Now*, please.'

The receptionist's attention was caught by movement beyond the doors to the car park. Relief flooded his face and he pointed to the driveway. 'The laundry van's just leaving. Hugo will be in the linen store.' He gave directions which Morgan didn't need. He had noticed the sign during previous visits. He led Spence to the conference suite corridor and through an open door on the left. They made their way round neat mounds of white laundry sacks into a room with banks of metal shelving. There were three washing machines at one end, next to two industrial-sized tumble dryers. The air was humid. There was an overwhelming smell of hot fabric.

Hugo Thorne had his back to them. He was diving into one of many dark blue laundry sacks and producing neatly folded towels, which he stacked on the shelves. He was singing softly.

'I'm sure you remember me, Hugo,' said Morgan. The singing stopped. 'I'm arresting you on suspicion of involvement in a sexual assault on Simon Dennison. I'm further arresting you for involuntary manslaughter of the same victim.'

Thorne's eyes widened. 'It's nothing to do with me. I don't have anything to do with any of it.'

Spence stepped over some piles of towels and reached to take hold of his arm but Thorne jerked it away from him. Spence sighed. He reached into his pocket. 'That was silly. Now I'll have to cuff you.'

'Cuff him to the rear,' said Morgan, 'and I'll walk through reception behind you. No point in making a bigger exhibition of this than we have to.'

Spence clicked the cuffs into place and raised a hand to hold Thorne by the elbow. He brushed some flecks of blue which had transferred from Hugo's sweatshirt to the sleeve of his dark suit. When he looked up, Morgan was watching.

'Wait,' said Morgan. He took his phone from his pocket and selected a number.

'It's DI Morgan here from Central and Southern MCU. Can you send a scene investigator over to East Gullhaven Country Club, please? Specifically, to the linen room. I want samples taken from the blue bath and hand towels, and a blue linen sack brought in for comparison analysis in a case of sexual assault. Victim's name is Simon Dennison.' He watched Hugo Thorne as he spoke, and thought he might have spotted a muscle twitch at the edge of his mouth. His next call was to the operations centre to arrange the urgent despatch of a uniformed patrol to guard the linen room until CSI could collect their samples. They would have to wait until the boys in blue arrived.

Chapter 85

Monday 20th April

Jenny Smart grabbed a sheet of paper from her desk and followed Morgan to his office.

'Well done on persuading Louisa Thorne to come in,' he said. 'Dave's just booking Hugo Thorne in downstairs. When he comes up, we'll talk through an interview plan.'

Smart nodded. 'You should be aware that I don't know how much we'll get from Louisa. When she admitted being at Dennison's flat, she got very emotional. It's not going to be an easy conversation. And her mum wants to sit in, although I'm not sure that'll help. They don't seem close.'

Morgan shook his head. 'We'll get an independent Appropriate Adult in. I don't want the mother to hear what Louisa has to say. She could be involved in what happened to Dennison. For all we know, they could all be involved.' He went on to provide an account of Hugo Thorne's earlier arrest at the club, including the dark blue laundry sacks filled with towels, and the blue fibres they were shedding.

'Like we found on Simon Dennison's sweatshirt?'

'And around his nostrils.'

Smart frowned. 'But he might have picked them up from towels in his room if he had a shower before he went to the beach.'

'I won't argue with that, but he also might have had a laundry sack pulled over his head and breathed them in.

Maybe we can conduct an experiment. You know how CSI love an experiment.'

'Well, isn't this the day that just keeps on giving,' said Smart, 'because I had a message when I got back from Chez Thorne.'

'I thought you were looking pleased with yourself. Lord Lucan turned up, has he?'

'Better than that. I've traced the ownership of the cuffs. At last.'

Morgan started to feel that tickle of anticipation he got when an investigation was coming together. 'Go on.'

'The print they found on the cuffs belongs to a retired officer from Manchester who died a few weeks ago.'

'I remember.'

'I couldn't get next of kin information from GMP, but I got a mobile number for the deceased officer. Don't look at me like that. I'm not telling you how. I left messages on that number and his son has rung me. He and his mum are just back from Tenerife. They were arranging the sale of his parents' holiday apartment.'

'And the cuffs?' asked Spence, keen to get her back on track.

'Sold using an online auction site before they flew out. He's going to text me the buyer's details when they've had something to eat and he switches on his computer.'

Morgan slapped his palms down on his desk. 'Christ, you wait weeks for a lead and three come along all at once. Now we just need Hugo Thorne to put his hands up and admit he assaulted Simon Dennison to avenge what happened to his sister, and if he also wants to admit the murder of Gary Fox for some reason we don't know, I won't stop him.'

‘Fat chance.’ Dave Spence’s voice came from the doorway to Morgan’s office. ‘My ears are bleeding from his protestations of innocence.’

Chapter 86

Monday 20th April

'Hugo Thorne. Is he yours?' The Custody Sergeant threw his eyes heavenwards. 'What a pain in the arse.'

'What's the problem?' asked Morgan. He was going to interview Thorne with Spence so that Jenny Smart could speak to Louisa.

'Refused point blank to have a solicitor. Kept saying he didn't need one because he's not done anything wrong. Even when he was told he was facing a serious allegation.'

'I'd rather have him represented,' said Morgan.

'Oh, don't worry. I spoke to Duty before she left and she's been with him for half an hour. Interview Room 4.'

'Great. Thanks.'

Spence led the way and opened the door. Morgan waited to be hit with the usual interview room smells: unwashed bodies, stale coffee and fear. He was pleasantly surprised to be greeted by a more acceptable perfume palette. Raspberry and honey with a hint of amber. Morgan appreciated it until he saw who was wearing the scent. Harriet Lees-Langham, his adversary from his first case at Gullhaven. The day which kept on giving had suddenly snatched it all back again.

'Hmph. I should have known you were SIO when I saw the paucity of the disclosure.' Lees-Langham's opening complaint was accompanied by a bad-tempered waving of A4 paper in the direction of the detectives. 'However, I've taken instructions from Mr Thorne and advised him of his rights.'

One glance at Hugo Thorne told Morgan that he'd made the wrong decision. He should have lined Jenny Smart up to accompany Spence into this room. This lad looked as if he'd been manipulated into taking on the school bully and fully expected a pounding. Smart would have given him her best calming smile before delivering that pounding, cleverly disguised as supportive listening and gentle persuasion. He thought about making a tactical retreat but his ego kept him in his chair. Lees-Langham would have seen his exit as a victory, and he wasn't about to give her the satisfaction.

'Would you like some water, Hugo?' asked Spence.

'No, thank you.'

'You've arrested my client for sexual assault and involuntary manslaughter,' said Lees-Langham. 'On what basis?'

'I'll come to that once he's answered some questions,' said Morgan. He turned his gaze to Thorne although he was still communicating with the solicitor. 'And if his answers to our questions indicate that he wasn't involved in the offences, we will de-arrest him and he'll be free to go. So I hope you can both see that it's in his interests to talk to us.'

He glanced back at Lees-Langham, who responded with a look that would stop global warming in its tracks. Spence started the recording and did the introductions. Thorne's stare didn't move from Morgan. He looked surprised when DS Dave Spence started to read from his notes.

'Simon Dennison died sometime on the night of 31st March and 1st April. We know he'd been drinking, and maybe using cocaine. We believe he was separated from colleagues at a beach party and assaulted with a dildo.

This caused him to vomit. We believe he was gagged at the time and because of that he inhaled his vomit and asphyxiated. What can you tell us about that?'

'Nothing. I was with my family in Dorset.'

'Yes, of course. The trip to prepare the holiday cottage.' Spence nodded and took his time before asking his next question. When did you last see Mr Dennison?'

'I think it was a couple of weeks before he died. I went out to admire his car, but also to ask him to move it. He was in one of the designated parking places.'

'Was he a friend?'

'He came to the club quite a bit, so I knew him by sight. I'd served him in the bar, but that's about all.'

'Were you on duty when he was here for the sales meeting back in September?'

'Probably. September was busy. We were all here for most of the time.'

'DS Spence, can you enlighten me? Where are we going with this? What has a sales meeting in September to do with the offences you've charged my client with?' Lees-Langham had paused her typing to intervene.

'I'm establishing Mr Thorne's relationship with the deceased,' said Spence.

'Well, I'm establishing that he doesn't have to engage with any of this,' she replied, staring at her client until he was obliged to make eye contact.

Morgan sat forward. He wanted to move this on. Thorne was sweating and it was time to apply a bit of pressure.

'When did you go to the holiday cottage?'

'Sunday afternoon.'

'And how long was the drive?'

‘Sixty miles, give or take. It took us an hour and three quarters.’ Morgan allowed himself a small smile. He sensed the glibness of a rehearsed alibi.

‘Which route did you take?’

‘What do you mean?’ asked Thorne. His brow furrowed and he pushed his glasses up his nose, made slippery with sweat.

‘It’s not a difficult question, Hugo. There are harder ones coming. Which route did you take?’

Lees-Langham must have sensed that this new line of questioning was heading for dangerous territory. She reminded Hugo again that he didn’t have to answer.

‘I don’t know. I was in the back listening to music. I can’t stand being in a car without music and Dad’s the opposite. I had my headphones on. Anyway, Dad was driving. He knows the way.

‘When did you set off?’ Morgan’s voice sounded gruffer.

Hugo shook his head. ‘I can’t remember.’

‘When did you arrive, then? Was it still daylight, or had it got dark?’

‘I’m not sure.’ He dragged each word out.

‘Come on, Hugo. It’s only three weeks ago. You must remember if it was dark when you got there.’

‘I don’t remember.’

‘No matter,’ said Morgan. ‘If you were listening to music on your phone, the cell site data will allow us to plot your route.’ He sat back again and Spence resumed the questioning.

‘What did you do when you were at the cottage? Young lad like you; not much entertainment out there. Did you have any evenings out?’

‘No. We were all very busy, so we vegged out in front of the TV in the evenings.’

‘To be clear,’ said Spence, ‘you’re telling us that you didn’t leave the cottage from the time you got there to the time you left?’

‘That’s not what he said,’ Lees-Langham chipped in. ‘Ask him a proper question.’

‘I will. If you’ll let him answer it.’ She pursed her lips and prepared to resume her typing.

‘From the time you arrived at the cottage on Sunday 29th March to the time you left on Friday 3rd April, did you leave the cottage for any reason?’

‘Dad and I went to the DIY store.’

‘How often?’

‘Twice.’

‘Were those two trips your only outings?’

‘Yes.’

‘Let’s talk about laundry bags,’ said Morgan.

‘What?’ The pitch of Hugo’s voice rose.

‘How many dark blue laundry bags does the club have on inventory?’

He shook his head. ‘I don’t know. It varies. At any one time, some are at the laundry and some are in transit.’

‘That doesn’t affect the inventory number, Hugo. The club buys these bags for their sole use. It’s got your logo on them. Someone must have placed an order for the bags; maybe more than one order. If I can find those orders and then trace where all your laundry bags are, am I going to find that one is missing?’

‘They get damaged. We buy more. There’s no way of knowing how many we have at any one time.’ He slumped down in the chair, but his answer seemed to satisfy him because he looked back at Morgan and Spence in turn, his face expectant.

'You spend a lot of time in the laundry, Hugo,' said Morgan. A statement, not a question.

'Not that much.' He replied as if he'd been professionally slighted.

'But you were there when we arrested you.' Thorne nodded before agreeing vocally for the recording.

'You were dealing with blue bath and hand towels, and some of the fibres and fluff had come off on your clothes.' No agreement this time. Not even acknowledgement. Morgan persevered. 'We found a significant amount of blue cotton fibres and fluff on Simon Dennison's clothes, and on his face. How would you account for that?'

'Perhaps he took a towel to the beach with him. I would if I was going swimming.' Morgan had to hand it to him. It was a plausible answer.

'We also found DNA on his fingertips. Is it yours?' He waited for an answer which never came. He sat forwards again. 'Well, we're going to know very soon, aren't we.'

'No comment,' said Thorne, and Morgan agreed to Lees-Langham's request for a break. He wanted a word with Jenny Smart before she spoke to Louisa Thorne.

Chapter 87

Monday 20th April

'You've just missed her,' said DC Lee Tyler. 'Mrs Thorne arrived with her daughter and she's gone to speak to her.

Morgan cursed. He'd wanted to remind her about not having Louisa's mother present at the interview. It could be a coincidence that the family cropped up so often in their inquiries, but his twenty-odd years in policing had blunted his belief in coincidence. He made his way back downstairs to the viewing room and turned on the screen in time to watch everyone settle into their seats.

Louisa Thorne took her seat opposite Jenny Smart, and although he had been warned, Morgan was shocked to see how thin she was. He zoomed in on her face and recognised that 'dead behind the eyes' look he had seen with other victims of abuse. He didn't recognise the other two women. One sat next to Louisa, and Morgan guessed that she was a solicitor; the other took the chair from its position beside Smart and moved it to the end of the table.

Smart started the recording system. She completed the formalities and got the introductions underway with her own details. She nodded to the solicitor, who followed suit. 'Also present is Sophie Jenner as Appropriate Adult.'

Morgan nodded. He was sorry he'd doubted her.

Smart took a bit of time to point out the cameras and explain what was being recorded. When Louisa confirmed that she didn't have any questions, Smart moved her laptop to one side and opened her folder.

‘When we spoke this morning, Louisa, you told me that you sometimes help your parents out at the club by working on the cloakroom desk. Do you remember?’ Louisa Thorne nodded before starting to gnaw at skin on the side of her left forefinger. The solicitor placed a hand on her arm and reminded her that she needed to answer in words, and loud enough for the recording.

‘Your mum told us that you were very good at it. You can even match coats to owners without the ticket.’ Louisa looked down at the damaged skin on her finger, which was starting to bleed. Sophie Jenner reached into her voluminous tapestry handbag and peeled a tissue from a generous pile.

‘How well do you remember helping out during last September’s busy time?’ Smart let her question lie there until Louisa was forced to look up to see if she was missing something. ‘You were at the club every night. Star performer. Then you went to a party at Simon Dennison’s flat and it all stopped. What can you tell me about that party?’

‘I’ve advised Louisa that she doesn’t have to answer your questions,’ said the solicitor.

Smart kept her eyes on Louisa. ‘She’s right. You don’t have to. But I think you’ll feel better if you do.’

Morgan watched Louisa shake her head. Her expression remained blank. She wasn’t in the room; she must be in some safe place they hadn’t reached yet.

Smart’s voice softened. ‘Is it easier if I tell you about the party?’

Morgan blew his breath out through pursed lips. ‘Steady, Jenny,’ he murmured.

‘I think it turned out to be a party for two.’ Jenny Smart’s voice was now little more than a whisper, but

Louisa's eyes widened as she spoke. 'I think Simon Dennison invited you to his party and when you got there you found yourself on your own with him. Am I right?' Louisa clasped the shredded tissue to her lips, but her eyes remained dry; focused on Jenny Smart.

'Maybe you weren't too worried at first? Maybe you were flattered? He treated you like a grown-up, didn't he?'

Louisa blinked slowly and Morgan watched tiny teardrops gathering at the corners of her eyes before they ran down her cheeks. Now she was back at that 'party', immersed in the memory. Sophie Jenner peeled another tissue off her pile and folded it into Louisa's hand. This time, she left the rest of them on the table.

'What did he give you to drink? Was it champagne?'

'Asti Spumante,' said Louisa. 'It was sweet. I didn't like it.'

Morgan reflected on the level of planning that had gone into the rape of this vulnerable girl. Plying her with sweet alcohol that he expected her to like.

'Do you remember how much you drank?'

'Not much. I didn't like it. He got a bit angry with me, especially when I kept asking when everyone else was going to turn up.'

'Did he give you anything else?'

'He brought me orange juice. He said it was just orange, but I could smell the alcohol. My parents are in catering. I've been around booze most of my life.'

'How much of that did you drink?'

'Two or maybe three. I don't know. Then I started to feel a bit woozy. I remember hearing him laughing, but not much more after that.'

'Do you remember sending a text to your mum?'

She frowned before shaking her head. ‘No.’

‘What else do you remember?’ Smart put her elbow on the desk and rested her cheek on her palm. Morgan nodded his approval. She was trying to fix Louisa’s attention on her to the exclusion of the other two women and the cameras.

‘When I woke up, it was daylight and Simon was dressed. He brought me tea and a bacon sandwich, I think. Yes, I definitely remember a bacon sandwich. The bedding was all bloody. I was bleeding. He told me he was sorry and that if he’d realised I was a virgin he wouldn’t have suggested sex. I didn’t even remember having sex. He gave me some ibuprofen for the pain and told me to get dressed so he could run me to the station. He told me I was a mistake.’

Morgan shook his head. Not even a lift home. What a bastard. He thought again about his daughter and what he would do to any man who treated her this way. When he forced his attention back on the screen, he saw that Louisa Thorne was dabbing her eyes with the tissue and that Jenny Smart was standing. She must have called a break.

When he heard the door to the viewing room open, Morgan didn’t need to look round. ‘Well done, Jenny. You’re doing a grand job.’

‘I don’t doubt it,’ said Dave Spence. ‘I wouldn’t want her interviewing me if I had something to hide.’

‘Sorry, I thought you were her.’

Smart appeared at Dave Spence’s shoulder and she closed the door behind her. Morgan repeated his congratulations as his detectives sat down.

‘How’s it going?’ asked Spence.

Smart updated him and he nodded his approval.

‘What do we still need from her?’ she asked. ‘I’ve got a feeling she’s going to clam up soon.’ She selected a new page in her book and clicked her biro in preparation.

‘When did she last lay eyes on Simon Dennison?’ suggested Spence.

Smart jotted it down before making a suggestion. ‘Maybe she was at the club when Forest-Fox had their Christmas do? Francine told us that they didn’t like leaving her alone, so they might have taken her to the club even if she wasn’t working.’

Morgan was pensive. He spoke slowly. ‘And I’d like to know a bit more about Louisa’s relationship with her father. He was furious with her about the so-called party, but they’re close now. What changed?’ He looked back at the screen. Louisa’s trembling hands were wrapped around a cup of something that was still steaming. She was staring directly into the camera, her haunted eyes drilling into him. He wished he could read her thoughts. He struggled to look away until her gaze moved to the solicitor, who must have spoken.

‘Have you asked Hugo Thorne about the argument with Gary Fox?’ asked Smart.

‘Not yet,’ said Morgan. ‘I’m figuring new arrest, new custody clock. Let’s make full use of the time we’ve got on this one first.’

Smart left to continue her interview with Louisa Thorne.

Morgan muted the volume of the audio and swivelled his chair round to face his sergeant. ‘Why do you suppose Hugo Thorne got so twitchy about the drive to Dorset? Let’s see where the techies have got to with the cell site data for his phone.’

‘Okay, but why don’t we ask Francine Thorne? She was in the car and she’s sat upstairs waiting for Louisa.’

‘That’s good thinking, Dave, but she’s unrepresented.’

‘Why would she need representation? It’s just a simple question about the route they took to Dorset.’

Morgan wondered if DCI Johnson would see it that way, then decided he didn’t care.

Chapter 88

Monday 20th April

Francine placed the cardboard cup on the table in front of her and looked up with a smile. When she saw Spence and Morgan, her face straightened. 'How much longer will my daughter be?' she asked.

'Francine, this is DI Morgan who is leading the investigation into Simon Dennison's death,' said Spence.

'How much longer?' she repeated.

'Louisa is in safe hands, Francine,' said Morgan. He sat opposite her. Spence leant on the doorframe.

'I know that you were all at the holiday cottage when Simon Dennison died, but it's part of my role to make sure we're not overlooking anything, so I'd ask you to humour me by answering some questions.' Her eyebrows and shoulders rose simultaneously in what Morgan thought epitomised a Gallic shrug.

'Were you at the cottage for the whole week? Sunday 29th March to Friday 3rd April?'

'My husband and son only returned on that Friday. Louisa and I stayed for a few more days.'

'And that was for shopping?'

'Yes. It also gave us some time together, which we don't get while I'm working.'

'How did you get to the cottage?'

'My husband drove.'

'In one car, then?'

'His car. Yes.'

'So how did you get back?'

'I drove Roddy and Hugo to the station and they came back by train. Louisa and I came back by car.'

'Which route did you take?'

Another shrug. 'Same one I always take. The A road to the motorway and ... If you provide me a map, I can show.'

'That's okay, Francine. What about your husband's route?'

'I don't know. I slept most of the way.'

Morgan felt that tingle at the top of his spine again. Francine Thorne was the second person who professed to have no memory of that journey. It must be significant.

'When did you leave?'

'I remember that. It was after Sunday lunch service, and I stayed to balance the takings.'

'Then you went home?'

'No. Roddy picked me up. I had packed the night before and Hugo and Louisa were already in the car.'

'At what time?'

'I don't remember. I'm sorry. I know it was later than planned.' Morgan thought she looked genuine, but she could just be a good actress.

'I remember waking up and not recognising where we were.' Francine Thorne became more animated. 'I know the route well because I have gone many times to sort out issues our clients report. Tap dripping; no hot water; things like this. When I asked, Roddy said it was a lovely day so he'd taken a detour.'

'When did you arrive at the cottage?'

'It was getting dark because I couldn't see the garden properly.'

'Sevenish?'

'Maybe. I don't know. I made up the beds when we got there and I got straight into ours and slept through until morning.'

'Is that normal for you?'

'I always sleep well at the cottages. It's the sea air, I suppose.'

'Did you have any reason to come back to Gullhaven during that week?'

She snorted. 'Of course not. There was enough there to keep us busy.'

'What about the others?'

'No. None of us had a reason to come back. Why would we?'

'Why would your husband take a less than direct route when you'd been late in leaving in the first place?'

Francine cringed and then smiled. 'Roddy likes to drive fast. He must have found a route without speed cameras. This would please him.'

Morgan thanked her and assured her that Louisa wouldn't be much longer, before he and Spence left her to the remains of her cold coffee.

'She was very convincing,' said Spence.

'I agree. But I'm interested in her speed camera theory. Why would you pick a route that takes a lot longer so you can drive outside the speed limit? Let me know when the cell site analysis comes in from Hugo's phone. He says he was listening to music all the way, so we should get a good idea of the complete journey.'

Chapter 89

Tuesday 21st April

DC Jenny Smart was on her phone when Morgan got to her desk the next morning. Her forehead rested in her palm and she looked exhausted. Morgan grabbed the vacant chair next to her and listened in.

'I understand that the shop is busy, but this is important. I'm investigating a serious assault that resulted in the death of a young man and –' She caught Morgan's eye and her expression changed to one that asked the Almighty to give her strength. 'Well, I may send a patrol to bring you in so you can make a statement, even if you do have to close the shop.' She slammed the phone down and swore. It was out of character and Morgan realised he wasn't the only person whose levels of frustration were peaking.

'The cuffs were delivered to a newsagent in Southampton. That's the only address the family who sold them have.' She pointed to the phone. 'That was the owner of the shop and he denies all knowledge. He insists that he wouldn't have time or resources to run a mailbox service. I'm paraphrasing here, his English isn't great.'

'That's a pity. I had hoped they were delivered to be signed for at the Thornes' house. The evidence trail would have been ace. Come on, I'll buy you a coffee and we'll see where we are.' He looked at his watch. 'We've got less than five hours on Hugo Thorne's custody clock and I need a decent coffee in me before I take what we've got to DCI Johnson.'

Smart looked reluctant to leave her desk.

‘Come on.’ Morgan got up and beckoned to Spence, who was walking towards them. ‘We’re going for coffee, Dave. Decent coffee. I’m buying.’

After two large cups of palatable coffee and an unpalatable encounter with DCI Johnson, Morgan rang round his troops to see if anyone had anything new to report. With nothing forthcoming, he cancelled the morning briefing and called Spence and Smart to his office.

‘John Jackson’s at the CPS desk today and I’ve had a word. He doesn’t think we have enough to charge Hugo Thorne. Not even if the blue fibres match up.’

‘What about the witness who heard him arguing with Gary Fox?’ asked Smart.

‘We haven’t talked to him about that, yet,’ said Morgan.

Smart’s phone pinged with an incoming email. ‘It’s Digital Forensics,’ she said. ‘Simon Dennison’s case.’ She scowled at her screen as she swiped. ‘I can’t read this on here. I’ll have to go to my desk.’

Morgan nodded his understanding. Phones were great when you were out and about, but some reports needed a full sized screen.

When she got to the door, Smart’s phone pinged again. ‘Hugo Thorne’s DNA results,’ she said. ‘I’ll read them at my desk and come straight back.’

When Jenny Smart returned, she was waving two printed sheets of A4. ‘I don’t know what to tell you first,’ she said.

Morgan stared at her. ‘Tell me something ... anything. I don’t care what order it comes in.’

She slapped a printout down on his desk. 'We've got the computer used to buy the cuffs. Well, not quite the computer, but the building it's in.'

'Please tell me it's not in an internet café in the middle of London,' said Morgan.

'It's in a house on the outskirts of East Gullhaven.'

He picked it up. The paper was still warm from the printer. The top half of the report comprised lines of meaningless data, the bottom half, a map. Dead centre was a red location identifier. 'That's the home of Mr and Mrs Thorne and their two offspring,' said Smart.

Morgan smiled, first at Smart and then at Spence. 'That's great news. Now, please tell me that the DNA on Simon Dennison's fingertips comes back to Hugo Thorne.'

She shook her head and he slumped in his chair.

'It's not his DNA, but the lab is reporting a familial match.'

'Francine or Roddy, then?' said Spence.

'Or Louisa,' said Morgan. 'I'm not ruling her out.'

Chapter 90

Tuesday 21st April

Samantha sat in the reception area of Silver Sands having discarded the well-thumbed magazine which had been thrust at her when she said she'd wait. She could feel her heart beating hard in her chest; hear it in her ears. Alex's confirmation that he had stayed with her mother had shocked her and she had been trying to prepare what she was going to say to her ever since. Nothing she came up with began to represent the anguish and panic she'd experienced while her own mother was ordering pizza and letting him sleep on her sofa.

She wasn't ready to talk to Nick about it – not yet, anyway. That conversation would be laced with 'Told you so' and 'Welcome to my world'. She wanted to confront her mother first. Maybe she would be able to justify it? But if that was the case, why had she gone into hiding?

When Samantha couldn't get a reply from her mother's mobile over the weekend, she'd rung Silver Sands and was told that Mrs Cooper had made a last-minute decision to join a residents' outing to York for a few days. She wouldn't be back until Tuesday afternoon. Samantha had been speechless. She imagined her mother sitting on a coach surrounded by fellow residents for whom she didn't have a kind word. With any luck, there had been endless choruses of 'Ten Green Bottles' on the coach, and compulsory bingo every evening. That would teach her.

She saw increased activity through the open door of the office before catching the unmistakable noise of a diesel engine. She got up and waited by the door. She was ready.

She watched as the coach disgorged its cargo of smiling residents. Some of the staff hurried out to help those who needed it, and she heard laughter and friendly banter through the open doors. No sign of her mother.

The driver crawled into the storage space at the side of the coach and pulled cases and weekend holdalls out, stacking them neatly. A young man dressed in overalls with the Silver Sands logo on his pocket appeared from the side of the building wheeling a large trolley, which he started to load. Samantha assumed this was Danny Easton's replacement.

As the coach driver said his goodbyes, Dorothy Cooper descended the steep steps and passed him without acknowledgement. She was carrying her travel bag, which she must have kept with her.

When Dorothy Cooper's eyes fell on her daughter, Samantha was pleased to see that she looked surprised and a little uncomfortable. Her earlier confident gait was replaced by the more hesitant steps she used when it suited her.

'I wasn't expecting you, dear,' she said, holding out her bag for Samantha to carry. 'You're looking haggard. Are you not sleeping well?'

Samantha hoisted her handbag over her head so she had both hands free. With one, she took the travel bag; with the other, her mother's arm. 'You and I need to have a word, Mother.'

Dorothy tried and failed to snatch her arm back. ‘I have just had a very tiring and tiresome weekend. This will have to wait.’

‘Not this time,’ said Samantha, and steered her towards the stairs.

Chapter 91

Tuesday 21st April

'We're not going to get the cell site information before Hugo Thorne's custody clock runs out,' said Morgan. 'Can you nip downstairs and release him under investigation, please.'

'Okay, but when are we going to speak to him about Gary Fox?' asked Smart.

'When we have a clearer idea about motive,' said Morgan. 'All we have is the financial adviser's statement that she thought it was Hugo, but really it could be anyone. It could even be Roddy Thorne.' The incredulity on Smart's face made him laugh. The idea of a man that size having a high-pitched voice wasn't likely. 'Okay, maybe not Roddy.' His phone rang.

'Yes, Ali? How goes it?'

Alison Goddard didn't answer immediately and he looked at his screen to check if the call had dropped.

'I've been trying to reach you,' she said.

'Sorry. I was in a meeting with Johnson about a suspect. I had my phone on silent. Did you not leave a message?'

'No. I wanted to tell you this myself.'

'Okay, I'm with Jenny.' He didn't think it harmed to let Alison know he was with someone, although he wasn't sure why it mattered. Their relationship was solely professional now.

'I spent an hour with one of the prosecutors this morning,' said Goddard. 'It's a no go with charges for Steven Cooper.'

'What? Nothing at all? Not even possession of the bladed article?'

'What she said was that none of the assault-related charges would stick because Danny Easton has already admitted to the stabbing and the suffocation.'

'But the knife must have got there somehow ...'

'No witnesses, no admissions, no evidence, no case. I pushed it hard, Nick, I really did, but she was adamant. She said that even if we limped it through the evidential stage, it wouldn't pass the public interest stage. She all but accused me of being over-zealous because I'm Acting DI and am trying to prove something.'

He heard the resentment in her voice and wondered if she thought he'd set her up.

'I'm sorry, Ali. I thought we had a case. I still think we do, but I hear what you're saying. Thanks for trying.'

'I'll see you later,' she said, and ended the call.

He sat in silence, racking his brain for another approach, another charge, some way he could implicate Steven Cooper in something ... anything. Some way he could hurt Dorothy Cooper for what she'd done to his family.

He heard singing and looked up at Jenny Smart. 'What the fuck ...?'

'It's from Disney. I've seen it twice with my nieces. I thought the words were relevant. *Let It Go*. And, if you don't, I'll start singing it again and neither of us wants that to happen.'

'Christ, you're not kidding,' he said, and relaxed, clasping his hands behind his head. 'Don't ever sing in my office again.'

They both laughed. ‘On second thoughts,’ he added, ‘don’t do it anywhere in this building. And that’s an order.’

Chapter 92

Wednesday 22nd April

Having dropped the twins off at school, Samantha headed for town. She had plans. Hairdresser, a new outfit, and food shopping. Special food shopping. When her phone rang she wasn't surprised to see that it was her brother.

'You'd better be at work,' she said.

'I've had a haircut and a shower and I'm in my black trousers and tie. I've even ironed my shirt. And yes, I'm sitting at my desk with newly sharpened pencils and my best sympathetic face on. How did you manage it?'

Samantha didn't answer his question; he didn't need to know. The expected argument with her mother hadn't happened. Dorothy had listened to her describe her trauma when Alex was missing without interruption. With growing confidence, she had moved on to her mother's obsessive hatred of Nick, again without a response. As her unburdening of years of resentments neared an end, she'd remembered that it was Steven who had insisted that Alex must return home immediately or God only knew how long her anguish would have continued. He deserved her gratitude and support and she told her mother to reinstate him in his role in the family business immediately because she wasn't going to be a part of it.

'When did she ring you?' she asked.

'Yesterday, at teatime,' said Steven. 'She said she'd spoken to you and that she'd decided to give me another chance.'

Samantha's mouth curled into a sneer rather than a smile. Trust her mother to put her preferred spin on it. 'Don't cock it up this time,' she said.

'I'll try not to. And can you thank Nick for me?'

'What for?'

'I heard from the detective that was dealing with the body in your bedroom. I'm not going to face any charges.'

'That's great news. Let's hope we can all move on now. I'm not going to let our mother wreck my marriage just because she wanted Graham as a son-in-law. And I suggest you grow a pair and stand up to her, too. What's that saying? Are you a man or a mouse?'

Steven replied with a high-pitched squeak which made her laugh.

'I'm making a special dinner tonight and I'm going to burn the draft divorce petition in front of Nick and the kids to show us all that things are going to be better. Why don't you come?'

'Love to. What shall I bring?'

'Just yourself. You can bring something when she's started paying you a salary.'

'Done.'

Chapter 93

Wednesday 22nd April

Morgan looked around the briefing room at what was left of his team. Since the murder of Gary Fox, it had almost halved in size as detectives and uniform officers had been reassigned to other more recent cases. Dave Spence stood at the door, not officially part of the team, but unable to stay away.

'Good morning, everyone, and thank you for all you've done so far on these cases.' It didn't harm to start a briefing with a positive message. 'You'll be aware that we released Hugo Thorne yesterday, but since then we've got details of the route that the family took between the club and their cottage when they drove there a few days before Dennison's death.'

He stuck a map on to the whiteboard. It showed the direct route in red and the route plotted from cell site information in blue. Next to it, he stuck a photo of a white Vauxhall family saloon. 'This is Roddy Thorne's make and model of car, although his is silver.' He stared at the pictures and saw that his audience were doing the same.

'They left late and arrived when it was getting dark. I'm estimating that the trip took somewhere between two and a half and three hours. Why? Why that route? Francine Thorne says it was to avoid speed cameras and she got me thinking. What if Roddy Thorne was looking for a route that avoided *all* cameras? That's what he'd need if his alibi was that the family spent the whole week in Dorset and that nobody travelled back to

Gullhaven.' Morgan turned to his team. 'What do we think?'

He had to ask the question. It seemed such a simple theory that he worried it might have a glaring flaw that he hadn't noticed. He looked across to the door where Spence was smiling.

'Volunteers to drive the scenic route and call in at any establishments with road-facing cameras, please. I need two per car; some of these roads are narrow and I don't want accidents, but I don't want to miss any cameras either. It's three weeks since Dennison died, let's hope there's CCTV still available.'

He read Maisie's text a few times. What did it mean? Was it a simple invitation for a coffee this evening? Was it the end?

Morgan jumped when DC Smart called his name. He was sure his face was flushed when he looked up, but so was hers.

'Got them,' she said, unable to suppress her smile.

'Where?' He didn't have to ask who she meant.

Smart opened a map of Dorset and spread it out in front of him. 'There's a T-junction here, with a pub on the corner. They have live music a couple of nights a week and the crime-prevention boys recommended CCTV to cover all exits and the car park to strengthen their entertainment licence application. Cars have to stop at the lights for the junction and we have Roddy Thorne's car at ten to two in the morning driving from the direction of Gullhaven towards their cottage. It looks like three up, or four. We've identified Roddy as the driver, just by the bulk of him, and the front-seat passenger is wearing glasses. When the car turns, there's a flash of reflected streetlight in them.'

Morgan rubbed his hands. 'Roddy and Hugo. That's great work, Jen. Just what we needed.'

'Shall we go and bring them in?'

He looked up at his office clock. He considered the time it would take to complete the required procedure before they would be able to start asking their questions. Find them; bring them in; process them; contact solicitors, and wait for those solicitors to take instructions. By then, they would be requesting a meal break, and soon after, time to sleep. They might get an hour of questioning in, but not much more.

'I think we'll do an early-morning wake-up call at home,' said Morgan. 'That way, we can search the home without a warrant.' He checked his watch. 'Can you arrange a briefing for five, please?'

'Got it.' Smart flicked her notebook closed and Morgan nodded decisively. He reached for his phone. He'd ring Ali Goddard first to request the loan of Dave Spence in the morning, then he'd update DCI Johnson. He would work on not sounding too smug before he made that call.

Chapter 94

Wednesday 22nd April

The atmosphere in the briefing room sizzled with excitement and Morgan struggled to get everyone to pay attention until he resorted to shouting at them.

'We're not there yet. There's still a lot of work to be done.'

'Tomorrow morning, we're going to arrest Roddy Thorne and his son, Hugo, under suspicion of their involvement in the sexual assault and involuntary manslaughter of Simon Dennison. Hugo was released under investigation for those offences yesterday, but we have new evidence today which puts the Thorne family car on the route from Gullhaven Cove beach back to the holiday cottage at ten to two in the morning that Dennison's body turned up. Evidence from Hugo's phone, as it happens.' He noted a couple of satisfied smirks. Officers loved it when a suspect supplied the evidence which led to their conviction.

'I want them brought in and processed separately. I'm sure there's already been enough coaching of alibis without us giving them an opportunity for revision. And once they've gone, I want a thorough, but tidy, search. Mrs Thorne and her daughter, Louisa, will still be there. The kid has mental health issues.'

'What are we looking for?' asked Lee Tyler, whose eyes were bright with excitement.

'There's a mobile phone, or a SIM card. It was used to send threatening texts to Simon Dennison at Christmas. He also took a call from that number at eleven p.m. on the night he died. That call was just under three minutes long and I believe it was the call that lured him to the beach. Gary Fox also received a text from the same number late in the afternoon on the day of his death. That text confirms a meeting at the club for eight p.m. that evening. I don't need to remind you that he didn't return from that meeting.' He consulted his notes. 'Next, we want the pink fluffy fabric they used to disguise the cuffs. And I want every mascara pack in the house. Someone snuggled up to Dennison before he died and I want to know who.'

'It still might have been a work colleague at the dinner,' said Smart.

'Or it might have been Francine Thorne,' said Morgan.

Spence's voice boomed from the back of the room. 'Or Louisa.'

'Thank you DS Spence,' said Morgan, who realised he'd probably had that coming.

'And I want all the phones, tablets, laptops and PCs. That should at least identify which of them was used for the purchase of the cuffs. A bottle of whisky for anyone who finds a dark blue laundry sack with Simon Dennison's vomit in it.'

'I don't know if one bottle's enough,' said Smart screwing up her nose.

The doorbell rang and Samantha put down her glass. The text from Nick had said he would be late but hopefully home before nine. He was cutting it fine: only fifteen minutes to go. And where were his keys?

'Sorry I'm late.' Steven thrust a bottle of fizz into her hands as he stepped over the threshold.

'You're not last,' she said, glancing down the drive. Her ears scanned for the sound of an approaching car but received only the waves crashing at the bottom of the cliffs. Thirteen minutes to go. 'The twins are starving. They've eaten every snack in the house. Alex has even had an apple, so it's not all bad.'

'Something smells good.' Steven hung his jacket on one of the hooks in the hall and she led him to the kitchen.

'It's lamb Wellington. I went to the farm shop to make it special.'

He crossed to the cooker and stirred the gravy. For a moment, she was offended. This was her house, her cooker and her gravy – but then she remembered she was just a custodian. At any time, Dorothy Cooper could change her mind and tell the Morgan family to get out because she preferred Steven to live there. Nick spoke often about getting something in writing and she had resisted it. Now, knowing what her mother was capable of, she was thinking he had a point.

The loud music coming from upstairs stopped and the twins appeared.

'We thought you were Dad,' said Alex.

'Sorry, mate. He must still be at work.' Steven waited until they came down before offering his nephew a high five and kissing Vicky on the top of her head.

Sam checked her watch. Seven minutes to go.

Maisie's duvet lay on the floor in an untidy heap.

'I can't reach it,' she said. 'And I'm too comfortable to want to move.' Her head nuzzled into his neck;

painted nails stroked his chest and her leg bent over his thighs. 'I don't ever want to move.'

He wrapped a muscled arm around her and kissed her cheek; a chaste kiss, in stark contrast to the passion they had just shared. 'I can't reach it either, but I don't want you to get cold.' When he attempted to sit up, she made a sound he normally associated with his daughter when she was sent to her room to get on with her homework. He eased his left arm down to the floor, stretching his fingers until the duvet was within grasp, and pulled it over their entwined bodies.

Maisie sighed. 'It's like our own little tent where the world can't reach us.' She moved her head and kissed his lips, her fingers tracking down his torso. 'How much longer can you stay?'

He reached his arm out again and patted the bedside cabinet until he found his watch. Nine twenty and time to make a decision. He stroked her cheek and ran his fingers through her hair, combing it back from her face. 'I have to go, Maisie. I'm sorry.'

'You don't have to be sorry. I know the score.'

He washed in her en-suite using the unscented soap she kept there for him, and wondered again if he should just get back into her bed and face the consequences another time.

He heard the vibration of an incoming text, but couldn't tell which of his phones had received it. Maisie appeared at the door and held out his personal phone. He read it.

Where the F are U?

He placed the phone, screen down, on the glass shelf above the sink and reached for her, pulling her into his embrace. He kissed her neck and lifted her chin so he could kiss her mouth. He led her back to bed. He sensed that those consequences might be coming sooner than expected.

Chapter 95

Thursday 23rd April

'I need DS Spence back.'

Acting DI Ali Goddard was the last person Morgan wanted to see in his office doorway.

'He's still at the Thornes' home, leading the search team.'

'I really need him now.'

'Sorry.'

'You wouldn't be getting away with this if DI Patel was here. You're taking advantage of our friendship. Just because I'm "Acting" DI doesn't mean my cases are less important than yours.'

'I'll ring him, Ali. Okay? I've got two in custody and it's all hands to the pump. Thank you for helping out.'

'And what about that petition? Have you sorted it?'

'Work in progress, Ali.'

When he'd got home in the early hours of this morning, the divorce petition had reappeared and was propped up against a pepper grinder in a prominent position in the kitchen. His meal was burnt beyond redemption.

His desk phone rang. Harriet Lees-Langham had taken instructions from Hugo Thorne and he was ready for interview. Jenny Smart was waiting for him in the custody suite.

Halfway down the last flight of stairs, Morgan's mobile rang.

'Yes, Dave.'

'No sign of the phone, or card. There's a lot of tech in that house, and it's all bagged up and on its way to

Digital Forensics. Eight black mascara wands ... if that's what they're called, found in the master bedroom and Louisa's room. They were in drawers and handbags. No laundry bags or pink fabric ... sorry.'

'That's good work, Dave. Thank you. Are you on your way in? Ali Goddard's been asking for you.'

'I'll be setting off in about ten minutes,' said Spence.

'How are Francine and Louisa dealing with the arrests and the search?'

'Louisa's just left for a bike ride and Francine's complaining about the mess we've left. That's all I know.'

Morgan finished the conversation as he entered the custody suite. He saw Jenny Smart inspecting the photos taken from the pub CCTV.

'Not brilliant, are they?' she said, offering them to Morgan.

'Good enough to rattle him.' Morgan let her precede him to the interview room.

The Custody Sergeant's phone was ringing as Morgan and Smart passed her desk. 'Interview Room 4,' she shouted after them.

Harriet Lees-Langham didn't greet them as they entered. Her eyes were on the screen of her laptop, her fingers poised above its keyboard. He took his seat beside Smart and sat back. She was going to lead the questioning.

Having completed the preliminaries, Smart reminded Hugo Thorne of his earlier interview.

'You told us that you didn't remember what time you set off and you also didn't remember when you got to the cottage. Is that still the case?' She was opening a blue folder as she waited for his response.

'Not again, DC Smart. My client has answered all of DI Morgan's questions about that.'

Smart gave her a nod. 'I have an aide-memoire for your client. You know what that is, don't you, Hugo. Your mum's French.' She slid an A4 sheet of paper from the folder and pushed it towards him. 'This is a road map which covers the area between Gullhaven in the east and your holiday cottage in the west. The red route is the most direct route from one to the other. You see?' She pointed to the paper and Hugo took off his glasses to look. 'And the blue route is the route you took on Sunday.' Her right forefinger traced across the paper. 'It's a long way off the main route. Why would you do that?'

'I wasn't driving, I was in the back,' said Hugo Thorne. 'You'd have to ask my father.'

'We'll do that, Hugo. Of course we will. But I'm interested in your thoughts as to why your father would choose that route.' She traced it again, Hugo's eyes following her finger.

'My client has answered your question. His father was driving. Please move on.'

'Okay,' said Smart. She selected another sheet of paper from her folder and placed it face down on the table. 'We know you have a smartphone, Hugo. In fact, it's data from that phone that gave us your route to the cottage. What other technology do you own?'

Lees-Langham reminded him that he didn't have to answer, but Hugo ignored her. 'A laptop and an Android tablet.'

‘And do you do much online shopping on any of your tech?’

‘DVDs, music, a few computer games.’

‘What about police paraphernalia? Are you a collector?’

‘Of course not.’

She turned the paper over and explained that it showed the purchase of police handcuffs by someone in his home.

‘Well, it wasn’t me,’ he said.

‘We’ll see,’ said Smart. ‘Let’s turn to the holiday cottage. You told DI Morgan that you made two outings from the cottage to a DIY store. Do you remember?’ He nodded. ‘For the recording, Hugo, please. You know the score by now.’

‘Yes.’ The reply was a snarl and Morgan could see that Hugo was starting to get angry.

‘Since you told us that, have you remembered any other trips that you may have overlooked?’

‘Definitely not.’

‘That’s very clear, Hugo. Thank you.’ She took the photo from the folder and placed it in front of him slowly and carefully. ‘This is your father’s car.’ She pointed to the number plate. ‘It was photographed at this T-junction.’ Morgan sat forward and placed his finger on the blue route of the map on the table.

‘It was ten to two in the morning. Not long after the pathologist’s estimated time of death for Simon Dennison,’ said Smart. ‘You can see your father is driving and that the front-seat passenger is wearing glasses. Are you that front-seat passenger, Hugo?’

Lees-Langham was staring at the picture. ‘That could be anybody. You can’t even see that it’s Mr Roddy Thorne driving.’

‘But there’s no report of the car being stolen, Ms Lees-Langham,’ said Morgan. She returned to her typing, fingers dancing across the keys, face expressionless, but he could see she was rattled. He knew she would be asking for a break at any moment and he wanted Smart to reinforce her point.

‘Is that you, Hugo, in the passenger seat of your father’s car at ten to two in the morning, on the route between Gullhaven Cove, where Simon Dennison was assaulted and died, and your cottage in Dorset?’

The room fell silent. Lees-Langham stopped typing. All eyes were on Hugo Thorne, who was staring down at the photo.

‘No comment.’ Relief flooded Lees-Langam’s face.

There was a loud knock on the door and Morgan rose to answer it. He felt Lees-Langham’s eyes follow him.

The Custody Officer handed him a sheet of paper. ‘DS Spence has called into the Ops Room,’ he said. ‘Your phone’s switched off.’ Morgan read the note. Two sentences. He read it again and swore. He handed the paper to Jenny Smart and heard her voice as he raced towards the custody suite exit.

‘DI Morgan has left the room. Interview suspended at 10.30 hours.’

Chapter 96

Thursday 23rd April

The rain battered on to Morgan's windscreen, unaffected by the efforts of his windscreen wipers' top speed. He leaned forward in his seat, struggling to see the road ahead. When he got to the clifftop he was able to park without difficulty. Dog walkers and pre-season tourists had anticipated this storm when the black clouds had descended and were back at home enjoying a cup of coffee and a biscuit. And this was a first: he'd arrived before DS Spence.

He looked across the grass and out to the bay. His heart sank. The area was deserted. He was too late. He stopped the engine and doused the lights. He'd have to get out and look more closely, including over the edge. She may have jumped.

The strength of the wind made it difficult to push his door open. It laughed at him for even considering fetching an umbrella from the boot. He would be soaked before he'd got it open. He got out and hurried to the pavement. The gutter was flooded; drains unable to cope with this unexpected deluge. He waded through, knowing that this was just an introduction to how wet he was going to get.

'Louisa!' It was as loud as he could shout, but the wind tossed his words back at him. He squelched across muddy grass. 'Louisa!'

There was a park bench by the side of the bite which nature had taken out of the cliff face. He hadn't noticed it when Gary Fox's body was found, but that day he'd been looking upwards from the beach path. It was more obvious from here.

As he got closer, he saw there was a bicycle leaning against the bench. It wasn't secured. If Louisa had abandoned it, she wasn't interested in protecting it against theft. She thought she no longer needed it. But she'd been here, he was sure of it.

Next to the bench there was a waste bin, two feet wide and about three feet high. He needed to see around it. He moved to the right and walked towards the cliff edge. Slowly; very slowly. If she was here, he didn't want to startle her.

He wasn't sure how to play this. He was used to negotiating with criminals, not tearful, terrified teenagers. Eight more steps and he would be level ... seven ... six …

The single *woop* from the ambulance startled him and he slipped in the mud. The grass here was worn away by paragliding pilots who congregated to share experiences and to take off. The edge of the cliff dropped straight down and provided an uninterrupted up-thrust of wind. Perfect conditions for them, but if Louisa was here, additional jeopardy for them both.

Something appeared around the edge of the bin: a small head; the eyes disproportionately large in the frightened face. Damn it! He'd hoped to get within grabbing distance before she noticed him.

The girl got to her feet and took a few steps towards the cliff edge. She turned her back to the bay and yelled at him: 'Go away. This is nothing to do with you. Who are you anyway?' The wind blew her words away from him and he struggled to hear them. He looked back towards the road, where two liveried police cars had arrived. He saw Dave Spence striding towards him; long, confident steps, unfazed by the slippery grass and rabbit droppings. Morgan extended a hand to discourage him from coming closer.

'My name's Nick, Louisa. I'm here to help you.' He made another move towards her and she stepped back without looking. Another one like that would take her over the edge. Morgan stopped. 'I'm here to help, Louisa.' He stretched out a hand but she was pointing towards the emergency vehicles and then to Spence.

'Are you with him? Are you police?'

He didn't reply. He didn't want to. If he confirmed her suspicion he knew she might jump. Maybe worse: maybe she would let herself fall backwards so that her head would make contact with the cliffs before the rest of her. 'I'm here to help,' he repeated.

'If you're police, then you're the reason I'm here,' she shouted. 'You arrested my dad and my brother. They didn't do anything. I did it. It was all me.'

A sudden gust of wind caught her and she screamed, dropping to her knees in panic. Morgan risked two more steps. It was a gamble, but he figured that if she'd intended to die she would have let the wind take her. He knelt down, not close enough to grab her, but close enough so they could speak without yelling.

'I did it. All of it. Nobody else is to blame.' Her hazel eyes fixed on him and he noticed her dilated pupils. Drugs or panic? Neither was good.

'I think Simon Dennison is to blame,' said Morgan. 'We know now that he was a serial sex abuser. We know he drugged and raped you. None of that was your fault.' His knees started to numb with the cold rainwater which wicked its way up his trousers. He moved so that he was fully seated in the mud. Colder; wetter; but a more stable position from which to reach out and grab her.

'My dad called me a slut.'

'He didn't know the full story then. And you're friends again now, aren't you?'

'He said it was my own fault. He said I was making up a story to put the blame on Simon ... but I wasn't.'

'How did you persuade him?'

'I filmed them. On my phone. He'd been looking at her all evening and I remembered that look. When she went out on to the picnic area and he disappeared, I followed her.'

'You filmed Simon Dennison with Claire Fox?'

'And I showed it to my dad. He blamed me for what that man did to me, and I was able to show him that I wasn't the only one who fell for it.'

'What happened after you showed your dad?'

'He said he was sorry and it's been okay since then.'

'But it hasn't, has it?'

She looked down and Morgan risked shuffling a couple of inches closer in the mud. She must have heard the splat, and backed away. She was even closer to the edge now.

'We can sort this out, Louisa. I know you want us to sort it out or you wouldn't have left the note for your mum this morning. I don't think you want to die today and *I* don't want you to die today. Let me help you to sort it out.' He extended a hand; his fingers stretched as far as he could reach.

She looked wary. 'You *are* police,' she said. Her voice was soft and low and the hairs on the back of Morgan's neck stood up. Her eyes were still on him as she put her palms down into the mud and eased backwards. She reached behind her again and her fingertips curled around the edge of the cliff. She smiled, those eyes now lit with the fire of intention.

'You don't have to do this, Louisa. Please don't do this.'

Louisa Thorne bent back from her waist. It was a slow and graceful movement.

'Now!' yelled Morgan.

Spence leapt forward, grabbed her arm and pulled her towards him. He dropped to his knees and folded her into his arms, her body convulsing with sobs.

'Well done, Dave,' said Morgan. 'I was scared she was going to hear you.'

Two paramedics ran across the wet grass. They wrapped Louisa in a foil blanket and the woman started to guide her towards their waiting vehicle. The man handed a blanket each to Morgan and Spence.

'We'll take her in and have her checked over. You said she'd been sectioned before?' His question was directed at Spence, who nodded. 'They'll likely do it again,' he said, pointing to the cliff edge.

Morgan refused his blanket, but thanked them. He looked down at his suit and then at Spence's. 'I hope DCI Johnson's got a decent dry-cleaning budget,' he said as they made their way back to the road.

Chapter 97

Thursday 23rd April

'This came in while you were out,' said Smart. 'I've just printed it. It's the vehicle examiner's report on Gary Fox's car.

'Anything interesting?' asked Morgan. He had showered in the locker room and put on the spare suit he'd carried in his car for the last five years on the off chance it might be needed. From the tightness of the fit, those five years had seen a widening of his waist. Dave Spence had gone home to shower and change.

'The report says that they believe the car has been recently valeted, inside and out. They mention that the boot is much cleaner than they would normally expect. They haven't found any hairs or skin cells; not even belonging to the owner.' She turned to the next page. 'The tyres have been cleaned, but they have found brick and concrete dust and the brick dust is consistent with the bricks they took from the build site at the club.'

Morgan smiled. Suddenly, his trouser waistband didn't feel quite so tight.

Smart turned to the third page. 'Blah blah blah – oh, that's interesting. Blue cotton fibres in the ridges of the brake pedal.'

'Interesting, but not conclusive. Gary Fox stayed at the club and would have used their towels.'

'I'm just reading it,' said Smart. She turned to the last page. 'The multimedia centre attempts connection to three phones. One of them is Gary Fox's Samsung. The second is a Samsung Galaxy S10 and the third is an iPhone 11.'

‘Get in touch with Claire Fox and ask her what model phone she’s using and if she has an explanation for the third connection.’

‘Hugo Thorne’s phone is an iPhone,’ said Smart. ‘I don’t know which model.’

‘And he doesn’t like to be in a car without music, does he? Let’s see if we can put him in Gary Fox’s car, especially on the night he was killed.’

‘Interview recommenced at 14.00 hours. I’m DC Jennifer Smart. Present also are DI Nicholas Morgan, Mr Hugo Thorne, and his legal representative, Ms Harriet Lees-Langham.’ Smart sat back in her seat aware that, for now, her contribution was over.

‘My client hasn’t been offered lunch,’ said Lees-Langham.

‘I apologise. There’s a lot going on at the moment. I will personally ensure that Mr Thorne is given his lunch as soon as we’ve asked a few questions,’ said Morgan.

‘Is my dad here?’ asked Hugo.

‘Should he be?’

‘There were two cars outside my house when you arrested me. Who was the other one for?’

‘Who do you think it should have been for?’ asked Morgan. He saw the anguish on Hugo’s face. Evidence which involved him in the deaths of Simon Dennison and Gary Fox was stacking up and he was about to add to the pile.

‘Can you tell us what car Gary Fox drove?’

‘I’ve no idea. Never seen him in a car.’

‘You’ve never been in his car with him, or driven his car?’

'No.' He was shaking his head as he answered.

'Was it you who contacted Mrs Claire Fox to ask her to come and collect Mr Fox's car from the club?'

'Yes. We needed the space for a wedding.'

How did you know it was Mr Fox's car? You've just told us that you don't know what car he drove.'

'Someone must have told me it was his.'

'I see. And why did you contact Mrs Fox? Surely you should have contacted the owner, Mr Fox. You had his mobile number and his office number. Would it not make more sense to ring him and get him to move his own car?'

Morgan kept his eyes firmly fixed on Hugo Thorne. 'Maybe you contacted Mrs Fox because you knew Mr Fox was already dead and his body was at the bottom of the cliffs at Gullhaven Cove.'

'That's crazy,' said Hugo. 'But you've reminded me: I called Mrs Fox to ask her to move the car because I heard Mr Fox's body had been found. The wedding wasn't affected and I needed the parking space.' The beginnings of a smile tickled at the edges of his mouth.

Morgan shook his head. 'We know when you rang Mrs Fox, because we were there when you spoke to her. We also know that you rang her before we released the name of the deceased. The only people who knew it was Gary Fox were the investigation team and whoever murdered him.'

Thorne's face coloured. He had started to sweat again. He took off his glasses and polished them on his sweatshirt.

'You promised my client lunch,' said Lees-Langham.

'He'll get it. But I've not quite finished,' said Morgan. 'Let's come back to the car. Gary Fox's car.

You've just said that you've never been in that car. Is that right?'

'Yes.'

'Our examiners have found blue fibre traces in the grooves of the pedals. See, we're back to those pesky blue fibres again. You seem to shed them wherever you go.'

'That's ridiculous, DI Morgan. They could have come from anywhere.'

'You're right, Ms Lees-Langham.' Morgan was rewarded with a disparaging look. He held out a hand and Smart passed him a printed email. 'So let's look at something a little more personal to you, Hugo. You already told us that you can't bear to be in a silent car. This report shows that your iPhone 11 connected to Gary Fox's car Bluetooth for a period of sixty-five minutes on the night he was killed. By my reckoning, that's about the time it would take to drive the car from the club car park round to the building site, pack Gary Fox's body in the boot then drive it to Gullhaven Cove and dump it over the cliff before driving back. What music did you choose for that trip? I'm fascinated to know.'

He waited. The silence got longer.

'For the recording, Mr Thorne hasn't answered,' said Smart. Morgan nodded at her and she continued. 'Hugo Thorne, I'm further arresting you on suspicion of the murder of Gary Fox and conspiracy to murder Gary Fox. You do not have to say anything ...'

Morgan tuned out while she finished the caution. He was surprised that Lees-Langham hadn't got anything to say for herself.

'I'm going to arrange for you to be taken back to your cell for some lunch. After that, you may wish to spend some time with your solicitor. We'll resume your interview after that.' Morgan pushed his seat back and the two detectives rose together. Smart left the room first and when Morgan reached the door, he turned back. 'You're right. I did arrange for two cars to be at your house this morning. I can at least assure you that Louisa wasn't put in the other one. Last I saw of her, she was being helped into an ambulance after she tried to throw herself off the cliffs this morning. Same place as Gary Fox's body was dropped over. Funny that.' He closed the door behind him and hurried a few steps to catch up with DC Jenny Smart.

Chapter 98

Thursday 23rd April

In spite of Harriet Lees-Langham's protestations about her client's delayed lunch, it turned out that Hugo Thorne wasn't hungry. He didn't want to speak to his solicitor, either. He wanted to speak to DI Nick Morgan, who was happy to oblige.

'I wasn't expecting that, were you?' asked Smart as she and Morgan made their way from the interview room to his office.

'I've never seen our Harriet look so pissed off,' said Morgan, the memory making him smile. 'Let's grab a drink and think through how we're going to handle Roddy Thorne.'

They got to Morgan's office door as Dave Spence was hurrying along the corridor towards them.

'What have I missed?'

'Hugo Thorne has confessed,' said Smart, raising her cardboard coffee cup in celebration. 'To everything. Dennison and Fox. Harriet Lees-Langham's spitting feathers.'

Spence stopped. 'But the photo shows that Roddy's driving the car, doesn't it? He's not completely innocent.'

'We're just about to have a word with him,' said Morgan.

Once the recording was underway, Roddy Thorne's solicitor cleared his throat before speaking. 'My client has decided to exercise his legal right throughout this interview to respond to your questions with the words "no comment".'

'Thank you, Mr Shah,' said Morgan. 'I don't intend to waste anyone's time here. Your client was arrested this morning under suspicion of the sexual assault and manslaughter of Simon Dennison. He is now further arrested for conspiracy in the sexual assault and manslaughter of the same victim. He is also under arrest for the murder of Gary Fox and conspiracy to commit that murder.' He completed the speech and sat down opposite Roddy Thorne.

'I've spent quite a bit of time today with your son and daughter. Your son has confessed to his involvement in the deaths of Simon Dennison and Gary Fox, and your daughter has tried to kill herself. Where would you like me to start?'

Roddy Thorne rubbed his chin and Morgan could hear the rasp of fingers against beard bristles. The arrest had come too early for Thorne Senior's morning shave.

'Here's what I know,' said Morgan. Your daughter was lured to Simon Dennison's flat and he had sex with her. She was fifteen and he was in his thirties, so, technically, rape.' Morgan watched Thorne's fists clench and he moved his chair a few inches back from the table before continuing.

'At Christmas, Louisa watched while Dennison lured another woman, Gary Fox's wife as it happens, out to your picnic area, where they had sex in full view of anyone who happened to be watching. I believe she showed you that movie to convince you that he'd tricked, and maybe drugged, her too. When you went to his room to have it out with him, he'd left early. Is there anything I've said that you wish to comment on?'

'No comment.'

'You sent Simon Dennison a couple of texts threatening his life from a PAYG phone. Then you started to hatch a plot. You wanted to make the punishment fit the crime. To do the same to him that he'd done to her. You bought a massive dildo. You also purchased police handcuffs. Let me save you the effort of those looks of incredulity. I can prove that they were bought from your home. I'm just waiting for our tech team to tell us which computer was used. Then you waited for the sales meeting. You booked leave so that the whole family were supposed to be in Dorset while Dennison was assaulted. Great alibi. But you all came back, using a route that you didn't think had any cameras.' Morgan nearly missed it. A concerned raising of those dark, hairy eyebrows. Gone now.

'You overlooked a camera, Roddy. I have a photo of you travelling back to Dorset just hours after you realised you'd killed Simon Dennison. You and Hugo in the front and the girls in the back. Hugo's admitted it, and after I finish with you I'm going to the hospital to speak to Louisa about her involvement.'

'Hospital? What hospital? Why is she back in hospital?'

'After we arrested you and Hugo this morning, Louisa cycled to Gullhaven. She left Francine a note telling her she couldn't stand the guilt any longer and she wanted to die. You used her, Roddy. You used her as bait to exact your revenge on Simon Dennison when she just wanted to forget it. There's DNA on Simon Dennison's fingertips and supermarket own-brand mascara on Dennison's shirt, both of which I'm sure will come back to Louisa. It strikes me that your wife's taste in mascara errs towards the more expensive brands.'

'He lured her. She lured him. Honours even, the way I see it,' said Thorne, crossing his arms.

'He died, she didn't.' Morgan shuffled the papers in front of him. 'Was it you who carried out the sexual assault on Simon Dennison?'

'Well, you can't think it was my excuse for a son. He ran away as soon as we got the hood on him.'

'That would be the laundry bag? Do you still have it?'

'Long since burned in my garden incinerator.' Smart made a note to check.

'When did you find out that you'd killed him?'

'He was wriggling and trying to yell when I started on him. Then he stopped. I was angry and I didn't stop. I kept pushing and pushing. When I couldn't push it any further, I dragged him off the rocks, untied the gag and took the bag off. His eyes had rolled backwards and he'd been sick.'

'Did you try to resuscitate him?'

'Nah. I dumped him in one of the old huts and I went back up to the car, where the kids were waiting. We all got in and I drove back to Dorset.'

'Where was Francine?' It was a question that had nagged Morgan from when they first traced the CCTV from the pub. Francine had seemed entirely unaware of the extensiveness of Louisa's assault. So why would she condone the violence of the revenge?'

'She was at the cottage.'

'That was risky. She might have woken up and missed you all.'

'Francine is very susceptible to the soporific qualities of antihistamines. I'd been feeding her small doses for a couple of days. She thought she was exhausted from working hard at the club. I wasn't worried.'

'That pretty much ties up with what Hugo told us. Now, what about Gary Fox?'

'He wanted money. Told me and Hugo that he'd seen everything and that he'd put us away forever unless we paid him compensation for the loss of his best salesman.'

'I have a witness that heard Hugo argue with Gary Fox.'

'Hugo knows we're in trouble financially. The build has broken us. Even if we wanted to pay Fox, we couldn't. The argument got heated and Gary Fox started to cry. Hugo took the piss and Gary went for him. I couldn't separate them. Gary was on top of my son and he had his hands round his throat. I hit him.'

'With a brick.'

'I had to stop him somehow.'

'Morgan looked at his watch. 'Is there anything you wish to add to what you've told us?'

'It wasn't meant to happen. None of it was meant to happen. And it wouldn't have happened if Simon Dennison had kept his hands off my daughter.'

'Interview terminated at 15.22 hours,' said Smart.

'I'm going to speak to the CPS. You'll be taken to a cell and someone will come for you when we're ready,' said Morgan. He was exhausted. He usually felt an element of jubilation when a case came together, but not this time. A father and son going to prison with long sentences and a daughter on suicide watch. Then there was Francine, left to pick up the pieces of something she didn't fully understand.

He thanked Jenny Smart and made his way to the stairs. DCI Johnson was about to have an uncomfortable phone call with the PCC.

Chapter 99

Saturday 25th April

The grass on the clifftop was still wet from the recent rain and Nick Morgan could see that Truffles was getting muddier with every step. He'd have to give him a good rub down with the towel that hung by the back door for that very purpose. The day was going to be traumatic enough without Sam screaming at him for doggy prints across the floor.

He wasn't sure when he'd decided to leave Samantha.

Was it the 'Where the F are U?' text? She'd sent worse.

Was it the divorce petition?

Or did it all come back to the night she spent with Graham Fletcher?

He threw the ball again and watched Truffles bound after it. It was anthropomorphism, but he'd swear his dog was smiling.

His dog.

His children.

He dropped down on to a bench and watched the patterns of sunlight on the waves as small clouds scudded over.

'I was watching you from our bedroom. You don't look as if you've just solved a big case.' Sam sat on the bench, closer than a stranger, but further away than a wife.

'We need to talk.' They said it together and both smiled, but there was pain.

'You first,' said Nick. He knew he wouldn't need to hear her news after he broke his own. He would be going home to pack.

'I'm pregnant.'

She reached out to stroke Truffles, but he passed her and lay across his master's feet.

'It can't be mine,' he said. 'I can't even remember the last time we slept together.'

'That's not very flattering.'

'And you're on the pill.'

'Maybe I forgot a few when you left me in charge of organising the move here.' Her voice was hard. She wanted it to be his fault.

'It's still not mine. It's his. Your oily solicitor friend.'

'You and I had sex a few days before the football dinner. At the park home. I haven't forgotten, it being such a rarity. So it's probably yours.'

'You can't be planning to keep it,' he said. 'You're forty-two.'

'It's my last chance to have a baby.'

He stared at her but she was looking out across the bay.

'I'm about nine weeks, so we can do a pre-natal paternity test. I need to provide a blood sample, but you just need a cheek swab.'

'Get him to do it.'

'Don't be childish, Nick. Anyway, we agreed I wouldn't be seeing him.'

'And yet he was at our house when Alex was missing. He knew before I did.'

'Well, now you know. I'd best get back. The twins will want breakfast.' She started to walk away before turning. 'Sorry. What was it you wanted to talk about?'

'It'll keep,' he said and stood. She was waiting. He could walk back with her and sit down to a weekend breakfast with his family. He looked down at the yellow ball in his hand and threw it as hard as he could for his dog to chase. In the opposite direction.

Chapter 100

Monday 27th April

He parked his black Range Rover on the double yellow lines by the school railings and waited. Moments later, the bell for lunch rang and doors opened, spewing kids into the grounds. He supposed that once you went to senior school, you were too grown up to call it a playground.

A small boy came and sat on his own on a bench near the fence. He wondered if the lad was bullied. Hoped not.

When JayJay appeared, he put his fingers in his mouth and whistled; a noise that pierced the enthusiastic yelling and made most of the children turn to look. He motioned to JayJay to come to the fence.

'Where's your little friend?' he asked.

'He doesn't talk to me anymore. His dad made him promise.'

'C'mon, JayJay. That's not how it works. Fetch him over.' He reached across for the battered mobile on the passenger seat and got out.

His little brother was arguing with Alex Morgan, who was shaking his head. He saw JayJay link his arm with Alex's and steer him to the fence.

'Hi Alex,' he said. 'I need your help again.'

'I can't. I got into so much trouble last time. They're all watching me.'

'Who's watching?' He threw an arm around. 'I can't see anyone watching.' When he turned back to Alex, the boy was looking down. 'I need you to go to the same place and pick up another packet and bring it to me.

Tomorrow. Take this.' He shoved the phone through the fence and held it, waiting for Alex to take it.

'I can't.'

'Designer trainers have to be paid for Alexander. And one trip doesn't cover it.'

'I don't have them anymore. My dad took them.'

'And you see that as my problem? Because I don't.' He pressed his face against the fencing. 'Take the fucking phone, or next time, my little brother will bring Vicky to the fence and you won't like what I'll do to her.'

Alex's small hand wrapped around the phone and pulled it from his hand.

'Here's the ticket. It's a day return, so make sure you don't try to use it before ten, or after four. Don't want to draw attention to yourself, do you. Ring the number that's in there when you get on the train back and I'll meet you in the station car park.' As he turned back to his car, he saw Alex punch JayJay's arm and walk away. He called after him. 'And that's an extra two trips you owe me. Nobody punches my little brother.'

Abbreviations

BOLO	Be On Look Out
CSI	Crime Scene Investigation/Investigator
DV marker	Domestic Violence marker
ELB	Extended Leave Break
GMP	Greater Manchester Police
IP address	Internet Protocol number
MAC address	Media Access Control address
MCU	Major Crime Unit
NPAS	National Police Air Service
PAYG	Pay-As-You-Go
PCC	Police and Crime Commissioner
SIM card	Subscriber Identification Module – stores the mobile phone subscriber's identity
SIO	Senior Investigating Officer
SIODP	Senior Investigating Officer Development Programme

DI Nick Morgan Crime Thriller Series Book 1

MAKE YOU SORRY

ONE CHANCE BEFORE YOU DIE

By CHRISTINE RAE-JONES

You feel him watching you. You know you've got one chance. One chance before you die.

When DI Nick Morgan relocates his family to south England's idyllic Gullhaven Cove, he is ready for a quieter life and a fresh start. His plans unravel when he discovers the body of a teenage boy in the master bedroom of his new home.

The death toll rises, including the decomposing corpse of a solicitor, dressed for her wedding which she failed to attend, local villains, and a predatory town councillor. Morgan is under pressure to replicate the success he enjoyed at the Met, but is distracted. He overlooks an important lead and is threatened with suspension.

Closing in on the perpetrator, he uncovers a secret which threatens his future happiness. If he tells – he will lose his family; if he doesn't – he will lose his career.

What would you do..?

DI Nick Morgan Crime Thriller Series Book 3

MAKE YOU CHOOSE

YOU LOVE YOUR BROTHER. HE WANTS YOU DEAD

By CHRISTINE RAE-JONES

Available Autumn 2021

Join the Reader Club at

https://www.christinerae-jones.com

for discounted pre-launch availability

Author's Note

Like DI Nick Morgan, I too have relocated to the south coast of England following a varied career in forensic toxicology, scientific instrumentation sales and professional skills development. I also served as a criminal court magistrate for a period of over ten years.

Throughout the novel I have used U.K. English spellings and colloquialisms and have taken a few liberties with the geography of Hampshire and Dorset as well as police structure of these two counties.

Acknowledgements

I've read that it's harder to write a sequel than to write a first novel. I'm not sure about that, but I can attest that it's definitely not easier.

"Make You Beg" is my second novel in the DI Nick Morgan crime thriller series and I would like to thank everyone who has encouraged and supported me during the writing process. My continuing thanks to those who provide insight into police service procedures and politics with a special mention for Graham Bartlett whose specialist writing courses have been invaluable.

I could not imagine a more appropriate cover for "Make You Beg" and am grateful to Debbie at The Cover Collection for her skills, and suggestions.

There are numerous friends who have again listened patiently while I agonise over plots and characters. Joyce & Ann, Mark, Audrey and Laura and, of course, my lovely mum – none of this would have been possible without you.

Printed in Great Britain
by Amazon

25236977R10235